Tales of the
Troubled Dead

To Nic
with love and thanks

Tales of the Troubled Dead

Ghost Stories in Cultural History

CATHERINE BELSEY

EDINBURGH
University Press

Edinburgh University Press is one of the leading university presses in the UK. We publish academic books and journals in our selected subject areas across the humanities and social sciences, combining cutting-edge scholarship with high editorial and production values to produce academic works of lasting importance. For more information visit our website: edinburghuniversitypress.com

© Catherine Belsey, 2019

Edinburgh University Press Ltd
The Tun – Holyrood Road, 12(2f) Jackson's Entry, Edinburgh EH8 8PJ

Typeset in Caslon
by Biblichor Ltd, Edinburgh

A CIP record for this book is available from the British Library

ISBN 978 1 4744 1736 5 (hardback)
ISBN 978 1 4744 1738 9 (webready PDF)
ISBN 978 1 4744 1737 2 (paperback)
ISBN 978 1 4744 1739 6 (epub)

The right of Catherine Belsey to be identified as the author of this work has been asserted in accordance with the Copyright, Designs and Patents Act 1988, and the Copyright and Related Rights Regulations 2003 (SI No. 2498).

Contents

Prelude. The Changing Shapes of Dorothy Dingley   1

   1. A Dead King Walks   11

   2. Haunted Pasts   33

   3. The Ghost of Mrs Milton   57

   4. Women in White   78

   5. Dangerous Dead Women   100

   6. Unquiet Gothic Castles   119

   7. Spectres of Desire   148

   8. All in the Mind?   175

   9. Listening to Ghosts   195

  10. Strange to Tell   215

  Coda. Figurative Phantoms   239

Sources   253

Acknowledgements   269

Credits   271

Index   273

The Changing Shapes of Dorothy Dingley

Strange news from Cornwall

Ghosts don't stay put. Seen by glimpses, they come and go unpredictably. And so, it seems, do their stories. The tale of Dorothy Dingley, due to evolve as time went on, first entered the written record in the seventeenth-century memoir of the Reverend John Ruddle.

On 20 June 1665 Parson Ruddle was unexpectedly drawn into a ghost story, when an elderly gentleman and his wife appealed to him for help with their son. The lad, once full of promise, was now in a serious decline. His parents suspected the boy of malingering. His reluctance to go to school might be the effect of laziness; perhaps he was in love; alternatively, it might be that he wanted an excuse to join his elder brother in London. But the youth himself maintained that he was haunted and they counted on the minister to talk him out of such fancies.

Left alone with the boy, the parson found him open and frank. For a year or so on his way to school, he claimed, a woman had passed him, sometimes more than once in the same field. At first, he had paid no attention, supposing her to be a local resident, but when he looked more closely, he recognised Dorothy Dingley, dead these eight years. He often spoke to her but she never replied. When he changed his route, she changed hers and met him in the lane.

To the boy's relief, Rev. Ruddle agreed to walk with him the next morning. And there, in a field well away from human habitation, was the woman, just as the boy had described. The minister had meant to address the ghost but somehow could not bring himself to do so, nor to look back at the departing figure.

Puzzled, but thoroughly enlisted in the adventure, he returned to the field alone as soon as other matters permitted, and there she was again, only ten feet away. A third time, the boy and his parents came too. On this occasion, she seemed to move faster. Ruddle and the boy turned to follow her but she crossed the stile and then vanished. He now noticed that she appeared to glide rather than walk. And a spaniel that had joined the company barked and ran away. The terrified parents, who had attended Dingley's funeral eight years before, had no wish to encounter the apparition a second time.

In the end, the clergyman resolved that he must speak to the ghost. At five the next morning he crossed the stile into the field. He spoke authoritatively to the dead woman and gradually, reluctantly, she replied. They met again an hour after sunset and, in the light of their exchanges, the spectre vanished for good. The testimony, committed to writing by Mr Ruddle himself, concludes with an assertion of its veracity. 'These things are true, and I know them to be so, with as much certainty as eyes and ears can give me.'

Ruddle dated his manuscript 4 September 1665, adding that, since he was young and new to the area, he thought it best to keep the story to himself. It appeared in print even so, but not until 1720, when 'A Remarkable Passage of an Apparition' was included, somewhat incongruously, in a pamphlet about a deaf fortune-teller, and then reprinted in a more substantial volume that same year, the second edition of *The History of the Life and Adventures of Mr Duncan Campbell.*

What prompted publication over fifty years on? In the early eighteenth century, accredited ghost stories had become highly saleable. For half a century or more, the Anglican Church had felt itself threatened by materialist Enlightenment philosophies that allowed no special place for the supernatural. If there were no ghosts, or no possibility of suspending the laws of nature, the way was open to declare that there was no God. In defence of religion, a number of divines took to promoting the apparitions that a century earlier Protestantism had denied as delusions of the devil. Stories of attested encounters with spirits, always popular, became exceptionally marketable.

So, at the same time, did anything written by Daniel Defoe. For many years, it was believed that the Ruddle memoir was actually the work of Defoe, master impersonator of other fictional storytellers, including the prostitute Moll Flanders, as well as the largely imaginary castaway Robinson Crusoe. Defoe was already known as the author of *A True Relation of the Apparition of One Mrs Veal.* Why not add, then, the record of an obscure Cornish clergyman's encounter with the supernatural? But that attribution is no longer secure and John Ruddle's authorship remains a distinct possibility.

The tale evolves

Ghosts exist in their stories, and Dorothy Dingley's did not end with publication in 1720. Instead, it was to survive as the theme of speculation and debate. Her tale would be variously defended as fact or enhanced as fiction, and would develop as time went on to accommodate new modes of storytelling. Dorothy's spectre slipped from memoir to history, and from there to romance, short story and, eventually, folklore, shifting in line with these distinct genres.

The narrative also changed with the times, marking new ways of understanding what it was to be a ghost. In addition, it came to focus more specifically on what might trouble a woman in the grave. As her tale was taken up, explained, embellished and elaborated, the matter that drove Dorothy to walk, unspecified in Ruddle's memoir, was gradually sexualised.

While her changing shapes demonstrate the power of ghost stories to seduce successive generations of writers and readers, they also throw into relief some of the difficulties we meet in engaging with the troubled dead. In 1817, nearly a century after its first appearance in print, the haunting made its way into local history. C. S. Gilbert reproduced the story in his *Historical Survey of the County of Cornwall*, adding that the boy's father, unnamed by Ruddle (now Ruddell), was Mr Bligh of Botathen. Seven years later, Fortescue Hitchins and Samuel Drew summarised the story in their own *History of Cornwall*. They too named the Bligh family but this time the ghost was identified as Dorothy Durant.

These historians evidently found the story sufficiently credible to merit such supplementary information. Drew, who edited *The History of Cornwall*, adds a note of personal scepticism: 'On this strange relation, the editor forbears to make any comment.' But he did not delete the narrative from the historical record. Gilbert, on the other hand, was inclined to take the matter seriously, as, from a different perspective, was T. M. Jarvis, who in 1823 included the tale among his *Accredited Ghost Stories*, a work designed to support the religious case for the immortality of the soul.

If the story proved attractive to local historians and defenders of the supernatural, it was even more seductive to writers of fiction. What mattered in 1720 was that a dead woman genuinely walked and the supernatural was real. In the epoch of the novel, however, the pressing question was *why* she walked. What so troubled Dorothy Dingley that she could not sleep in her grave? In 1845 Anna Eliza Bray took Ruddell's account from Gilbert's history and included it in her romance, *Trelawny of Trelawne*. Mrs Bray was more alert than Hitchins and Drew to the nuances of the record. In Gilbert, as in the Ruddle memoir he repeated, the boy's mother was a 'gentlewoman', the ghost a 'woman'. Bray's novel makes Dorothy a servant. Her guilty secret, revealed at last in the field to the minister, is that she once concealed documents proving that the haunted boy was in reality the true heir to a landed estate. Years later, the dead nursemaid walks the field to meet her former charge. Eventually, she tells Mr Ruddell where to look for the papers and justice is finally done.

This avowedly fictional explanation was not to be the last, however. In 1867 R. S. Hawker published what has since become a canonical Victorian chiller. 'The Botathen Ghost' first appeared in Charles Dickens's journal *All the Year Round*. There Hawker claims to have had access to the original 'diurnal' of Parson Ruddall, as the vicar has now become. On the basis of this journal, Hawker resets the story in winter, the appropriate time for apparitions. He also reduces the interval between the funeral and the sighting to three years, within the likely reach of a schoolboy's memory. The allusion to tradition, along with increased probability of detail, brings the tale into line with the conventions of nineteenth-century ghost stories.

Moreover, since ghosts are dedicated followers of fashion, the spectre now adjusts her appearance accordingly. The solid revenant that the lad initially mistook for a local woman has here taken on the wraithlike features of a properly Gothic ghost.

Dorothy (now Dinglet) has a 'pale and stony face' with 'strange and misty hair'. 'She floated along the field', the minister records in Hawker's version, 'like a sail upon a stream, and glided past the spot where we stood, pausingly. But so deep was the awe that overcame me', he continues, 'as I stood there in the light of day, face to face with a human soul separate from her bones and flesh, that my heart and purpose both failed me.' Hawker's ghost is a phantom, visible but not to be mistaken for a living body, at once perceptible and insubstantial, of a different composition from her material surroundings.

A sexual secret

As this development implies, the supernatural has a history. Ghosts change their nature from one epoch to the next. And that differential history also redefines the nature of the trouble that wakens the dead. While any kind of unfinished business might keep male ghosts from resting in peace, by the nineteenth century what had come to trouble women most was their sexual past. Hawker's fictional parson notes that, on recognising Dorothy Dinglet, the boy's elderly father, Mr Bligh, shows signs of anxiety. When the clergyman finally persuades the ghost to speak, she confesses to 'a certain sin', although the minister does not name it. Since 'Pen and ink would defile the thoughts she uttered', those thoughts remain veiled. At evensong, the minister has a long talk with 'that ancient transgressor' Mr Bligh, who shows 'great horror and remorse'. Satisfied with his penitence, the ghost is duly laid to rest.

Whose was the unspeakable sin? Mr Bligh's, evidently. But was Dorothy his victim, or his willing partner? The story does not say. We are invited to construe that the sin was sexual – and our guess may be a good deal more lurid than anything that could be spelt out in a Victorian journal for family reading. In the story the facts remain elusive, shadowy and uncertain – like ghosts, perhaps. If sex has now become the female secret, it remains undefined, suggested in hints for imagination to work on.

Oddly enough, however, part of Hawker's fiction resurfaced in the twentieth century as popular local legend and, in the process, Dingley's story acquired a more specific sexual core. In 1940 Christina Hole incorporated 'The Botathen Ghost' into her *English Folklore*. This book, claiming the story as Cornish belief, actually reproduced word for word Hawker's description of the apparition, complete with the stony face and misty hair. But it omitted the guilty secret. Thirty years later, when the renowned folklorist Katharine Briggs repeated Hole's account in her four-volume *Dictionary of British Folk-Tales*, she tentatively adduced a different cause for the dead woman's restlessness. Briggs stated in a footnote that, according to 'Hunt', Dorothy had had an affair with the elder brother of the boy she haunted.

But it turns out that Robert Hunt, author of *Popular Romances of the West of England*, published in 1865 and frequently reprinted, had made no such claim. On the contrary, he abridged, with acknowledgement, the account given by the historian, C. S. Gilbert, which matches the first printed version of 1720, and makes no reference whatever to a troubled past for Dorothy. What could have prompted the scholarly Briggs to suppose he did? By this time, there were in circulation several versions of the earliest printed account. Was the affair between Dorothy and the elder brother a creative misreading of John Ruddle's memoir? Romance, after all, came into that story, however obliquely. The worried parents thought love might be to blame for the boy's decline. He also had an elder brother who had gone to London. Had these two pieces of information somehow been elided?

Indeed they had, but not, in the first instance, by local legend. Instead, they were brought together in 'The Woman in the Way', a short story by Oliver Onions and published in 1924 in a collection called *Ghosts in Daylight*. Here the tale is presented as fiction and the storytelling is as ingenious as the sexual politics are misogynist. 'The Woman in the Way' begins with John Ruddle's memoir. It pays close attention to the particulars of the narrative, points to the gaps there and fills them with what it explicitly calls conjecture. It inventively coaxes the memoir to reveal that the boy's mother 'wears the breeches' in the household. When her elder son shows signs of wanting to make his fortune in the big city, what would she do but find him a nice local girl to marry instead? But suppose he had already contracted a relationship of his own with Dorothy Dingley? And what if Dorothy, scorned by the family as not good enough for their son, chose in anger to lead him on? We cannot be sure, the story continues, whether the elder son left for London teased but rejected, or whether, on the contrary, he prevailed with the young woman and departed in triumph. Either way, Dorothy died but, after seven years, returned to set about a vengeful seduction of the younger boy in his turn. No wonder the parents were frightened when they recognised her in the field.

Truth

In the fiction of the roaring twenties, then, the ghost has become a vamp – and half a century later Dorothy's sexual relationship with the elder brother has entered Briggs's *Dictionary* as folklore. In the three hundred years since 1720, a tale that, in the first instance, may or may not have been invented passes into history and, from there, back into fiction, which then reappears as local legend. The story of Dorothy Dingley/Durant/Dinglet is still told in the neighbourhood of Launceston and in some current versions she died in childbirth, after a sexual relationship with the boy's brother, who abandoned her and disappeared in London.

Where, if anywhere, does the truth lie? Is there anything here that we can safely believe? Did Dorothy Dingley ever live? If so, did she walk after her death? Did John Ruddle/Ruddell/Ruddall lay her ghost to rest and record the encounter but not what she said? At the heart of this evolving story is a spectral woman who cannot rest until she tells her secret. Her motive for walking might or might not be a troubled sexual past. But her existence, real or imagined, depends on a memoir, itself conceivably genuine, but possibly not. All we have is the version of it printed in 1720. The original manuscript of this memoir, dated 1665, remains as spectral, as uncertain, as the ghost herself.

What do we know for sure? It turns out that the Reverend John Ruddle existed – and the variations in the spelling of his name are not out of the ordinary. He was vicar of Launceston at the date of the haunting until his death in 1698. But did he write about the ghost, and was his record put into print in 1720? Dingley was a common name in the neighbourhood. The topographical accuracy, such as it is, remains remarkable: the author seems to have known the neighbourhood.

But it remains a puzzle that the Cornish manuscript should have come into the possession of a London publisher so long after the events in question and in defiance of the secrecy Ruddle had thought prudent. On the other hand, by 1720 John Ruddle had been safely dead for more than two decades, and the hauntings had taken place over thirty years before that. No one was likely to complain at the release of his secret; equally, no one was likely to be in a strong position to challenge the veracity of the published tale.

During the nineteenth century, various respectable people claimed that others, equally impeccable, had seen the original memoir. Evidence for the truth of the record, stoutly declared incontrovertible, was in practice thin, and no manuscript has been produced. In the event, when it comes to apparitions, it may be that the truth is not an option. Facts are elusive; too much is lost in the telling and retelling.

Fabrication, on the other hand, belongs to a distinct category. That the truth is out of reach or uncertain does not mean that there is no difference in principle between attested narratives and stories that are simply made up. It is too easy to assume that, if truth cannot be guaranteed, 'it's all fiction', as they say. Even if the line between the two is not always hard and fast, there is a distinction between accredited stories and inventions. The difficulty, however, as Dorothy Dingley's story demonstrates, is to tell one from the other.

While truth remains an object of desire, it does not necessarily lie waiting for us on the other side of writing or speech. The troubled dead walk in their stories, and perhaps only there. Those tales have a history and, as the consecutive revivals and rewritings of this one imply, a strong and continuing appeal to readers and listeners. That history and that appeal are the main concerns of this book.

ONE

A Dead King Walks

A tale comes to life

'Who's there?' At midnight on the battlements, a sentinel patrols the margin between safety inside the fortress and danger from the outside world. There is feasting inside, perhaps to excess, but beyond the walls, darkness and the unknown. Here, in between, the ramparts of the Danish castle bear witness to an unnamed fear. And yet nothing has so far disturbed tonight's sentries: 'Not a mouse stirring.' With the changing of the guard, there are two sentinels, as well as the prince's friend, Horatio, keen to dispel anxiety. He dismisses their apprehensions as groundless but the soldiers want him to listen to their story. Although the night is bitter cold, 'Sit down awhile', one of them improbably urges, and let me recount again what we have seen these last two nights.

His narrative will stretch belief. The late king cannot rest, it seems, in his tomb but walks this very platform at the dead of night. Ghost stories inevitably feature among the tall tales conventionally recounted after dark on long, cold nights. A few years earlier, Christopher Marlowe's Barabas remembered old wives who used to tell him 'winter's tales, / And speak of spirits and ghosts that glide by night'. Soon Shakespeare's Lady Macbeth will deride her husband's reaction to the blood-stained spectre of the dead Banquo;

such terror befits 'A woman's story at a winter's fire'. Apparently ready to suspend his guard duty, Barnardo is offering to tell a winter's tale, while Horatio and Marcellus gather round to listen.

Despite the unlikely setting for their own story, then, Horatio and the guards are re-enacting a familiar ritual. In 1601, the conjectural date of *Hamlet*, England was still a mainly agricultural society. When the frozen soil was unresponsive, people filled the dark evenings with games and pastimes, among them storytelling. Shakespeare's own *Winter's Tale* would concern a riddling oracle, the recovery of a long-lost child and a miraculous resurrection from the dead. But, in the opinion of the play's little Prince Mamillius, 'A sad tale's best for winter', especially one 'Of sprites and goblins'. These are not the disarming mischief-makers of the Victorian nursery but ghosts and demons. The boy's contribution to the genre begins as a winter's tale well might: 'There was a man . . . Dwelt by a churchyard.'

Such narratives were fireside diversions, pleasurable for the contrast of their gloomy settings with warmth and safety indoors. But there is no such shelter on the battlements where the Danish guards keep watch, and here on the outer walls of the castle they are face-to-face with the cold – and perhaps worse. Besides, they are supposed to be alert, keeping watch. In the interests of probability, some modern directors cut the injunction to be seated, but all three early modern editions of *Hamlet* are consistent on this issue. 'Well, sit we down', Horatio agrees, 'And let us hear Barnardo speak of this.' Evidently, in Shakespeare's play the conventions governing winter's tales override an emerging realism.

No sooner has Barnardo set the scene – last night, at this very hour, when the clock struck one – than an armed figure walks towards them in the shape of the dead king. This apparition quite overcomes Horatio's disbelief; it harrows him, he admits, with fear and wonder. The first edition of the play, published in Shakespeare's lifetime, intensifies the verb: 'It horrors me', Horatio declares. Either way, what began as a ghost story has come to life in the telling.

As the figure approaches the three, something new happens on the English stage and in the history of ghost stories. *Hamlet* gathers up a range of threads from distinct traditions to weave a tale that continues to haunt the imagination of the modern world. On those grounds, if no others, this play marks a critical moment in the development of the genre – and an appropriate starting point for a discussion of ghost stories. Their continuing vitality indicates that their kind remains compelling today, just as they held the attention of our ancestors beside the winter hearth. Do tales of the troubled dead have anything to tell us that might matter in these rational, sceptical times?

'What art thou?'

I believe they do but it may take the length of a book to put forward some tentative answers. Let's begin, then, with *Hamlet* and some of the inferences about ghost stories we can draw from the play. The dead walk when they are troubled; they return because they must. Hamlet's fellow-student, the educated Horatio, should be the one, the guards believe, to find out why this Ghost has returned: 'Thou art a scholar, speak to it, Horatio.'

But the scholar begins with a still more pressing question, 'What art thou?' In Shakespeare's time the phrase can be used interchangeably with 'Who are you?' The proper reply might be a name, a profession or a social status. At the same time, the question also carries its modern charge. What is this thing that the guards call 'it'? Horatio is asking about the identity of the Ghost. Is it really the dead king of Denmark? At the same time, however, he is probing what the Ghost – or what any ghost – is. Two years before, Shakespeare's Brutus, suddenly aware of an apparition in his tent, had put the same question to the spirit of Julius Caesar, 'Speak to me what thou art.'

In the earlier play Brutus is afraid, he says; his blood runs cold, his hair stands on end. Horatio is harrowed (or horrored); he trembles and looks pale. Why should it be frightening to see a ghost? After all, neither Caesar nor King Hamlet offers any threat of violence. But the fear is not in these instances physical, however physiological its symptoms. On the contrary, spectres are unnerving in so far as they shake the norms that allow us to understand what exists – and, by extension, what we ourselves are. Ghosts defy the categories we take for granted, the distinctions we appeal to in finding our location in the world. Buried and yet there to see, neither wholly dead nor truly alive, belonging to the past but evident here and now, unreal but visible, at once human and inhuman, ghosts defy the laws of nature as well as the principles of logic. Figures that are out of place and out of time disturb all that is habitual and reliable, the sureties we count on: the apparition is – and cannot be – present. Ghosts unsettle what we know.

As inhabitants of a realm beyond access – and perhaps beyond belief – they suspend the assumptions that guarantee the customary order. Ghosts demonstrate, as Hamlet will in due course assure his friend, that 'There are more things in heaven and earth . . . Than are dreamt of in your philosophy.' That 'your' may point to Horatio's scholarly doubts or, used colloquially, to the limitations of philosophy in the wider sense. As a threat to all that reason relies on, an apparition means that what is outside the framework of knowledge has made its way in; the unknown has intruded into the familiar. Incompatible with good sense, incommensurable with reality, ghosts stretch what it is possible to grasp; they prompt, as Hamlet also declares, 'thoughts beyond the reaches of our souls'.

And so Horatio's question is the first and most pressing one: 'What art thou?' How is he to understand a ghost, to accommodate the occult in his scheme of things? But the Ghost does not reply. Refusing to gratify curiosity, either Horatio's or the playgoer's, the figure stalks away, 'offended' by the scholar's challenge. When after an interval the apparition returns, Horatio has grown bolder. He now intercepts it with a series of questions that show an astute grasp of popular ghost lore. Is the spectre troubled in a way that he can help to relieve? Has it come to warn of a political crisis? Or does it want to reveal the location of treasure hidden in its lifetime? But the cock crows for dawn and the Ghost turns away once again. Eager to detain it this time in the hope of an answer, at first the men agree that Marcellus should bar its way with his spear. But then they reflect that such physical interventions will have no effect, 'For it is as the air, invulnerable'.

What is a ghost made of? Is the solid, warlike figure before them material, as they initially suppose, or insubstantial, impervious to their weapons, able to be everywhere and nowhere? ''Tis here' . . . ''Tis here' . . . ''Tis gone.' At the Globe Theatre, playgoers might well have been as undecided as Horatio and Marcellus on the question of the Ghost's materiality. The ghouls that haunted winter's tales at this time were most commonly cadavers come out of their graves to confront the living. As young Mamillius hints in Shakespeare's own *Winter's Tale*, cemeteries were especially ominous places, particularly during the hours of darkness, until daylight drove the revenants back under the earth. In *A Midsummer Night's Dream* Puck reminds Oberon of the coming sunrise, 'At whose approach, ghosts wandering here and there / Troop home to churchyards'.

In some respects, Shakespeare's armed Ghost resembles a corporeal revenant of this kind: he too goes back underground as dawn breaks. Hamlet himself seems to share the traditional belief when he appeals to the apparition to say why its corpse, duly swathed for burial, has burst its wrappings and left the tomb. Franco Zeffirelli's film of the play, made in 1990, emphasises the point with a solid and recognisable Ghost, when we have already seen a massive tombstone placed over the dead king as he lies in his grave.

And yet, at other times, the spectre behaves like an insubstantial soul indifferent to materiality. On the battlements, it fades away, Marcellus observes. Drawing on a range of conventions, not always compatible with each other, and performed at a transitional moment, *Hamlet* is pivotal in this ambiguity. Playgoers might be expected to understand either version of what it was to be a ghost; Shakespeare was not compelled to choose between them. And the uncertainty deepens the enigma that surrounds his Ghost's identity.

Some modern directors apply much ingenuity to the construction of an armed ghost that at the same time meets modern expectations of an ethereal presence. Film, itself in so many respects a spectral medium, is able to do it well, especially with the aid of music. Darkness, distance, mist, a silhouette all combine to maintain the ambiguity of the apparition. Laurence Olivier's black and white version, made in 1948, reduces the Ghost to a remote outline until, for a moment, we glimpse a face so gaunt that it resembles a skull. Later directors often prefer chain mail to plate armour, however. In our own times, Olivier's warrior phantom, its voice hoarse from the grave and hollow behind its chin guard, inescapably risks evoking Darth Vader. The similarity is still more apparent in Grigori Kozintsev's Russian film version of 1964. There the Ghost is encased in black metal, while his cloak billows out behind him.

But the first *Star Wars* movie was made in 1977, and the comparison was not available to Kozintsev's first audiences – nor to Shakespeare's at the Globe, where the likely associations of the visual image would include the effigies on patrician tombs. The gentry, those entitled to bear arms, might choose to display their lineage in death, and their monuments often showed a recumbent figure in full armour. William Clopton, who died in 1592, was commemorated in this way in Stratford-upon-Avon, while Shakespeare might also have found elegant earlier examples in the Warwick parish church some six miles away. But there is no need to reach for local instances: this widespread tradition stretched back as far as the 'crusader' knights on their thirteenth-century monuments.

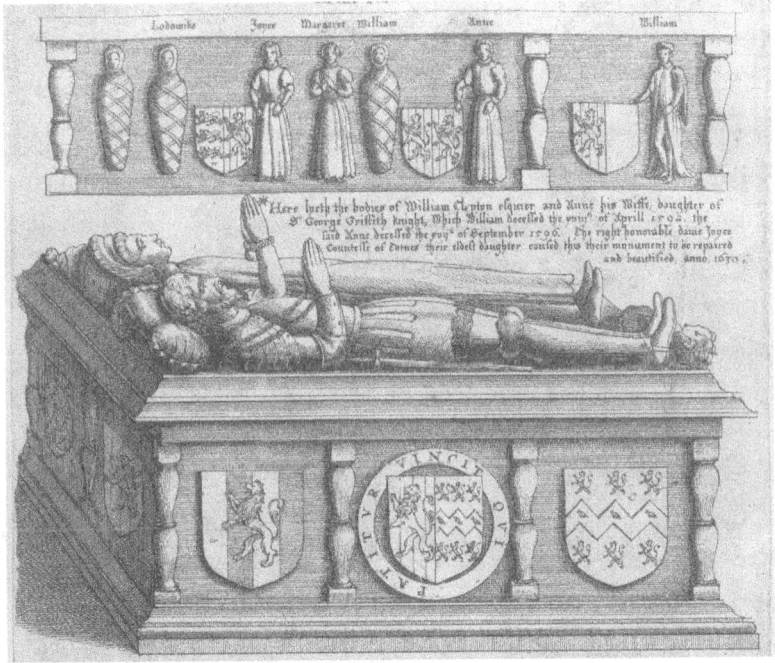

Figure 1 An armed effigy in Stratford-upon-Avon, 1590s

That either an effigy or the dead man it depicted might rise from the tomb to walk by night would have deepened the eeriness of the apparition. It is worth remembering that Shakespeare's Ghost was required to appear in broad daylight at the Globe play-house. Perhaps that is why the play dwells on the mystery of its being. Since lighting effects are not available, the play relies on words to provoke the imagination of the audience. In addition, a convention of counting on the ghost-seer to convey terror goes back at least to the late seventeenth century, when Thomas Betterton as Hamlet was famous for his skill in making the dead king as frightening to the spectators as he was to the prince.

At his third appearance, Old Hamlet speaks volubly of the assault on his life and the obligations of his son to avenge it. And yet he remains reticent when it comes to his own condition. He is kept, he says, in fires until his sins are burnt and purged away. This has led those interested in Shakespeare's religious affiliations to see the dramatist as hinting at his own closet Catholicism. That conjecture seems to me to overload the allusion, which is more hermetic than theological. The Ghost gives no further inform-ation but instead tantalises the audience with what he withholds. He is forbidden to reveal the secrets of his prison to the living, or he would tell his son a real winter's story: 'I could a tale unfold whose lightest word / Would harrow up thy soul, freeze thy young blood.' When it comes to the supernatural, suggestion encourages a more powerful response than exposition.

'What art thou?' But Shakespeare's Ghost evades definition. Enigmatic, an invulnerable spirit, an effigy come to life, a dead body out of the grave, a soul back from purgatory, or each of these at different moments, perhaps, Old Hamlet does not allow us to decide. Classification would bring the being of a ghost within a framework that would begin to make the apparition intelligible.

To the degree that they remain undefined, ghosts solicit more than a slight adjustment of what we thought we knew. The troubled dead prove most unnerving when they keep us guessing.

'Wicked or charitable'?

The Ghost in *Hamlet* also unsettles conventional ethics; its moral status remains as unresolved as its identity. Victorian critics, certain that fathers ought to be obeyed even from beyond the grave, had no doubt that the Ghost was right. The question for them was why Hamlet didn't just do what he was told and avenge the dead king by killing his murderer. Evidently, there was something wrong with the prince, a malady of the mind, perhaps, a fatal indecisiveness. But the play is by no means so ready to sanctify the Ghost. 'I'll cross it though it blast me', Horatio bravely declares at its second appearance. He has good reason to fear the worst. Ghosts in fireside tales were commonly dangerous; popular revenants were capable of force. In some instances, their decomposing flesh spread disease; in others, they came to summon the living, and people who saw them might expect to die within days.

The imagery of the play links the dead king with misfortune and misdeeds. Spirits that walk by night are 'extravagant and erring', Horatio claims, straying outside their proper bounds, misled and misleading. When the cock crew to herald the return of daylight, the Ghost 'started like a guilty thing', he recalls. And Marcellus adds that Christmas banishes all spirits, who dare not then stir abroad: instead, at that holy time 'The nights are wholesome.' As it happens, Shakespeare seems to have invented this belief: in the fireside tradition ghosts were particularly active at Christmas – and would remain so once Dickens had re-energised the convention in *A Christmas Carol*. But in *Hamlet* their supposed expulsion reminds playgoers of the traditional link between ghosts and pollution. To Marcellus, the apparition shows that 'Something is rotten in the state of Denmark.'

Although Hamlet refuses to be deterred by such considerations, he acknowledges a related anxiety: 'I'll speak to it though hell itself should gape.' Is the Ghost a demon loosed from the next world? In medieval images of God's Last Judgement, commonly painted above the chancel arch in the parish church for all the congregation to see, entrance to the infernal region was through an open mouth, the jaws of hell. Into this huge maw, demons propelled sinners towards a range of graphically depicted tortures. From the 1530s on, the Protestant Reformers demanded that images of the deity be whitewashed over, but some inevitably survived and more lived on in the cultural memory. In 1598, Philip Henslowe recorded among the props of the Rose theatre 'one hell mouth', which was probably in use for performances of Marlowe's *Doctor Faustus*. 'Ugly hell, gape not', cries Faustus, as the devils come to claim him as their prey. Hamlet's allusion suggests that hauntings might reverse the process: ghosts could be emigrants from a gaping realm of the damned.

The prince had a case. Reformation orthodoxy resolutely denied the existence of ghosts; seeming revenants were impersonated by devils, who borrowed likenesses of the departed with malign intent. We need to go back in time to make sense of this insistence. In ancient Rome the dead walked, especially if their burial rites had been inadequate or incomplete. But St Augustine, perhaps the most influential among the thinkers who put together a theology for the early Christian Church, was anxious that the new religion should turn its back on all things pagan. There were, he therefore declared, no ghosts. The dead were indifferent to this world; their concerns were with the next.

But even Augustine conceded that semblances of the dead might appear in dreams, although there was no possibility that this took place with the knowledge of the deceased themselves. Other Church Fathers were not so sure that there was no return. Gregory the Great was not above telling vivid cautionary tales of ghostly bath attendants compelled to come back in this lowly employment to atone for their sins. Meanwhile by the fireside, apparitions persisted and winter's tales did not always take account of Christian teaching. Since the troubled dead refused to rest in their graves, purgatory was made official in the twelfth century in order to give ghosts a home – and to make money for the Church in the process. The returning dead were entitled to solicit payment for masses and, in due course, indulgences, to reduce the term of their enforced purification.

The Protestant Reformers, however, deplored this practice; they also greatly admired Augustine and invoked him as an ally against what they saw as Catholic corruption of the integrity of the early Church. Salvation was a matter of faith; it could not be bought. In Protestant regimes, from the mid-sixteenth century on there were no ghosts and no purgatory to house them.

Once again, however, winter's tales proved tenacious, despite the best efforts of the clergy. In fireside culture, the troubled dead continued to leave their graves, perhaps with a view to putting things right in some of the ways Horatio lists, or perhaps purely out of reluctance to let go of this world. To the despair of the Church, the old beliefs did not melt away in the face of doctrinal exposition. A letter probably written in 1564 by the Bishop of Durham to the Archbishop of Canterbury gives an indication of the difficulty. Church teaching didn't seem to be making much headway against traditional convictions, the bishop reported. He had just visited Lancashire and the many problems he had found in that county included a young man, 'fantastical (and as some think a lunatic)', who claimed to have held a number of conversations with a neighbour dead for four years or more. Sometimes he took with him the curate, the schoolmaster and various other members of the community, all of whom confirmed his story.

'Fantastical' the young man might have been, but his worthy companions should surely have known better. And the bishop concludes querulously, 'These things be so common here', and the people in authority so reluctant to contradict superstition, 'that everyone believes it.' Accordingly, Reformation theology bowed to popular opinion just far enough to concede that, while there were no ghosts, demons from hell might impersonate them to lure the living into error. They might even give an honest account of the past. 'Oftentimes', as the living Banquo sagely observes in *Macbeth*, 'to win us to our harm / The instruments of darkness tell us truths.'

Although in England the Reformation of the 1530s had got off to a shaky start, the accession of Elizabeth I in 1558 had done a good deal to cement Protestant beliefs. In 1601 Shakespeare's guards are cautious: they speak of the apparition as 'it'; the figure *resembles* the late King Hamlet, they note; at his first address, Horatio asks who or what it is that 'usurps' the form of the buried sovereign. At the same time, *Hamlet* is a work of fiction, set in a remote Scandinavian past, not a treatise on current Christian doctrine. In other instances the play treats the Ghost simply as the dead monarch. Offended by the suggestion that he is not a true revenant, the figure stalks away. When Horatio reports the apparition to Hamlet, he says he thinks he saw his father. Hamlet, meanwhile, suspends judgement. On the one hand, 'If it assume my noble father's person, / I'll speak to it though hell itself should gape'; on the other, and within ten lines, 'My father's spirit – in arms! All is not well.'

The prince's reaction to the first sight of the Ghost also keeps the options open:

> Angels and minsters of grace defend us!
> Be thou a spirit of health or goblin damned,
> Bring with the airs from heaven or blasts from hell,
> Be thy intents wicked or charitable . . .

This may be a wholesome visitant from the past, eager to bring to light a crime; it may also be a malevolent tempter impersonating a beloved father to endanger his son. When the apparition impels Hamlet to follow it on his own, the sentries and Horatio all doubt its motive: suppose it lures him towards the cliff edge, only to 'assume some other horrible form' in order to drive him mad and tempt him to jump. Once again, they are in tune with popular lore: shape-shifting was widespread among fireside apparitions. But the prince is not to be restrained – and at last the Ghost delivers its message.

When it does so, is the distrust of the sentries proved right or wrong? Is it, as Hamlet himself will go on in due course to wonder, a devil that abuses him to damn him? The Ghost tells a tale of murder and illicit desire; Hamlet's role is to punish the offender. But what this armed Ghost wants is violence. The vengeance demanded by the spectre (either father or demon) would involve a repetition of the first crime, another family murder that is also regicide. Does the Ghost ask his son to bring a criminal to justice, or to retaliate by re-enacting the original offence? And if Hamlet dies in the process, as is more than probable since treason does not go unpunished, will he face damnation in consequence? That is what the prince (along with the audience) has the rest of the play to decide: whether it is more honourable to put up with a villainous new king, or to obey the Ghost against all odds; 'Whether', in other words, ''tis nobler in the mind to suffer / The slings and arrows of outrageous fortune, / Or to take arms against a sea of troubles.'

Whatever simple truths the Victorians may have taken for granted about the obligation to obey a father, Elizabethan revenge plays struggled with the ethics of personal vengeance. At a moment when the early modern state was doing its best to bring private quarrels under the control of the law, Hamlet's own extant stage predecessors could not bring themselves to avenge cruel injuries while in their right minds. Shakespeare's Titus Andronicus and Thomas Kyd's Hieronimo both hold out for legal remedies, until repeated denials of redress drive them mad. In what follows, the excesses of their crazed retribution align revenge with horror, not justice.

When it comes to *Hamlet*, the playwright intensifies the problem. Drawing in Act 1 on different elements of existing ghost lore, he leaves open to doubt the identity, provenance and authority of the Ghost, and in the process sets up a dilemma for his hero that will take the prince four more acts to resolve. In this play Shakespeare stages a new kind of ghost story – and tales of the troubled dead would never be quite the same again.

Suspense

Since *Hamlet*, we have known how much a good ghost story owes to the telling. If we put aside the modern requirement for trans- lucent phantoms to walk through walls, if, that is, we succeed in coming to terms with the seeming solidity of Shakespeare's armed apparition, we can see that the play builds a special kind of suspense. The Ghost's first appearance is fleeting, only long

enough for the spectre to be recognised and addressed. At the
second, it seems about to speak when the cock crows for dawn to
drive it away. The play makes the audience wait. The third time,
the figure defers revelation still further by beckoning Hamlet to a
more remote place. Only then, at the end of the Act 1, is its
purpose made clear.

The suspense deepens when the uncanny gives way for a time
to the everyday. From the viewpoint of the playgoers, these
strange midnight encounters are contrasted with all that is habitual and well lit. The first scene of the play introduces the Ghost.
But the next moves the action from the castle walls to the court
within, from the spectre of a dead king to his living successor,
busily hearing petitions and issuing orders. The Ghost is not
forgotten, however: at the end of that crowded episode, Horatio
and the guards report what they have seen to the prince, who
instantly resolves to join their watch at midnight. But before he
can do so, the scene shifts again to the domestic relations between
Laertes and Ophelia, and the prosaic instructions of a thoroughly
conventional, living father. As the settings alternate, the play
repeatedly reaffirms normality, only to plunge us back with a
renewed shock into awareness of the occult.

Shakespeare's Ghost made its mark at the time. No sustained
commentary on *Hamlet* survives from the seventeenth century
and we know of its influence only from scattered allusions, parodies and imitations. These indicate that the skull, Hamlet's
assumed madness and the Ghost were the features that attracted
most attention. In 1709 the playwright's first editor, Nicholas
Rowe, claimed that Shakespeare had himself played the Ghost, as
'the top of his performance'. The story that the dramatist took the
role may or may not be true. What invests it with a certain interest
is Rowe's evident view that the Ghost was a strong part for a

dramatist whose century-old works were worth editing. And he went on in his comments on *Hamlet* to declare that 'no dramatic writer ever succeeded better in raising terror in the minds of an audience than Shakespeare has done'.

The evidence we have suggests that no previous dramatic writer had ever made much effort to frighten playgoers with the uncanny, although brute horror was a speciality. If we suspend the insoluble problem of an earlier play called *Hamlet*, possibly by Thomas Kyd and now lost, ghosts on the Elizabethan stage, though plentiful and frequently murderous, were not generally eerie. Eager to construct their plays in the light of theatrical tradition, early modern playwrights put their education to work and looked mainly to the Roman dramatist Seneca for inspiration. In the unenviable post of tutor and then adviser to the Emperor Nero, Seneca had produced a series of bloodcurdling tragedies that were widely read when they became available in translation in Elizabethan England.

Seneca's ghosts, however horrible, are not uncanny. They inhabit a separate plane from the living characters. No one is haunted; the dead do not interact with the living. In two instances, ghosts appear as prologues, without introduction or build-up. They have come from the dark underworld, they tell us, to watch with relish the downfall of those left behind. Far from withholding the secrets of the afterlife, they describe them in detail, as a prelude to prophesying vengeance. Here, for example, is the dead Thyestes in full spate at the beginning of Seneca's *Agamemnon*: replete with hatred, he has returned to the threshold of his brother's palace, a place he detests. Ought he not to go back to the equally hateful lakes of Hades, where crime meets with due punishment? There Sisyphus hopelessly pushes his rock up the hill, vultures endlessly devour the liver of Tityos and thirsty

Tantalus cannot reach the water that surrounds him. But Thyestes is distracted from this thought by the memory of his own crimes, which far outdo the evils of those he has named. He has devoured his own sons and fathered a child on his daughter. Still more grisly events are to come, however, he promises: soon the palace will swim in blood, a king's head will be split open . . .

English imitations of Seneca are generally less gory but the same pattern is perceptible. Ghosts are largely confined to prologues, choruses, dumb shows or dreams. They foretell conflict and then stand aside to watch the action. In the late 1580s, Kyd's dead Andrea tells his story at the opening of *The Spanish Tragedy*: he died in war and journeyed through the underworld, where the classical torments he describes were supplemented by scenes from medieval depictions of the Christian hell. When Old Hamlet claims to come from purgatory, he updates the netherworld Seneca's ghosts had described in such graphic detail, as well as Kyd's partial Christianisation of Roman convention.

From the perspective of storytelling, rather than theology, only a temporary prison-house of purgation is consistent with Hamlet's indecision. A providential spectre sent back from heaven would have to be obeyed without question – but would be most unlikely to recommend murder and regicide. Conversely, Hamlet would be wise to shun a damned soul from hell – and the play would be over before it had got under way. Only an intermediate state leaves open the question of whether the Ghost's intents are wicked or charitable, and faces Hamlet and the audience with the imponderable question of what he ought to do.

In *The Spanish Tragedy* Andrea has returned, with his companion Revenge, to witness earthly retribution for his death. The pair remain as spectators throughout the action of the play, but they take no part in it. Something new to the drama occurs, however, in Shakespeare's *Julius Caesar*, when on the eve of the battle of Philippi a ghost interacts with a living man. Brutus alone remains awake in his tent; the taper dims and an apparition that makes his blood run cold speaks to him directly. This ghost draws on the fireside tradition.

Julius Caesar was performed in 1599, two years or so before the probable date of *Hamlet*. The later play refers back to its predecessor: Polonius once took the part of Caesar, he reveals; Brutus killed him in the Capitol. Was this an in-joke? Did the same actor play Caesar and Polonius at the Globe? It seems likely that Richard Burbage played Brutus, who stabbed Caesar, as well as Hamlet, who will go on to run through Polonius. Either way, the Ghost of Old Hamlet, while much more fully developed, evidently belongs to the genre that emerges in *Julius Caesar*. A spectre confronts the living, evoking terror and dismay. Seneca is not forgotten but winter's tales also go into the making of this uncanny spectre – and, at the same time, the Gothic is suddenly in sight.

Death

Indefinite, unnerving, enigmatic, ghosts give form to what little we know of death. It is not easy to accept the prospect of extinction, our own or other people's. Rationally, we know that death will occur – preferably at a safe distance. Woody Allen notably wasn't afraid of it: he just didn't want to be there when it happened. It is hard to believe that the self before which the world has played out its many pageants should simply cease to be, while the spectacle carries on regardless. Sigmund Freud puts it well:

> It is true that the statement 'All men are mortal' is paraded in
> text-books of logic as an example of a general proposition; but

no human being really grasps it, and our unconscious has as
little use now as it ever had for the idea of its own mortality.

Such minimal account do we take of what we know to be true,
he notes, that we find it impossible to imagine our own death,
and 'whenever we attempt to do so we can perceive that we are
in fact still present as spectators'. If Freud is right, we hover
by our own projected deathbeds, unable to leave the world
behind. In other words, we conceive of ourselves witnessing our
death as our own ghosts. No wonder ghost stories have proved
so enduring.

What defies imagination is not the process of dying but annihilation viewed from the other side of it, from the perspective of
the dead. All we know is life. Death, the state of being dead, is a
secret, an 'undiscovered country', as Hamlet puts it. And what
remains concealed from our knowledge generates fear. In *Measure
for Measure* Shakespeare's Claudio names the anxiety about what
follows as he foresees his own execution:

> to die, and go we know not where;
> To lie in cold obstruction, and to rot;
> This sensible warm motion to become
> A kneaded clod.

So much, at least, for the body. And Claudio runs through the
fates different cultures have prescribed for the soul: to be confined
to fire or trapped in ice, to be blown about in the wind, or, worst
of all, to howl in hell. The most wretched life we can imagine is 'a
paradise / To what we fear of death'. Hamlet says something
similar in 'To be or not to be': who would bear the miseries of this
life but for dread of the next?

Religions step into the breach in our knowledge, promising a variety of afterlives. Oddly enough, they do not seem to appease either Claudio or Hamlet, even at a time when atheism was only just thinkable. Is there something unsatisfying about doctrinal certainty, ready answers to the question death presents? Ghosts, by contrast, while they imply a form of survival, leave its character imprecise, unresolved. They half-tell the secret of what is to come – and then vanish. For centuries, ghost stories have maintained their hold, now in harmony with orthodoxy, now in opposition to it, as a parallel way of delineating what we can't know, while at the same time preserving its uncertainty.

Although we can have no experience of our own death, the death of others brings home to us the reality of loss, especially when those others are close to us, or the model of what we may become. 'I'll call thee Hamlet', says Hamlet to the Ghost, when for a strange moment it is as if he addresses himself in the father whose name he bears. And, indeed, the play that follows might be viewed as a sustained meditation on the prospect of death. If 'To be' contemplates the fate that may afflict the soul, Hamlet's reflections culminate in the exchanges in the churchyard. There the prince examines Yorick's skull at close quarters and asks the gravedigger searching questions about the decomposition of the body. How long, he wants to know, does it take for the corpse to rot. 'If it be now, 'tis not to come', he finally reasons; 'The readiness is all.' On one reading, the tragedy is about the reluctant achievement of that readiness.

From the beginning of the play, Hamlet is in mourning, his grief for his father compounded by absence of sorrow in the person who should properly feel it most. The widow's hasty remarriage betrays a loving husband and cuts short the period custom allocates to commemoration. Most cultures greet loss with rituals,

burial practices, funeral gatherings, monuments, elegies, obituaries and stories – in the first instance, tales of happier times, the
achievements and virtues of the deceased. All these go to invest a
life and its conclusion with meaning. And yet deep mourning,
experienced as profound loss, is not felt only at the level of such
representations. Something more visceral cannot quite be allayed
by memorial rites, especially when these are abruptly terminated
or interrupted.

Revenants speak to the bereaved on this less than rational
plane; they meet a deeply held desire to bring back the dead.
Hamlet, most hesitant of heroes, does not pause for thought
before resolving to seek out the Ghost; the combined efforts of his
companions cannot prevent him from following its summons.
Objects of fear, ghosts can also be magnetic: they tug at the imagination, and not only of the bereaved themselves. Perhaps, after
all, they unsettle our certainties for better, not worse. Tales of the
walking dead offer clues to the secret that experience itself can
only withhold.

Are they and their stories consoling, then, after all? Sometimes,
to the degree that they seem to fulfil a longing for contact or reassurance. But, paradoxically, such contact is generally arrested,
attenuated, incomplete. When Hamlet calls death a country from
which no traveller returns, critics see an inconsistency. Has he
forgotten the Ghost? But 'return' in that context is ambiguous.
The Ghost cannot come back to the world of the living, take up
his former position, reinstate himself in the life of the castle.
Although he appears in Gertrude's closet, he does not belong
there and, indeed, the queen cannot see him. She has a new
husband, Denmark a new king. The Ghost is now more fully
immaterial in every sense of that term, not only insubstantial but
also irrelevant, out of time and out of place.

For that reason, spectres mark not the restoration of the deceased but a loss that cannot be repaired. In the event, the dead prove irrecoverable, their phantoms incompatible with the everyday. Since they breach the laws of nature and logic, apparitions defy the possibility of restitution. Shakespeare's Ghost, who reappears in the closet in order to strengthen his son's resolution, threatens only to weaken it, Hamlet says, as vengeance gives way to tears of mourning. Even while they seem to promise presence, ghosts have the effect of affirming what is missing.

And narratives about them? What, since accounts of revenants are in the end so rarely reassuring, can be the perennial attraction of ghost stories for listeners, readers and viewers? No doubt, people are drawn to winter's tales for a range of reasons. Possibly ghost stories seem to counter the threat of death; perhaps they ward off the finality of loss, or at least hold it at bay. Sometimes they offer fragments, however chilling, of news from the unknown. At the same time, they register a resistance to the limits that stout common sense imposes on thinking, stretching speculation beyond the maps culture provides and allowing a brief engagement with undiscovered countries, those mysterious terrains that exceed our names for them.

TWO

Haunted Pasts

The record

Like Dorothy Dingley, the armed figure of Old Hamlet would resurface in the future, sometimes in unfamiliar guises, with repercussions for the evolution of the genre. *Hamlet* brings together much that we have come to expect from ghost stories, including suspense and the uncanny. It presents apparitions as a puzzle, while linking them with both bereavement and the fear of death. The play projects a form of survival and yet maintains the secrets of the grave. Stamped with Shakespeare's authority, *Hamlet* goes on to exert a powerful influence on tales of the supernatural, so that, for all these reasons, the play threads its way through this book.

I have introduced it as a starting point for my history of ghost stories because it brings together in one place so much that had gone before. And I continue my own account by considering, in a series of flashbacks, the range of traditions that led up to the play. Ghost stories go back a long way. All the evidence points to a widespread belief in tribal cultures that the dead survive in some form. But, while folklore may keep alive the contours of old tales, only societies with writing preserve ghost stories intact.

Although many parts of the world have a rich supernatural heritage, oral and written, here I confine myself mainly to the West. This is not out of indifference so much as the fear of gate-crashing. Where possible, past cultures are best explicated by those who inherit them. Besides, keeping the lineage of *Hamlet* in view helps to focus my narrative. The troubled dead returned, then, in ancient Greece and Rome; they did so with a difference in Northern Europe. Classical and Norse traditions both played a part in medieval storytelling, as did the other worlds where ghosts lived on, sometimes celebrating but more commonly in distress.

Greek and Roman ghosts

A range of troubles brought back the dead of the classical past. Most notably, in ancient Greece and Rome they could not move on to the next world without full funeral rites. The Greek Patroclus, killed by Hector in the Trojan War, returned to his friend Achilles as he slept, Homer records. In the dream, the ghost of Patroclus looked exactly like himself, dressed as was his custom in life. He was refused admission to the underworld, he complained, kept out by the bodiless spirits of the dead, who would not let him join them. His last request was that his bones should share an urn with those of his old friend and comrade. Achilles held out his arms for one final embrace but the apparition vanished. It was nothing but a wraith, the semblance of a man.

In the classical world, any sudden death risked inadequate ceremonial and that in turn barred access to the next world. Homer's young Elpenor fell from the roof of Circe's palace while the Greeks were beating a retreat in too much haste to stage a funeral. Elpenor's ghost begs Odysseus to burn his body and raise a mound for him where he died. The drowned Palinurus, haunting the banks of the River Styx, makes a similar plea to Virgil's Aeneas, when the living hero visits the underworld. Surly Charon will not ferry souls across the river to the netherworld while their bones remain unburied.

But not all revenants sought burial. Suppose, besides Patroclus, other Greeks from the Trojan War were able to return from the dead. What stories they could tell! In his Greek prose work *On Heroes* Flavius Philostratus recounts the tales told to a visiting Phoenician sailor by a local vine-dresser. Protesilaos, this cultivator of grapevines tells the visitor, was the first of the Greeks to die. Killed as he leapt ashore onto Trojan soil, Protesilaos was still able to observe mortal affairs. Now he passes on to his living friend stories about the war.

The Phoenician isn't convinced by the vine-dresser's source: he has outgrown the tales of the returning dead he heard from his old nurse. On the other hand, since he likes a good story, he over-comes his doubts to let the vine-dresser, on the authority of his ghostly companion, retell what Homer's *Iliad* omitted or misrep-resented. Actually, the gossipy storyteller confides, the Trojans hated Helen, whose abduction from Greece had started the war; they didn't let her live in Troy; instead, she was exiled to Egypt. The Greeks didn't want her back, either; it was Trojan wealth they were after. She and Achilles went on to be lovers after their death and lived happily together on a secluded island.

Writing in the third century CE, Philostratus could count on his readers' familiarity with a long tradition of Greek and Roman ghost lore. Protesilaos had access to information lost to the living. Since from early times the classical dead were widely thought to know more than we do, it was not unusual to approach them as authorities on the future, as well as the past. One example of such a consultation is dramatised in the ancient Greek play *The Persians*. Hearing that their army has been put to flight by the Greeks at the battle of Salamis, the Persians summon their dead king Darius to give them advice.

Darius comes up to the daylight, rising from his tomb in response to the appeal of his compatriots. The king's ghost knows nothing of current events on earth, but he remembers a prophecy that his country would pay a price for overreaching itself. He little thought the prediction would be fulfilled so soon, he admits. But now the Persians must never take on Greece again. They will lose once more to the Greeks at the battle of Plataea. His wise counsel once delivered, the dead Darius returns to the dark. The battle of Salamis took place in 480 BCE and Plataea in the following year. Seven years later Aeschylus, who fought for the Greeks at Salamis, won a prize in Athens for four plays, including *The Persians*.

Oracles, too, could foretell the future, if often in riddles, by summoning the spirits of the dead. Alternatively, ghosts might use their foreknowledge to confer a blessing. Virgil's defeated Trojan hero Aeneas flees from the burning city, carrying his aged father and holding the hand of his little son, with his wife Creüsa following behind them. Hearing the tramp of Greek soldiers at his back, Aeneas darts down unfamiliar by-ways, only to find himself separated from the wife he loves. When he plunges back into the scene of destruction, desperately calling her name, what he finds instead is her shade, larger than life. Now his terror increases and his hair stands on end, but the ghost speaks to allay his fear. The gods have decreed that his wife should be lost, she says. Perils await him but he will come through the ordeals and find a new wife. Then Creüsa vanishes, urging him to take good care of their child.

Grateful revenants sometimes came back to return favours or to comfort the bereaved. But other ghosts have less benevolent intentions. Victims of homicide, for instance, may seek revenge on their killers. Clytemnestra pursues her son Orestes, who killed her to avenge the murder of his father. In *Octavia*, attributed to Seneca, Nero's mother reappears to promise he will pay for putting her to death.

Outside the epic and dramatic traditions, ghosts could be violent. The town of Temesa was pestered by the spectre of a Greek sailor who had got drunk and raped a virgin. The local people stoned him to death but his ghost killed their townsfolk until they appeased him annually with a new sacrificial maiden. One year, however, the Olympic champion boxer Euthymus fell in love with the maiden, fought the revenant and drove it from the land for good. Philostratus – or his vine-dresser – tells how the dead Achilles once asked a visiting merchant to bring him a Trojan girl. As the merchant sailed away, he heard her agonised cries from the shore, while the ghost of the Greek hero tore her limb from limb. A century earlier, Phlegon of Tralles had recorded the case of a revenant who ate all but the head of an intersex baby, perceived as a monster.

These grim tales attest to a popular repertoire that barely surfaces in the poetic tradition. But perhaps it lived on. Fireside narratives are known to survive only when they make their way into the written record. It was not until the fifteenth century that accounts began to circulate in writing of the *vrykolakas*, a dangerous undead corpse shared by Greek folklore with Slavic tradition – and perhaps with northern Europe as well.

Nordic noir

In the north, tales of revenants were put on record in the Icelandic sagas. These dead were corporeal and threatening; they came out of their graves to harass the living; they could not be appeased and were best laid by physical means.

According to one of these Norse stories, when the Icelander Grettir was shipwrecked on an island off the coast of Norway, Thorfinn took him in. A local resident told Grettir how Thorfinn had come by his land. At first, he and his father owned a single farm. But the father's corpse walked after his death until he drove out all the other farmers and now Thorfinn had possession of the whole island. Grettir instructed his new friend to meet him at the father's grave mound with digging tools. In spite of the danger, he descended into the barrow, while his companion held the rope that would help the Icelander back to the living world. In the grave the hero found horse bones, as well as treasure, and a man sitting in a chair. As he carried the treasure to the rope, something seized him. Grettir fought back fiercely and, after a bitter struggle, the grave-dweller fell dead. Hearing a thud from the barrow, his friend turned and fled. Grettir cut off the head of the corpse and placed it against the buttocks – then returned with the treasure.

Grettir's Saga was written in the early fourteenth century but the origins of the narrative are probably much older; its setting is over three hundred years earlier, when Christianity was new to Iceland. That the dead walk is taken for granted: mounds and cairns were designed to keep them underground. It is odd to reflect that our own gravestones, placed as memorials, also hark back to a time when the main imperative was to stop cadavers from returning. The revenant is physically powerful: Grettir's companion runs away from the graveside, assuming the ghost's superhuman strength has prevailed in the struggle. Such walking corpses ravaged the countryside and killed without remorse.

Larger than life, these pre-Christian ghosts had also lost all normal human sympathies. Former ties were forgotten in an unmotivated malevolence. Saxo Grammaticus, the twelfth-century chronicler of Denmark, tells the story of Aswid and Asmund, friends who, swearing undying brotherhood, promised to be buried together. When Aswid died, Asmund kept his promise, and entered the cave of death alive with the corpse, along with Aswid's horse and his dog. Swedes who broke open the barrow soon afterwards, hoping for treasure, found instead the pale, bleeding Asmund with one ear missing. Aswid had returned from death in his tomb, devoured the horse and the dog, and then fallen upon his friend. But Asmund retaliated, finally cutting off the head of the revenant and staking his body.

If they threaten living people, these Nordic dead are best dismembered or burned. But only a hero stands a chance of defeating them. Grettir's fight with Thorfinn's dead father was not to be his last encounter with the supernatural. It turned out that ghosts besieged the farm belonging to Thorhall, especially in winter. Workers would not stay at Thorhallstead and in desperation Thorhall appointed the Swedish Glam as his shepherd. Thorhallstead was Christian but Glam rejected all religion as mere superstition. On Christmas Eve he died in a snowstorm and began to walk in his turn, killing the livestock. The following Christmas Eve the new shepherd disappeared. He was found by Glam's grave mound, every bone in his body broken. When Glam killed the old cowherd, Thorhall left for the rest of the winter.

It was Grettir's own idea to intervene. The dead Glam had taken to sitting astride the roofbeam of the farmhouse, riding the hall like a horse and beating on the ceiling with his heels. Although the revenant had grown to the size of a monster, Grettir had skill and cunning in addition to strength. After a long struggle at the dead of night, the ghost fell to the ground but at that moment the clouds parted and the moonlight shone full on the spectre's eyes. Appalled by what he saw, the hero paused long enough to hear the ghost prophesy his future. Grettir's exploits would turn to misfortune and the gaze of the revenant would always be within his view. While Glam was speaking, Grettir recovered his powers. He killed the ghost with his short sword, placing the severed head beside the buttocks. The corpse was burned to ashes but ever afterwards Grettir was afraid of the dark, which he experienced as haunted by apparitions. To this day in Iceland, 'Glam's sight' denotes a propensity to see beyond what is there.

Medieval revenants

Stories of corporeal revenants lived on. In mid-twelfth-century England, Geoffrey of Burton recorded the history of two dead peasants from Stapenhill, who terrorised the neighbourhood. The men had had the effrontery to move to Drakelow, preferring the lordship of the secular Count Roger to the jurisdiction of Geoffrey's own superior. Once there, they stirred up trouble between the layman and the Abbot of Burton. God's vengeance was ruthless: the peasants were struck down dead and their bodies were taken back for burial in the churchyard at Stapenhill, where they belonged. That very evening, however, the two irrepressible runaways came out of their graves, hoisted their coffins onto their shoulders and set out for Drakelow.

They walked through the village all night, shouting and banging on the walls of the houses, sometimes taking the forms of bears, dogs and other animals. After successive nights of this, all but three of the villagers fell ill and died. With the bishop's permission, the corpses of the two peasants were dug up. Their heads were cut off and placed between their legs, and their hearts were extracted and set on fire. When the hearts cracked, everyone there saw an evil spirit in the form of a crow fly out of the flames.

A few years later, William of Newburgh put on record the story of a worldly priest who walked after death both inside and outside the convent. He had been the chaplain of a pious lady, who found him groaning outside her chamber. When she appealed to a friar for help, this clerical Grettir set up a vigil with three stalwarts in the graveyard. The four waited for the ghost to emerge but, when by mid-night nothing had happened, the other three retreated to the warmth of a nearby house. Seizing his chance, the revenant now rose out of his tomb. When the terrified friar struck at him with an axe, the wounded monster turned back, howling. The grave opened to receive its occupant and the mendicant was left shaken but victorious. On the following morning, the corpse with its wound was exhumed and burned. Its ashes were scattered and the hauntings ceased.

Encounter with a revenant portended death or sickness. In particular, the dead were known to spread pestilence. It was equally common for ghosts to change into one frightening shape after another, as the Drakelow peasants did and as Horatio fears Old Hamlet may. In about 1400 the story of Snowball the tailor was recorded by a monk of Byland Abbey on the spare pages of an old manuscript. Snowball was attacked on his way home by a raven that turned into a dog. At their next meeting the ghost took the form of a she-goat. After each encounter, the innocent Snowball was ill for some days.

Eventually, the she-goat morphed into a tall man, who resembled the picture of 'one of the dead kings'. The kings in question were the Three Dead, who encountered the Three Living in illuminated manuscripts and on any number of fourteenth-century church walls. These grisly manifestations of the destiny that awaits the living have returned from the grave to warn their successors of what will become of them. 'As I am, so you will be', they announce. Mirroring the inevitable fate of the living kings, the ghosts wear tattered shrouds that disclose their entrails, often worn away or devoured by worms. In John Awdelay's early fifteenth-century poetic narrative of 'The Three Dead Kings', the Dead reveal that they are the young men's fathers, come from their past to show them their future.

Figure 2 The Dead show the Living kings their own future, about 1310

The next world

When historical cultures have imagined ideal life forms, they have made them immortal. On Mount Olympus, the deathless Greek gods spend delightful days in the clear, cloudless air, in command of the winds and seas. Any troubles are of their own making. Adam and Eve lost both a fertile paradise and immortality when they disobeyed the word of an eternal God.

Since then, human beings have lived in the shadow of death, projecting an afterlife designed to allay the fear of annihilation. The grave goods uncovered by archaeologists attest to a widespread belief in the realm of the dead. But images of it vary. For the ancient Egyptians the next world was much like this one, although they had to win the right to go there. In other instances, the dead inhabit a sunless place, drained of all vitality. Although the most illustrious of the Nordic dead feasted with Odin in Valhalla, Hel was the dismal destination of ordinary Viking ghosts.

The world where mortals live on is often a place of judgement and retribution. When the next world is seen to put right the injustices of this one, it includes torments, as well as rewards. One fear then comes to replace another, as the dread of extinction gives way to the threat of suffering. 'Men fear death, as children fear to go in the dark', Francis Bacon noted in his essay 'Of Death', 'and as that natural fear in children is increased with tales, so is the other.' Stories about the next world that set out to counter the fear of death may have the paradoxical effect of intensifying anxiety about what is to come.

A strange netherworld features in the oldest epic we have. Gilgamesh was king of Uruk in Mesopotamia in about 2800 BCE. His story circulated first in oral form and then in fragments of script. The Babylonian *Gilgamesh*, possibly put together by a single author, was committed to clay tablets in about 1700 BCE. A separate tablet, probably older in origin, records how the king's friend Enkidu descends into the netherworld, where he is taken captive but permitted to report to Gilgamesh. The ghosts of the sick are not healed in the underworld but stillborn children do well. Otherwise, sex in this life is the main key to success in the next. Eunuchs and childless women are cast aside; virgins of both sexes weep. Fathers are rewarded, however, according to the number of their sons. Those with two sons eat bread and those with three are given water. But fathers of seven male children sit on thrones among the minor deities. While the ghosts of those accursed by their parents are compelled to wander, people who died by fire have no ghosts.

Already, it seems, the afterlife is conceived as better than no life at all but, because it allocates rewards and punishments, even if in accordance with a set of cultural values we might now find somewhat arbitrary, the other world is as much a threat as a promise. Fear of death is displaced onto the half-life that follows it. Homeric ghosts are no more enviable. Unlike the Mesopotamian dead, who eat and drink if they have proved themselves virile enough to merit such pleasures, the inhabitants of Homer's other world have no bodies and no consciousness.

When Odysseus visits their realm, he fills a trench with libations and adds the blood of two sheep. Then the place of darkness and mist is filled with ghosts, fluttering and moaning round the trench. Only those who are permitted to drink the blood regain their wits and recognise the living hero, among them his mother. After an exchange of news, Odysseus longs to hold her. Three times he moves towards her with arms outstretched; three times she slips through them, like a shadow or a dream. He fares no better with his old comrades, although he is glad to hear their stories. Agamemnon would embrace him but all the strength has left his arms. Surely, Odysseus urges Achilles, you are a great prince down here? But his friend is not reconciled to the afterlife. Better, in his view, to serve on earth than reign in Hades.

Ghost lore is rarely systematic, however, and later in the same book of the *Odyssey* Homer's disembodied shades are seen as subject to physical torture, providing the material Seneca would in due course recycle. Minos sits in judgement on the dead as they present their cases to him and the sentences he delivers are carried out on their bodies. Tityos lies on the ground, his endlessly regenerating liver devoured by vultures. Tantalus stands in water that he cannot drink, surrounded by fruit he cannot reach. Sisyphus forever pushes a boulder up the hill but, each time he reaches the top, the rock topples back to the ground. And if this picture seems to contradict the image of the ghosts as immaterial wraiths, perhaps the undecidable character of the afterlife only replicates the unknowable condition of death itself.

Epic heroes are tested to the limit when they visit the under-world as living beings. To go there is easy; the hard part is to return. Odysseus survives the experience, as does Orpheus and, in his turn, Aeneas. Virgil echoes Homer in many respects. The dead are 'shades', 'spirits'; when Aeneas wants to fight the monsters that live in Avernus, his guide the Sibyl reminds him that they are no more than images, bodiless lives with only the semblance of form. He cannot embrace his beloved father: there is nothing substantial to hold. On the other hand, Minos gives his verdicts and Tityos is subject to the familiar torment, as are other notorious offenders.

Purgatory

Old Hamlet fasts in fires until his crimes are burnt and purged away. Some accounts of the next life also include an intermed-iary state of purification between reward and punishment. The eighteenth-century Protestant Enlightenment, recoiling in equal measure from superstition and popery, convinced itself that ghosts had their origins in the medieval Catholic doctrine of purgatory. Nothing could be further from the case.

Like ghosts themselves, purgatory, or something that points to it, goes back much further. According to the *Phaedo*, Plato's moving account of the judicial execution of Socrates, before he takes the hemlock the philosopher gives a mythological account of the afterlife. Those who have practised virtue (philosophers, for instance) will live on in the next world, bodiless, in the open air. The incurably wicked will be condemned to Tartarus, never to emerge. But those whose lives have been mixed will undergo a period of purgation before returning to live again in the world.

Socrates does not go into detail, but Virgil's *Aeneid* develops the geography of the netherworld. Once across the River Styx, Aeneas passes weeping infants and those falsely condemned to die. Next come suicides and betrayed lovers, including Dido, abandoned by Aeneas. Then he finds warriors, his own friends among them. But this is only the approach road. Soon the way parts. To the right is Elysium, where heroes disport themselves in groves and meadows, while on the left stands Tartarus, a prison-house of torture, where the wicked are punished for ever. But in a third space the mortal body is refined by exposure to winds, floods or fire as a prelude to eventual reincarnation. The souls of the dead are cleansed as crimes done in their days of nature are purged away. Shakespeare would probably not have known Plato but he had studied Virgil at school. Old Hamlet did not need to invoke a closet Catholicism: he could have found in the *Aeneid* all that he needed to justify his hints about the nature of his afterlife.

When Dante came to journey through the Inferno, Purgatory and Paradise, it was Virgil he chose for his guide. Dante's sophisticated reimagining of the medieval cosmos elaborates the topography of these other worlds in *The Divine Comedy*. The universe is conceived as a sphere with the earth at its heart. Descending circles of hell reach the centre of the earth but from there the poets begin their journey upwards to the other side, through purgatory, a mountain that culminates in the earthly paradise. After that, the purified soul ascends through the successive heavens to the Empyrean, home of God. Hell is vividly depicted: marshes and swamps give way to boiling blood and excrement, to be followed in the lowest circle by absolute winter. Purgatory is a place of sorrow and penitence, where the soul is prepared for eventual redemption.

But purgatory had been a latecomer to Christian theology and it is not clear how far it permeated fireside culture. Where Dante systematised the next world, popular storytelling was unsystematic – and macabre. Some of the stories recorded by the Byland monk in about 1400 entirely ignored the official account of the afterlife. James Tankerlay, for instance, once rector of Kirby, took to leaving his grave outside the Byland chapter house and making his way back to his old parish, some five miles away. One night, he mysteriously 'blew out' the eye of his former mistress there. At this point, the Byland monks had his body dug up and instructed Roger Wainman to cart it to the remote Gormire Lake. The story ends as the coffin was lowered into the water, when the oxen pulling the wagon practically drowned for fear. Father Tankerlay walked but, cleric though he was, the story gives no hint that he came from a realm independent of the grave itself.

In other medieval instances, the dead return from a penitential afterlife, but it can be hard to tell the difference between purgatory and hell. In *The Adventures of Arthur at Tarn Wadling*, also composed around 1400, Queen Guenevere's dead mother appears to her daughter to complain of the pains she endures. The queen and Sir Gawain have hung back from the hunt so that Guenevere can rest. All of a sudden, the sky darkens and a figure appears in the likeness of the devil. It wails and sobs like a mad thing. While the living Guenevere is dressed in a shimmering gown, adorned with furs and rich jewels, the ghost is bare to the bone, and plastered with mud. The dead woman offers herself to the queen as a mirror of her future. 'I was once as fair as you, and still wealthier', she declares; 'See what death has done to your mother.' So far, it seems that she comes from the grave rather than another world.

On the other hand, the ghost adds, 'Cherish the poor while you have time. Their prayers may buy you peace when, like me, you make your bed in the ground.' Evidently, if her body belongs in the earth, her soul is in a place from which release is possible. Thirty trentals would help her towards bliss, she urges. Thirty masses made up a trental and thirty trentals was a common request.

Theologically speaking, then, this soul must be in purgatory, since there is no redemption from hell, but it is not clear how far *The Adventures of Arthur* distinguishes between the two states. The story does not name the dead woman's place in the next world. Though she walks by God's grace to warn her daughter, the spectre has fallen into a lake with Lucifer; indeed, she looks like Lucifer, she says. She dwells in a dungeon, a prison house where the fiends of hell hurl her and hack at her; she burns in brass and brimstone.

This sounds very like hell itself. Perhaps she's not sure. Other ghosts were also subject to confusion. A usurer of Liège, who had been through it, mistakenly took purgatory for hell. On his death, the usurer's selfless widow shut herself up in isolation to secure his salvation by prayer, fasting and alms-giving. After seven years, the dead husband appeared dressed in black to acknowledge her efforts. Thanks to her, he had been spared the worst. Another seven years of self-immolation from her would set him free. At the appointed time he returned in white to announce his deliverance – from hell. The thirteenth-century theologian Caesarius of Heisterbach, who tells the story for the instruction of novices, takes care to set the record straight: the usurer had got it wrong; he had been in purgatory; the damned cannot be saved.

And yet even Caesarius wobbles. Everwach the steward was a good man at heart but, hounded by people trying to prove his accounting false, he sold his soul to the devil in a panic. In due course, he went to hell and suffered the usual torments. However, God remembered his earlier virtues and released him to atone. Where was he? Not in purgatory, apparently, since only the elect go there.

These tales give every indication of their origins at winter hearths, where there may have been only a shaky purchase on

Church doctrine. Purgatory featured in medieval wills, when it must have seemed prudent to take every precaution on behalf of the soul. Tombs and brasses, too, invited the living to pray for the dead. But it is not clear how much impression the idea of this intermediate state made on everyday life. Instead, it was the Last Judgement that was most commonly depicted on the ceremonial west door of the church, or above the chancel arch, where the painting was visible to the laity as they worshipped on Sundays.

These vivid images showed the dead pushing their way out of their graves on the last day to be assessed. Below the throne of God, St Michael weighed their souls, and directed them to the heavenly city or consigned them to devils, who dragged them through the gaping jaws of hell. This was a place of eternal punishment, where fiends tossed the damned with pitchforks, scandal-mongers' tongues were pulled out, toads and snakes clung to lechers of both sexes, and money-grubbers swallowed molten gold.

Purgatorial ghosts featured in sermons but all the evidence indicates that, when it adopted purgatory as doctrine in the twelfth century, the Church largely appropriated a storytelling energy derived from popular culture. Since the people were not willing to surrender visitants from another world, best to provide a home for ghosts – and an income for a Church that now took control of the dead, as well as the living. The doctrine of purgatory was not the cause of ghost stories; on the contrary, ghost stories helped to promote purgatory.

The Church takes over

Meanwhile, deadly corporeal revenants survived well into the sixteenth century. When the Catholic priest Thomas Pilchard was subjected to a botched execution in Dorchester in 1587, his ghost secured an immediate revenge. Several officers died on the way home, complaining that they were poisoned by the smell of his drawn entrails. The same evening, the governor of the prison saw Father Pilchard in the garden. The governor died, as did another prisoner, and the wife of yet another, who lost her life in childbirth.

But other influences had been at work in popular medieval lore, making for uncertainties and ambiguities. In some cases, revenants were visible to all; in others they were spirits, perceived only by those chosen to see them. Some ghosts vanished unaccountably, or turned out to be able to pass though physical obstacles. Individual medieval ghosts were already impervious to earthly weapons. It was impossible to wound the wicked Henry Nodus of Trèves, who haunted his daughter's house. Caesarius, whose novices must have loved the fireside tales that illustrated his teaching, records that, when attacked, this ghost simply gave off the sound of a soft bed being struck. And a (very) short story noted down at Byland Abbey concerned a woman who carried a ghost into the house on her back. Witnesses observed that her hands sank deep into its flesh, as if it were putrid, and not solid but phantasmic. Putrid, or insubstantial, or illusory? The story leaves unresolved the question it seems to pose: either rotting flesh or no flesh at all. The impossibility of deciding leaves this visitant especially uncanny.

Perhaps the educated clerics who wrote down these stories retained a memory of disembodied classical wraiths. Or perhaps the Christian dualism that distinguished between body and soul gradually remoulded pagan beliefs. The stories permit us to glimpse moments when orthodoxy can be detected in the process of appropriating pre-Christian ghost lore. William of Newburgh records that in twelfth-century Buckinghamshire a dead husband returned to the conjugal bedroom and lay on top of his wife, threatening to crush her with his weight. In due course, he went on to harass the whole community, at first by night and then increasingly by day. The matter eventually reached the ears of the Bishop of Lincoln, a saintly Frenchman, who was advised that the usual remedy in England was to exhume the corpse and burn it. But the bishop felt such practices were uncivilised and instead prepared a scroll of absolution that was placed on the dead man's chest. The hauntings then ceased.

This was now the proper Christian way to lay a ghost. As time went on, revenants were increasingly driven by the desire for absolution. Two tales recorded in North Yorkshire, a couple of centuries apart, show the difference the Church made. Both stories are written down by monks, literate members of the medieval community, but with the passing of time the institution takes control of the conventions. In Newburgh Priory in 1198, William repeated a story from Berwick. A worldly, wealthy man, duly dead and buried, took to coming out of his grave by night and wandering round the town, followed by the sound of loudly barking dogs. Everyone feared a violent attack. What was to be done? The townsfolk agreed that ten sturdy men should exhume the corpse, dismember it and burn the pieces.

This duly brought the hauntings to an end. But two or three miles away at Byland Abbey – and two hundred years later – the attentive monk transcribed the story of Robert of Boltby, who walked by night, frightening the villagers and causing the dogs to bark. The community agreed that their young men should apprehend him. When the revenant came out of his grave, Robert Foxton captured him and held him on the church stile. This corporeal ghost did not slip through anyone's grasp. On the other hand, he was laid not by physical means but by the priest summoned to give him absolution. When his confession was made, the hauntings ceased.

The same Byland monk admitted to anxiety about the story of Father James Tankerlay, disposed of in Gormire Lake after blowing out the eye of his mistress. At the end of his narrative, the monk adds, 'Let me not be in any danger for writing such things, since it is only what I have heard from my elders.' Was he apologising for putting on record the behaviour of a renegade priest, who might, he piously hoped, be saved despite his posthumous violence? Or was he acknowledging that solving the problem by incapacitating the body was now seen as a pagan practice?

Unfinished business

Absolution promised rest. Ghosts lamented the trouble that brought them back. In the Byland tales Adam de Lond's sister returned from the grave in the hope of persuading her brother to return to her impoverished family land she had made over to him in her life. Her callous brother was unimpressed. 'If you walk forever, I will not give the deeds back.' Groaning, she answered that she would have no peace until Adam's death – and after that he would walk in her place.

It was a severe threat. 'Why hast thou disquieted me to bring me up?' demands the biblical Samuel, summoned from death by the witch of Endor. 'Oh who sits weeping on my grave, / And will not let me sleep?' asks the dead lover reproachfully in *The Unquiet Grave*. 'Rest, rest, perturbed spirit', Hamlet urges his father, and Horatio wishes as much for the dead Hamlet: 'flights of angels sing thee to thy rest'.

But like Old Hamlet, like Banquo, ghosts remained troubled in their graves by the injustices of this world. In fireside tales, as in

the plays, they walked to put things right, exposing misappropriation, revealing murder. At the same time, there was considerable
theological doubt about who or what permitted them to intervene
in the world they had left. Would God let the dead leave their
allotted place in the afterlife? Were they really allowed to concern
themselves with earthly matters, or were the ghosts actually devils
impersonating the deceased? St Augustine thought so. William of
Newburgh was not sure by what agency the dead walked, but he
thought the Berwick ghost and the dead chaplain had Satan's help.
John Mirk's fourteenth-century compilation of sermons includes a
story of the third of three brothers, who died without the last rites,
like Old Hamlet 'Unhouseled' and 'unanealed'. In consequence,
the fiend was able to take possession of the corpse, which left its
grave to the horror of the townsfolk. Challenged, the devil admitted that he could not touch the soul, but he could make use of the
supposed revenant to delude and endanger the living.

Doubt

In the end, the only safe generalisation about ghost stories is that
no generalisations hold. Perhaps it is because the walking dead
cannot be neatly classified that they retain their power to disturb.
In the long medieval period, distinct conventions blended or
collided, sometimes within the same narrative. Undecidably flesh
or spirit, pagan or Christian, the material of fireside tales or
sermons, ghosts followed their troubled path through different
modes of storytelling, defying our desire to reduce them to order.
In this respect, ghost lore differs from religion. Divinity also
embraces the supernatural, but to offer an alternative discipline,
codes of ethics, laws and rituals. The walking dead, by contrast,
go their own anarchic way. If religion generates doctrine and

appeals to theology, it is above all when ghost stories refuse our intellectual mastery that they most touch the uncanny.

Where religion demands faith, ghost stories incorporate the possibility of disbelief. It is tempting to suppose that our predecessors were more credulous than we are and took the walking dead for granted. Perhaps some did, but there was room for dissent. The scholar Horatio does not at first believe in ghosts. Like many sophisticated Elizabethans, he knows a winter's tale when he hears one. His incredulity was shared by a number of Shakespeare's contemporaries. Reginald Scot, for instance, who in 1584 published a detailed denunciation of the witch craze, had no patience with 'absurd' accounts of souls returning from heaven or hell. These were nothing more, he insisted, than 'old wives' fables'. A knave in a white sheet was the most likely explanation for a so-called apparition. On a dark night, a shorn sheep would pass with the gullible for the soul of their father, especially in a churchyard. Ten years later, Thomas Nashe was just as derisive. Phantoms were mostly delusions, he maintained, monstrosities forged by our own brains. Where Scot sets out to persuade, Nashe takes for granted an audience that shares his witty dismissal of ghost stories as products of an overheated imagination.

While in one way or another, then, Horatio is of his time, his inclusion in *Hamlet* also makes for good storytelling. Horatio's disbelief allows a space for any incredulity in the audience, all the better to dispel it when the time comes. While many recent ghost stories follow this model to found the improbable on doubt, it might come as a surprise to learn that a similar strategy seems to have appealed to the monk of Newburgh Priory in the late twelfth century, when he brought ghost stories into his *History of English Matters*. After recording the tales of the Buckinghamshire husband and the wealthy man of Berwick, William disarmingly concedes that they are hard to believe. Who would credit that the dead should come out of the ground to terrorise the living and return to a grave that opens to receive them? But, in the light of so much current testimony from trustworthy people, he will include, as a warning to posterity, just two more of the many narratives he has heard.

The use his future readers are to make of this warning is not entirely clear. Instead, it is tempting to conclude that here, as in *Hamlet*, misgivings are duly acknowledged, only to be outweighed by the power of the tales. A ghost story from ancient Rome is also framed by doubt. About 100 CE, Pliny the Younger, senator, lawyer and general man-about-town, wrote to a friend to ask his opinion on the existence of phantoms. Were they real, or did they arise from our fears? Pliny is inclined to believe in them, he says, for several reasons, including a story he has heard of a haunted house.

A building was offered at a rent below market rates because of its ghost. In the tale Pliny tells, Athenodorus the philosopher undertakes to lay the spectre. He refuses to be alarmed by strange noises in the house at the dead of night. Instead, calling for writing materials, he busies himself with his studies to keep his mind occupied, as a good philosopher should. A clanking sound gradually advances into the room where he sits at work. Athenodorus eventually turns round to see a filthy and emaciated old man beckoning with his finger. The philosopher gestures for the figure to wait a little, and calmly carries on writing, but the apparition remains, determined to secure his attention. At last, Athenodorus agrees to follows the ghost. When it suddenly vanishes at a place in the courtyard, the philosopher marks the spot. The next day he gives instructions to exhume human bones there and give them proper burial – with the result that the haunting comes to an end.

Can this story be true, Pliny wonders? 'Please bring your learning to bear on this question', he presses his addressee. 'Do not
leave me in suspense and uncertainty.' The reply is not on record.
Evidently, the existence of ghosts is controversial and, on the face
of it, Pliny's doubt prompts him to recount what he has been told.
On the other hand, his *Letters* are elegant compositions, published
by their author. It might have been hard to resist the impulse to
repeat the well-rounded tale of a gruesome shade faced with an
imperturbable philosopher. In storytelling practice, does the
desire to tell the tale come first, even while the writer wants to
avoid looking naïve? If so, scepticism presents an excuse for the
narrative; the affirmation of his own reservations permits Pliny to
relay a memorable ghost story.

Either way, pleasure in stories does not require conviction but
only, as Coleridge put it, the willing suspension of disbelief. This
is not a book about what people believed. Opinions are elusive –
like ghosts themselves – and perhaps as evanescent. Scot is surely
right that what can be ruled out by daylight may look more plausible in a churchyard at midnight. But the tales people tell can
reveal something else. While a history of ghost stories presup-
poses nothing in particular about convictions, it does concern
desires, expectations, regrets and anxieties. Perhaps winter's tales
register hopes and fears that go deeper than any formal view on
whether the dead genuinely walk.

THREE

The Ghost of Mrs Milton

Paradise regained?

A fter Shakespeare had drawn on a range of options to make his troubled Ghost, the history of the genre moved on. We have not generally thought of John Milton, author of *Paradise Lost*, as a writer of ghost stories. But one of his sonnets, conventionally numbered 19 (or, in some editions, 23) records an apparition of his dead wife. In a dream the widower seems to regain a personal paradise, only to lose it a second time when he wakes. It's an occurrence familiar to the bereaved. Sleep brings some relief from sorrow and in the dream the loved one is restored, or still there. Waking then proves all the more painful, when loss demands recognition all over again.

As luck – or cultural history – would have it, this poem belongs to a new turning point in the history of ghost stories, when the walking dead were in the process of rehabilitation as evidence for the existence of God. Suddenly, increased numbers of virtuous phantoms returned to comfort the bereaved. Consoling ghosts come in waves. They multiplied in the wake of the First World War, when spiritualism undertook to reassure those left behind that the dead were not lost for ever. And there was a new vogue for benign ghosts in the fiction of the early 1990s, when British and American movies brought lovers back as mentors in *Ghost* (1990) and *Truly Madly*

Deeply (1991). Perhaps at times of crisis we need whatever reassurance we can get. In the nineties it was a recession (minor by later standards); in the 1650s England's brief period of republicanism generated an existential anxiety. But Milton's ghost story also has a more specific place in the evolution of the supernatural.

There are some puzzles in Milton's poem, a complicated sentence structure and one or two unfamiliar references. But they are not enough to obscure the account of a ghost who brings comfort to the bedside, and yet leaves behind her the sorrow of renewed privation.

> Methought I saw my late espoused saint
>> Brought to me like Alcestis from the grave,
>> Whom Jove's great son to her glad husband gave,
>> Rescued from death by force though pale and faint.
> Mine as whom washed from spot of childbed taint,
>> Purification in the old Law did save,
>> And such, as yet once more I trust to have
>> Full sight of her in heaven without restraint,
> Came vested all in white, pure as her mind:
>> Her face was veiled, yet to my fancied sight,
>> Love, sweetness, goodness in her person shined
> So clear, as in no face with more delight.
>> But O as to embrace me she inclined
>> I waked, she fled, and day brought back my night.

Back from the dead

'Methought I saw my late espoused saint.' The dead wife is a saint in the Reformation sense of that term: she died in the faith. Protestantism rejected as idolatry the Catholic practice of prayer to the saints: only God deserved worship. What was more, the canonisation of selected individuals was not a matter for human institutions: only God knew the workings of the heart. Since salvation was secured by faith, all who died a godly death were by definition saints. Where stories of malevolent spectres register the menace of the unknown, saintly ghosts familiarise the terrain that lies on the other side of death. They are more like us than we expected, the place they come from less frightening. But reassurance does not erase their difference completely. The apparition keeps a degree of distance. She does not speak; the embrace she offers does not take place; at dawn she vanishes as suddenly as she appeared.

The dead wife is brought from the grave like Alcestis, rescued from death by the son of Jove. Alcestis was an ideal wife, named in Plato's *Symposium* as the woman who laid down her life for her husband, when all his kin refused to do so. The gods so approved her action that they let her return to earth – but as a living being, not a ghost. In the story as Euripides dramatised it, King Admetus is doomed to die unless he can find a substitute. His parents and friends make excuses until, sadly, graciously, his wife Alcestis opts to take his place. As she dies, the desolate husband begs her to visit him in dreams and gladden him.

On that very day, however, it happens that the god Heracles comes to visit. He is the son of Jove himself, the king of the gods. Hospitality must prevail over mourning, and King Admetus tells his distinguished guest nothing of the tragic death that has taken place in the palace. But a servant lets the story slip and the mighty Heracles resolves to win the queen back from Death by force. When the god reappears with a veiled figure, Admetus fears she must be a phantom. But Alcestis is alive and well and returns to take her full place in the family. This traveller has miraculously returned from the undiscovered country: she is here to stay.

In the sonnet, 'Jove's great son' brings Alcestis back to the king. By analogy, Milton's wife, we are entitled to understand, is brought to him by the authority of the Son of God, who promises life after death to all the faithful. But the woman restored in the play is neither pale nor faint: she lives. When he rewrites the story as an analogue of his own experience, Milton invests Alcestis with a ghostliness foreign to the Greek tale. His dead wife, by contrast, cannot come back to stay. Ghosts stand in for a loss beyond repair. The poet's encounter with his dead wife's 'Love, sweetness, goodness', however precious, remains momentary, their full reunion deferred until the next life and a matter for 'trust'.

Dreams are fleeting. While the last line of the sonnet confirms that the apparition took place in sleep, the opening words already foreshadow a dream: 'Methought I saw . . .' If the allusion to Alcestis is classical, the vocabulary here is English and traditional. *Methought*, it seemed to me, already slightly archaic by the 1650s, has a long ancestry as a prelude to dreams and visions. 'Methought the souls of all that I had murdered / Came to my tent', shudders Richard III, recounting his dream on the eve of the fatal battle; 'Methought their souls whose bodies Richard murdered / Came to my tent and cried on victory', counters Richmond in Shakespeare's strange, split-stage dream scene. Chaucer's *Book of the Duchess* records the sleeping poet's encounter with a knight in mourning for his lost lady. The record of the narrator's dream begins, 'Me thoghte'.

Changing times

There has been some biographical discussion of the date of Sonnet 19, which was not published until 1673. Does it concern Milton's first wife, Mary Powell, who died in 1652, three days after the birth of a daughter, or his second, Katherine Woodcock, who died

in 1658, four months after giving birth, when the period of
'Purification in the old Law' had had time to elapse? In their
account of *John Milton: His Life, Work, and Thought*, Gordon
Campbell and Thomas Corns plump resolutely for the later date.
Milton's first marriage did not go well and ended in an obscure
burial; the second, by contrast, was painfully sad and concluded
with a grand, heraldic funeral.

In November 1656, Milton, then aged 48 and blind, with three
small daughters, married Katherine, who was 28 years old. Soon
she was pregnant and little Katherine was born in October 1657.
The following February she died, and six weeks later, the baby
died too. Campbell and Corns are clear that Sonnet 19 must be
about Katherine. The play on purity and purification alludes not
only to the ceremony of churching after childbirth but also to the
Greek etymology of her name: *katharos* means pure. Moreover, in
the dream she is veiled, not only in imitation of Alcestis, not only
because women wore a white veil to be churched after childbirth,
but also because Milton had never seen her. Campbell and Corns
regard the evidence as conclusive.

Biographical speculation is not my main concern, however. In
the history of ghost stories, what counts here is the date. If the
sonnet was written in 1658 or soon after, it coincides with a rehabilitation of the walking dead that began in the second half of the
seventeenth century. Forgive me if I recapitulate the story so far.
Like Homer, Virgil tells of disembodied shades who, as it happens,
will turn out to play a part in our sonnet. St Augustine, banishing
pagan lore in favour of Christian theology, firmly repudiated
ghosts. God would not let the dead return. Funeral rites, the
condition of access to the classical underworld, were now purely
for the comfort of the bereaved; in Augustine's account, they
could not affect the fate of the dead.

The Augustinian position, which came in due course to prevail in the Christian Church, exerted only a limited influence, however, on popular storytelling, which took for granted that the dead were all too ready to come out of their graves and haunt the living. Eventually, with the doctrine of purgatory, the Church conceded the existence of ghosts and put them to work to solicit money from the bereaved. But the Reformation did away with that practice. Augustine's authority was now higher than ever and salvation was not for sale. In the sixteenth century there were once again officially no ghosts, though demons might impersonate them to delude the living.

Just as before, repeated clerical injunctions had very little effect on popular culture. Sceptics – Reginald Scot and Thomas Nashe among them – denounced superstition, but they demonstrated in the process that, in the world of those they derided the old beliefs persisted, to the despair of the authorities – and to the advantage of Shakespearean drama, as well as generations of old wives spinning yarns by the fire.

In other words, when Hamlet first confronted his dead father at the Globe in 1601, there were three distinct positions on offer: first, official Church insistence that ghosts didn't exist; second, popular consensus that they made for good stories; and third, contempt for superstition. As the seventeenth century wore on, however, it was the last of these that began to bother orthodoxy most. With the advent of Enlightenment thought, disbelief was multiplying. Reginald Scot's sceptical book was reprinted in 1654, seventy years after its first publication, in support of a new generation of doubters.

But to query the supernatural was to risk questioning the existence of God. The final straw, from the point of view of the Church, was the philosophy of Thomas Hobbes. In *Leviathan*, published in 1651, Hobbes argues that the laws of nature, including human nature, are ultimately rational; human behaviour can be explained in materialist terms, references to spirits are to be understood metaphorically, and ghosts are purely imaginary. Worse, whatever Hobbes himself may personally have believed, his philosophy does not rely, as did Descartes's, on the existence of God.

'No spirit, no God'

The 1650s, then, were turbulent times for English Christianity, already in a state of upheaval as radical sects multiplied in Oliver Cromwell's Commonwealth. Materialist philosophy made atheism a distinct possibility. In 1653, two years after the appearance of *Leviathan*, the Cambridge Platonist Henry More issued one of several counterblasts on behalf of divinity. *An Antidote against Atheism* invokes a series of arguments for the existence of God, among them the evidence of the supernatural in general and spirits in particular. There were, More maintained, insubstantial beings of many kinds, ready and able to intervene in earthly affairs. Their existence was crucial to his case for a supreme intellect, independent of the physical world, that supervises its development. As well as intelligent design, this was intelligent day-to-day management. Human souls, separable from their bodies, are the image (or, as More puts it, the effigy) of the divine. And he concludes with a flourish: 'that saying was nothing so true in politics, *No bishop, no king*, as this is in metaphysics, *No spirit, no God*'.

The view, if not so neatly put, would be widely echoed as the century wore on. 'No bishop, no king' had been James I's response to the Presbyterian policy of abolishing the bishops. The abolition of authority in the Church, he believed, would threaten authority in the realm. Now, half a century later, More appropriates the phrase to make a parallel point: to deny the supernatural is to threaten the existence of God.

As it happens, James I is part of our story. In 1597 in his book *Daemonologie*, James VI of Scotland, as he was then, had taken issue with Reginald Scot's sceptical *Discovery of Witchcraft* and, when he acceded to the English throne in 1603, the new king ordered all available copies of Scot's book to be burnt. The main issue at that time was whether witchcraft worked. James I claimed that witches were not deluded: the spirits they conjured came from the devil, and he insisted that by vindicating the witch craze he was defending the faith against what he called 'the old error of the Sadducees, in denying of spirits'.

In this, he was ably supported, oddly enough, by a French Catholic, Pierre Le Loyer, whose *Treatise of Specters* appeared in English translation in 1605 with a dedication to the king. *Spectres* at this time included apparitions of any sort. But while, to defend the faith, any spirit was better than none, neither author was prepared to go so far as to support the existence of ghosts. As a good Augustinian, James took the official clerical view that apparitions of the dead were sure to be the devil in disguise. True, the devil can masquerade as a virtuous revenant, exposing a crime, announcing a death, or revealing a bequest or a murder, but this is done to delude people, and James was adamant that 'neither can the spirit of the defunct return to his friend, or yet an angel use such forms'.

In the changed climate of 1658, the likely year of the sonnet, however, Thomas Bromhall brought out a new *Treatise of Specters* to suit 'these so much Sadducean and Socinian times'. The biblical Sadducees had denied the existence of spirits; Socinians argued against the divinity of Christ. To confute these dangerous doctrines, Bromhall reprinted two chapters of Le Loyer's original *Treatise of Specters*, but the bulk of his long book consists of stories concerning miracles, predictions, omens, prodigies, familiars – and now ghosts.

Among Bromhall's ragbag of magic tales, some that betray a popular origin bear comparison with Sonnet 19. These include the story of a Bavarian widower who so grieved for his dead wife that she returned to earth, on condition that he gave up railing and blaspheming. Although she remained wan and sad, like Milton's Alcestis, the restored wife was corporeal enough to bear him several children. One night, however, the husband came home drunk and swore at the maid, whereupon his wife vanished, leaving her clothes behind her where she stood. She was never seen again. The earthy details of Bromhall's story – the drink, swearing, the empty garments – throw into relief the idealisation that makes Milton's sonnet special.

At intervals, Bromhall remembers Augustinian orthodoxy and insists that the point of his narratives is to remind us of the lengths the devil will go to in confirming superstition and reinforcing idolatry, but a reader could be forgiven for taking most of his tales as evidence for constant supernatural intervention of every kind in human affairs. Henry More is much more circumspect, but his new book, *The Immortality of the Soul*, published in 1659, addressed once again to those who preferred reason to religion, and to Hobbes in particular, now also adduces as evidence the walking dead. More takes for granted his readers' familiarity with ghost stories: 'Such instances', he says, 'are infinite.'

Ethereal ghosts

Henry More did a great deal to promote the translucent, ectoplasmic phantoms later generations took for granted. Drawing on his classical learning, and at this stage a strong admirer of Descartes,

More gave a theoretical account of ghosts from the perspective of a thoroughgoing mind–body dualism. Spirit and flesh were distinct substances. Spirits could make themselves visible to mortals by creating a form out of air. Composed of ether, they were able to assemble their airy bodies at will.

Nor are the returning dead always as dangerous or as troubled as they once were. Since, from More's point of view, ghosts are part of a God-given order, the stories he invokes are generally benign and providential, as, for example, 'those wherein the soul of one's friend, suppose father, mother, or husband, have appeared to give them good counsel'. Dead wives are evidently beneath the gaze of the philosopher, but they are surely included by implication in this list of domestic mentors. As for the Reformation argument that apparitions are manufactured by demons, this now seems to him absurd. Directly contradicting the orthodoxy of the previous century, More argues that ghosts who reveal murderers, call to account untrustworthy executors, or advise the bereaved are evidently performing 'just and serious' tasks wholly unlikely to be carried out by the devil.

Not all his allies were as consistent. Bromhall's spectres are a disorderly crew, although they do include St Augustine who was seen by a monk on the day he died, sitting among the clouds 'all in glorious white'. If ghosts were to be effective in countering the many Sadduceans, Socinians, Epicureans and atheists who were threatening the Christian faith, it was necessary to give prominence to virtuous examples. When in 1691 Richard Baxter assembled empirical evidence for *The Certainty of the Worlds of Spirits*, he lamented the dwindling number of modern miracles he was able to include. There were, he was obliged to concede, more bad spirits than good. But where a hundred years earlier James I had declared that all spirits were sent by the devil, Baxter was clear that God's messengers could intervene in this world, and there was no reason why these emissaries should not include blessed souls too, since they were equal with angels.

Ghosts, in other words, were officially back and were now at least potentially respectable. If Sonnet 19 was written in 1658, the poem was of its moment, if not slightly ahead of the curve, although it is worth acknowledging that Milton hedges his bets by confining his ghost to a dream. In an earlier generation, this might not have made much difference. Richard III and Richmond both take their dreams to heart. While the parade of the king's dead victims leaves the waking Richmond joyful, Richard himself is not reassured when Ratcliffe dismisses his as no more than shadows. 'Shadows tonight', the king retorts, 'Have struck more terror to the soul of Richard / Than can the substance of ten thousand soldiers.'

There will be more to say about dreams in Chapter 7. But when the walking dead began to take on the burden of proving the existence of God, the distinction between dreams and reality would gradually come to matter. In due course, people who saw ghosts, even those visited in their beds, would be inclined to insist that they were wide awake.

At the same time, on biblical authority dreams were still best not ignored. In 1662, the Anglican minister Isaac Ambrose reminded his readers that there were 'such dreams as come into us by God's special, and sometimes extraordinary work of providence' and these 'challenge our very serious consideration'. The possibility that the dead might speak in dreams was allowed even by the sceptical physician John Webster, who in 1677 denied that souls returned.

Webster rejected what he called Henry More's 'Platonic whimsies'. On the other hand, a neighbour, Webster noted, had dreamt that John Waters had been murdered, and was able to lead the constable to his body. In consequence, Anne Waters duly confessed that she had conspired with her lover to kill her husband. How could this be, Webster wonders. Evidently, 'it was brought to pass by the finger of God . . . or by the ministry of a good angel'. Milton's poem invests its ghost with the authority of Jove's great Son, but at the same time places her in a dream and so evades the question of her empirical reality.

Providential spirits

There is no need to see Milton's sonnet as participating directly in the arguments for and against the existence of ghosts. On the contrary. But providential phantoms were newly in the cultural air that anyone might breathe in the late 1650s and would remain there for many years. The fourth edition of Joseph Glanvill's expanding compendium of the supernatural was published in 1668 under the title *A Blow at Modern Sadducism*. Here, those Sadducists who wickedly deny the reality of spirits include Hobbes once more, as well as Reginald Scot, whose work was reissued yet again in 1665. Glanvill's counter-evidence embraces apparitions, but it was not until 1681, in the fifth edition of his book, now called *Saducismus Triumphatus* and published after the author's death with a prefatory letter by our friend Henry More, that Glanvill took on the ungodly by assembling a selection specifi- cally of ghost stories. Such narratives, Glanvill insisted, should not be dismissed as 'mere winter tales and old wives' fables'; instead, people must be 'brought to be afraid of another world'.

By the end of the century, the question of visitants from another world was keenly debated. A shared preoccupation with the problems of 'Sadducism and Hobbism' drove the popular coffee-house periodical *The Athenian Mercury* to turn over the issue of 31 October 1691 to stories of nine apparitions, as recorded in the words of those who saw them. Their testimonies included a tale about another family member who brings comfort to the bedside. This time, a wayward son, persuaded by his mother to reform his life shortly before he died, draws back the bed curtains to assure her that he is at rest and will trouble her no more.

The Athenian Mercury takes such tales seriously, on the basis that they 'have been credited in all ages'. Anyone who disbelieves them risks denying the soul's independence of the body, and 'if that once is admitted, farewell all moral virtues', the hope of heaven and the fear of hell, allowing 'by consequence an inlet to the most profligate base things whist [known] here, that human nature can possibly stoop to'. An advertisement follows for Richard Baxter's new book, *The Certainty of the Worlds of Spirits*.

John Aubrey, on the other hand, seems to have been more interested in a good yarn than in promoting the existence of spirits when in 1696 this snapper-up of unconsidered stories told another tale about a dead wife who brought comfort to a widower:

Mr. T. M., an old acquaintance of mine, hath assured me that about a quarter of a year after his first wife's death, as he lay in bed awake with his little grandchild, his wife opened the closet door, and came into the chamber to the bedside, and looked upon him, and stooped down and kissed him. Her lips were warm; he fancied they would have been cold. He was about to have embraced her, but was afraid it might have done him hurt. When she went from him, he asked her when he should see her again. She turned about and smiled, but said nothing. The closet-door striked [scraped], as it used to do, both at her coming in and going out.

Mr T. M.'s account records intimations of anxiety absent from Milton's poem: his ghost kisses her husband but he fears to embrace her. And the domestic details, including the ill-fitting door, are a long way from the elevated register of the sonnet. But there is in both stories a reaffirmation of love, as well as a similar allusion to the future. Mr T. M. wants to know when he will see his wife again. No Christian ghost can legitimately promise reunion in the afterlife, pre-empting God's Judgement, but Mrs T. M. can encourage her husband's faith with a smile, just as the poet's dream of perceiving his wife's love confirms his trust that he will see her in heaven. Both ghosts, like More's, do God's work.

The beatific ghost goes back at least to Dante's last vision of Beatrice, who looks at him with a smile in *The Paradiso*. Such images survive the centuries to offer more secular reassurance. In 1757, Thomas Hussey pulled aside the curtains round his daughter's bed at Upwood House in Cambridgeshire. He smiled and then dissolved back into the dark. This was, she later learned, the moment of her father's death in London and with his last words he had withdrawn his opposition to her choice of husband.

While the circulation of benign ghost stories increased, the disputes between the anti-Sadducists and the sceptics remained unresolved well into the eighteenth century and beyond. In 1705 Daniel Defoe joined in with *A True Relation of the Apparition of One Mrs Veal*. The day after her death, Mrs Veal returned to fortify her old friend Mrs Bargrave. Defoe may also have been responsible for the story of Dorothy Dingley, published in 1720, although that remains open to doubt.

Either way, in 1727 he went on to make clear his general opinion on whether the dead walked. In *An Essay on the History and*

Reality of Apparitions Defoe reflected that, on the one hand, so many stories could not be ignored, while on the other, many of them seemed highly improbable. The messages brought back from the grave were often trivial. Was supernatural intervention seriously to be harnessed for such purposes as indicating the place where a few shillings had been buried and forgotten, or to put right a false executor's theft of £10? Wickedness was so common that if the dead walked to seek retribution for every concealed wrong, there would no space left on earth for the living.

As a good Augustinian, Defoe argued that souls could have no motive strong enough to make them leave heaven – and they would not be permitted to come back from hell. In sum, the dead do not return: 'the good would not if they could, and the bad could not if they would'. But, while there were no walking dead, it was more than possible that spirits of other kinds thronged the air under the ultimate control of God. It followed that an apparition was either angelic or devilish, and more likely to be providential.

These debates, esoteric to our ears, concerned nothing less than what it meant to be human. Are we, as Hobbes argued, material beings, here on our own, making what provision we can to protect ourselves from an indifferent cosmos, or are we, as the divines insisted, souls first and foremost, sharing our air with millions of providential spirits placed there to sustain us? The question is still not settled to everyone's satisfaction. Despite the Enlightenment, the supernatural has not gone quietly, even if its last major stronghold is fiction. However strenuously science takes possession of dark corners, it seems that intense experiences – bereavement among them – can bring us up sharply against what we don't know for sure. Ghosts offer one way of giving a form to what still eludes rational definition.

When in the 1760s the Methodist preacher John Wesley came to read Baxter and then Glanvill, he wasn't certain what to make of them. Some of what they say is credible, he thinks. Wesley will try to keep the middle way. He is sorry the learned are so ready to dismiss the supernatural as 'mere old wives' fables'. But then such people realise that if they allowed one ghost story to stand, what he calls their whole materialist castle in the air would fall to the ground.

Wesley was therefore fascinated to take down the record of another comforting domestic ghost, strange though it was, and to transcribe it in full in his journal for 25 May 1768. An orphan, brought up in Sunderland by her beloved uncle, Elizabeth Hobson had seen dead people since her childhood. The experience was so common that she made little of it. When she was sixteen, the uncle she loved fell ill; three months later, he died in her arms. Deeply distressed, she too grew very weak until it was thought she would die. But in her sickness her dead uncle visited her bedside each night and stayed till cock-crow, bringing whatever she needed without her having to ask. Every morning, as he left, he waved his hand and she heard singing.

After six weeks of this supernatural nursing, Elizabeth recovered and began to wonder whether it was right to want the dead man to come back. As she was resolving to leave the matter to God, her uncle returned one last time.

> But he was not in his usual dress: he had on a white robe which reached down to his feet. He looked quite well-pleased. About one, there stood by him a person in white, taller than him and exceeding beautiful. He came with the singing as of many voices and continued till near cock-crowing. Then my uncle smiled and waved his hand toward me twice or thrice. They went away with inexpressibly sweet music, and I saw him no more.

Loss

This ghost restores Elizabeth to health; it goes without saying that her uncle's angelic companion brings divine grace. But Milton's poem does not end so happily. In the last two lines of Sonnet 19 consolation gives way to reiterated loss. Unlike Alcestis, this dead wife is not back for good – and unlike Bromhall's Bavarian husband, the poet does nothing to provoke her disappearance. The apparition is all too brief, and the bleak monosyllables of the final line, not to mention the native English sentence structure after so much Latinate syntax, confirm the sorrow it leaves behind: 'I waked, she fled, and day brought back my night.'

Short of a miracle, there is no permanent return from the undiscovered country and the immortality of the soul does not wholly allay the pain of bereavement in this life. One of Glanvill's family narratives registers something of the same conjunction of comfort and sadness. Six months after his death, Mr Watkinson appeared to his daughter, Mary. 'On a night when she was in bed, but could not sleep, she heard music, and the chamber grew lighter and lighter, and she being broad awake, saw her father stand at her bedside.' They talked long and earnestly, and Mary told him she had lost a baby in the interim. 'He bade her speak what she would now to him, for he must go, and that he should never see her more till they met in the kingdom of heaven.' This ghost does venture a prediction, but the consolation Mary experiences is tinged with regret: 'So the chamber grew darker and darker, and he was gone with music. And she said that she did never dream of him nor ever did see any apparition of him after.'

Are we to understand that, like Elizabeth Hobson, Mary no longer needed her ghostly comforter? Or does the encounter set the seal on her loss? The bright light he brings is gradually extinguished, reinstating the darkness of the bedchamber. In Milton's case, 'day brought back my night'.

Where the revenants of the old wives' tales could be physically violent, these orthodox ghosts largely evaded physical contact, as the failed embrace of Sonnet 19 indicates. Aubrey's Mrs T. M. kissed her husband, but he refrained from putting his arms round her out of fear. The poet wakes before his wife can clasp him. Campbell and Corns suggest a more specific interpretation of Milton's missed encounter. Churching, the purification named in the poem, put an end at this time to the ritual period of recovery from childbirth, and in the process legitimised the resumption of marital relations between the couple. The ceremony required a white veil and was regarded by the devout as a kind of second wedding. A sexual reunion, Campbell and Corns propose, is the embrace averted without warning when the poet wakes up.

No one knows more about the period, or is less subject to flights of fancy, than Campbell and Corns. I think we can trust them. And if so, the two lines on purification, that stand out so oddly to modern eyes, take their place in the story, while the white garments also make double sense. The consensus has been that white wedding dresses were a Victorian invention, but in 1595 the bride in Spenser's *Epithalamion* wears white, while the Princess Elizabeth wore white when she married the Elector Palatine in 1613. Both acted on scriptural authority: according to the book of Revelation 19.8, the Church was arrayed to marry the Lamb in 'fine linen, clean and white'. Milton's young wife, relinquished once to death, is now lost a second time – on the brink of a second 'marriage'.

In the dream, the poet can see but not touch. Among the classical ghosts repudiated by St Augustine, those familiar to Milton from the epics of Homer and Virgil were immaterial shadows. But there is a specific Virgilian parallel in the sonnet that Milton, steeped in classical epic, is not likely to have ignored. When the dead Creüsa appears to the widowed Aeneas, her mission is to dispel his anxiety. 'What use is it to give way to this frantic grief, my sweet husband? These things do not happen without the will of heaven.' His wife's ghost yields the founder of Rome to his destiny and then draws back into thin air. Three times he tries to throw his arms round her neck but, Aeneas records, three times the form, clasped in vain, 'fled from my hands as light winds, and most like a winged dream'. Although Creüsa promises Aeneas eventual happiness, there is pain to come first and much travail. 'Long exile is your lot, a vast plain of the sea you must plough.'

This prophecy must have resonated with a middle-aged poet, who had three young daughters to bring up and important poetic work to do, in spite of his blindness. Indeed, in an earlier sonnet addressed to Cyriack Skinner on this last issue, Milton himself had defined his own state in similar terms. For three years, he says, he has seen nothing, 'Of sun or moon or star throughout the year, / Or man or woman'. Yet, he insists, 'I argue not / Against heaven's hand or will' but, echoing Creüsa's nautical allusion, 'still bear up and steer / Right onward'. And what sustains him? The defence of liberty, he replies. Like Aeneas, Milton too had a destiny, if in a rather different sphere.

'This dark world'

Even so, 'day brought back my night'. The final line of the sonnet surely points in the unassuming word play to a double meaning. The night that paradoxically returns with the day to leave the poet in such understated desolation suggests not only the darkness of bereavement but the perpetual night of blindness. Unbearably, sightlessness erases the elementary distinction between the light of day and the undifferentiating dark.

Is this, perhaps, after all, what Sonnet 19 has been about all along? With the recognition of that meaning of the final line, doesn't another poem begin to take shape as we look back through the sonnet we have been reading? What is it that is momentarily restored in the dream, if not sight itself? 'Methought I saw . . .' And what is it that will be recovered in heaven, but 'full sight . . . without restraint'? In the dream the poet can see the ghost's white garments, and if the face he has never seen remains veiled, 'yet to my fancied sight, / Love, sweetness, goodness in her person shined / So clear'. That precious clarity of vision is abruptly confiscated as, ironically, the familiar darkness reasserts itself when morning returns. The poet's days are lightless; only his dreams are full of sights.

What, then, is it that Sonnet 19 records? Is the lost object of desire recovered in the dream a dead wife, or the ability to see? I can't find any way to resolve that question but perhaps there is no need to choose. The point about ghosts is that you see them. Mary saw Mr Watkinson stand by her bed. 'If I stand here, I saw him', insists Macbeth, when Banquo is invisible to everyone else. Sit down and hear again, the guards urge Horatio, 'what we two nights have seen'; 'Methought I saw'.

A ghost may affect the other senses: a sudden chill, a rustling sound, a hollow whisper, the touch of a cold hand may accompany the apparition. But, without at least the glimpse of a shape, a supernatural visitant might be a poltergeist but it barely qualifies as a full-scale phantom. The English language bears this out: we think of the credulous as *seeing things*, psychics as having *second sight*. Mrs Milton's ghost gives a form to a double bereavement, conjoining both of the poet's losses, a beloved wife and the power to see. Both are restored in the dream; both will surely be recovered in heaven; both are snatched away a second time in the moment of waking.

Curiously, however, as it ends, the poem, sad as it is, seems to me to offer as much pleasure as grief. If you agree, why is this? Partly because it records a familiar experience of dispossession temporarily repaired in a dream. Partly, too, because it tells a ghost story – and one that turns out to be more complex than it seemed. But above all, I suggest, because its eloquence culminates in the final line, where the poem pits against the pain of deprivation the supreme resource available to human beings, asserting the power of words in a triumphant pun that has the effect of defying the inevitability of loss. Day brings back the poet's night, but that paradox itself marks a victory for the human exercise of the remarkable capabilities of language, putting our best invention to work in a tale that can still engage readers long after Milton himself is also in his grave.

FOUR

Women in White

What Jacob Postlethwaite saw

In the evolving history of ghost stories, certain conventions have emerged to repeat themselves with a difference across the generations. There have been spectral hunts, death coaches, hooded monks, wounded cavaliers – and women in white. Mrs Milton consoles her grieving husband 'vested all in white'. In the first instance, white dress implies purity. But while women in white might come back to do good, they could in the process threaten to undermine the authorities. They would also, paradoxically, have their work cut out to take control of their own stories. But when they did, women in white might, it turned out, be dangerous after all.

The subset of women in white was well enough established to give Wilkie Collins the title of his sensational novel in 1860. In *The Woman in White* little Jacob Postlethwaite stands in the corner of the village schoolroom in disgrace because he claims to have seen a ghost. Here the story brings official scepticism face to face with popular tradition. The fictional moment is 1850 and the schoolmaster is adamant: there are no ghosts; such things cannot possibly be; Jacob must be punished for refusing to submit to rational authority. But the boy persists in his belief. The figure was all in white, as a ghost should be. And he saw her at twilight in the churchyard, where a ghost ought to be. Jacob is convinced he has seen a good woman back from the dead.

Anne Catherick, the woman in white of the novel, is not in the event a phantom and yet from the beginning she is described in terms derived from ghost stories, so that the reader is half encouraged to share Jacob's belief. She first appears out of nowhere, just after midnight, at a place where four roads meet. Crossways, we know, are often haunted by the restless spirits of those refused Christian burial, interred there to confuse them about the way back home. In the novel, as Walter Hartright walks alone by moonlight towards the city from the uncultivated land of Hampstead Heath, he feels a hand laid lightly on his shoulder.

> There, in the middle of the broad, bright high-road – there, as if it had that moment sprung out of the earth or dropped from the heaven – stood the figure of a solitary woman, dressed from head to foot in white garments; her face bent in grave inquiry on mine, her hand pointing to the dark cloud over London.

Anne has a meagre appearance with large, wistful eyes; her hand, when Walter touches it, is cold and thin. She is a living being but, as the novel goes on, it becomes clear that her troubled nature sets her apart in a borderland between life and death, while her resemblance to Laura Fairlie lends her the strangeness of all doubles. Glimpsed, like countless spectral figures, in liminal places, solitary, longing to be at rest, the woman in white is driven by a desire to protect a living relative. After her death, Walter reaffirms the supernatural comparison: 'So the ghostly figure which has haunted these pages as it haunted my life, goes down into the impenetrable gloom. Like a shadow she first came to me, in the loneliness of the night. Like a shadow she passes away, in the loneliness of the dead.'

If Jacob Postlethwaite is technically wrong in believing the woman in the graveyard is dead, his ghost lore is beyond reproach. Women in white walk for good in any number of stories – among them Hermione, who appears to Antigonus in a dream in Shakespeare's *Winter's Tale*. She is clothed 'in pure white robes', a mother speaking on behalf of the baby daughter that Antigonus has been told he must expose to take her chances in the wild. Winter's tales, as we know, relish the far-fetched and, although this is probably not the place to discuss whether Hermione 'really' dies in the play, at the moment when he recounts his dream, both Antigonus and the audience believe the queen is dead.

On the stage nearly 200 years later in *The Castle Spectre*, M. G. Lewis raises the dead Evelina to protect her daughter from rape by her own killer. Lewis is never knowingly understated. Only the words of the stage direction can do full justice to the apparition of the murdered mother. In the oratory

> stands a tall female figure, her white and flowing garments spotted with blood; her veil is thrown back, and discovers a pale and melancholy countenance; her eyes are lifted upwards, her arms extended towards heaven, and a large wound appears upon her bosom.

Evelina expands on a figure from the author's own runaway success *The Monk*, published a year earlier. There Elvira returns from the dead in white to warn her daughter of impending danger.

As a village boy, Jacob himself would know nothing about these classic victims of male misogyny, although it is highly likely that his author did. But in their case the literary tradition simply elaborated what it found in popular legend, where, like Hermione, like Elvira and Evelina, women in white are often called back by care for their children. From the seventeenth century on, until a restoration replaced the east window of Trinity Church, Micklegate in York, three phantoms were regularly visible in or just beyond the glass. A Victorian clergyman who saw them described a mother in white, her child and a nurse. The adults moved to and fro, apparently lamenting the fate of the baby.

Women in white multiplied in the nineteenth century when, once again, ghost stories stood to counter a crisis of Christian faith. Victorian biblical criticism queried the authenticity of the sacred texts, the fossil record cast doubt on the book of Genesis, and evolutionary theory was to challenge creationism. In 1848 Catherine Crowe published *The Night Side of Nature*, designed, like Joseph Glanvill's book nearly two centuries earlier, to reaffirm the supernatural. Crowe included an account of Miss L. of Dalkeith, who dreamt she saw her aunt 'dressed in white, and looking quite radiant and happy'. The next morning Miss L. heard that the aunt had died in the night.

This time, the Anglican clergy were on the whole less sympathetic: it was spiritualism and its variants that were more likely to confirm such benign apparitions. The theosophist Reverend C. W. Leadbeater relayed a story of a mother who died abroad, anxious, she declared, for one last sight of her children in Torquay. On the day of her death, 10 September 1854, she appeared in the English house, gazed at them for a few minutes, smiled and then vanished into the next room. The older children recognised their mother; the younger ones and the nursemaid all 'saw a lady in white come into the smaller room, and then slowly glide by and fade away'.

As the psychic industry got under way, ghosts were not only seen but photographed with a view to convincing those left behind. Ectoplasm was generally white. The spirits summoned in seances to comfort the bereaved commonly took on the form of the departed in white muslin, cheesecloth or cotton wool.

Spectral dress codes

Ghostly dress codes vary. In ancient Greece and Rome, the dead often walked in black. Alternatively, to assist recognition, many later spectres were dressed in the clothes they habitually wore when they lived. Material and solid as they seemed, it might not be immediately apparent that they were ghosts at all. Dorothy Dingley at first passed for a local resident. Mrs Veal, whose apparition was recorded by Daniel Defoe, wore her riding habit when in 1705 she visited Mrs Bargrave the day after her death. Although she evaded her friend's welcoming kiss, Mrs Veal did place her hand on her friend's knee; her silk gown, too, was tangible. Other ghosts authenticated their identity by wearing the dress shown in their portraits. The Brown Lady of Raynham Hall, who died in 1729, walked in the brown brocade she wore in her painting.

As the corporeal revenants of medieval tradition gave way to less substantial figures, grey clothing also came to prominence. A female ghost that terrified Edward Drury in Willington on the Tyne in 1840 was only one of many spectres 'attired in grayish garments'. The ghost of Ravenclaw Tower in *Harry Potter and the Deathly Hallows*, who glides through walls without touching the ground, is known as the Grey Lady. An American short story of 1912 spells out the reason for this trend: 'her garments were gray, the color of a mist that the sun is about to pierce, wavering, luminous'. Modern ghosts are translucent, indistinct, ready to fade into their surroundings.

But there are enough tales of women in white to form a sub-genre worth attention in its own right. When in 1983 Susan Hill calls her novel *The Woman in Black*, she knowingly draws on the contrast between benevolent and dangerous apparitions.

Unlike the mothers who return to rescue their daughters, her perverse woman in black snatches other people's children in compensation for the loss of her own. The film, which differs in a number of respects from the novel, makes the point even more sharply. In contrast to the thwarted mother in black, when the hero's dead wife returns at the end to reunite the family, she wears white.

Viewers who take this contrast for granted are drawing on traditional ghost lore. William Lovett, setting out on an empty, moonlit road in the second decade of the nineteenth century, found he was catching up with a woman in white but was able to reassure himself that she would do him no harm: malign spirits wore black, after all. (As it turned out, the figure was not a ghost at all but a woman leaving a secret sexual liaison.)

The assumption William Lovett made reached back through the centuries. Medieval souls in purgatory commonly appeared to their relatives in black to ask for their help in releasing them from punishment for their sins; like the usurer of Liège, they often reappeared later in white to show that the intercession of the living had been effective. After the Reformation the sceptical Reginald Scot told his sixteenth-century readers derisively, 'They say that you may know the good souls from the bad very easily. For a damned soul hath a very heavy and sour look; but a saint's soul hath a cheerful and a merry countenance: these also are white and shining, the other coal black.'

A saint's soul. The texts confirm the lineage Scot is mocking. Hermione is dressed in white 'Like very sanctity'; Milton's white-clad wife is his 'late espoused saint'. The Book of Revelation consistently clothes the blessed in white. When St John saw the elect in heaven, they wore white robes, washed clean in the blood of the Lamb. Angels, too, were dressed in pure white linen; the angel who rolled away the stone from Christ's tomb was radiant like lightning, while his raiment was white as snow.

There was no very clear demarcation between saints and angels. In their lives medieval saints saw angels; in death, according to some theologians, at least, they joined their ranks. Angels were spirits but, when they appeared to mortal eyes, they might wear any colour they chose, as medieval and Renaissance art attests. White in particular registered angelic purity, however. 'Spirits of peace' appear to the dying Queen Katherine in Shakespeare's *Henry VIII*. These figures, 'clad in white robes', bring her the promise of eternal bliss. The dead pearl-maiden, who consoles the poet dreaming beside her grave in the anonymous fourteenth-century *Pearl*, wears shining white linen and a gleaming white mantle.

Gleaming white would have been a luxury in a world before chemical bleaching. For centuries, cloth was whitened in the sun, or treated with lye, but the process could be long and costly. No wonder, then, that the garments of the saints displayed a brightness barely known on earth. According to *The Golden Legend*, Saint Elizabeth of Hungary appeared after her death to cure a sick monk in the shape of an honourable lady clad in white. And thanks, no doubt, to the biblical tradition, virtuous apparitions in white survived the Reformation. The innocent heroine of *The Lady's Tragedy*, Thomas Middleton's play of 1610–11, comes out of her tomb 'all in white, stuck with jewels and a great crucifix on her breast'. In *The Virgin Martyr*, by Thomas Dekker and Philip Massinger a decade or so later, Dorothea reappears after her execution to bolster the faith of the living. She wears a white robe decorated with crowns and a crown on her head. Her acolytes follow, also in white 'but less glorious', the stage direction indicates.

Women with authority?

These female figures possess a certain authority in death. The pearl-maiden reconciles the dreamer to his loss and teaches obedience to God's will; Milton's dead wife confirms his faith. Other women in white walked to warn of a death. Since the fifteenth century the White Lady of Neuhaus in Bohemia had been haunting the various homes of the Prussian royal family to prepare them to die well. Her last appearance was in 1879. Nearer home and lower down the social scale, on 25 July 1837 Polly Allen, aged 3, who had been playing in front of the family cottage, ran indoors to tell her mother she had seen a tall woman in white coming down the hill opposite. When the child insisted, her mother went to look but there was nothing to see. On that day Polly's father John was drowned while he was cutting reeds in the river Stour. Some six or seven months earlier, he had reported seeing something that told him he had not long to live.

But female authority provoked clerical unease. The minister who tells John Allen's tale believes the child was mistaken: the apparition in white was not a woman at all but the spectral form of Allen himself, appearing at the moment of his death. This member of the clergy is evidently more open to the supernatural than the village schoolmaster who punished Jacob Postlethwaite, but he shares an inclination on the part of male orthodoxy to rewrite the story: many in command were reluctant to believe that the unearthly possessor of hidden knowledge could be a woman.

Consolation was one thing, women as God's emissaries quite another. Early in the seventeenth century Sir Thomas Wise saw a female figure in white and shining raiment at the foot of his bed. She remained there for half an hour or so and then vanished. Unsure what to make of the experience, Sir Thomas consulted the archdeacon, who concluded that, since the apparition did him no harm, it was probably an angel. The godly cleric Daniel Featley, however, strongly opposed this view: it couldn't be an angel. For one thing, miracles had been superseded by the Scriptures, which revealed all we needed to know. For another, the apparition brought no message. Finally, it was unheard-of for an angel to adopt the form of a woman.

When medieval artists imagined a higher life form, they frequently depicted angels as sexually ambiguous. Milton declared that spirits could assume whichever sex they chose. But some Reformation divines were made of sterner stuff. An unpublished manuscript of the early 1590s takes a firm line on the gender issue. Randall Hutchins, rector of West Tilbury, wrote a Latin treatise *Of Specters*, explaining, in accordance with the Protestant ortho-doxy of the time, that there were no ghosts. There were, however, spirits, intelligences that might take forms we recognise to make themselves accessible. Hutchins does concede the possibility of angelic visitations but heavenly spirits commonly appear as men, opting for the ideal human body. We read 'almost nowhere', he continues, of good spirits 'in a woman's form or in that of any beast whatsoever, but invariably in the aspect of a man'. Demons, however, often appear as women and beasts.

There was clearly anxiety here. On the one hand, angels could adopt any form they chose; on the other, the Bible always calls them 'he'. Perhaps the gender issue deepened another clerical worry: it was bad enough that direct encounters with angels threatened to by-pass the authority of the parson; female messengers from God would turn the all-male ministry of the Church upside down. On 10 June 1788 Margaret Barlow told John Wesley that she had been visited by an angel for more than a year. Her face, she affirmed, 'is exceeding beautiful, her raiment . . . white as snow, and glistering like silver; her voice unspeakably soft and musical'. The angel

foretells the future, warns of death to come and prophesies the Last
Judgement. In his journal Wesley wonders what to make of this.
Evidently, the doctrine is sound; perhaps the apparition really was
an angel but it couldn't at the same time be a woman; on the other
hand, Margaret might have been wrong about the sex.

While some of the clergy withheld power from female apparitions, fiction continued to align itself with tradition. The protagonist
of Tennyson's *Maud* is led by a shadow that resembles his love 'in a
cold white robe'. In due course the dead Maud will seem to detach
herself from 'a band of the blest' and send him off to the wars to
redeem his crime. Meanwhile, wrestling with the imperative to
part from Mr Rochester, the orphan Jane Eyre dreams that a ray
penetrates the darkness of the night. Eventually, a light

> broke forth as never moon yet burst from cloud: a hand first
> penetrated the sable folds and waved them away; then, not a
> moon, but a white human form shone in the azure, inclining
> a glorious brow earthward. It gazed and gazed on me. It spoke
> to my spirit: immeasurably distant was the tone, yet so near, it
> whispered in my heart –
>
> 'My daughter, flee temptation.'
> 'Mother, I will.'

Jane's mother appears as a direct descendant of Hermione, Evelina
and Elvira.

Inconsequential

So far, so clear-cut and, you might want to add, so predictable:
white dress for virtue, black for evil – if with the added curiosity
of male incredulity towards attempts to ascribe supernatural

authority to women. But it's not, in the event, that simple. Ghosts belong in stories, whether these announce themselves as true or fictitious. Outside the narrative that presents them, spectres barely exist. 'Let me tell you . . .' people say, and what they tell is a story. But good women don't necessarily make for good narratives, living or dead. In most of these instances, the women in white have no more than walk-on parts – more or less literally.

By contrast, a malevolent dead woman – and there are many – has standing as the hero's antagonist. While Susan Hill's woman in black makes things happen, terrifying a whole town, many women in white do no more than inform, admonish, instruct, confirm, reassure, comfort the living or simply perpetuate their own sorrow, then vanish, leaving others to drive the plot forward. How many readers of *Jane Eyre* remember the apparition of her mother? We are more likely, I suspect, to carry away the memory of another figure that initially seems supernatural: when the vengeful Bertha Mason appears in Jane's bedroom the night before her wedding, she too, ironically, wears white.

Good women in white are to varying degrees incidental and inconsequential. Even Anne Catherick, who constitutes the impetus for the plot of Wilkie Collins's novel, does little more than trigger the events that follow. The agents of the story are the amateur detectives, Walter and Marian, and their main antagonist, the appalling Count Fosco. If the woman in white is the enigma that draws us into the tale, she is at the same time what Alfred Hitchcock would call the McGuffin. Like Rosebud in *Citizen Kane*, or like the Maltese falcon, she represents the mystery that motivates a quest pursued by others.

In one instance, a woman's disappearance determines the tale of 'The Mistletoe Bride'. Haunting the house is her only option; discovering her must be the work of others. Kate Mosse rewrites for a twenty-first-century audience the Victorian ballad of a bride who played hide and seek, only to be buried alive when the lid of the old chest she had chosen clicked shut. Many years later, when the cover was finally raised, 'a skeleton form lay mouldering there, / In the bridal wreath of that lady fair'.

According to the modern version, a woman in white is said to walk the corridors where she would have been mistress. The ghost plaintively records her longing to be found. Has someone heard her footsteps? But no, 'I sigh. As always, hope is snatched away before it can take root.' On her wedding day, she danced with her bridegroom, already unconsciously anticipating her fate: 'I am lighter than air, he says, barely there at all, and I can see this pleases him.' In the event, she lies full-length in her coffin-container, until 'I died as I had lived. Quietly, gently, leaving little trace.'

Barely there, leaving little trace, women in white drift in and out of view, playing an attenuated role in their own stories, as does Rose Velderkaust, the white-robed spectre of J. Sheridan Le Fanu's 'Schalken the Painter'. Rose is sold as his bride to a demonic old man in a transaction conducted entirely between men, including, without his knowing it, the young artist who loves her. They are the protagonists of the story; the living Rose's part in her own tale is confined to pleading in vain for her guardian's protection, while the motives of her ghost remain ambiguous.

Other stories are even less conclusive. In the 1850s, HMS *Asp* was haunted by a woman in white who pointed towards heaven. A traveller on the ship had once had her throat cut. Was this figure her ghost seeking justice? The question stays unanswered. Highlow Hall in Derbyshire was haunted by a white lady, who walked through the courtyard and up the stairs with a rustle of silks. Sometimes bumps were heard on the staircase. Legend had it that her unidentified murdered body was being dragged to an unmarked grave.

Such figures retain their mystery. In Edinburgh in the first half of the nineteenth century a young man and his sister, warming themselves at night by the kitchen fire, looked up to see a female figure in white gazing at them from the doorway. When the young woman screamed, the spectre crossed the kitchen towards a closet and vanished. The apparition remained unexplained. An unnamed woman in white was known to haunt the dark glen at Raven Rock near Washington Irving's Sleepy Hollow, and to shriek before winter storms. A headless woman in white on a white horse was the talk of the local pub in Victorian Lark Rise. She crossed a bridge nightly as the clock struck twelve.

On occasions, reports of an apparition in white would bring down the rent of a property; conversely, sometimes it constituted a visitor attraction. At Glamis Castle the ghosts never appeared to family members. Undeterred, at least one visiting relative strained her eyes 'for a glimpse of the white lady, a most harmless apparition, who is supposed to flit about the avenue', recorded Mrs Maclagan, wife of the then Archbishop of York, in the late nineteenth century.

Flitting about, evanescent, anonymous, often victims of violence, sometimes headless, phantom white ladies offer an emblem of the female condition in misogynist cultures. Unaccounted for, ineffectual, detached from their own stories, such figures only duplicated the role of living women, angels in the house who left little trace outside it. Caring they might be, but if they were not to be eclipsed by their dangerous sisters, women in white needed to find a way to assert themselves – with a little help from their storytellers. Even when their tales afforded them a purpose, they were not well equipped to compete on the ground of the uncanny.

Clerical reservations notwithstanding, they were just too orthodox. Ghost stories in general promise their audience tentative access to the unknown; they offer glimpses of what customary wisdom leaves obscure, unnamed or inexplicable. In addition, malign ghosts repudiate humanity. The walking dead are most unnerving when they are beyond the reach of ethics, as well as logic. Ghosts animate both the lure and the menace of a terrain that remains unmapped by science, philosophy or theology, giving flickering, indefinite form to the perils that hover on the outer edges of what we think we know. In that sense, many ghost stories, even when they're clerically authorised, find themselves in competition with orthodoxy: they maintain the possibility of enigma in the face of a world conformity longs to render fully intelligible.

According to Virginia Woolf, ghosts are present 'whenever the significant overflows our powers of expressing it; whenever the ordinary appears ringed by the strange'; their stories are most compelling when 'something remains unaccounted for'. But, even while they remain enigmatic, the harmless adherence of random white-clad figures to the habits of a conventional femininity brings them closer to a realm that is all too familiar. To the degree that women in white return to comfort, nurture and warn, they perpetuate the ordinary – and protective mothers, wives, aunts and daughters are not always quite strange enough to thrill. When they vouch for the existence of a happy afterlife, women in white go some way towards domesticating the unexplained, retaining a foothold in a predictable cosmos.

Recovering the uncanny

How, then, to invest benign female revenants with their own fearful tales? Ambrose Bierce, master of the missed encounter, finds a way in 'The Moonlit Road' in 1907. Like *The Woman in White*, this short story is told in the first person by a succession of participants: the son, the husband and finally the dead wife herself, who finds a voice through a spiritualist medium. And like *The Woman in White*, the tale concerns, as the title indicates, a late-night apparition by moonlight, although this time the narrating son sees only the effects, his father, 'standing rigid and motionless in the centre of the illuminated roadway, staring like one bereft of sense'. Even so, the uncanny is registered in the son's record of a sudden chill: 'It seemed as if an icy wind had touched my face and enfolded my body from head to foot; I could feel the stir of it in my hair.' Meanwhile, his father, driven to madness by the apparition and thus bereft of sense in perpetuity, will remember only 'the gleam of white garments', and then the eyes of his dead wife fixed on his with the 'infinite gravity' of recognition.

But it is the wife's narrative that offers to haunt the reader long after the tale is told. Innocent though she is, this ghost is no smiling saint from a radiant eternity. On the contrary, her world is the one she has lost – but drained of sunlight, warmth or companionship, utterly without difference, apart from the absolute division between the living and the dead. Not knowing who killed her, this woman in white walks to give her husband the traditional consolation and sympathy – but his awareness of his own guilt for her murder leaves him able to greet her only with terror.

How, even so, could he have misread her purpose? The answer lies in a different strand of ghost lore. Whether or not he knows of the tradition of saintly women in white, the husband almost certainly remembers another. White dress may be no more than a winding sheet. In *The Monk*, Elvira's is her shroud. When Jane Eyre sees Bertha Mason, she notes, 'I know not what dress she had on: it was white and straight; but whether gown, sheet, or shroud, I cannot tell.'

As Jacob Postlethwaite knows, revenants are most commonly to be found in the churchyard, where they are understood to have come not from a brighter future but out of their graves. Burial clothes were traditionally white and children dressing up have long known how to turn themselves into ghosts with a sheet. Fragments of white shroud cling to medieval images of the Three Living and the Three Dead, while in *Hamlet* Horatio talks anachronistically of the 'sheeted dead' who left their graves to walk the streets of Rome, presaging Julius Caesar's death.

The Induction to the late sixteenth-century play *A Warning for Fair Women* derides the practice of bringing in 'a filthy whining ghost / Lapped in some foul sheet'. Indeed, the sceptical Reginald Scot thought that many a so-called ghost was nothing more than a knave in a white sheet. In 2017 David Lowery's film *A Ghost Story* conceals its spectre, increasingly adrift in time, under a white sheet with eye holes; in one of M. R. James's best-known stories, animated linen bedclothes alone arouse terror.

E. Nesbit's 'From the Dead', published in 1893, records another failed encounter. After a series of misrepresentations and misunderstandings, it is not clear whether the husband or the wife is more to blame for a separation both bitterly regret. As the husband lies in bed, wishing and fearing she would come back from the dead, the figure of his wife enters the room 'in its white graveclothes, with the white bandage under its chin . . . Its eyes were wide open and looked at me with love unspeakable'. But his terror prevails and, ironically, he covers his face with his own bed sheet, winding it round his head and body to keep the ghost at bay.

Both these women offer consolation in vain, but the motives of other dead women in white are more suspect. Caesarius of Heisterbach tells how a pale woman in a white dress caused the extinction of neighbouring families. She came from the graveyard and simply looked at them. At Easter 1650 Susan Lay, former servant, now reduced to sleeping in her master's barn, testified to an Essex court that her mistress Priscilla Beauty, buried three days earlier, had appeared to Susan all in white. The haunting continued for three consecutive nights and, on the third night, the apparition called out her name and pinched her arm.

The living servant, it turned out, was the mother of two children, now dead, one, she claimed, fathered by Priscilla's husband and one by his son. Both men had promised to marry Susan but in the end they had cast her out and she faced a life of vagrancy. Was Priscilla's ghost remorseful because she had failed to protect her servant from her predatory menfolk? Or was she, rather, vengeful because Susan had wanted to take her place?

The record doesn't say, but grave clothes are compatible with revenge. A law of 1660 imposed a fine on all who chose to be buried in imported linen rather than good English wool. When the dead Lady Sadleir avenges the theft of her contraband seventeenth-century works of devotion in M. R. James's 'The Uncommon Prayer Book' in 1921, it is as a five-foot roll of shabby white flannel that she delivers the fatal snake-bite. Japanese women traditionally wear white kimonos in death. One of the most unnerving of all Japanese movies, *Ring*, directed by Hideo Nakata in 1998, shows the vengeful daughter issuing from the television dressed in white.

Fairy ladies

Conventionally enough, the ghost of Ogmore Castle once revealed hidden treasure, telling her interlocutor he could have half of it. Less predictably, when he came back for the other half, this female figure in white nearly tore him to pieces with her claws. Equally conventionally, a young Welsh squire betrayed the servant girl he had promised never to leave. But when she returned in white to his sick bed with her baby, neither had a face. The squire cried that he would not go with her – and died. Catrin Wen, lost in a mountain mist, was violent and noisy after her death. She was seen placing a small white bundle at her feet.

The Welsh connections may not be accidental: Celtic tradition had another way of putting women in white at the centre of their own stories. It seems that the Ladi Wen is not necessarily a ghost at all but belongs to a distinct tradition of fairy ladies possessing magical powers. The Welsh white lady may also be related to the Irish banshee, who comes with fearful shrieks to portend a death. When Lady Fanshawe visited Lady Honor O'Brien in nineteenth-century Ireland, she saw a female figure standing in the window recess. The vision was 'attired in white, with red hair and a pale and ghastly aspect'. That night one of the O'Briens died.

White ladies, then, might owe as much to the fairy tradition as to ghost stories. In 1830 James Hogg exploited the chilling potential of the uncertain boundary between the two in 'The Mysterious Bride'. There, in what Hogg's narrator calls his 'winter evening's tale', the young laird repeatedly encounters a seductive young woman, who walks the local hills in white gauze. Ominously, her accessories are green, the fairy colour. Enchanted by her beauty, and puzzled by her sudden disappearances, the hero thinks of her as an angelic phantom. Against all reason, in due course the two plight their troth and, at the hour appointed for the wedding, they are seen together on the back of his horse, riding through the town at breakneck speed. But the horse is found dead at the stable door, while the corpse of the young laird is recovered at the wild place where the lovers were accustomed to meet. His father and grandfather had died at the same spot.

In the event, an old woman of the neighbourhood knows why. Jilted and murdered by a former laird, the entrancing spectre in white lures his descendants to their death in revenge. The mysterious bride is as far as can be from the shining visions of the saintly tradition. Unlike these figures, who dutifully maintain after death their caring destiny as daughters, wives and mothers, she is a bride but no wife, and her beauty is deadly to the degree that it proves irresistible. What is more, she is the protagonist of the tale: her consecutive manifestations determine the shape of the narrative; the young laird features as little more than her dupe, while the other characters simply provide circumstantial detail.

The Wili

At about the same time, coincidentally or not, something was stirring at the Paris Opéra. In 1831 the theatre put on *Robert le diable* with music by Giacomo Meyerbeer. At the end of the third Act of this story of passion, dark forces and a projected pact with the devil, Carmelite nuns in white rose from their graves to dance by moonlight, singing in praise of sin. This sensational episode initiated the tradition of *ballets blancs*, where, in the new point shoes, supernatural women in filmy white dresses seem to glide and float, skimming a stage bathed in a blue, lunar light.

Among the most influential of these *ballets blancs*, *Giselle* turns over its second half to these spectral figures. *Giselle* was conceived when the poet Théophile Gautier read in the work of his friend the poet Heinrich Heine about the Wili of Slavic folklore. So that there could be no mistake, Heine's account was printed in the libretto on sale in the lobby of the theatre when the work was first performed in 1841. The Wili, he declared, are brides-to-be, dead before their wedding day, driven out of their graves by an unfulfilled desire to dance. At midnight the Wili haunt the roads, and woe betide any young man who meets them: he has no choice but to dance with them until he drops exhausted to his death. Wearing white bridal dress, with chaplets of flowers in their hair, these ghost-maidens are pale but beautiful, their seduction impossible to resist.

In *Giselle*, then, the tradition of dead women in white joins another convention of supernatural women as tempters, possessed of a dangerous sexual energy – sirens, mermaids, the demons who beset male saints – reversing expectations of the customary consolation and rescue. But the story of the ballet manages to have it both ways. If the Wili are dangerous and deadly, Giselle's benign ghost, also in white, intercepts their overtures to her living lover. Refusing the imperative to join them, she shields him from the Wili until the sunrise returns them all to the tomb. In the process, she consoles him, reconciling him to life without her.

Giselle was a triumph. Within a year it was performed in London and was regularly revived thereafter. Plays, too, reimagined the story: as so often, adaptations of the work did much to popularise its theme. I can't resist a speculation that the Wili were domesticated in the phrase, otherwise unaccounted for etymologically, *to give someone the willies*, meaning to unnerve or unsettle. But, if so, that was not the end of their influence, since they were to resurface as the Veela, the Bulgarian mascots who perform before the Quidditch match in *Harry Potter and the Goblet of Fire*. The Veela are the most beautiful women the 14-year-old Harry has ever seen – although they don't seem quite human. As they dance faster and faster, he and Ron feel a strange compulsion to hurl themselves from the top box into the stadium below.

The end of the line

The Wili have died as brides-to-be and set out to destroy young men. In Castleton, Derbyshire, the Castle Inn is haunted by a jilted bride, who walks in white towards the dining room, where her wedding breakfast was prepared but never eaten. James Hogg's mysterious bride never reaches the altar – and will continue to seduce the heirs to the title until the line is extinct. In Edgar Allan Poe's 'The Fall of the House of Usher', published in 1839, the unmarried lady Madeline comes back from her tomb, still in her shroud, with 'blood upon her white robes'. Was she buried alive? Her return brings with it the death of her twin brother, the end of the lineage and the collapse of the ancestral mansion.

Is it possible that these figures – or some combination of them – age into Dickens's Miss Havisham, another vengeful virgin who figuratively buries herself alive and finally brings the house down about her? Here is the young Pip's first vision of her in *Great Expectations*, published in 1860–1:

> She was dressed in rich materials – satins, and lace, and silks – all of white. Her shoes were white. And she had a long white veil dependent from her hair, and she had bridal flowers in her hair, but her hair was white.

In this instance, however, the body is withered and emaciated and the fabrics are reduced in many places to yellowing rags, so that Miss Havisham's garments, designed for the wedding that never took place, evoke at the same time the tattered winding sheet of the medieval tradition. Like her near-contemporary, Anne Catherick, Miss Havisham is not literally a ghost and yet this most Gothic of Dickens's fictions teases the reader by allowing the resemblance to play its macabre part in the story. Defying nature and logic, time has stood still in Miss Havisham's room: the past inhabits the present. Cobwebs and decay combine to evoke the decomposition of the tomb in this borderland between life and death. And Pip comments,

Without this arrest of everything, this standing still of all the pale decayed objects, not even the withered bridal dress on the collapsed form could have looked so like grave-clothes, or the long veil so like a shroud.

So she sat, corpse-like.

As he lies dying, Miss Havisham's brother, who played a part in the plot to jilt her, sees the spectre of his sister in white by his bed. She has come to drag him from this world. There are drops of blood where her heart was broken.

In its way, *Great Expectations* invokes and remodels the entire tradition of women in white. Miss Havisham exercises her own form of enticement: at first she seems a benign influence, Pip's benefactor, perhaps even a surrogate mother to the orphan boy, but she turns out instead to have lured him only to his own destruction. Seductive at one remove through her adopted daughter Estella, wronged, a bride and no wife, she is also a travesty of a mother, who brings up a beautiful young woman to break hearts, not only Pip's but in the end her own. Eventually, Miss Havisham sets fire (deliberately or not) to herself and the room that has for so long entombed her alive. Although Pip rescues her, the reprieve is fleeting – and after her death her house is fit only to be pulled down. As a powerful, menacing woman in white, in every sense unorthodox, Miss Havisham is surely too consequential for readers to ignore or forget.

FIVE

Dangerous Dead Women

Precious fabrics

S ome female ghosts were just plain menacing – and deadlier, perhaps, than the males. Did they have grounds? We can begin to think about this by going back in the first instance to the Icelandic sagas, where a high price was paid for the neglect of Thorgunna's last wishes. Thorgunna was in her fifties when she arrived in Iceland from the Hebrides, bringing with her two chests full of fine garments and elegantly worked bedclothes of a quality the local people had never seen before. Thurid, wife of the farmer at Froda, thought she might eventually coax the newcomer into parting with some of them and invited her to stay at the farm. In exchange for her keep, Thorgunna would work at haymaking and weaving.

The entire household kept its distance from the stranger. On her death bed Thorgunna gave strict instructions to Thorodd, the farmer, concerning the disposal of her body and her worldly goods. Thurid was to have her scarlet cloak, Thorodd was to take whatever he liked of her property to cover any expenses he incurred but, to avert disaster, her bed and bedclothes were to be burned. It would be a mistake to disregard her wishes in this matter. Thorodd built a bonfire ready to obey Thorgunna's instructions but Thurid would have none of it. Such beautiful fabrics, she insisted, should not be wantonly destroyed. Reluctantly, Thorodd yielded to his wife's coaxing: he burned the bed and the pillows but allowed Thurid to take charge of the bedclothes.

Thorgunna's body was prepared for the journey to her chosen burial site, stripped of all but a linen cloth. When, on the way, an inhospitable farmer refused to provide the funeral cortège with an evening meal, the travellers made shift to find resting places in the hall, while the local inhabitants went to bed. Moments later, loud noises were heard in the kitchen. A woman, stark naked, was preparing a dinner which, in due course, she served to the burial party, with the result that everyone got a good night's sleep. It seemed that the dead Thorgunna was not prepared to let her bearers march on an empty stomach. News of this ghostly intervention spread rapidly and other farmers were alarmed into proving more welcoming.

Soon after the burial party returned to Froda, people began to die, first among them a shepherd. Then one night Thorir Wood-leg, who had got on badly with Thorgunna, went outside to relieve himself, as was the custom. When he tried to return, the dead shepherd beat him black and blue against the door. Thorir died of his injuries and from then on he and the shepherd were repeatedly seen together, to the terror of the neighbourhood. More members of Thorodd's household fell ill, until six were lost in a matter of weeks. Just before Yule, Thorodd himself and five more of his companions were drowned in the course of an expedition to fetch dried fish. On the night of their funeral feast the dead men came and sat in the hall, soaking wet. The revenants stayed until the fire burned down, then took to coming back every night in their wet clothes.

In due course they were joined in the hall by Thorir Wood-leg and the dead farm workers, muddy from their graves. The living residents of Froda eventually moved into the smaller room, leaving the main hall to the nightly visitors who came to sit by the fire.

But this was not the end of the story. More people died and others fled, in the process reducing a staff of thirty to no more than seven.

When Thurid herself became ill, Thorgunna's bedclothes were finally burned. In a court of law convened for the purpose, the ghosts were convicted on counts of trespass and murder. Grudgingly admitting in public that they had outstayed their welcome, the revenants stood up one by one and left. A priest performed Christian rites, Thurid recovered, and the farm at Froda gradually returned to its former prosperity.

These events, said to have taken place in Iceland around 1000 CE, were written down in *Eyrbyggja saga* in the thirteenth century. If Thorgunna's story marks a moment in cultural history when Christianity was in the process of coming to terms with the pagan past, it also points to a continuing fear of reprisals on earth from beyond this life. There is a degree of ambiguity about whether the hauntings represent Thorgunna's revenge for the hostility she has experienced, or whether her death-bed instructions are designed to avert disaster from another unnamed cause. Either way, failure to execute her will incurs a fearful retribution.

Six hundred years later, in 1868, and quite coincidentally, I believe, Henry James published a short story, 'The Romance of Certain Old Clothes', that tells how a young woman, dying after childbirth, implores her husband with peculiar intensity to keep the silks and satins of her grand trousseau in store for their daughter when she grows up. The wife's sister, Viola, is to have her blue and silver brocade but the rest of her clothes are to be locked away in a great chest until the child is old enough to wear them. Not long after, the widower marries Viola herself, who cannot bear to leave such rich fabrics unused in an attic. She eventually prevails on her new husband to surrender the key but his perfidy, like Thorodd's, has tragic consequences. As the story ends,

The lid of the chest stood open, exposing, amid their perfumed napkins, its treasure of stuffs and jewels. Viola had fallen backward from a kneeling posture, with one hand supporting her on the floor and the other pressed to her heart. On her limbs was the stiffness of death, and on her face, in the fading light of the sun, the terror of something more than death. Her lips were parted in entreaty, in dismay, in agony; and on her bloodless brow and cheeks there glowed the marks of ten hideous wounds from two vengeful ghostly hands.

A changing history

The parallels between these two stories, products of such different cultures and widely separated moments, might seem to point to an unchanging misogyny. Both depend on a feminine love of finery, a husband at the mercy of a manipulative wife, and a monstrous penalty for ignoring a woman's final request. But, at the same time, the historical differences between the saga and the short story are striking. The Icelanders have no defined inner life: the record confines itself to their actions. Henry James's central figures, by contrast, are closely characterised: Viola's bitter rivalry with her younger sister for possession of this socially desirable husband is etched in persuasive detail.

The horror of the nineteenth-century revenant is also registered psychologically: Henry James does not allow readers to see his ghost. As Sir Walter Scott, himself no slouch in the genre, had argued in 1827, 'The marvellous, more than any other attribute of fictitious narrative, loses its effect by being brought much into view.' The option of concealing the source of terror remains at the disposal of the best Hollywood directors. Like them, Henry James plays on the power of the imagination to create phantasms that exceed the power of words or images, when he allows the appalling nature of the apparition to register in the response of the victim: 'on her face . . . the terror of something more than death'.

Henry James's phantom leaves physical marks on Viola and vanishes. But the Icelandic revenants are solid physical presences. The dead Thorgunna's cookery is duly nourishing; the shepherd's ghost beats a man to death. And they return direct from their resting places. Thorgunna is naked from her bier; the dead sailors' clothes are drenched with sea water; the farm hands bring with them earth from the grave. These medieval revenants mingle with the living and occupy the same plane. At Froda the walking dead take possession of the domestic space and either drive out the staff or seize them to become their companions. Evidently, the bereaved co-exist with the ghosts, however uneasily. And although the priest plays a part in their exorcism, the Froda revenants are effectively driven away by a legal process conducted in an earthly court.

Dead women strike back

There could be no clearer evidence that both ghosts and ghost stories have a history. At the same time, however pronounced the historical differences, there is one major link between the saga and the nineteenth-century tale. Both stories allow us to see these female revenants as avenged not only for the neglect of their final wishes but also for a lifetime in which their hopes have been of equally little account. If Henry James is an expert in psychology, he is also a specialist in power relations. The dead wife of his story is called Perdita, *the lost girl*, in memory of a baby sister who died in infancy. Named from birth as a substitute, not the thing itself, Perdita grows up less imperious than her elder sister. In death she retaliates.

But Perdita's lack of consequence in life goes deeper than eclipse by the overbearing Viola. In practice, neither sister has much scope for imposing her wishes. Although the story makes clear that both are cleverer than their better educated brother, it also notes that they are culturally required to restrain their native curiosity: 'in those days' the narrative voice reminds us, 'a well-bred young woman was not expected to break into the conversation of her own movement or to ask too many questions'. When it comes to their contest for a husband, they are powerless in the courtship process:

> a young girl of decent breeding could make no advances what-
> ever, and barely respond, indeed, to those that were made. She
> was expected to sit still in her chair with her eyes on the carpet.

Living in what is presented as an American colonial backwater, Viola and Perdita spend their days 'stitching and trimming', each hoping that her appearance alone will select her for marriage by the wealthy English visitor. If the model woman in this society was to all intents and purposes a kind of ghost already, the story-teller evidently doesn't share that ideal.

Perhaps, then, the danger ghosts represent may be inversely proportional to the level of their power in life: the less their living authority, the more menacing they become after death. Thorgunna's story supports that idea. The status of women as depicted in the sagas is by no means negligible. Like Thorgunna herself, women work outdoors, as well as at more traditionally feminine tasks; widows may run farms and often play a major part in the events recorded, for better or worse. *Laxdaela saga*, in particular, depicts a succession of formidable matriarchs.

But these powerful figures remain an exception to the general rule. Both men and women have their conventional place. The men are generally busy farming, heroically lopping off each other's limbs, or combining to make legally binding decisions at the Althing, the annual assembly of the Icelanders and an ancestor of all parliaments. Meanwhile, the ideal woman is a wife who excels in her domestic duties, defined poetically as 'goddess of table-games' or 'goddess of the drinking-horn', 'linen-goddess', 'fir-tree of the tapestry', and 'she who spreads the cloth / over the wide bed'. She also bears rich gold, putting on display the family's wealth in the form of bracelets and rings. In command in her own household, she is not expected to intervene directly in the affairs of the wider world, and if she wants revenge for injustice, she usually incites men to exact it.

Thorgunna, however, is already middle-aged when she arrives in Iceland. Whatever the explanation for her rich possessions, she is now a lone woman. At Froda she is also an outsider and few people befriend her. The events after her death signally reverse the neglect she has experienced.

Injured wives

Although the varieties of ghost stories defy generalisation, tales of women overshadowed in life and avenged in death constitute a category we might call the return of the oppressed. Curiously enough, one of the oldest recorded ghost stories also concerns unburnt fabrics. According to the Greek historian Herodotus in the fifth century BCE, the dead Melissa turned the tables on her husband, Periander, the tyrant of Corinth. A guest had left something with Periander but, after his wife's death, he couldn't find it. When the tyrant sent to ask her through the oracle of the dead, Melissa's ghost refused to help, on the grounds that she was cold and naked: her clothes had not been cremated with her and were therefore no use to her in the afterlife. To prove her authenticity, Melissa hinted in the message conveyed by the oracle that her husband had had sex with her corpse. Duly convinced that this was the real Melissa, Periander made all the women in Corinth strip naked so that he could burn their clothes to appease his wronged wife. Only then did she tell him where he had put the lost object.

It also continued to be dangerous to neglect an undertaking. The Scottish writer David Person told in 1635 of a man who broke his promise to bury his wife in the churchyard. In consequence, she returned to haunt the family, frightening them to the point where there was no rest for them at any time.

But all guilty widowers should beware. In England in 1700 a dead wife left her husband covered in blood after she had returned to beat him. As she lay dying, he had thrashed her in the belief that she had hidden money from him. Her ghost was evidently just as corporeal as the Icelandic revenants. A Danish folktale wife also comes back to avenge years of ill-treatment. When her husband begs her on her grave to rid him of his new wife, her cruel successor, the ghost reappears, to break *his* neck instead.

In ancient Egypt, it seems, the mere return of a dead woman prompted her husband to examine his conscience. A papyrus left in her tomb begs the Lady Onkhari to leave her widower alone. His late wife has haunted him ever since she died, he complains, disturbing his house. 'What wrong', he asks, 'have I been guilty of that I should be in this state of trouble?'

At the trial of George Burroughs for witchcraft in Salem in 1692, it was brought in evidence against him that his two successive dead wives blamed him for their deaths. If Burroughs denied this, their ghosts might well testify in court. He had treated them as slaves in life and sworn them to secrecy about his wicked practices.

During the trial one of the people bewitched by Burroughs saw the dead women crying for vengeance against him. Others, brought in for the purpose, saw the apparitions too, although the accused claimed he did not. Burroughs was convicted and executed on 19 August, still protesting his innocence.

If mistreatment of wives is perilous, divorce offers no solution. 'Black Hair', a Japanese folk tale recorded by Lafcadio Hearn – and dramatised in 1964 in Masaki Kobayashi's stylish film *Kwaidan* – concerns a samurai who abandoned his good and faithful wife for a more advantageous marriage. Years later, repenting of his error, he returned to the house where they had lived so happily together. Still beautiful, the first wife now forgives him and, as they talk lovingly together, he falls asleep beside her. The morning sun, however, reveals a different companion in his bed: a faceless corpse, little more than a skeleton, with tangled black hair.

Love betrayed

Unfaithful lovers are also pursued from the next world. In a Latin elegy from about 16 BCE, Cynthia returns in a dream to complain bitterly that she was neglected in life and in death. Now the poet loves another – but soon Cynthia alone will hold him; her bones will be the ones to embrace his. Seventeen centuries later and in a different social key, the ballad of *Two Unfortunate Lovers* tells how the inappropriately named John True, a shoemaker from Coventry, abandoned Susan Mease for another woman. When Susan died of love, her ghost spoke from the grave to summon the remorseful John, who followed her into the afterlife two weeks later.

This warning against betrayal was published in the 1680s, but another ballad, this time of *Fair Margaret and Sweet William*, was already familiar in London in 1607, when a snatch of it featured in Francis Beaumont's play, *The Knight of the Burning Pestle*. In Beaumont's version,

> When it was grown to dark midnight,
>   And all were fast asleep,
> In came Margaret's grimly ghost
>   And stood at William's feet.

Not long after, the faithless William died of sorrow.

The tale was still in circulation in the eighteenth century, when David Mallet rewrote the story to include Margaret's reproaches:

> Bethink thee, William, of thy fault,
>   Thy pledge and broken oath:
> And give me back my maiden vow,
>   And give me back my troth.

But it can't be done. Margaret compounds her complaint by describing her state:

> The hungry worm my sister is;
>   This winding sheet I wear:
> And cold and dreary lasts our night,
>   Till that last morn appear.

William rises from his bed, maddened and shaking, to go straight to the churchyard, where he lies on Margaret's grave and never speaks another word.

Such desertion must be one of the commonest reasons why dead women seek revenge. In 1860 Mary Elizabeth Braddon's

'The Cold Embrace' portrays a young artist who abandons the cousin he has loved, with the consequence that, after her suicide, he cannot escape the icy hands that clasp his neck whenever he finds himself alone.

Sometimes the lover's crime also runs to homicide. In the early 1630s, Anne Walker, pregnant by a kinsman and murdered on his instructions, returned from death to accuse her killers, who were tried and executed for the crime. M. R. James, who had read this story in Glanvill's *Saducismus Triumphatus*, rewrote it as 'Martin's Close' in 1911. His version depicts a young gentleman pursued to the point of dread by the ghost of Ann Clark, a simple country girl he had first betrayed and then killed. More recently, a rejected mistress returns to fetch her killer in the film *What Lies Beneath*, directed by Robert Zemeckis in 1999, a detailed recapitulation of the theme in elegant modern American dress.

First partners

In other instances, the husband's crime is no more than remarriage. First wives, it seems, do not like to be replaced. Perdita punishes Viola for marrying her husband. According to English folklore, a widower out courting another woman just after burying his wife saw the face of the deceased through the window. Within two weeks he too was dead.

Edith Wharton's story 'Pomegranate Seed' in 1931 records the struggle between two wives, one living and one dead, for possession of their husband. Kenneth, happily remarried after two years of widowhood, receives at intervals a succession of letters that mysteriously appear at dusk in pale grey envelopes. The first arrives the night he returns from his honeymoon. Each consecutive letter drains him of further vitality. When eventually Kenneth disappears altogether, his second wife tears open the latest of the letters. The writing is so faint as to be barely visible: all she can provisionally see are the words 'mine' and perhaps 'come'.

A wife returns to deter her former husband from consummating his second marriage in May Sinclair's 'The Nature of the Evidence' (1923). The 'Secret Chambers' depicted by Mrs Wilson Woodrow in 1909 are haunted by a first wife, Adele, in much the way that the dead Rebecca would continue to possess Manderley in Daphne du Maurier's novel of 1938. The contest takes comic form in Noel Coward's comedy of 1941, *Blithe Spirit*, where the protagonist's first wife returns to kill the second, who then walks in her turn, taking up spectral residence in the house alongside her predecessor. *Blithe Spirit* is attentive to the tradition it parodies: if the emphasis is on the absurdity of ghost stories, the plot is well established in the genre.

An unconquerable female sexuality refuses to give way to a second wife in Edgar Allan Poe's 'Ligeia' in 1838, where, unless we ascribe the horrifying outcome to an opium dream, the former wife poisons her successor and takes possession of her corpse to effect an appalling resurrection. In 2009, Ligeia's modern descendant, Audrey Niffenegger's Elspeth Noblin cannot allow her partner to move on in *Her Fearful Symmetry*.

Nearest and dearest

In the end, all family relationships are dangerous. The chest full of finery was durable enough to resurface in Elizabeth Bowen's short story 'Hand in Glove' in 1952. Ethel has been keeping her aunt locked up in her room. Now, genteel but impoverished, Ethel badly needs evening gloves to go to a ball. The aunt's death gives her sudden access to the trunk in the attic containing the perfectly preserved trousseau of a generation ago. But the precious materials the niece eagerly pulls out seem oddly resistant to her grasp – until 'the spotless finger-tip of a white kid glove appeared for a moment, as though exploring its way out'. That eerily animated accessory goes on to seize the predator by the throat, avenging years of cruelty to the aunt who owned it.

Like Viola and Perdita, siblings may carry their romantic rivalries beyond the grave. The old ballad of *The Twa Sisters* exists in a range of versions, but each tells of young women who compete for the same man. When the lover makes his choice, the forsaken elder sister pushes the younger into the sea. But a harp is made from parts of her corpse, sometimes the breast-bone, sometimes locks of her yellow hair, and the music reveals her murder, in some variants at her sister's wedding.

Vengeance is long deferred in Elizabeth's Gaskell's 'Old Nurse's Story' of 1852. But although not swift, it remains sure. Miss Maude and Miss Grace, sisters in love with the same man, are both forbidden to marry him by an imperious father. Maude, the elder, prevails with the lover, but Grace betrays them to her father, and a ghostly re-enactment of the scene on a winter night leaves the now ageing Grace struck down with a death-palsy.

Maude sends her spectral daughter back to entice living children to join her in death. An unrelenting elder sister forces Susan Hill's woman in black to give up her little boy for adoption, leaving her powerless to intervene as she witnesses his drowning, but the little boy still inhabits his nursery, while the deadly revenant seeks living replacements for the child she has lost.

Elsewhere, vengeance belongs to the child. In 1998 the murdered illegitimate daughter of a socially rejected mother retaliates with a curse that can be survived only by passing it on in *Ring*. A phantom child comes back to claim her killer in Toni

Morrison's *Beloved*, which won the Pulitzer Prize ten years earlier. This ghost grows up to damage her mother and sister until her presence has the paradoxical effect of reuniting the African American community to support what remains of the family.

Malign power

These injured ghosts are unforgiving. Death undoes their humanity. The dead Elspeth Noblin seems to have lost what her lover calls 'compassion, or empathy, some human thing'. The face of Susan Hill's woman in black reveals

> a desperate, yearning malevolence; it was as though she were searching for something she wanted, needed – *must have*, more than life itself, and which had been taken from her. And, towards whoever had taken it she directed the purest evil and hatred and loathing.

In the stories, the terror of monstrous female revenants is seen as well founded: many of them now possess a mortal power unimagined in their lifetime. Henry James's dead wife kills the sister who has replaced her in her husband's affections. The anonymous folktale woman whose widower betrays her on the day of her funeral summons him to join her; ghostly arms dance the faithless artist to death in 'The Cold Embrace'. George Burroughs is executed; Anne Walker convicts her murderers; sightings of Ann Clark are instrumental in bringing her lover to the gallows. Thorgunna's revenge, if that is what it is, kills Thorodd, but not before effecting the systematic elimination of most of those who keep his farm in operation. Hill's woman in black terrorises a whole neighbourhood when she returns to snatch its children.

Coincidentally or not, the woman in black had her predecessors in ancient Greece. *Lamias* and *mormones* were demonic women who flew by night to kill or devour babies and girls. The children of Lamia and Mormo had died young, and after death these cheated mothers took to killing other children out of envy. Greek folklore also included a special category of *gelloudes*, ancestors of the Wili. These were maidens who had themselves died untimely deaths before achieving their proper status as wives and mothers. In consequence, they had no honoured place in the underworld and could not find rest there from their hatred of others who had fulfilled the true destiny of women. Inhabiting the margin between life and death, and appeased only by similar unhappiness among the living, these revenants brought about miscarriages, death in childbirth, stillborn children and infant mortality. They had their own formidable goddess, Hecate, leader of ghosts, who dwelt at crossroads, on tombs and near dead bodies. Hecate taught witchcraft and necromancy.

What motivates so many stories of menacing women? Were there more malevolent female ghosts, or were they more monstrous than their male counterparts? In the absence of accurate statistics, which is to say without a record of all the ghost stories ever told, it might be hard to know for sure. But dangerous dead women seem to hold an exceptional and shocking place, perhaps because they contradict the stereotype of femininity as caring and nurturing.

And possibly that stereotype itself goes some way to account for the prevalence of the stories. Caring and nurturing are good things but throughout much of history they have been left to women, as wives, mothers, housekeepers, ladies' maids, nurses or governesses. And nurturing may have been highly valued but it has not been highly paid – when it is paid at all. The angel in the house has not traditionally exercised much power outside it.

The prevalence of these stories at such a wide range of cultural moments could be ascribed to straightforward misogyny. When they repudiate their allotted role, women turn into monsters. But an alternative explanation is slightly more complex. So many tales of dangerous dead women can be seen as the result of a shared social anxiety. Societies that allocate a subordinate place to part of the population are haunted by terrifying phantoms who, released in death from the humane inhibitions that bind the living, wreak an appalling revenge on those implicated, whether personally or cultur-ally, in the practice of their oppression. By rehearsing these tales to itself, orthodoxy betrays its own guilt, and an awareness that its constraints are fragile. The unequal distribution of power generates the fear of a deadly retribution all the more shocking to the degree that women are culturally required to be life-giving and loving.

Not all the many dangerous dead women I have mentioned have been individually oppressed. Some of them are seen as just plain malign. Some are victims of other women. And it is not clear that first wives have a claim to fidelity beyond death – unless in the unease of their successors. But a long history of menacing female revenants registers a broader fear that sooner or later the oppressed group will escape their culturally prescribed place. You will judge how far we have now begun to call the living to account in more legitimate ways than walking after death.

Old wives

If this is how we read the tales, perhaps old wives had an interest in telling them. Traditionally, it was women who spun their yarns at winter firesides, holding their audiences rapt. The sources are constant and all-but unanimous in attributing ghost stories to women. It was old women who used to tell Marlowe's Jew of

Malta winter's tales; Macbeth's fear of Banquo would suit 'A woman's story at a winter's fire, / Authorised by her grandam'. While there might be ministering spirits, there were no ghosts, Daniel Defoe maintained: 'all the old women's stories, which we have told us upon that subject, are indeed old women's stories, and no more', he insisted.

This ascription of tall tales to women remains constant, regardless of the value judgement it entails. In ancient Rome, Persius, the first-century Stoic, thought it right to root out all foolish notions inculcated by old wives (literally, old grandmothers). 1500 years later, the sceptical Reginald Scot holds 'our mother's maids' responsible for transmitting supernatural nonsense. Conversely, the Phoenician of Philostratus, who first heard such yarns from his nurse, concedes that she cleverly kept him amused by this means. In the seventeenth century John Aubrey praises the skill of his old nurse in recounting the stories.

Philosophers rebutted the challenge of the supernatural to Enlightenment wisdom by dismissing ghost stories as the province of uneducated women: 'The ideas of goblins and sprites have really no more to do with darkness than light', John Locke argued. 'Yet let but a foolish maid inculcate these often on the mind of a child and raise them there together, possibly he shall never be able to separate them again so long as he lives.'

As Locke indicates, the young were widely seen as the most susceptible listeners to winter's tales. When in 1711 Joseph Addison spent an evening with his landlady's daughters and their friends as they told ghost stories by the fire, 'with many other old women's fables of the like nature', a little boy who was present was especially attentive to every story. Addison reverted to this issue in a later essay: ghost stories were first heard in childhood from 'nurses and old women'.

And, as Locke also indicates, they tended to stick. Accordingly, M. G. Lewis's innocent Antonia remains open to superstition because of the stories she heard from her nurse. To Anne Brontë's young Gilbert Markham, the appearance of Wildfell Hall stood to confirm 'the ghostly legends and dark traditions our old nurse had told us respecting the haunted hall and its departed occupants'. Confined to the red room at Gateshead, the terrified Jane Eyre recalls the 'evening stories' of Bessie the nurse. In her subsequent illness, she hears Bessie discussing her panic with the housemaid: 'Something passed her, all dressed in white, and vanished' . . . 'A light in the churchyard . . .'

Handbooks repeatedly instructed servants not to spread such fears. Conversely, defenders of the genre allowed women and children a special access to realms beyond the immediate. The Enlightenment was mistaken in its belief that no one credits tales of the supernatural but the very young and old women, insisted Catherine Crowe in her nineteenth-century collection of attested ghost stories. Women and children are simply more receptive, more intuitive; the wisdom of this world is foolishness with God; faith is a pre-condition of awareness, and the uneducated are most open to occult beliefs.

Although not all writers of ghost stories were women, some concessions were made to the oral convention in the narratives themselves. It is a destitute old woman who explains the story of 'The Mysterious Bride'; a local peasant woman knows that armed effigies walk on All Saints' Eve in E. Nesbit's 'Man-Size in Marble'. Elizabeth Gaskell calls her contribution to the genre 'The Old Nurse's Story'; the servant Nelly Dean recounts much of *Wuthering Heights*. Two early twentieth-century American short stories are recounted by servants, Edith Wharton's 'The Lady's Maid's Bell' and Josephine Daskam Bacon's 'The Children'.

Suppose, then, that in the light of the consensus that old wives and maidservants are the source of ghost stories, we allow the attribution to stand. What had women to gain from relaying such tales? In the first place, the limelight. Working and elderly women were probably not used to much attention in other contexts but here was one place where they could hold centre stage, commanding audiences with their eloquence. In addition, ghost stories defy in a society that aligned itself with reason, science or theology the limits of the knowledge that identified old women themselves as ignorant and uneducated. But above all, stories of dangerous dead women assert a female power disallowed by misogynist cultures. They permit women to demonstrate from beyond the grave an energy greater than any that might have been acknowledged in their lives. As sources of terror, malign female ghosts might well compensate in the tales for any slights and exclusions their story-tellers experienced in reality.

And their audiences? If the tales a culture tells itself register anxieties that might not find a name in other genres, the circulation of these ghost stories marks an uncertainty about what women just might be capable of if pushed too far.

SIX

Unquiet Gothic Castles

A new genre

It is a truth universally acknowledged that a Gothic castle must be haunted. While spectral stereotypes emerged and evolved through one epoch after another, at a specific moment in the eighteenth century a fledgling genre made its way into public consciousness. Just when the philosophers were urging old wives to keep their tales to themselves, and John Wesley was wondering how far to believe Joseph Glanvill, novel-readers were lining up to buy the prototype of a new kind of ghost story. Horace Walpole's best-selling *Castle of Otranto* was published in 1764.

Thirty years later, in Ann Radcliffe's blockbuster *The Mysteries of Udolpho*, the now familiar outlines of the Gothic novel are sketched by Mademoiselle Bearn, who has missed her friend. 'I had begun to think some wonderful adventure had befallen you, and that the giant of this enchanted castle, or the ghost which, no doubt, haunts it, had conveyed you through a trap door into some subterranean vault.' Mademoiselle Bearn light-heartedly names most of the props of this particular strand of English story-telling – and links it with fairy tale. The castle is under a spell, while its ghost is interchangeable with a giant.

As she undoubtedly knows, *The Castle of Otranto* had intro-duced a figure that was both spectral and huge. A classical education would have inculcated from Virgil the idea of a larger-than-life shade and at the end of Walpole's novel, published, appropriately enough, on Christmas Eve, the gigantic phantom of Alfonso materialises in arms to resolve the questions that have accumulated in the course of the story.

Ghost stories reinvented to gratify an emergent novel-reading public would go on to register anxieties about the market economy, as well as the supremacy of reason. In due course, they would also relegate but not replace traditional winter's tales. The new genre was not immediately named as Gothic, however. Its first title page identified *The Castle of Otranto* as the translation of a sixteenth-century Italian tale. But four months later, when Walpole's second edition subtitled his nightmarish confection *A Gothic Story*, the term was designed to place the improbable events in the barbarous – but fascinating – Middle Ages. Walpole's novel, an instant sensation, was thought to be one of a kind but there followed in 1777 Clara Reeve's *The Champion of Virtue: A Gothic Story*, now better known by the title of its second edition, *The Old English Baron*.

Reeve declared in the preface that her novel, written on the same plan as *The Castle of Otranto*, would be more instructive and altogether more credible. Credible or not, her Castle of Lovel also has its ghost, whose role in the story was important enough to justify his depiction in the frontispiece to the retitled second edition. From then on, no Gothic castle was complete without its phantom. Another ghost terrifies the dastardly Walter in the castle of Anne Fuller's *Alan Fitz-Osborne* in 1787, while the murdered owner of *Mort Castle* walks in an anonymous novel of 1798. Meanwhile, Dark Lord Erick comes back from the grave to reveal a treasure chamber that will save the castle in Sir Walter Scott's unperformed play *The Doom of Devorgoil*. In 1847 G. P. R.

James's *Castle of Ehrenstein* promises supernatural residents in the subtitle: *Its Inhabitants Earthly and Unearthly.*

Early in the development of the genre, ominous preparatory sights and sounds tend to build expectation gradually, but by 1862 a novel bluntly titled *The Haunted Castle* can go straight to the central issue. Replying to the opening request for directions to Llewellen Castle, a local resident corrects the visitor: it is known in these parts as the haunted castle. The equally perfunctory way this engaging romance introduces its macabre apparition invests the uncanny with a paradoxical predictability. By now, after nearly a hundred years of Gothic fiction, as soon as the reader has been led into a fortified medieval dwelling, spectral terrors are the order of the night.

In other words, fortresses, once built to keep out marauders, now find themselves threatened by irrepressible powers from within. Even when castles are not actually troubled by ghosts, they are widely believed to be. Ann Radcliffe has the best of both worlds, creating terror without in the event confirming a super-natural origin. It is not until Emily St Aubert reaches the Italian castle in volume 2 that the uncanny begins to feature seriously in Radcliffe's 4-volume *Mysteries of Udolpho*. At first its source is Annette, the French lady's maid, who repeats the gossip of the servants as she helps Emily find her way to the heroine's allotted bedroom. But it gradually influences Emily too, helpless in the power of the unpredictable Montoni, the castle's current proprie-tor and the heroine's adoptive uncle.

Once they reach the remote and gloomy chamber where Emily is to sleep, she finds herself reluctant to be alone, and Annette settles down by the fire to tell her a ghost story. The tale, punctu-ated by the teller's anxious insistence that she has heard a noise, or that the lamp is burning blue, concerns Signora Laurentini, the former owner, who refused the hand of the young Montoni and spent her days in deep melancholy. One winter evening, the Signora went for a walk in the woods – and never returned. The servants say her spirit has been seen in the building; it comes and goes unaccountably, but never speaks.

Castles were not unique. Other old and isolated edifices were also haunted, most notably ruined abbeys, not least because they once housed tombs and monuments to the dead. This tradition goes back at least to John Webster's play *The Duchess of Malfi* in 1614, where the widowed Antonio hears his wife's voice from her grave in an echo among the remains of an abbey. The play was performed in the open air, but also by candlelight in the indoor playhouse at the Blackfriars, itself a former convent restored as a theatre. Webster in turn probably took his cue from John Marston's *Antonio's Revenge*. This play, contemporary with *Hamlet*, similarly shows a son confronting the apparition of a murdered father. Marston's ghost rises straight from his coffin in St Mark's Church to demand revenge, perhaps taking advantage in the process of the playhouse's own location inside the cloister of old St Paul's. Two centuries later, Radcliffe and Lewis both exploited the eerie potential of monastic buildings in bestselling novels, while the practice was parodied by Jane Austen in *Northanger Abbey* and Thomas Love Peacock in *Nightmare Abbey*.

Oddly enough, however, in what looks like a minor concession to the preferred setting, Nightmare Abbey is 'castellated'. In this Peacock is faithful to the novels he mocks: Radcliffe's Abbeys of St Augustin and St Clair are both provided with battlements. These textual parapets feature as a Gothic extra, since medieval monasteries were not defensive structures. True, their gatehouses might be fortified, while church towers were often decoratively crenellated, but much castellation took place in the course of nineteenth-century restoration or Gothicisation.

Eventually, battlements with or without their attendant castles will come to provide the proper setting for ghosts. In 1898, the narrator of *The Turn of the Screw* first sees Peter Quint on one of the towers at Bly, 'incongruous, crenellated structures', 'architectural absurdities' added to the house in the romantic revival.

Knights in armour

Castles, in other words, held a special place in the Gothic imagination, to the point where in 1813 a spoof of the genre was entitled 'Il Castello di Grimgothico'. Medieval ghosts had no particular association with specific buildings or social classes. The Gothic preferred its ghosts aristocratic, however, as well as archaic. In consequence, a good many apparitions were now clad from head to foot in arms. Like Walpole's Alfonso, Dark Erick walks in outsize armour to save Scott's Devorgoil Castle. Clara Reeve's Lord Lovel also wears plate mail to guard his burial chamber. When in 1794 James Boaden rewrote Radcliffe's novel *The Romance of the Forest* as a stage play called *Fountainville Forest*, he included the ghost of the heroine's father – in armour. It is at Têtefoulques Castle that Washington Irving's Don Luis is confronted by the ghost of Foulques Taillefer (Fulke Hack-iron, the story helpfully translates), 'armed cap-à-pie' in 'The Knight of Malta'. The haunted hall of Ehrenstein Castle reveals 'a tall and lordly looking man, clothed in arms from head to heel'.

These metal-clad ghosts are warriors for justice. *Gaston de Blondeville*, not published until 1826, after Ann Radcliffe's death, centres on an armed knight who appears in Kenilworth Castle to expose his own murder. Unlike the work Radcliffe chose to publish, *Gaston* does not explain its ghost away. The author had already rehearsed the outline of this story in the old Provençal tale

Figure 3 The late Lord Lovel guards his burial chamber in *The Old English Baron*, 1778

incorporated into *The Mysteries of Udolpho*. There, a stranger habited like a knight drew a baron to the forest where he found the knight's corpse. As the horrified baron recognised the stranger's features in the body on the ground, the knight's form gradually faded away to nothing.

Real or hypothetical, armed ghosts are chivalrous, heroic, authoritative. In M. G. Lewis's play *The Castle Spectre*, a painting of Earl Reginald, victim of his brother Osmond, shows the late owner in armour. The servants believe that the figure in the picture walks in Conway Castle. Lewis introduces a new twist on the familiar convention when the living hero conceals himself in Reginald's armour and comes down from his pedestal. Distracted by this seeming apparition, the guilty Osmond lets his niece escape his unwanted attentions.

Garrick's Hamlet

It was Henry Fielding's Partridge who in 1749 had unwittingly confirmed the inspiration for so many armed phantoms. When Tom Jones takes his guileless companion to see David Garrick play Hamlet, Partridge is justly impressed by the protagonist's terror at his first sight of the Ghost. Garrick's performance at this moment was legendary: startled, he turned to face the spectre with arms outstretched, as if to fend him off; he may have worn a fright wig that made his hair stand on end as he staggered backwards. 'His whole demeanour is so expressive of terror that it made my flesh creep even before he began to speak', commented a German visitor to London. Partridge refuses to concede that Garrick's behaviour owed anything to acting skill: self-evidently, the little man on the stage was genuinely frightened, he maintains; Partridge himself would have responded in exactly the same way to an apparition. But he is surprised by what he hesitantly recognises from pictures as armour. Although he himself has never seen one, Partridge knows what belongs to revenants. 'No, no, sir, ghosts don't appear in such dresses as that.'

Historically speaking, he is broadly right. With a handful of exceptions, fireside revenants wear either their shrouds, perhaps torn and muddy from the grave, or the clothes they habitually wore in life. In the eighteenth century, more sophisticated critics than Partridge were also puzzled by Old Hamlet's armour. But Gothic novels were not winter's tales. Popular oral ghost stories were now in the process of relegation to the world of the artless – to be artfully reinvented as multi-volume romances for an expanding readership. As a villager, Partridge knows his ghost lore. But to gratify the tastes of a wider reading public, the new genre made a bid for a higher status and grander influences went into its making.

Shakespeare, highly regarded at this time, was well on his way to becoming the National Bard, with a good deal of help from Garrick. And while, faithful to Enlightenment values, the emerging novel preferred plain truth to life in the highly successful work of Defoe and Richardson, Gothic fiction was able to justify its embrace of the supernatural by reference to Shakespeare. Shakespeare's plays included ghosts; our greatest writer therefore anticipated the Gothic; Shakespeare legitimated Gothic ghost stories. When Old Hamlet appeared on the battlements of Elsinore Castle, he was clothed 'cap-à-pie' in armour; Gothic ghosts therefore surprised no one who knew their Shakespeare when they too appeared in fortified dwellings, armed from head to foot.

Garrick's interpretation of the play prevailed for more than thirty years from his first appearance as Hamlet in 1742; his

Figure 4 Garrick on the battlements of Elsinore Castle

performance was definitive for the second half of the century. A widely circulated print, made in 1754 from Benjamin Wilson's painting, shows Garrick's Hamlet facing the Ghost against the backdrop of a shadowy Elsinore castle, its battlements in evidence behind the terrified prince.

The appeal of Hamlet

Other Shakespearean ghosts were available – and were cited. But *Hamlet* had a special appeal. First, it was Shakespeare's most detailed ghost story. Scattered references indicate that for a century following the first performances of the play, the Ghost made a striking impression. And, as ghost stories went, this one was held to excel. In 1711 the Enlightened editor of *The Spectator* took an equivocal position when it came to ghosts on the stage. On the one hand, the supernatural was no more than good box office. 'A spectre', Joseph Addison noted archly, 'has very often saved a play, though he has done nothing but stalked across the stage.' On the other hand, Addison is full of admiration when it comes to *Hamlet*, where the Ghost is 'a masterpiece in its kind, and wrought up with all the circumstances that can create either attention or horror'. Old Hamlet's initial silence, the suspense, the reaction of the prince, all conspire to intensify anxiety, he maintains.

Many critics agreed. In 1736 George Stubbes praised the opening scene of the play for the way it persuades viewers to suspend their incredulity and believe they actually see a phantom. The general mid-century view is that the dramatist's imaginative presentation makes the improbable convincing. The play was also enlisted in the culture wars against French neoclassicism. Classical deities have lost their power to thrill, argued Elizabeth Montagu; Shakespeare, by contrast, drew on native English superstitions and his genius made them credible. Her essay concludes with an enthusiastic account of the ghost scenes in *Hamlet*.

But it was Ann Radcliffe herself who proved most eloquent in Shakespeare's praise. The dialogue between Mr Willoughton and Mr Simpson that frames *Gaston de Blondeville* shows the strongest approval fending off scepticism. Simpson has his doubts about the supernatural in general. But Shakespeare's magical creatures are made plausible by their settings, appearance and manner of speaking, Willoughton insists. In his view, 'Above every ideal being is the ghost of Hamlet, with all its attendant incidents of time and place.' And Willoughton proves himself no mean critic, alive to the way the play builds a context for Barnardo's ghost story, which breaks off only with the appearance of the spectre that ratifies it as truth. 'Oh, I should never be weary of dwelling on the perfection of Shakespeare, in his management of every scene connected with that most solemn and mysterious being.'

The rightful heir

Besides its exemplary dramatisation of the supernatural, there was more for the period to find in *Hamlet*. Any number of Gothic hauntings had the effect of uncovering the legitimate owner of the property. Here is the climactic disclosure in *The Castle of Otranto*, when Alfonso comes from his tomb in the church of St Nicholas:

> A clap of thunder at that instant shook the castle to its foundations; the earth rocked, and the clank of more than mortal armour was heard behind ... The moment Theodore appeared, the walls of the castle behind Manfred were thrown down with a mighty force, and the form of Alfonso, dilated to an immense magnitude, appeared in the centre of the ruins.

Behold in Theodore, the true heir of Alfonso! said the vision: and having pronounced these words, accompanied by a clap of thunder, it ascended solemnly towards heaven, where the clouds parting asunder, the form of Saint Nicholas was seen; and receiving Alfonso's shade, they were soon wrapt from mortal eyes in a blaze of glory.

Dismembered parts of this more than mortal armour, stripped from Alfonso's effigy in the church, have already terrified the inhabitants in parts of the castle: a vast helmet in the courtyard, a leg in the great chamber, and a hand on the staircase. Now the ancestral ghost appears in his entirety to announce that the present proprietor has no title: contrary to expectation, the castle belongs to young Theodore.

Hamlet, too, drew attention to the misappropriation of the prince's title. At any time before the Romantic epoch, audiences would have taken for granted that his uncle has taken illicit possession of the hero's inheritance. True, Denmark is technically an elective monarchy. But, while Hamlet was pursuing his studies at Wittenberg, Claudius has 'popped in' between the election and his hopes, the prince complains. To deflect Rosencrantz's questions, Hamlet tells him, 'I lack advancement.' 'How can that be', wonders Rosencrantz, when you have the support of the king for your succession? But while the grass is growing, the horse has nothing to sustain it, the prince replies. 'I eat the air, promise-crammed', he tells Claudius. And he adds, 'You cannot feed capons so.' Capons are castrated cocks, fattened for the table. His uncle, Hamlet implies, is inhibiting the line of descent, obstructing the legitimate transmission of his title. Although this is not the whole story, the assumption pervades the play that Claudius is a usurper who has stolen Hamlet's throne. Pronouncing the prince's obituary, Fortinbras affirms that 'he was likely, had he been put on, / To have proved most royal'.

Hereditary titles – entitlements to land – meant wealth and power. But as the eighteenth century wore on, mounting social and economic unrest on the other side of the English Channel threatened to destabilise the dynastic order, and in 1789 it became clear that, in France at least, the worst fears (or best hopes, according to taste) were capable of being realised. In the next five years, the French king was executed, countless land-owners were beheaded and fear of revolution spread through Europe. Meanwhile, in Britain in particular, more gradual changes were also threatening the aristocracy, as a market economy turned land into a commodity. Property, traditionally passed on by inheritance, was increasingly for sale to the highest bidder. In these circumstances, perhaps only the supernatural could preserve the old ways and guarantee succession by birth.

In many Gothic romances, it does: the apparition ultimately brings about the reinstatement of the rightful owner. As in the fairy tales that went into the composition of Gothic fiction, the desert of the true-born heir has always been evident as a natural nobility that shines through a humble or neglected upbringing. At the end of *The Old English Baron*, the castle doors fly open of their own accord to welcome their proper master. 'I accept the omen!' comments Edmund piously, before leading the way to the haunted apartment to reveal the skeleton of his father, the late Lord Lovel. Marriage follows, a son and heir is born and the dynasty is secured.

In 1798 *Edgar; or, The Phantom of the Castle* brings many of the threads together, if in some confusion. Castle Fitz-Elmar is held by the wicked uncle who has killed Edgar's father. But much of the action takes place in a nearby ruin, initially a 'priory' but at intervals a 'castle'. There Edgar finds his father's armour dislodged by a crash of thunder. In order to secure this precious legacy, Edgar slips it on, inadvertently convincing his uncle that his victim has returned from the grave. Frightened literally to death, the murderous uncle makes way for this latter-day Hamlet to come into his property.

But the Gothic is not always so nostalgic for a hierarchic past, or so seemingly oblivious of contemporary issues. In *The Castle of Wolfenbach* Eliza Parsons tackles them head-on. Published in 1793, this novel takes time out to distinguish between Britain and pre-revolutionary France, where the love story is set. In France the foundling Matilda cannot marry the Count de Bouville without dishonour to his family. But the Count has been visiting England, the land of law and liberty, where they arrange things so much better, achieving an exemplary harmony between classes. Merchants there, for example, are highly regarded, we learn, because they sustain the economy; the nobility do not scruple to marry them, it seems. After all, the middling ranks are better looking, since the aristocracy ruin their complexions by late hours and dissipation.

The want of noble birth is no bar to alliances where there is merit, the Count continues. Manufacture is encouraged and with better management of the many charities, there would be no poverty. Parsons's middle-class British readers are thus reassured that there is no good reason for revolution to cross the Channel. They are also offered the double gratification of rubbing shoulders with continental aristocrats at the same time as recognising their own unqualified superiority.

Here, true to the principles of romance, the problem is resolved when Matilda's title is discovered. Hamlet is not so fortunate. Strangely, however, *Otranto* is indirectly closer to its tragic original. The walls of the castle are thrown down and the ghost of Alfonso, dislodged by his chamberlain, appears amid the ruins. His rightful heir, Theodore, lives to take over the principality but the loss of the woman he loves cannot be repaired. He marries Isabella, who loved her too, with a view to indulging in his wife's companionship 'the melancholy that had taken possession of his soul'.

In this instance, anxieties about the transmission of property are not entirely dissolved. Part of the structure Edgar inherits also collapses in *The Phantom of the Castle*. But the fullest exploration of the effects of middle-class encroachment on aristocratic entitlement occurs in 1819 in Scott's *The Bride of Lammermoor*, his own reinvention of *Hamlet*, complete with a ghost, a brooding hero and a graveyard scene. Displaced by Mr Ashton, who has bought the castle with the fortune he made as a lawyer, the impoverished Lord Ravenswood has retreated from Ravenswood Castle to Wolf's Crag, a lonely tower that stands tall and grey, itself 'like the sheeted spectre of some huge giant'.

The novel, faithful to *Hamlet*, centres on the question of revenge. Ravenswood himself bears a striking resemblance to an armed portrait, relegated by the Ashtons to the laundry room in Ravenswood Castle. This picture prompts speculation among the maids. Generations ago, Sir Malise Ravenswood killed a man; worse, he is expected to return, claiming in a hollow voice, 'I bide my time.' But for love of Lucy Ashton, Ravenswood renounces vengeance. On the other hand, the ghost of old Alice implicitly confirms her living warning that any attempt to unite the two families will lead to destruction. Ghosts can be relied on to know – and neither family long survives the madness of Lucy/Ophelia. In the present of the frame narrative, Ravenswood Castle is now a ruin. Despite the optimistic account Eliza Parsons gives of English social relations, in Scotland Scott seems to see no possibility of reconciliation between hereditary titles and the market economy.

The threat of reason

Paradoxically, the Gothic flourished in the age of reason. If Hamlet's story appealed on the grounds of its concern with the transmission of property, it also offered access to a realm of experience that was under threat from the Enlightenment. Was it possible to have too much rationality? Is Joseph Addison pleased or sorry in 1712 to report that not a village in all England lacked its ghost, 'before the world was enlightened by learning and philosophy'? 'The churchyards were all haunted', he remembers. But fiction was there to preserve the supernatural. Our poets, he continues, are experts in it, and among them Shakespeare has incomparably excelled.

Enlightenment thought delivered a radical challenge to credulity. René Descartes had hoped to clear the decks of the medieval obscurity that could lead only to error. We are in essence thinking beings, he claimed and our ideas are credible to the degree that they are clear and distinct. God would not support confusion. Unless ideas are clearly and distinctly presented to the understanding, we cannot take them to be divinely endorsed. Clarity is a criterion of truth: 'Only the things I conceive clearly and distinctly have the power to convince me completely', he insisted. Scepticism towards the supernatural could only deepen as the influence of Descartes spread. Phantoms, after all, are anything but clear and distinct. Creatures of darkness, shadowy and evanescent, they puzzle the senses; they also baffle reason, defying the oppositions between reality and illusion, presence and absence, life and death.

Meanwhile, at the moment when Joseph Glanvill and his colleagues were dedicating themselves to assembling ghost stories in defence of the supernatural, the Royal Society was founded in 1660 to promote the value of experimental science. The laws of nature did not allow for ghosts. Interest in 'natural philosophy' was not confined to academic specialists. While early members of the Society included the chemist Robert Boyle and the physicist Isaac Newton, Samuel Pepys the diarist was also a member, as was John Dryden the poet. Oddly enough, Glanvill himself was also on the list – but then, after all, his quest was for empirical evidence to support what he believed. So, too, was our old friend John Aubrey who, among his other activities, collected winter's tales. Natural philosophy was a theme of discussion in sophisticated circles, in journals, over dinner and in the new coffee houses.

From the perspective of Enlightenment science, ghost stories were superstitious nonsense. They were also associated with popery. After the expulsion of the Catholic James II in 1688 and the Jacobite risings of 1715 and 1745, sectarian hostility continued below a surface tolerance. Purgatory was a Protestant stick to beat papists – and so was cemented as history the Reformation ascription, still supported by some, of ghost stories to medieval Catholicism. In an essay written in 1741, the youthful David Hume denounced superstition as both Catholic and dismal. Occult beliefs were brought on by misfortune or melancholy, he held. In this unhappy state of mind, 'infinite unknown evils are dreaded from unknown agents'. And Hume goes on to explain that 'where real objects of terror are wanting, the soul . . . finds imaginary ones, to whose power and malevolence it sets no limits'.

We might have some sympathy with this psychologising account of what it means to be haunted but Hume's rhetoric, based on oppositions, propels his reader towards a stronger inference. To the degree that they are unspecified, evils and agents are illusory; the unknown, aligned with the occult and populated by the imaginary, is contrasted with the real. Hume's essay leaves itself open to the interpretation that the unnamed is outside reality; what we don't know doesn't exist.

Enlightenment scepticism provoked an equal and opposite reaction, however. In 1754 the even younger Edmund Burke launched a defence of obscurity and confusion when he called them sublime. Burke's *Philosophical Enquiry into the Sublime and the Beautiful* puts forward an alternative to the Cartesian view. His human beings do not live by thought alone but are motivated by the passions, and the strongest of these are pain and terror. However unpleasant they are in themselves, pain and terror experienced at one remove can give delight, Burke maintains, as they do, for example, in tragedy. Whatever is grand, vast, powerful or overwhelming generates intensity. The unknown, the unmastered, darkness, uncertainty, astonishment are all sublime. In short, while on the basis of clear and distinct ideas, the Enlightenment builds a mappable world founded on reason and the laws of nature, Burke insists that our strongest emotions are enlisted by what is wild and uncharted. In his account, 'dark, confused, uncertain images have a greater power on the fancy to form the grander passions than those have which are more clear and determinate'.

Burke would not go so far as to endorse ghost stories. On the contrary, he called them 'idle'. But he did concede that the impossibility of reducing ghosts to clear and distinct ideas contributed to their power in the minds of people who believed in them. His book thus provided oblique support for a mode of self-proclaimed fiction that extended its reach into the undiscoverable realm unacknowledged by Enlightenment orthodoxy.

Burke's account of the sublime crystallised a value that was in the air at the time. Shakespeare's work, eighteenth-century critics had always maintained, was sublime. The word resonates through their discussion of the plays. Shakespeare's ghosts are so well presented as to escape censure. Ghost stories, told by a bungler, are ridiculous, but in the hands of a master storyteller they are 'noble and sublime'. Shakespeare is a master; *Hamlet* is sublime; 'the sublimest scene in this whole piece', added George Stubbes, is the encounter between the prince and the Ghost.

A special virtue of Shakespeare's Ghost is 'the uncertainty of the thing described'. Ann Radcliffe's Willoughton calls in Burke by name: uncertainty expands the soul. 'The union of grandeur and obscurity, which Mr Burke describes as a sort of tranquillity tinged with terror, and which causes the sublime, is to be found only in *Hamlet*, or in scenes where circumstances of the same kind prevail.' Eventually, in 1818 Coleridge delivered his critical verdict on the contest between Enlightenment philosophy and *Hamlet*: 'Hume himself could not but have had faith in this Ghost dramatically, let his anti-ghostism have been as strong as Samson against other ghosts less powerfully raised.'

Perhaps human beings cannot bear too many clear and distinct ideas. Without necessarily subscribing to Burke's view that we delight in pain and terror, without wanting (and I don't) to appeal to the overworked sublime, we might concede the lure of the unknown. The knowledge generated by reason, indispensable as it is, depends on the unknown for its existence. Modern science acknowledges that what we don't know is the motive for further investigation. Ghost stories remain intriguing, if they do, not because they advance our knowledge but to the degree that they don't: they meet enquiry with a question, not an answer. In so far as ghosts remain undefined, unaccountable, unpredictable, or in Burke's word uncertain, they offer an alternative to the plenitude of information that presses in on us from books, lectures, the media, Google.

But that alternative is not another orthodoxy. Instead, at its heart lies the undecidable. Ghosts represent a way of naming what we don't know and their stories give a shape, but an enigmatic one, to what remains unidentified or unacknowledged by the prevailing culture. Ghost stories at once augment and subtract from the comfortable convictions of the everyday. They provoke – and it was Hamlet who said so – 'thoughts beyond the reaches of our souls'.

Ethereal ghosts

Even so, some Gothic ghost stories made concessions to Enlightenment scepticism. Ann Radcliffe, for instance, at least in the novels published in her lifetime, generally appeased rationality by explaining away what at first seemed supernatural. Signora Laurentini, thought by the castle servants in volume 2 to haunt her old home of Udolpho, turns out, although not until well into volume 4, to be alive and, if not well, at least surviving in a convent in France. Her mysterious disappearance was a deliberate move in her secret plan to murder her lover's wife. Others who followed Radcliffe's example supplied their readers with a similar frisson without yielding to the charge of superstition.

Cartesian philosophy paradoxically confirmed the immateriality of the ghosts it denied. Since, according to Descartes, we were in essence thinking beings, it followed that, if any part of us lived on, it must be consciousness or the soul. This was the period when corporeal revenants, back from the grave, widely yielded pride of place to immaterial, translucent spectres gliding noiselessly through walls. Magic lantern shows and phantasmagoria projected ethereal ghosts on gauze screens. The introduction of footlights at Drury Lane in the 1760s and a darkened auditorium would already have helped to dematerialise the Ghost in Garrick's production, while the steel-blue satin costume that stood in for armour must have made it easier for Old Hamlet to glide on noiselessly and vanish at will. The ghost in James Boaden's play *Fountainville Forest* seemed to float, appearing, as he did, behind a curtain of gauze.

Even so, the turn to insubstantial spectres was more easily accomplished in writing than it was on the stage. Shakespeare was read, as well as performed, and many admiring accounts of *Hamlet* at this time refer to the experience of the reader, not the audience.

Visual images of the returning dead take on increasing unearthliness. Henry Fuseli's larger-than-life Old Hamlet stands with the moon behind his head, but instead of silhouetting a darkened shape, the light shines through the armour and the glaring eyes. A Richard Westall engraving made in 1802 shows the apparition of the dead Caesar to Brutus on the eve of the battle of Philippi. This menacing figure, which glares at a stoical Brutus, floats weightlessly behind his chair, as if it inhabits a different plane from the solid helmet and sword in the foreground.

Influenced by the fireside tradition of walking cadavers, but in the light of classical ghosts who slip through the embrace of the living, Shakespeare's *Hamlet* kept the options open. Should the guards strike at the Ghost, or was it 'as the air invulnerable'? Old Hamlet is a 'spirit', on the one hand, but comes from the tomb on the other; why, the prince asks, have his father's bones burst their wrappings to revisit the earth? The eighteenth century, however, wanted its spirits to be fully immaterial. Dr Johnson was by no means the only critic of the period to puzzle over Hamlet's idea of a phantom that had bones. The prince, he concluded, must be confused, 'confounding in his fright the soul and body'.

Figure 5 Richard Westall's ethereal Julius Caesar, 1802

Already in its issue of 31 October 1691, *The Athenian Mercury* had undertaken to explain to its popular readership the theology of apparitions. Spirits were disembodied. Had not the risen Jesus insisted that he was not a ghost, when he invited his disciples to touch him – 'For a spirit hath not flesh and bones, as ye see me have'. The religious justification for telling ghost stories was to demonstrate that the soul could live on without the body. But it wasn't, apparently, quite that simple: fireside convictions die hard. The same issue of the journal recorded the apparition of Madam Bendish, 'like a shadow', to persuade an old gentlewoman to win back her recalcitrant son. When this was accomplished, the ghost was grateful, but that did not stop her returning to give the old gentle-woman a blow that hurt a little, almost turning her out of bed.

Popular culture had evidently not entirely absorbed the new philosophy of disembodied spirits. In the early eighteenth century a reader of the *Norwich Gazette* wrote in with a question. A friend had seen his wife sitting in her usual place in the parlour, wearing her habitual clothes, three days after her burial. Was she, were such figures, not in their graves, the writer wanted to know? And if not, how did they get out? Apparently, this correspondent had not succeeded in divorcing the insubstantial spirit from the material body. It would be many years before walking corpses disappeared entirely from winter's tales if, indeed, they ever did. They still feature in American horror films.

Although fireside culture was slow to change, the novels demonstrated a shift in emphasis from revenants to phantoms – and from the unlikely to the indefinite. The old material ghosts already manifest their own improbability: suddenly, there is something where there ought to be nothing. Walking cadavers are sharply outlined, substantially perceptible as if they were alive, crossing the boundaries between present and past, reality and unreality, life and death. They defy expectations, materialising, changing shape and vanishing unaccountably, to the perplexity of those who see them. Immaterial ghosts do most of this but they also go further, marking themselves as unknowable. Misty, elusive, diaphanous, at once visible and translucent, unimpeded by physical obstacles, they refuse the test of empirical observation.

Even the ghost stories approved by authority reject good sense, customary understanding and the world people take for granted. When the Church supports supernatural intervention, it does so to show that religion is not reducible to the everyday. The successive understandings of the spectral are not unrelated but they resist different cultural allegiances: on the one hand, simply by being there, walking corpses contradict what is believed possible; on the other, only uncertainly there, immaterial phantoms call in question what is either known or knowable.

Scepticism recurs from one epoch to another but it defends different values at different historical moments. While medieval sceptics deny the capacity of the dead body to return from the grave or the next world, modern sceptics disavow whatever is not available to rational, scientific knowledge. There and not there, ethereal ghosts defy systematic analysis by the consciousnesses the Enlightenment insists we are.

Antiquarianism

Gothic fiction came into existence in a context of an antiquarianism it must also have promoted. Castles, for instance, had become a tourist attraction. On the way to Pemberley, Elizabeth Bennet and the Gardiners visited several heritage sites, including Kenilworth and Warwick. From the early eighteenth century, Windsor Castle had been open to visitors, while travellers could expect to be shown round Warwick and Alnwick castles. These were well maintained but ruins were popular too. At the height of her fame in 1795, Ann Radcliffe herself published her own record of a journey through Holland and Germany, with a tour of the Lake District. Most of the English section centred on the romantic scenery but historic buildings also received their share of attention. A young woman from a nearby farm acted as guide to the ruins of Brougham Castle, where at twilight the superstitious eye might take the ash saplings 'for spectres of some early possessor of the castle, restless from guilt'.

Antiquarianism also prompted a desire to recover a disappearing folk culture. In 1760, James Macpherson had put out *Fragments of Ancient Poetry*, elegiac compositions based on Highland myths. These lyrical laments include many ghosts, attenuated figures, hardly distinguishable from the winds that bear them or the Celtic mists they inhabit. Next, despatched to find Scotland's lost epic, Macpherson came back with the works he ascribed to 'Ossian', published as *Fingal* in 1761–2 and *Temora* in 1763. There, the dead return among the clouds and ride on meteors. Encouraged, no doubt, by Ossian's phenomenal success, in 1765 Thomas Percy brought out his *Reliques of Ancient English Poetry*, including a number of traditional supernatural ballads.

Fireside tales became collectables, objects of knowledge for the elite. Joseph Addison observed his landlady's daughters and their young friends, while they entertained one another with 'dreadful stories of ghosts as pale as ashes that had stood at the feet of a bed, or walked over a churchyard by moonlight'. And he adds that 'at the end of every story the whole company closed their ranks and crowded about the fire'. Aware of his own supposedly rational and literate readers in *The Spectator*, the rational and literate Addison distances himself from the circle of storytellers by taking a book from his pocket. At the same time, he only pretends to read. Apart, and yet evidently fascinated, he stays to hear the tales they tell.

Winter's tales

Meanwhile, in 1762 an artisan ghost was reported in Cock Lane, London. This proved to be a fraud, but not before it had deceived a good many eminent visitors. While spectres haunted aristocratic castles in middle-class fiction, attested apparitions were increasingly relegated to the lower orders. It is the laundry maids who expect the return of Sir Malise Ravenswood. In *The Mysteries of Udolpho* Emily catches her fear of supernatural visitants from her attendant Annette, source of gossip from the servants' hall. In such settings, as well as by cottage firesides, in taverns, at fairs and markets, and in chapbooks and popular periodicals, the traditional tales continued to circulate.

There, only the names were altered. Graveyards and crossways remained fearful; ghosts still changed shape, warned of death, and sought reparation for those they had wronged. Anti-Sadducist divines also maintained an interest in recirculating popular ghost stories in defence of God. It was recorded in 1752 that a number of dead people had played a part in convicting murderers; one spectral victim had appeared in court to elicit a confession. A few months before *The Castle of Otranto* was published, a member of the clergy wrote a pamphlet called *The Ghost* to vindicate the hanging of John Croxford for the particularly bloodthirsty murder of a pedlar. After his execution, there was some dispute about Croxford's guilt. But he returned, by divine permission, not only to confess to the crime but to prove his own authenticity by telling the clergyman where to find a ring that had belonged to the pedlar.

In many cases, popular ghosts remained solid and capable of shapeshifting. Later in the century, *The Arminian Magazine* printed the tale of a Catholic spectre that had given a great deal of trouble to a family in Newcastle twenty-five years before. The recusant was as violent as any medieval revenant. He murdered the cat and dragged the children from their beds. Once, he appeared as a brown and white calf that grew to the size of a horse.

If clerical orthodoxy was hostile to popery, it was also inclined towards conservatism in politics. In 1793 'A Most Holy Person', unnerved by the French Revolution, put into print the story of a pale, shrouded ghost with gory locks, who came back to warn against sedition. Resistance to the secular powers, it declared, would incur damnation.

Whether they were recycled from conviction or for profit, many of the old tales remained marketable. T. M. Jarvis published *Accredited Ghost Stories* in 1823, including some of Glanvill's narratives, as well as the record of Dorothy Dingley. Two years later John Timbs's *Signs before Death, and Authenticated Apparitions: In One Hundred Narratives* reproduced the familiar stories, including Dorothy Dingley's. By now, in other words, there were two distinct and identifiable genres, on the one hand Gothic novels, marketed as fiction and, on the other hand, winter's tales, dismissed by sceptics, promoted by believers and absorbed, we may guess, with a mixture of credulity and doubt – and a thrill of horrified pleasure.

In practice the two genres overlapped thematically. The transmission of property may have taken on a peculiar urgency in the late eighteenth century, but it had also been a recurrent concern of the fireside tradition. Misappropriation was a preoccupation of medieval ghosts too. In about 1230, Caesarius of Heisterbach provides evidence of the torments of the afterlife with a story that makes no effort to conceal its folk origins. The ghost of a landowner bore with him the effects of his exploitation of the poor. Erkinbert, a citizen of Andernach, saw a dead knight on a black war horse, whose nostrils shot smoke and flames. He recognised the noble Frederic of Kelle, but was surprised to see him clothed in sheepskins and carrying a load of earth on his shoulders. Unlike the knights who haunted Gothic castles, Frederic was guilty. In order to lessen his pains, he urged Erkinbert to beg his sons to restore the sheepskins, now red-hot, that he stole from a poor widow, and to return to its owners the land he took from them. The sons refused, however: they would rather he suffered than give up any part of their inheritance.

In England two centuries later, the Bishop of Lincoln appeared to one of his squires after his death. He was unable to leave the hunting ground he had created by dispossessing the tenants. But he would have rest if the canons of Lincoln gave back the land. They did. In eighteenth-century Wales, the Reverend Edmund Jones recounted the story of Thomas Cadogan of Llantarnam, who had moved his landmarks to enclose the property of a widow. After his death, Cadogan appeared to a woman of the neighbourhood by night to beg her to see that his error was corrected. The message delivered, he vanished; only then did the woman remember he was dead. The widow got her land back but Cadogan's family was punished for his rapacity: his three daughters all married badly and the whole estate was lost.

Second marriages threatened to cheat the rightful heir. One of the Glanvill narratives that resurfaced in Jarvis's collection, and again among the hundred tales retold by John Timbs, suggests that the disposition of their estates in such circumstances had continued to trouble the dead at other lower social levels than Hamlet's. The apparition that accosted the serving man Francis Taverner at a crossroads one windy night in 1662 was concerned for his son, cheated of his legacy by the boy's stepfather. The ghost, on horseback and in a white coat, claimed to be James Haddock, five years dead; he wanted to ride with Francis, who spurred on his own horse in terror until, to his relief, the cocks crew. But Haddock's ghost persisted, reappearing several times in a succession of terrifying shapes to urge Francis to intervene among the living. Mrs Haddock had remarried and her new husband had appropriated a lease that justly belonged to James Haddock's son. Eventually, the ghost threatened to tear Francis to pieces if he failed to deliver the message. Francis duly obeyed.

Shakespeare drew on the fireside tradition for his Ghost. The Gothic drew on Shakespeare but, even in doing so, the new genre never wholly lost the link with the fireside tradition. Gothic novels are to varying degrees romances, melodramatic tales of adventure and mischance, fidelity and betrayal, elaborately recounted and often minutely attentive to landscape and psychology. By contrast, the fireside narratives are more often brief and bluntly told, lacking in circumstantial detail. They commonly take settings for granted and leave the feelings of the protagonists to the imagination of the listener. But both kinds reveal a desire for social justice, however conceived.

They also maintain a profound interest in what defies customary knowledge. The stratification of society that took place with the rise of commerce and the industrial revolution complicated the history of ghost stories, while Enlightenment philosophy fostered a continuing scepticism. But neither succeeded in erasing the lure of the unaccountable.

SEVEN

Spectres of Desire

The nun's story

Ghost stories envisage a special relationship between love and death. *The Monk*, M. G. Lewis's Gothic novel of 1796, repeatedly brought desire and mortality together, not least in the spectre of a bleeding nun, who spoke to her culture so powerfully that in no time she took on a half-life of her own. In Lewis's lurid story, the living Agnes changes places with the dead nun. Agnes impersonates the ghost to elope with Raymond but, when the ghost reaches him first, Raymond unknowingly exchanges vows with the nun. Since her lover has broken his promise to her, Agnes herself now becomes a nun. But, seduced in the convent garden by Raymond, she breaks her own vow of chastity to incur a living death in the vaults of her convent.

Lewis's bleeding nun has everything: sex, violence, treachery – and Catholicism, for some, in the wake of the Jacobite risings, at least as bad as any of the others, and associated with all of them. Sister Beatrice left the convent, we learn, to indulge her desires; then she murdered her lover for the sake of his younger brother. Once he had inherited the castle by this means, the usurper killed her with her own dagger: 'He plunged it, still reeking with his brother's blood, in her bosom.' At once a murderer and a victim of murder, the nun returns as an animated corpse, haggard, pale and hollow-eyed, forever bleeding from the mortal wound that is the consequence of a faithless love, itself betrayed in its turn. In the castle of Lindenberg she haunted her killer, the usurping heir. Now she haunts Raymond, depleting his strength with her nocturnal visits. 'Raymond! Raymond! Thou art mine! / Raymond! Raymond! I am thine', she declares. Never properly buried, Beatrice cannot find rest until she is finally exorcised by the Wandering Jew, who bears the Mark of Cain.

This sexually charged ghost immediately acquired a huge following. A spectral nun had already appeared in 'The Abduction', one among a collection of German folktales by Johann August Karl Musäus in the 1780s. Lewis's addition of blood trickling from the wound in her breast eroticised her past, as well as her present, turning her into an instant sensation. Although the nun's story formed a minor episode in *The Monk*, within two or three years her tale had been issued in a cheap, abridged edition as an independent work, *The Castle of Lindenberg; Or, The History of Raymond and Agnes*. Soon after this, there appeared *The Bleeding Nun, or, Raymond and Agnes: A Romance*, while *The History of Raymond and Agnes; Or, The Castle of Lindenberg* followed in 1803. Clearly, in those days of weak copyright, perming any two from three plot strands licensed a new publication.

Conflating the characters worked, too. Agnes and Beatrice are combined in *The Bleeding Nun of St Catherine's*, included in a popular anthology of *Romances and Gothic Tales* in 1801. Abandoned by the baron she has secretly married, the heroine dies in the vaults of St Catherine's convent, but returns to haunt her husband with her stillborn child. She is not noticeably bleeding but by now the title term evidently names a generic category.

Shortened and redacted versions of the tale accumulated and new episodes emerged, mostly without the blessing of Lewis himself. The story first appeared on the stage as early as 1797, set to music without words as a ballet pantomime. A version with dialogue was performed in 1809. An unsuccessful opera by Edward Loder was staged in 1855, although *La Nonne sanglante* with music by Charles Gounod did better in Paris in 1854.

Such was the tale's popularity that 'Raymond and Agnes' featured as a country dance in 1798. Meanwhile, the bleeding nun went on to triumph in magic lantern shows and phantasmagoria, where moveable lighting and translucent screens set wraiths in motion. She also featured as a novelty cut-out. I have a very fine reproduction of a cardboard doll that was sold for one shilling in 1817, a gift from my friend Jennifer Fellows (who has been generous with any number of other sources for this book). My nun is 21.5 cm high (8.5 inches); she carries a lamp and a dagger, as the novel requires; a moveable tab on her back gives her alternative faces, one living, one a skull. Deft use of a flashlight or a candle can make her throw a perfectly horrific shadow on the wall. 'Raymond, Raymond, I am thine, / Thou art mine', she affirms, with a credit to *The Monk*.

A year after the novel had established his notoriety, Lewis himself reprised some of the nun's story in his own *Castle Spectre*, the runaway success of the London stage in 1797. Although Evelina, one of the women in white of Chapter 4, is not a nun but a virtuous mother, who emerges from her 'oratory', to the strain of heavenly music, her dress is spotted with blood, and 'a large wound appears upon her bosom' – the mortal thrust she took when she intervened to save her husband from his murderous younger brother.

But perhaps the most interesting adaptation was Lewis's own retelling in his *Tales of Wonder*, five years after the publication of the novel, where the nun's story appears as a free-standing poem. Here the extravagance of the first version is austerely pared down.

In the novel the nun first appears in Agnes's comic rendering. Agnes has no patience with superstition, and the tradition of 'her ghostship' seems to her absurd – but worth putting to good use if it secures her escape with her lover. Raymond learns of the nun from Agnes as comedy – and lives to find his scepticism confuted. The reader shares Raymond's delusion that his nun is Agnes in disguise, until the carriage begins to move with unnatural speed, the horses run out of control and a storm breaks. When their conveyance crashes, Raymond is stunned; he comes round to find that his companion has disappeared. But as he lies convalescing, heavy footsteps on the stairs cause a sudden chill . . .

The poem, by contrast, has borrowed from the medieval ballads. Lewis had a gift for pastiche. In the new version there is no comedy and no scepticism. The narrative is more elliptical and the refrain, 'I am thine, and thou art mine, / Body and soul for ever!' takes on the character of a riddle for the reader to solve. Now it is Raymond who makes the plan to elope. The nun has no past; no explanation is given of her deadly designs; there is no exorcism, no rest for her and no release for her mortal victim.

Desire and death

In both instances the dead nun is a substantial, corporeal figure with lustreless eyes, 'ghastly, pale, and dead'. The epigraph to the chapter in the novel quotes Macbeth's horrified reaction to Banquo: 'Thy bones are marrowless; thy blood is cold; / Thou hast no speculation in those eyes / Which thou dost glare with!' Physical contact with the nun appals Raymond. She has icy fingers and cold lips; 'The spectre again pressed her lips to mine, again touched me with her rotting fingers', Raymond records with revulsion.

Was this deadly sexuality perversely exciting, even so? The extensive afterlife of the story suggests that readers found it compulsive. In the first instance, a nubile nun exerts a special fascination, especially in an anti-Catholic culture. Catholic spectacle and incense seem designed to excite a particular emotional and physiological intensity. Perhaps the imagination is ready to see the fervour of a bride of Christ redirected as carnal desire. More simply, a vow of chastity represents a challenge. In the fantasies of others, those who take it must be possessed by dark longings and secret impulses, as is Sister Beatrice's male counterpart, the monk of Lewis's novel. Erotic tales of convent life found wide circulation in the course of the eighteenth century.

But what links sex with death? William Hogarth had seen a connection between popery, carnal love and spectrality. In a print of 1762, he shows a couple embracing in a pew below the pulpit. Around them are figures in various stages of transport, while a minister delivers a hell-fire sermon. Such is the Evangelical preacher's ardour that his wig slips off to reveal the tonsure of a closet monk. The woman in the foreground has her hands clasped in prayer but her open mouth turned to her lover's. He caresses her neck with one hand, while the other slips a miniature ghost between her breasts. The little revenant, recognisable from the standard image in pamphlets of the period, is a shrouded figure holding a lighted taper to indicate darkness.

Desire and death, apparently polar opposites, seem, paradoxically, capable of overlapping. Passion – which still retains a trace of *suffering*, its old meaning – only deepens with impediments to gratification. The *Liebestod*, the shared death of lovers, has a long history from Pyramus and Thisbe through *Romeo and Juliet* to Wagner's *Tristan and Isolde*. Even at a more everyday level, romantic love can often defy the norms that bind society together;

Figure 6 A little replica ghost excites desire in Hogarth's satirical print, 1762

marriage, which promises peace and harmony, may in practice turn possessive, controlling, jealous, vengeful; desire can be reckless, destructive and self-destructive.

Biologically, reproduction and death form a couple: death makes way for the new generation. When in 1920 Freud wrote *Beyond the Pleasure Principle* in order to settle once and for all the distinction between the sexual imperative and the death drive, he found that, without losing their difference from one another, they kept getting intertwined. Did one work in the service of the other? If so, he was not sure which obeyed which.

Was sex more powerful than death, or did death prevail? Ghost stories, too, pose the question. One of the oldest surviving examples can be read either way. A servant is surprised to find the dead Philinnion in the guest room where a young man is lodging with her family. On the following morning, the ghost has gone, leaving behind her love tokens that her mother reluctantly recognises as her late daughter's. The next night, Philinnion returns. She greets her family but, since they grudge her regular visits, she will not come again – and she stretches out dead in front of them. On the bier in the family tomb where she was buried nearly six months before, there is nothing to be found but the gifts the young man has given her in exchange for hers. Philinnion's parents burn her body and offer sacrifices to the gods.

On the one hand, an irrepressible desire drives the young woman's return from the grave. On the other, her lover kills himself – though whether out of longing or shame is not on record. Most cultures prohibit necrophilia. 'The dead and the living can never be one: God has forbidden it', exclaims poor Rose Velderkaust in Sheridan Le Fanu's 'Schalken the Painter'. The innocent Rose belongs to another time and place: her dead husband fills her with horror. On the other hand, like the story of the bleeding nun, both tales attract audiences, perhaps because each in its own way points to a relation between desire and death. Does the prohibition on desire for the dead intensify curiosity?

Philinnion's story proved durable. It seems to have been a fragment of an ancient folk tale, written down by the Greek Phlegon of Tralles in the second century CE, but reaching back to a much earlier period. Unlike the disembodied ghosts of classical epic, Philinnion is a revenant from the tomb and fully substantial. She eats and drinks with her lover and embraces her parents. A summary of her story was later recorded by Proklos in the fifth century CE. According to Proklos, the dead Philinnion was a newly-wed deprived of gratification by death.

When in 1797 Goethe rewrote this story as 'The Bride of Corinth' for a Romantic public, the contest between love and death remained unresolved. Goethe added explanatory details that filled the gaps in the old tale. Now the young man arrives from another city to perform the marriage arranged for him when he and his promised bride were both children. Their parents drifted apart when hers converted from paganism to Christianity, but he hopes their union will heal the breach. On his first night as a guest in her parents' house, a young woman steals into his room in a white dress and veil. He desires her and, although she is icy cold, his passion warms her. Her mother, surprised to overhear their exchanges, bursts into the chamber, only to recognise her dead daughter, reproachful that she has been denied the love she was led to expect.

The young woman is driven from her grave to seek her lover and suck his heart's blood. Christian orthodoxy does not override the oath made years before in the temple of Venus, when the two were betrothed to each other. Instead, an older law demands its due, the dead fiancée insists:

'The droning hymns of priests have little worth,
And their blessings carry little weight.
Neither salt nor water cool
What young ones feel;
Ah, the very earth dampens not a love this great.'

Passion triumphs over death, it seems. And yet, unless both bodies are burned on a funeral pyre, the ghost must go on to find another partner in due course. Love forces open the grave, only for death to prevail in the end.

Rose Velderkaust is evidently right: the living and the dead cannot be united, at least in this life. A curious variant of Philinnion's story was published in 1924. The protagonists of Rudyard Kipling's 'A Madonna of the Trenches' are middle-aged; they belong to another class and context; their desire is adulterous. But once again passion both transcends and entails death. The young Cockney witness breaks off his own sensible engagement when he sees what he perceives as the real thing. 'The reel thing's life an' death. It *begins* at death.'

This is 1918. The ghost of the young man's aunt appears in the trenches on the day she dies in London. She has come to claim for herself the living sergeant, another woman's husband. The ghost and the sergeant look at each other as if they would devour one another but the condition of their union is his death. 'I saw 'er', the shell-shocked nephew insists. 'I saw 'im an' 'er – she dead since mornin' time, and he killin' 'imself before my livin' eyes so's to carry on with 'er for all Eternity.' The sergeant takes the ghost into the dug-out with two charcoal braziers and seals the door to guarantee their joint suffocation.

Demon lovers

In these instances, the sexual energy that outdoes death is at the same time itself deadly. Perhaps Freud had a point: the antithetical imperatives are not always distinct. And the returning lover was not always a woman. M. G. Lewis, who told the story of the bleeding nun, also published one of several English translations of the German poem *Lenore* in his *Tales of Wonder*. Lenore's soldier-lover does not return from the war and the promised bride refuses to be consoled, until a knight appears at midnight to take her on horseback to his dwelling:

> 'And where is, then, thy house and home,
> And where thy bridal bed?'
> ''Tis narrow, silent, chilly, dark;
> Far hence I rest my head.'

The knight spurs his horse furiously in the moonlight until they reach a distant graveyard, where his armour crumbles to dust and his steed vanishes from under them. Then Lenore knows that her own hour is come.

Lenore in turn owes something to a folktale known all over Europe and already invoked in Lewis's own ballad of *The Bleeding Nun*. A phantom conveyance, horse, coach or ship, speeds by night to bear a living lover towards the tomb. Sometimes suitors come back from death to reclaim a bride who has betrayed her promise. In a ballad James Harris, drowned at sea, returns after seven years for Jane Reynolds, now a wife and mother. Jane is never seen again. The most famous version of the story is Sir Walter Scott's in *Minstrelsy of the Scottish Border*, where the dead lover leads the woman to his ship. The pair have set sail before she glimpses his cloven hoof.

This convention is wittily – and eerily – updated in Elizabeth Bowen's wartime story, 'The Demon Lover', where in 1941 capable, prosaic Mrs Drover finds a letter reminding her of a tryst with her soldier fiancé, killed in the previous conflict in 1916. They were to meet in a quarter of a century. He had always been frightening, somehow unearthly; she can no longer remember his face. Mrs Drover, now happily married, takes a taxi to escape the place where the ghost has threatened to find her but, as the driver turns round, she screams – and the cab accelerates remorselessly.

The Dance of Death

Desire and death meet in the dance. A ballad included in *The Monk* tells how the dead Alonzo, cheated in life of his promised bride, reclaims her on the day of her marriage. Now, four times a year they are seen to dance at midnight in the abandoned castle where once she feasted. The ghost in her white bridal dress shrieks as the skeleton knight spins her round among prancing phantoms. When the 16-year-old Dante Gabriel Rossetti translated *Lenore*, he showed her, too, caught up in a fatal dance:

> The churchyard troop – a ghostly group –
> Close round the dying girl;
> Out and in they hurry and spin
> Through the dance's weary whirl.

In a distant echo of the Wili, these dead dancers have turned the age-old rite of courtship, socially approved model of the sexual relation, into the figure of mortality.

The spectral dance binds lovers inexorably to one another and, like the plunging horses that bear away the ghost's living prey, takes them under its relentless control. The unfaithful lover in Mary Elizabeth Braddon's 'The Cold Embrace' feels chill arms round his neck: 'they whirl him round, they will not be flung off, or cast away; he can no more escape from their icy grasp than he can escape from death.' Dancing, conventionally the prelude to sex as the source of life, flips over into the sport of death.

This sport had been familiar in the Middle Ages. The *Danse macabre*, dance of the dead, shows mummified corpses coaxing or dragging living partners into the round. Most famously depicted in the cloister of the Holy Innocents in Paris in 1424, and then along the walls of the old St Paul's churchyard in London, the Dance of Death was copied and elaborated all over Europe and remained familiar well into the seventeenth century. The living were called from their everyday pursuits to dance with their dead counterparts, emaciated revenants who accosted royalty and peasants alike, popes and beggars, compelling them all to join in. Resistance was vain. Paradoxically, the vitality of the images belongs to the capering cadavers, as their victims hang back, clinging to life.

Here conflict yields to the parallel between desire and death, as mortality itself is sexualised. One inescapable force draws on the imagery of another irresistible imperative. Desire and death join forces to take possession of the living. A corpse surprises Hans Holbein's Duchess in her daybed to tear at her clothing, while another serenades her in a parody of seduction. Offering no defence, her pet dog cowers at her feet.

In Holbein's image of the Duchess from his *Dance of Death* sequence, the measure itself has left no more than a trace. Death

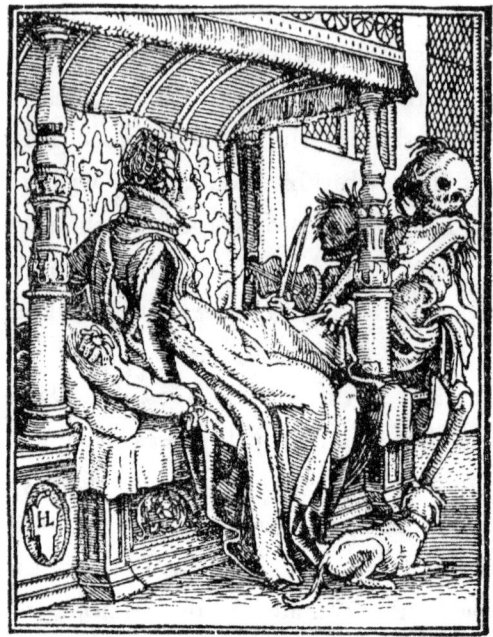

Figure 7 Death seduces the Duchess in Hans Holbein's *The Dance of Death*, 1538

as a partner already leads an erotic life of his own. Why does Juliet still look so life-like in the tomb, Romeo wonders. Perhaps her beauty is preserved for the most macabre of reasons. 'Shall I believe / That unsubstantial death is amorous, / And that the lean abhorred monster keeps / Thee here in dark to be his paramour?'

Romeo draws on a tradition of the amorous dead that was already widely familiar. Sebald Beham's engraving of *Death and the Lascivious Couple* in 1529 shows the shrunken corpse still capable of sexual arousal. Death reacts to the living couple as to pornography. But while he has one grasping palm on the young man's buttock, the other proprietary hand on his shoulder indicates where power ultimately lies.

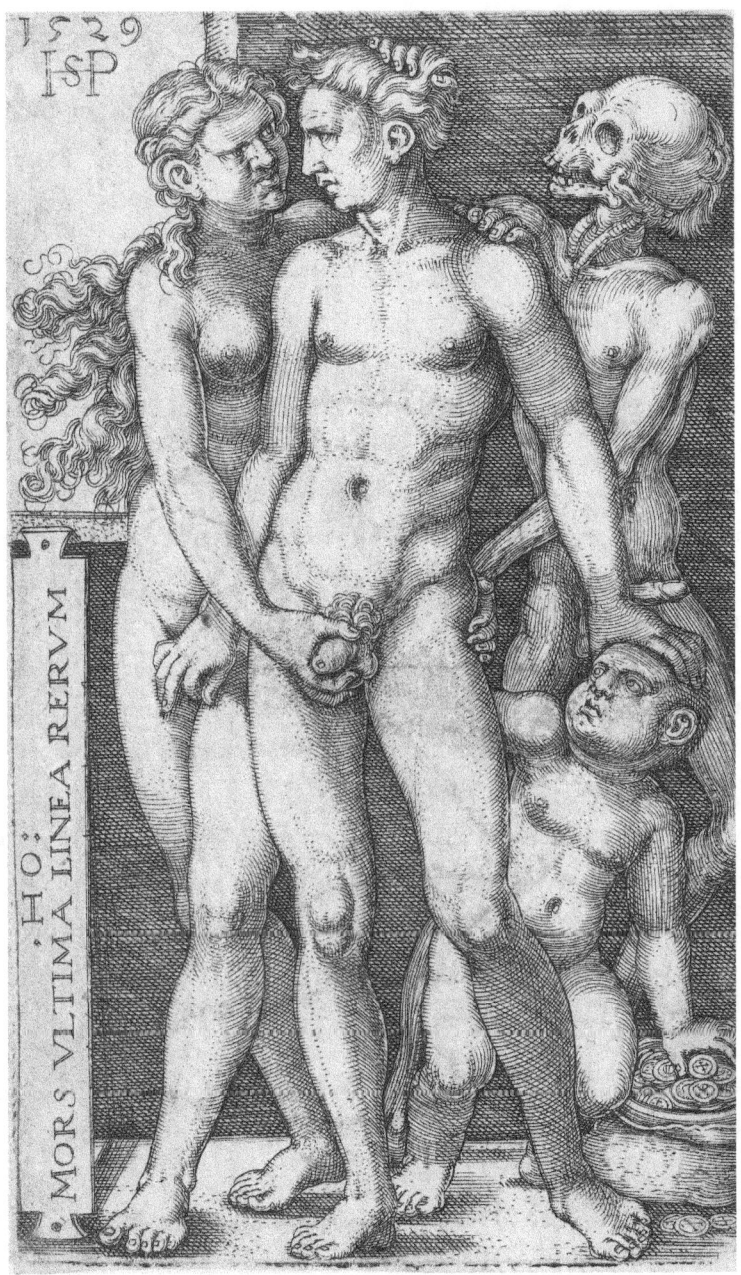

Figure 8 Desire arouses Death in 1529

Women in black

In 1849 Maria Manning was hanged with her husband in London for murdering her lover. Twenty years later the Swiss adulteress reappeared at the window of a house in Bermondsey, where crowds gathered to see her ghost in the same black satin dress she had worn to die. Fallen women, in disgrace for succumbing to their desire, haunted the society that so fiercely repudiated them. Whatever licence was allowed to men, women were officially condemned for sexual activity outside marriage. And yet at the same time, the culture was fascinated by their condition as outcasts. In Henry James's *The Turn of the Screw* the dead governess, seduced and driven out, returns with a distinctive melancholy grandeur to take her former place in the schoolroom as a tragic figure, 'Dark as midnight in her black dress, her haggard beauty and her unutterable woe'.

Such distress outlasts death. In *The Turn of the Screw* Miss Jessel's design – or so, at least, the narrator of James's equivocating tale believes – is to take possession of her former pupil, the 8-year-old Flora. In 1969 Rosemary Timperley's 'The Mistress in Black' exploits the double meaning of 'mistress' to define the fallen woman who haunts a school for girls, where the new English teacher finds the black-clad ghost of her predecessor in her place in the classroom. Miss Carey, it seems, conducted a secret liaison with a married man, until at last he repudiated her. In her bitterness, she set fire to the school gymnasium, where she herself burned to death, in company with a devoted pupil who followed her there. And now she walks to seek exoneration 'with beautiful but very unhappy dark eyes'.

Is the black dress penitential, provocative or simply funereal? Susan Hill's woman in black is in mourning for her own little boy when she returns to steal other people's children. *The Woman in Black* was published in 1983 but set much earlier, with a nod to

'The Giant Wistaria', a story published by Charlotte Perkins Gilman in 1891, when the wishes of lone mothers stood no chance against the rigid proprieties of the time. Hill's culprit is not only the dead woman's severe sister, who adopted the child, but, like Gilman's, a dogmatic culture that condemns single parenthood.

In line with Miss Jessel and Miss Carey, Hill's woman in black bears traces of her former beauty. Terrifying, she is at the same time compelling, an enigma that cries out to be deciphered. Arthur Kipps confesses: 'I had fallen under some sort of spell . . . I felt . . . half fearful, half wondering, excited, completely in thrall.' Although the dominant feeling is horror, his condition is also oddly akin to romance: 'I was living in another dimension, my heart seemed to beat faster, my step to be quicker, everything I saw was brighter.'

Illicit female sexuality proved seductive. While propriety demanded chaste virgins and faithful wives, the levels of prostitution in Victorian cities imply that conformity failed to satisfy male sexual imperatives. Desire can relish its own recklessness in the pursuit of forbidden pleasure. The nineteenth century imagined women who, flouting conventional restraint, thrilled their lovers with their supposed immorality.

Such women also appalled them when they threatened masculine self-control. Men who succumbed to an irresistible passion risked losing their authority, their own agency and even, perhaps, their reason. A woman in black had already driven Gottfried Wolfgang mad in Washington Irving's short story of 1824. The impressionable German student whose adventure the tale records moves to Paris at the time of the French Revolution. Women become subjects of reverie and a particular face of transcendent beauty begins to haunt his imagination. One stormy night, he sees a woman lamenting at the foot of the guillotine and bearing the face of his dreams, 'pale and disconsolate, but ravishingly beautiful'. He takes her back to his lodgings, where in no time the two pledge their troth 'for ever'. But the next morning he finds her a corpse, the head held in place only by a black band round her neck. The student goes mad, convinced that he is in the grip of an evil spirit, driven to distraction by a heady mixture of love and death.

The femme fatale

In the overwhelmingly heterosexual spectral community, the counterpart of the demon lover is the phantom femme fatale. Back from the dead, her powers of seduction undimmed, she lures men to their own death. Vernon Lee's *Hauntings*, published in 1890, includes 'Amour Dure', the story of a bewitching phantom dressed in black. When she lived in the Renaissance, men who found Medea da Carpi impossible to resist lost their own lives in consequence. Duke Robert, however, steadfastly refused to set eyes on her. Fearing, even so, to meet her in purgatory, the duke had an effigy of his soul concealed in his statue, to await the Last Judgement.

Medea's motto is the punning 'Amour Dure': love lasts, cruel love. (A purist might query her grasp of French gender.) Now her ghost wants a young Polish academic, 'wedded to history', to steal Robert's soul for her. Captivated, just like all the others, by the promise she holds out, the living historian knows the risks he faces:

> The love of such a woman is enough, and is fatal – 'Amour Dure', as her device says. I shall die also. But why not? Would it be possible to live in order to love another woman? Nay, would it be possible to drag on a life like this one after the happiness of tomorrow? Impossible; the others died, and I must die.

But the happiness of tomorrow, so eagerly anticipated, is either undelivered or – strange thought – proves so overwhelming as to cause the young man's death.

Toni Morrison's *Beloved*, published in 1987, deserves a book of its own. Even so, it belongs here briefly as a ghost story that puts the tradition of the dead femme fatale to work in a denunciation of the ultimate oppression. Killed by her mother to save her from slavery, the beautiful Beloved returns dressed in black to avenge her death. She seduces her mother's lover, does her best to break up what remains of the family and absorbs her mother's energy, depleting her strength. Ironically, Beloved replicates the enslavement she was killed to evade – demanding, proprietary, destructive, draining. Beloved does not in the end prevail but slavery is not forgotten. It haunts the African American community – and still, we might want to add, American culture.

Perfect union

The narrator of E. Nesbit's story of 1893, 'The Ebony Frame', cannot forget a portrait that once enthralled him. In the deep, luminous eyes of the pre-Raphaelite beauty in black velvet depicted there, he refound a love he did not know he had lost, a perfect union with another: 'our two souls in that moment met, and became one'. Is one source of desire's interdependence with death to be found in that merging of identities, the lover absorbed in another to the point of annihilation? Such complete oneness can only be a phantasm; the abolition of difference lures to deceive. Its outcome is the obliteration of the self in madness, extinction or disenchantment. Only death can do away with the ultimate separateness of the individual, reuniting us with the earth in what Hamlet calls 'a consummation / Devoutly to be wished'.

Perhaps the desire for union with another stems from a recollection, ill-defined but pressing, of an older separation. An infant, at first continuous with the sources of its own sensations, only gradually learns to distinguish inside from outside, the self from the world. The recognition of difference allows a degree of self-determination, but at a price we don't know we pay – until the promise of oneness with another revives an old memory of severance. Freud saw the uncanny as at once strange and oddly familiar. Perhaps ghosts return to consciousness from a time in our lives before consciousness truly existed, a country only seemingly undiscovered that, in practice, we have once lived in but dismissed from awareness. Language and culture called on us to leave it behind and yet the choice we had no option but to make leaves an imprint of loss.

Conformity does not satisfy the intense desire to restore lost union. When the portrait is destroyed in a fire, the narrator of 'The Ebony Frame' reluctantly makes do with the ordinary, settling down to become stout and dull. His everyday prosperity is now no more than a dream, he maintains. In 1847 Emily Brontë's Catherine Earnshaw also finds herself unable to reconcile desire with convention. Edgar Linton has all the qualities requisite in a husband, including devotion to his wife but, impelled in the end to opt for either Linton or Heathcliff, the civilised interiors of the Grange or the wildness of the Heights, she dies baffled by the obligation to choose.

From then on in *Wuthering Heights*, Heathcliff, familiar with ghost lore, begs Catherine to haunt him. 'You said I killed you . . . The murdered *do* haunt their murderers. I believe – I know that ghosts *have* wandered on earth. Be with me always – take any form – drive me mad! Only *do* not leave me in this abyss, where I cannot find you!' This novel, which remakes the conventions in so many ways, rewrites with a difference the story of a fatal love. A fevered Catherine has already sworn not to rest until Heathcliff joins her in the grave. Does she come back to reclaim him?

Heathcliff believes so. Part romantic hero and part villain, violent and brooding, like his Gothic predecessors he sees a ghost. Or almost sees her. Driven by desire, Heathcliff spends eighteen years beguiled 'with the spectre of a hope' of reunion. He senses Catherine's presence and longs for a glimpse of her, always to be disappointed. When he sleeps in her bedroom, she is there in his mind, 'outside the window, or sliding back the panels, or entering the room, or even resting her darling head on the same pillow as she did when a child'. In the end, he exhumes her body and secures his place in the grave beside her to die, haunted, drained and haggard, but strangely exhilarated. Although Nelly and Lockwood don't believe it, the country people are convinced their spirits walk.

Official Victorian culture moralised desire, brought it firmly within the safe confines of marriage and the family. Catherine chooses that safety but remains discontented: for women, too, it seems, desire exceeds the limits imposed by domesticity. But what kind of passion is it that joins these lovers in life and, apparently, beyond it? Devotees of *Wuthering Heights* – and it still has many – will remember their declarations: his 'I *cannot* live without my life! I *cannot* live without my soul'; her 'Nelly, I *am* Heathcliff – he's always in my mind . . . as my own being'; 'he's more myself than I am'. In their only love scene, immediately before Catherine's death, they cling to one another, static in a long embrace. Nelly's account reveals an oddly symbiotic couple, as if to confirm the oneness they have asserted.

But it is a strange union and unexpectedly impersonal. As children, they were 'very thick', Nelly records; it was a punishment to keep them apart. Catherine's diary depicts their shared seclusion under the dresser concealed behind a curtain made from their pinafores. But that is before Thrushcross Grange separates them from one another, to socialise Catherine and exile Heathcliff. As grown-ups, they don't seem to like each other all that much. Catherine calls her love for Heathcliff 'a source of little visible delight, but necessary'. 'He's always in my mind – not as a pleasure, any more than I am always a pleasure to myself – but as my own being.' Are we to think of this as the height of romantic love? If so, it seems a long way from the idealisations of conventional romance.

On the contrary, it is Edgar Linton who is handsome and charming. Catherine marries him, she insists, for what distinguishes him from Heathcliff: 'Whatever our souls are made of, his and mine are the same, and Linton's is as different as moonbeam from lightning, or frost from fire.' Romantic love relies on difference. This need not be anatomical (it does not entail heterosexuality) but the enigmatic otherness of a separate person. In Victorian fiction, romantic courtship leads to marriage and parenthood. It forms, in other words, the proper prelude to sex. The love between Catherine and Heathcliff, by contrast, comes across as curiously sexless, although no less intense for that. Their inseparability reaches back to a lost past; when Heathcliff shuts his eyes, he sees Catherine's head on the pillow of her girlhood; the ghost at the window in Lockwood's dream is a child.

As luck would have it, Nelly lulls the motherless Hareton with a ghost story, a ballad recorded by Sir Walter Scott. 'The Ghaist's Warning' concerns a mother driven to return from the dead when a new wife neglects the stepchildren. In the two lines Nelly quotes, the children's cry reaches their mother beneath the earth. Such bonds are absolute. Perhaps the connection between Catherine and Heathcliff is unbreakable in a similar way.

Does it resemble the love that brings Cordelia back to an irascible father, or the tie that compels Antigone to bury her treasonous brother in defiance of Creon's law? These unconditional commitments reach beyond liking or pleasure; they persist across time. Catherine's love for Linton, she maintains, is like foliage, subject to change. By contrast, 'My love for Heathcliff resembles the eternal rocks beneath.' Isn't this bond, forged in infancy, older and more durable than romance, prior to sexual difference and to the fine discriminations language introduces? If so, it repudiates the distinctions we have to learn to make in order to live in the world, refusing a severance only death can undo.

The unnameable

If the loss of oneness with the world is hard to bear, if union with another cannot repair it, could we retreat to a realm prior to difference? Not fully: language gets in the way. May Sinclair's story, 'The Intercessor', published in 1911, suggests that, even if it could be achieved, to go back would provoke as much terror as joy. In infancy, outside language, absences cannot be accounted for, presences are unexplained. Some of the most frightening ghosts come from an archaic place without names, where experiences are not yet defined or intelligible. 'The Intercessor' calls this space 'a borderland of fear'.

Sinclair, whose book on the Brontës does full justice to the supernatural in Emily's novel, begins her remarkable tale by remaking *Wuthering Heights*. In 'The Intercessor' Mr Garvin seeks lodgings in an isolated, forbidding Yorkshire house, where the surly inmates are burdened by their own oppressive history. But this is not a mere retelling. Instead, the house is in the Bottom, not up on the heights, the date over the door is 1800, not 1500, and the inmates are Falshaws (fall-sures?), not Earnshaws.

Like Lockwood's, Garvin's bedroom attracts a pitiful wraith. But he does not share Lockwood's terror and revulsion. What he sees in this spectral child is her anguish, beyond definition, 'thinkable only as a cry, an agony, made visible'. If the child is not herself horrific, however, she is surrounded by a menacing shadow, a borderland of fear that Garvin cannot explain or name. When its inhabitants become visible, such is Garvin's sympathy with the little girl that he witnesses the scene from her point of view, sharing her terror. A spectral Falshaw is there with a woman but not his wife. Seeing as a child sees, 'He couldn't say what it was he saw, what was done by those two, but he knew that it was evil':

> It was monstrous, unintelligible; it lay outside the order of his experience. He seemed, in this shifting of his brain, to have parted with his experience, to have become a creature of vague memory and appalling possibilities of fear . . . The feeling was unspeakable. Its force, its vividness was such as could be possible only to a mind that came virgin to horror.

Later, the local doctor will give form to this spectral scene, explain in words the family history that has led to an adulterous coupling, incomprehensible to an infant. A grown-up would recognise the illicit desire of others but, seeing as the child saw, Garvin seems to himself in the moment to have lost his power to understand: 'a whole tract of knowledge – clean gone'. The doctor, professionally detached, has interpreted what he has observed on his visits, but Garvin has witnessed it, known at first hand 'the unnamed, unnameable secret of pity and fear'. What breaks in on his consciousness is the manifestation of a tragic eroticism that does not yet make sense to a child, terrifying because immediate, not named in language or defined by culture.

The touch of fear

This primal condition is full of menace. Indeed, the horror of the realm without names, of appalling possibilities, surely points to one secret of the peculiar unease evoked by the ghost stories of M. R. James. In the early years of the twentieth century his central figures, frequently desiccated antiquarians or academics, are thrown off balance by a sensuality that evades or precedes sexual difference. While demon lovers and femmes fatales generally have the grace to groom their victims, James's bookish narrators suddenly find themselves objects of desire for predatory creatures that defy definition. An unspecified sexuality informs the crumpled sheet that erects itself unaccountably on the spare bed, fracturing the mind of Professor Parkins in 'Oh, Whistle and I'll Come to You, My Lad'.

Worse, the reliable, scholarly Mr Dunning of 'Casting the Runes' finds a creature inside his own bed. Reaching for his watch, he 'put his hand into the well-known nook under the pillow: only, it did not get so far. What he touched was, according to his account, a mouth, with teeth, and with hair about it, and, he declares, not the mouth of a human being.' Post-Freudian explanations of this mouth as vaginal do it less than justice: it is not, we are to understand, human.

And the shock is prompted by touch, a sensation that precedes definition. Professor Parkins also recoils from the touch of his animated linen apparition. It succeeds in cornering him because 'he could not have borne – he didn't know why – to touch it; and as for its touching him, he would sooner dash himself through the window than have that happen'. 'Now I venture to state boldly', notes Lafcadio Hearn in 'Nightmare-Touch', 'that the common fear of ghosts is *the fear of being touched by ghosts*, – or, in other words, that the imagined supernatural is dreaded mainly because of its imagined power to touch'.

Isn't touch among the most primal of senses? Newborn babies don't understand words, they don't yet see clearly, their taste buds recoil from flavours that will later delight them, but they respond to touch, for better or worse. Caresses remain a source of pleasure into adulthood, and abrasions continue to cause pain, but in later life the touch of an unknown substance can still be unnerving and unwanted sexual touching repels.

'*Gare à qui la touche*', beware of touching: this motto guards the treasure of James's Abbot Thomas. When, undeterred by the warning, Mr Somerton pulls towards him what seems to be a shapeless leather bag, 'It hung for an instant on the edge of the hole, then slipped forward on to my chest, and *put its arms round my neck.*' This time, the creature is even less certainly human. 'I was conscious of a most horrible smell of mould, and of a cold kind of face pressed against my own, and moving slowly over it, and of several – I don't know how many – legs or arms or tentacles or something clinging to my body.'

'The Nameless' is Lafcadio Hearn's label for the ghostly tormentor whose touch he so fears. Like the aggressor of 'Oh, Whistle', 'it' is sexually undifferentiated. In 'The Treasure of Abbot Thomas' Mr Somerton's quasi-erotic assailant is the appointed guardian of the treasure. And is it gendered? The pronoun puzzles the antiquarian protagonist. *Gare à qui la touche.* Abbot Thomas adopted this as his own device – 'though it doesn't quite fit in point of grammar'.

But doesn't it? James has constructed a neat, multilingual cryptogram of his own that would no doubt have delighted the original donnish audience gathered round a single candle in his rooms at King's College, Cambridge. Deciphered, the message that leads him to the treasure reads, '*Decem millia auri reposita sunt in puteo in atrio domus abbatialis de Steinfeld a me, Thoma, qui posui custodem super ea. Gare à qui la touche.'* In English, the Latin reads, 'Ten thousand pieces of gold are laid up in a well in the court of the Abbot's house of Steinfeld by me, Thomas, who have set a guardian over them.' And then, *beware whoever touches it – or her.* The motto doesn't fit in point of grammar only if Somerton assumes that the feminine singular *la* is supposed to apply to the ten thousand pieces of gold (*ea*, them, neuter plural). But *custos* (singular), the appointed custodian of the gold, can be masculine or feminine. According to the motto, the body of the questing antiquary is enfolded in the repulsive embrace of a female guardian of the treasure, human or otherwise.

James revisited the ambiguities of spectral identity ten years later in 'An Episode of Cathedral History'. This time, the ghost is 'A thing like a man, all over hair, and two great eyes to it'. A thing, or a man? But after the apparition, an epitaph is applied to the tomb: 'IBI CUBAVIT LAMIA' (Here the lamia has rested). The lamia is a Greek night-hag, or a serpent-woman; in Keats's poem about her, Lamia is a femme fatale. Is the revenant that haunts James's story male or female? Is it human? Primeval? In some threatening way sexual? The story doesn't say for sure.

Pleasure

Where, since James's ghost stories remain popular more than a century on, lies the pleasure for readers in tales of these horrors? Perhaps it is paradoxically reassuring to be reminded in safety – and in words – of a wordless infancy, when the differences we now take for granted were not yet given. Instead, we were at one with an unnamed world, simultaneously inside us and outside, unpredictably gratifying or predatory. It may be that access to language and culture only represses a condition that is never completely surmounted. If so, the uncanny recalls something of what it was like to be without that named world, not yet capable of systematic thought processes, a little human animal at the mercy of the nameless.

Both May Sinclair and M. R. James were contemporaries of Freud, although James would have repudiated any connection. Lafcadio Hearn, who died in 1904, was (just) another. Hearn concluded 'Nightmare-Touch' with a speculation that might have been endorsed by the author of *The Interpretation of Dreams* and 'The "Uncanny"'.

> It may be that profundities of Self, – abysses never reached by any ray from the life of the sun, – are strangely stirred in slumber, and that out of their blackness immediately responds a shuddering of memory, measureless even by millions of years.

Is it possible that, like dreams, ghost stories invoke those abysses and stir the shudder of a memory from our own prehistory? M. R. James's central figures are pursued by an undefined and engulfing eroticism that threatens their lives or their sanity. Conversely, those seduced into seeking a repair for past loss by pursuing the desire for perfect union with another want a consummation no longer available in life. For grown-ups, such oneness with the world has become the property of death.

EIGHT

All in the Mind?

Doubt

If ghost stories allude to our own forgotten past, doesn't it follow that spectres belong to the mind of the ghost-seer? Enlightenment philosophy preferred to blame psychology for the walking dead. How far do storytellers themselves permit us to understand apparitions as illusions of our own making? The question goes back to some of the oldest recorded tales. In ancient Rome Pliny framed his with the question whether ghosts arise from our fears. When Brutus, in the Greek Plutarch's version of his story, reports to Cassius that he has faced an evil spirit, his friend does his best to reassure him. We don't always see what we think we see, Cassius urges. Our senses can delude us; our thoughts can influence imagination to the point where we perceive what isn't there; surely, Brutus is just overtired.

Pliny and Plutarch both leave the issue unresolved. *Hamlet*, too, allows for more than one possibility. The armed figure on the battlements first appears to the guards, who have no motive for summoning the dead king. Later in Gertrude's closet, on the other hand, no one else sees the apparition that his mother immediately ascribes to Hamlet's madness. 'Look you, how pale he glares', the prince insists, 'Do you see nothing there?' 'Nothing at all', replies the queen, 'but all that is I see'; 'This is the very coinage of your brain.'

All three early versions of *Hamlet* direct the Ghost to appear on the stage at this moment. The first of them, Q1, adds a detail: 'Enter the Ghost in his night gown.' Evidently, the spirit has shed his armour as inappropriate to the domestic setting. But, since he is invisible to Gertrude, is Old Hamlet a figment of his son's imagination, apparent to the audience only as the content of a fantasy? In Richard Eyre's stage production of 1980 Jonathan Pryce played a Hamlet projecting the spirit of his father throughout. Encountering the Ghost in Act 1, the prince, alone on the stage, spoke both sets of lines, the Ghost's in sepulchral and agonised tones, Hamlet's breathless with intensity.

Old Hamlet haunts the battlements at one in the morning, 'the dead waste and middle of the night'. Like Julius Caesar and Pliny's ghost, many spectres walk after sundown, when people are most subject to anxieties. We are, after all, more vulnerable in darkness and, paradoxically, more capable of 'seeing things' when visibility is reduced. Besides, moonlight throws strange shadows. It was often while travellers were making their way home after dark near medieval Byland that they were pursued by shape-changing revenants.

Like Thomas Nashe before him, David Hume attributed preternatural emanations to the emotions; they were prompted, he argued, by misfortune or melancholy. At the beginning of the nineteenth century, when psychiatry became a medical discipline and psychology the central concern of the novel, mental states began to take an even greater responsibility for the uncanny. Ann Radcliffe's Gothic heroines are more prone to let superstition conquer reason when they feel at their most isolated and helpless. From this perspective, weakness succumbs to a credulity that is best countered by stoical rationality.

Other Enlightenment thinkers took a still harsher line: Kant blamed fraud and imposture. But Kant's admirer Friedrich Schiller

allowed psychology to play its part in creating the illusion of apparitions. His novel *Ghost-Seer: An Interesting Tale from the Memoirs of
Count von O***, published in 1798, begins in mystery but leads on to
a detailed exposition of the conjuring tricks practised by a so-called
sorcerer. The illusions all depend on deceiving the senses. Invented
ritual, manufactured thunder and lightning, smoke and mirrors
combine to convince the bystanders that they have seen a phantom
by distracting their attention from the mechanics used to produce it.

In practice, however, such apparatus may prove unnecessary. A
fireside circle telling ghost stories late at night can excite enough
shared apprehension to suspend disbelief. Thomas Peacock's satirical *Nightmare Abbey* shows such a group exchanging anecdotes
until midnight strikes. Mr Flosky (aka the poet and philosopher
Coleridge) is approaching his grand rhetorical conclusion that all
phantoms inhabit the mind – in that sense, he himself lives in a
world of ghosts, he sees a ghost at this moment – when the door
opens and a figure in white with a bloody turban on its head
comes into the room. The entire company, believers and sceptics
alike, take to their heels, only to learn in due course that the
apparition was the steward, sleepwalking in a red nightcap.

By this account, the stories themselves are to blame for filling
with fearful phantasms the vacancy left by the dark. It is her reading of Gothic novels that misleads the innocent heroine of Jane
Austen's *Northanger Abbey*. But on occasions such scepticism pays
tribute to the success of tall tales in making error convincing.
Washington Irving's 'The Spectre Bridegroom', a story dating
from 1819–20, tells how an arranged marriage is prevented by the
death of the prospective husband on his way to claim his bride.
When his friend arrives at the castle to deliver the sad news, the
company, who have never seen the fiancé they await, mistake
the friend for the bridegroom. While the handsome visitor and the

blushing bride fall silently in love with one another, the Baron entertains the gathering with the tale of Leonora, 'a dreadful, but true story, which has since been put into excellent verse, and is read and believed by all the world'. The tale gives the friend an idea.

The Baron's Leonora is none other than our friend Lenore, whose soldier-lover returns at midnight to carry her off to his grave. In Irving's witty remake of the story, when the living visitor finds that everyone takes him for the prospective husband, he prolongs the impersonation for a while. He cannot marry, he insists: instead, he must return to the tomb that has now claimed him. But, careful to be seen haunting the castle grounds, he eventually carries off the young woman – only to come back in due course, fit and healthy, with his newly married wife.

This supposed haunting is motivated. In E. Nesbit's 'Number 17', first published in 1910, it is the story itself that has designs on the circle of travellers round the hearth. The grisly tale of the haunted bedroom secures the best room in the hotel for the teller, when a ghost, invented for the purpose, impels the current occupant to move to another room. The mind plays tricks on us, these tales propose. Encouraged by ghost stories, thinking conjures up apparitions where none exist outside our own heads.

In dreams

As psychology turned the mind into a more layered place, phantoms began to inhabit a deeper region. And when Freudian theory took hold in the twentieth century, ghosts were increasingly identified as projections into the external world of unconscious desires. Shirley Jackson's Hill House can be seen as genuinely haunted. But it might alternatively be interpreted as playing host to a woman on the verge of a nervous breakdown.

In Freudian theory, thoughts inadmissible to the waking mind find a way to make themselves felt as demons of the night and the dead return as revenants in the true sense of the term, back from a place in the unconscious that they had never truly left. *The Haunting of Hill House* was published in 1959. When in 1968 Jonathan Miller adapted M. R. James's 'Oh, Whistle' for television, he excised all independent witness to the apparition and characterised his professor of philosophy as deeply repressed.

Here the apparition is generated in the unconscious mind. Psychoanalytic theory proposed that the best means of access to the unconscious was the interpretation of dreams and Freud's big book on this topic was published in 1900. From the point of view of psychoanalysis, ghosts that appeared in dreams revealed more about the individual sleeper than they did about the occult. How far do ghost stories themselves bear out the case?

From early times ghosts had appeared in sleep but, although in a post-Freudian world it is tempting to psychoanalyse the dreamers, the oldest stories do not immediately appear to justify this approach. Instead, such ghosts offer access to knowledge not available to the living. When Homer's Patroclus appears to Achilles in a dream, the effect is to convince the dreamer that there is an afterlife. 'So then it is true', exclaims Achilles, 'something of us lives on.' The Trojan hero Hector returns from the dead in a dream to alert Virgil's Aeneas to a burning Troy. Aeneas does well to act on his warning.

Classical ghosts, it seems, had information to impart. A story in circulation in ancient Rome concerned a man who dreamed his friend called for help when he was threatened with murder. It was only a dream, the man reflected, and went back to sleep. But when he then dreamed the friend's ghost was calling on him to bury his body, he took the apparition seriously, led the authorities to the corpse and brought the perpetrator to justice.

At the same time, Rome had its doubters. Not everyone was ready to treat dreams as messages from the dead. Cicero, who records this tale of the murdered friend in the first book of his *On Divination*, spends the second book denouncing all superstition. Sceptics, then and into the Middle Ages, were more likely to ascribe dreams to indigestion or an imbalance of the humours, than to either messages from the afterlife or unconscious wishes. The debate is replayed as comedy in Chaucer's *Nun's Priest's Tale*, complete with the dream of the friend's murder.

And yet in Chaucer's story Chaunticleer's dream of a fox proves prophetic. As the entire chicken run learns from experience, to ignore a dream can be dangerous. Thomas of Woodstock, hero of a play of the 1590s, does not believe in ghosts or the truth of dreams. When the ghost of his brother, the Black Prince, appears in thunder and lightning to warn Woodstock in a dream that he is threatened with murder, the spectre is too weak to wake the slumbering man: 'Still dost thou sleep? Oh, I am nought but air!' he exclaims. The Black Prince is followed in Woodstock's dream by the shade of Edward III, come 'from his quiet grave' to alert his son. This time, 'O good angels, guide me – stay, thou blessed spirit!' Woodstock exclaims, recognising his father. But no, he reflects, awake now and rational; the room is empty, after all; it was only his fancy. Waking reason misleads Woodstock, however. The ghosts of his dreams were right all along and the murderers return to carry out their task.

At about the same time, Thomas Nashe, predictably, dismissed dreams as 'a bubbling scum or froth of the fancy'. He allowed them no independent significance. But a new, psychologising alternative was already beginning to emerge. When the dead victims of Shakespeare's Richard III have filed past one by one to curse the king and urge on his opponent, a stage direction indicates that

'Richard starteth up out of a dream.' In the moment of waking, Richard sees himself at the heart of the coming battle: 'Give me another horse! Bind up my wounds!' But then he reassures himself: 'Soft, I did but dream.' And yet the dream has shown Richard that he is indeed the villain the ghosts have proclaimed him: awake now, and alone with his conscience, he begins to see his crimes for what they are. Whether or not the ghosts are real, in his sleep they have revealed a truth beyond illusion.

The Atheist's Tragedy of 1611 introduces the possibility of accounting for apparitions in psychological terms, when Charlemont puzzles over the reason for his dream. There his father has declared himself dead and Charlemont disinherited. No one else has seen the ghost. Could he himself somehow have generated the manifestation, the soldier wonders. But he has had no recent news of his father; he has not been worrying about him. Charlemont must have spent too much time in the company of war and death, he reasons, ruminating on the strange powers of fantasy to confuse and falsify impressions.

Evidently, in anticipation of the Freudian view, it is already thinkable that dreams spring from parts of the mind not amenable to conscious control. But the drama was not yet ready to let go of the supernatural. Like Woodstock's, Charlemont's waking scepticism proves mistaken. The ghost reappears and this time a Musketeer sees it too. When he fires at it, the shot goes straight through the spirit of the dead man. In these instances, the dreamers are wrong to doubt their supernatural visitants: the ghosts are indeed in possession of more than mortal knowledge.

Even so, in *The Atheist's Tragedy* the possibility has explicitly arisen that apparitions are projections of the dreaming mind. Can we be sure that Shakespeare's Brutus, surrounded by sleepers, has not himself nodded off and dreamt he sees the spirit of Caesar?

Even if the religious authorities of the period allow dreams authority, does Milton's dead wife really exist outside a wish made visible in his dream?

Keeping the options open

Julius Caesar and Milton's Sonnet 19 allow the playgoer or reader a degree of choice about what to make of them. Dreams can disclose information but they may also delude the dreamer into taking them for reality. In any number of ghost stories the seer is in bed, on the verge of sleep, or suddenly roused to confront the uncanny. How far can we trust the storytellers, when they insist that they were wide awake? Joseph Glanvill's Mary Watkinson saw her dead father one night when she could not sleep. Aubrey's Mr T. M. was awake in bed when he saw his dead wife. Alternatively, in 1879, 'He dropped off to sleep quickly, but woke with a start ten minutes afterwards', records Mary Elizabeth Braddon's 'The Shadow in the Corner'. 'On the night of the following Friday, I started suddenly from my sleep. An unaccountable horror was upon me', declares Washington Irving's Don Luis in 'The Knight of Malta'. In 'Pirates', a short story of 1934, E. F. Benson's Peter Graham 'woke very suddenly and completely, knowing that somebody had called him'.

Perhaps, and perhaps not. The conventions of sleeplessness and sudden waking allow sceptical readers to enjoy the pleasures of a ghost story without feeling any obligation to subscribe to the supernatural. 'While such pleasing reflections were stealing over my mind, and gradually lulling me to slumber, I was suddenly aroused by a sound like that of the rustling of a silken gown.' This is how General Browne begins the narrative to his friend Lord Woodville of his disturbed night in 'The Tapestried Chamber' in 1829. Has Walter Scott's Lord Woodville really allowed the general, as an intrepid soldier, to confirm the story that the room is haunted by a wicked ancestress of the family whose portrait hangs in the gallery? Or has the ancient bedroom itself provoked a bad dream that subsequently attaches itself to an old painting?

In Guy de Maupassant's 'The Dead Woman', in 1887, a desolate lover resolves to spend the night in the cemetery where his beloved mistress lies buried. Lost in the necropolis and overcome with terror, he rests on a tombstone, only to find corpses and skeletons rising from their graves to rewrite the flattering epitaphs recorded on their memorials. The dead now tell the truth, recounting lives of malice, deceit and shame. The lover's mistress, too, returns to tell her own tale: it was after going out in the rain to deceive him that she caught cold and died. Was the lover dreaming? 'The Dead Woman' can be read as a ghost story, or as a comment on love's blindness, as a satire on fulsome epitaphs, or, finally, as the nightmare of a lover who cannot let go.

Mourning

Maupassant's lover is in mourning. Is it possible that grief itself provokes apparitions? Hamlet sees the Ghost when he is in mourning for his father; he fears that the devil is taking advantage of his melancholy to mislead him. When Patroclus dies at the hands of Hector, the anguish of Achilles knows no bounds. Not content with killing Hector in return, Achilles subjects his corpse to every indignity. But his grief is still not allayed; instead, it absorbs him. Summoned to a feast, Achilles has no appetite; he won't even wash his battle-stained body until he has accorded his friend a proper funeral. That is the night that Patroclus visits him in a dream to ask for burial. Would we, then, be wrong, after all, to think the ghost called up by his friend's dearest wish?

Perhaps the Roman poet Propertius agreed. At any rate, he echoes the exclamation of Achilles as a prelude to the return of his dead mistress in a dream. 'Sunt aliquid Manes', he begins. 'So ghosts exist . . .' or 'Ghosts are something.' And 'death does not end it all', he goes on. But the poem that follows recounts a more or less self-evident fiction in which Cynthia recalls their past and his neglect.

Cynthia also complains that her lover has skimped on her burial rites. Patroclus, too, wants a proper funeral, as does the ghost in Pliny's tale of the haunted house in Athens. Meanwhile, the mourning rites for Old Hamlet have been curtailed by the precipitate remarriage of the widow. Could there be a genuine link between apparitions and inadequate death rituals?

On the basis of one of Freud's suggestions, the French psychoanalyst Jacques Lacan thought so. Bereavement makes a gap, 'a hole in the real', as he puts it, that cultures do their best to fill with ceremonies, rites, eulogies, mourning dress, flowers left at the spot, notices in the paper, obituaries, elegies, wakes, memorial gatherings, anniversaries, burial mounds, pyramids, gravestones, monuments, posthumous medals, blue plaques, commemorations in high places . . . But nothing quite makes up for the loss to those who most loved the dead person. Hamlet's 'inky cloak' doesn't tell the whole story of his grief, the prince insists. Instead, 'I have that within which passes show.'

Even after due honour is done to Patroclus, Achilles still weeps for his comrade. Only when he has returned Hector's body with honour to the Trojan king is he free to sleep soundly. In modern terms, Achilles has at last acknowledged a loss that cannot be repaired by ritual or redressed by revenge. If the sorrow goes deep, the hole in the real can become a place of phantasms – hallucinated satisfactions, Freud calls them. In this view, the dead return because we want them back. Perhaps the intensity of Heathcliff's longing summons Catherine in *Wuthering Heights*. Spiritualist seances placate the bereaved.

But, as so often, generalisations do not hold: there are counter-examples. No one seems to want the return of the ghost Athenodorus lays. The anonymous hooded monks and headless cavaliers of popular fiction are mourned by no one living. And the ghost in *Ghost* is not a hallucination. Molly is in mourning, left desolate by the sudden death of Sam Wheat in this hugely successful movie, directed by Jerry Zucker in 1990. But *Ghost* is also a thriller: Sam has matters to put right, a crime to solve and punishment to supervise. His insubstantial presence is sensed first by the cat (animals always know) and then by a medium, who reluctantly co-operates in hunting down his killer. Molly is the last to be convinced of his return, consoling though she finds it. Sam, we are invited to believe, leads a spectral life outside Molly's mind.

Ghost's only marginally more bracing near-contemporary *Truly Madly Deeply* is more elusive, however. This film, directed in 1991 by Anthony Minghella, acknowledges the psychoanalytic account of the response to sudden death. Freud's essay 'Mourning and Melancholia' treats bereavement as a source of conflict between what we know to be the case and what we want to believe. When a lover dies, reality impels us to withdraw desire from its object. But that period of gradual retraction, while feeling is slowly detached from each of the memories and hopes involved in a partnership, can also be a time of haunting. In the movie, Nina doesn't want to let go of the dead Jamie. Her fragile autonomy is invested in a new flat he did not share, where nothing quite fits or works. Nina contemplates the resident rats with indifference. Her living space puts on visual display, it seems, her desolation and despair. Efforts to draw her out of seclusion fail; she is fully absorbed in mourning.

Jamie's ghost fulfils a deeply held wish. When he comes back, Nina is overjoyed. She tells no one, and the dead man obligingly hides from visitors. But as his spectral friends progressively take over the domestic space, as Jamie comes to dominate the flat, Nina begins to realise that her existence has been turned over to the ghosts. Like all mourners, in other words, Nina eventually faces a choice between renouncing life to cling to the dead person and resuming it by assenting to the loss.

It is possible to tell a parallel story from the point of view of the dead themselves, who want the living to let them go. In the ballad of *The Unquiet Grave* the lover mourns for a twelvemonth and a day but, at the end of that time, the dead woman pleads to be left at rest in her burial place. There is said to be a Breton belief that sorrow on the part of the bereaved intensifies the distress of the dead. A young woman, inconsolable after the death of her mother, wept without ceasing. One evening she remained in church until midnight, when she saw a procession of the dead walk down the nave. Her mother came last, struggling under the weight of a pail full of tears. Only when the ghost told her of the pain she was causing did the daughter stop crying. The following night, her mother led the procession, her face bright and shining.

Against every impulse of self-immolation, mortality demands acknowledgement as a fact of life. *Lincoln in the Bardo*, which won the Man Booker Prize for George Saunders in 2017, records Abraham Lincoln's grief for his dead son Willie on a night in the cemetery where the President visits the boy's body. By revealing the state of mind of the dead (troops of them, it seems) *Lincoln in the Bardo* inventively turns the mourning process inside out. In this instance, the ghosts themselves do not name their own condition. They evade the word *death*; coffins and tombs are 'sick boxes' and 'stone homes'. But while they continue to disavow their state, the dead, just like the bereaved themselves, are trapped in a darkness in the margins of this world. Willie cannot move on while he believes his father will come back for him.

It is tempting to linger on the details of this witty, incisive and humane ghost story – and not least to reveal how it ends. But what matters here is that, while the ghosts do not appear to President Lincoln and are in no sense creations of his mind, it is as if they work as projections of ours. They give readers access to both Lincoln's pain and the meaning of death. And in the process they invite us to acquiesce imaginatively in what we already know rationally, that no amount of wishing reinstates the dead.

Fear

Absorption in mourning brings dangers. Nina badly wants Jamie back, until he begins to threaten her already tenuous sense of self. Lenore longs to be reunited with her soldier-lover, until she discovers that this means being buried with him. In *The Unquiet Grave* the living lover begs for one last kiss, but 'If you have one kiss of my clay-cold lips', the ghost replies, 'your time will not be long.'

The living establish relationships with the dead on conditions that the dead lay down, and their terms are not ours. Since we cannot resurrect them as fully living beings, we can rejoin them completely only in their world. While the death of others generates grief, our own death most commonly provokes fear. Does the degree of comedy that goes into many modern ghost stories, including *Ghost*, including *Truly Madly Deeply* and *Lincoln in the Bardo*, serve as an apology for introducing the supernatural in our scientific, rational age? Or, alternatively, does laughter work in these instances to deflect the terror conventionally aroused by the returning dead?

If our minds create ghosts, they form them as projections not only of a wish but also of fear. While there are benign ghosts, dead saints, women in white, spiritualist emanations that claim to be well and happy, most cultures have regarded the walking dead as objects of dread, to be kept at bay or, at best, appeased. Cairns, pyramids, barrows, tombs, gravestones, while they memorialise the dead, also keep them away from those left behind, prevent them from returning to bring misfortune, disease or death. In Australian aboriginal cultures, naming the dead might bring them back, interrupting their journey to the ancestors and causing mischief or sadness for the living. The dead are *taboo*, Freud says, at once sacred and unclean, forbidden. People are wise to recoil from contamination by the touch of their clay-cold lips or, perhaps worse, some indefinite, unidentifiable alternative.

As the spectre of the father he loves bears down on Charlemont, 'He fearfully avoids it.' The fear of ghosts is visceral, experienced bodily, paralysing. Rudyard Kipling's 'My Own True Ghost Story' defines the special terror engendered by the supernatural: 'Not ordinary fear of insult, injury or death, but abject, quivering dread'. In 'Nightmare-Touch' Lafcadio Hearn also notes the singular anxiety ghosts provoke. 'It is a peculiar fear. No other fear is so intense; yet none is so vague.'

Isn't there a connection between the intensity and the vagueness? Ghosts are no longer identical with their living counterparts. What, after all, are they now? They are familiar and yet alien, dead but not lifeless. Flickering unpredictably on the edges of vision, ghosts evade definition, calling into doubt the distinctions we rely on. If they stand in for what we fear of death, their very evanescence incites us to face the possibility of our own fading into dissolution. The dead Banquo 'unmans' Macbeth, unpicks the fabric that makes him human. In the presence of the evil spirit, Walter Scott's old soldier feels his manhood melt from him.

On this reading, ghosts project outwards as uncanny manifestations all that we dread of the ultimate unknown. And their stories offer readers, viewers and playgoers access to the depiction of that visceral dread – while preserving, as stories, a safe distance from the thing itself.

Guilt

Fear invests ghosts with a superhuman power, whether physical or spiritual. Like mourners, then, perhaps malefactors too, ironically, solicit the return of their victims in all their fearfulness, prompting the parallel suspicion that ghosts are no more than projections of their own guilty minds. In this case, the motive is not consolation but terror of unearthly retribution. Any number of Gothic younger brothers tremble at the sight of the rightful owner's spirit, real or impersonated. How often do unfaithful lovers imagine their own haunting? How many false executors, who have ignored the deceased's last wishes or the laws of inheritance, are pursued by phantoms of their own creation? Daniel Defoe tells a tale of a man tried for murder. It seemed that he would be acquitted for lack of evidence, when a further witness appeared on the stand. But the newcomer was visible only to the defendant, who was induced by this spectral presence to confess.

Defoe explicitly blames the phantom on a tormented conscience. If crime is not brought to justice, the criminal is 'haunted with the ghosts of his own imagination, and apparitions without apparition. The murdered person is always in his sight, and cries of blood are ever in his ears.' When Banquo haunts Macbeth, does the spectre exist outside Macbeth's own guilty mind? 'Thou canst not say I did it!' cries Macbeth to the ghost. 'Never shake thy gory locks at me.' His wife is obliged to make excuses. The apparition is imaginary, she insists, no more real than the dagger he once saw before him. Such terrors befit old wives' tales, 'A woman's story at a winter's fire, / Authorised by her grandam'.

Macbeth is not reassured. His fear is palpable, but is the revenant real, or is Lady Macbeth's diagnosis the right one? With a proper respect for the power of fiction, Shakespeare's play leaves the question in the balance as Macbeth implores the apparition to leave him alone, but in terms that seem to concede his wife's point: 'Hence, horrible shadow, / Unreal mockery, hence.' As in the case of Old Hamlet in Gertrude's closet, the original stage direction is clear: 'Enter the Ghost of Banquo, and sits in Macbeth's place.' Simon Forman, who went to the Globe in 1611, saw the dead Banquo take Macbeth's chair. But then, how else can the stage show the source of a delusion?

Even so, the Enlightened eighteenth century preferred its spectres imaginary. In the 1790s, both James Boaden and M. G. Lewis had great difficulty in persuading their respective theatre managers to allow them visible apparitions on the stage. And while the public loved these ghosts, critics were much more grudging. Shakespeare was allowed a special dispensation at the time: everyone, it was mistakenly held, believed in ghosts in his barbaric day. But now, in the age of reason, fiction should confine itself to imitating reality, and what does not exist should not appear. As a concession to this new orthodoxy, John Philip Kemble produced *Macbeth* at Drury Lane with an invisible Banquo – and a correspondingly crazed protagonist. The critics hailed the innovation but audiences were not impressed, and the dead man continued to appear on stage in rival productions at Covent Garden.

Subsequent ghost stories may keep us guessing about which of them invest the supernatural with an independent existence and which concern visions that beset a mind out of control. Mrs Henry Wood (née Ellen Price) weaves a tale round the question in 'Reality or Delusion?' in 1868. Does Maria Lease really see Daniel Ferrar half an hour after he hanged himself, or is his ghost a figment of her remorseful imagination? In a story from 1872, Sheridan Le Fanu's Mr Justice Harbottle, a notorious hanging judge, is brought to a state of terror when he dreams he is condemned to death for the murder of a forger he convicted in his own court. In the dream, he is to be executed on the tenth day of the month. Gouty, as well as guilty, and correspondingly morose, he finds it hard to shake off the anxiety generated by the dream. On the night of the ninth, the servants witness unaccountable events in his house and the following morning the judge is found dead, hanged by the neck from his own bannisters.

Was it suicide, or supernatural retribution? The judge had already received a summons to appear in court in a letter signed by Caleb Searcher, 'Solicitor in the Kingdom of Life and Death'. But this document survived only in a copy made by Harbottle himself. The fictional narrator of 'Mr Justice Harbottle', who himself relays the tale at second hand, supposes the original letter to be a figment of the judge's imagination, the effect of brain disease. But it is not clear that we can count on a narrator so distant from the events to know for sure.

Does the Spanish film *The Orphanage* in 2007 depict the revenge of the dead children, or the mounting delusions of an adoptive mother, guilty because she slapped her little boy? In these cases, the stories do not always resolve the question they present. Sometimes the balance tilts one way, sometimes another. And in some instances, readers and viewers are left to form their own opinions.

Understanding

Is the difference, in the end, important? Does it matter whether the dead walk in the world or only in the mind? Yes and no. In 1882 the Society for Psychical Research was founded to subject the supernatural to the scrutiny of science. But no conclusive evidence ever confirmed the survival of the dead. If ghosts exist independently, the world includes a terrain that remains, despite the most enlightened efforts of this organisation, unmapped and unknown, perhaps unknowable. But when the Enlightenment placed ghosts in the eye of the seer, it moved the occult from the world to the mind. If ghosts are deceptions of our own making, it follows that rational thinking does not define us after all. Instead, in a space beyond the reach of reason, we generate visions we cannot explain or control.

Either way, apparitions call into question what passes for knowledge – whether of the cosmos or of ourselves. In that sense, surely ghosts have something to tell us about the limits of our understanding – at least, on condition that they belong to the world of storytelling. Each era seems fond of saying that in previous, more superstitious times, everyone thought the dead walked. The Enlightenment never tired of repeating that belief in ghosts went unquestioned in the past. The Enlightenment was wrong about this: scepticism goes back a very long way. But as realism became the preferred narrative mode, it seemed as if ghost stories had to imply a faith in the supernatural: people who enjoyed ghost stories must think that ghosts were real.

The naivety of this conviction becomes apparent when we reflect that pleasure in Aesop's fables does not depend on supposing that animals actually talk. Remarkably, very young visitors can recognise and still enjoy the inventions that make up

Disneyland. Do grown-ups have to believe there is life on other planets to enjoy science fiction?

But ghosts differ from talking animals and cartoon mice in that people not only relish tales about them; they also claim to see them (and aliens, of course). Such sightings testify either to a world that is more mysterious than we know, or to a mind that perceives more than the facts presented by the senses. In 1937 Oliver St John Gogarty, Irish doctor and poet, had it both ways. 'I believe in ghosts', he asserted – and immediately added, 'that is, I know that there are times, given the place which is capable of suggesting a phantasy, when those who are sufficiently impressionable may perceive a dream projected as if external to the dreamy mind: a waking dream due both to the dreamer and the spot.'

'The mind is its own place', Milton's Satan proposed, at a moment when consciousness was beginning to take centre stage as an object of knowledge, 'and in itself / Can make a heaven of hell, a hell of heaven.' Satan's view is that thinking can transform the realm in which we find ourselves, for better or worse. It is not entirely clear that we can trust the speaker here: he is comforting his fallen troops in hell. But he has a case. Milton's contemporary, Andrew Marvell, called the mind an ocean where all things in the world are replicated. 'Yet', he adds, in what might be read as a refinement of Satan's view, 'it creates, 'transcending these, / Far other worlds and other seas.'

Marvell's point is that what we can imagine exceeds what we know. Two and a half centuries later, psychoanalysis extends the range of the mind to unconscious processes that may be concealed from consciousness itself. If psychoanalysis is right, we are not sure what we are capable of experiencing, for better or worse, or how far the mind may transform the realm we inhabit. Ghost stories register that uncertainty, an acknowledgement that there may be, if not out there in the world, perhaps inside our heads, far other worlds that lie beyond the reach of rationality.

If so, what we know is haunted by what we don't, and although this reflection credits imagination with creativity, it also acknow-ledges the mind's capacity to deepen anxiety. Mortality gives us an investment in evidence that something of us survives it. But ghosts threaten at least as often as they reassure. While their stories imply that death is not final, they all too commonly treat what follows as a clay-cold continuity or worse, in the process confirming for the living the fear that belongs to the unknown. If we invent ghost stories, we do so as much to our own disquiet as by way of consolation.

Storytelling, however, allows for the suspension of judgement. Despite calls for realism to confine itself to what exists, narrative has no obligation to replicate the outside world, or to restrict the tales it invents to a faithful representation of the life we know. Instead, if ghosts belong in the mind of the seer, their stories bring to light what takes place there. Read in this way, ghost stories contribute, however obliquely, to an understanding of the conditions mortality is heir to, including bereavement, the fear of death, or remorse. As stories, no more and no less, they offer their audience a range of provisional relationships with death – and at the same time they let us live to tell the tale.

Psychological explanations, in other words, do not disparage or dismiss ghost stories. Choosing to locate ghosts in the mind does not explain them *away*. On the contrary. And in what follows I go on according their stories the respect I believe they deserve. In other words, I continue to take them seriously on their terms as much as mine.

NINE

Listening to Ghosts

Speech

'What brings you here?' asked the manager of a hotel in North Yorkshire. 'Ghosts', I replied and before I had time to explain that my project was – ahem – research, she told me the hotel had a ghost. When I involuntarily looked behind me, she added, 'There's nothing to be frightened of. As my old granny used to say, you just ask them politely what they want.' I was not entirely reassured. Some ghosts undoubtedly want to be invited to talk – to explain the past, put things right, induce the living to join them, or just to relieve their own isolation by telling their stories.

And some don't. At its first two appearances on the ramparts, the Ghost in *Hamlet* is silent. Like so many spirits, it comes and goes unaccountably, all the more unnerving to the degree that the apparition remains unexplained, as well as unearthly. 'It would be spoke to', asserts Barnardo and, as if to support the conviction of the hotel manager's granny, Marcellus too urges Horatio to question it. The guards are half right: when the Ghost finds the right listener, it is eager to tell its story.

What do the dead have to say for themselves? What do their voices sound like and what can they reveal of their world? What impels their return? Do they come back for good or ill? And what, in deference to the hotel manager's granny, do they want from the living? Perhaps listening to ghosts as they tell their own tales offers insights into the practices of storytelling in general. If so, listening attentively may also cast light on the practice of reading.

There is a widespread belief that ghosts don't speak first, borne out by the sad tale of William Clarkson. According to a rambling and oddly inconclusive account of an attested ghost, recorded in 1826, William Mann, who lived in North Yorkshire, saw Clarkson, his dead lodger, every other night for about a week and then nightly for about a month. The living man, increasingly drained by these supernatural visits, tried to address the ghost but found he was too frightened to speak. Eventually, however, one evening when his wife and a niece were with him on the way home from Ripon, he summoned the courage to ask the spectre what it wanted. The dead Clarkson replied, 'Willy, thou hast kept both thyself and me unhappy, by reason of not speaking before now.' The ghost's will isn't being executed in accordance with his wishes, he complains; his goods are to be sold; the sale must be stopped if possible. But sadly it is too late: the haunted man has waited too long to ask the revenant what troubled him.

On the other hand, if there is such a thing as ghost lore in general, its only rule is that beliefs about the walking dead are not consistent. Spectres, subsisting on the outer limits of the world charted by cultures, don't obey recognised norms. Instead, the walking dead hover uncertainly between improbabilities. Some speak when spoken to – and some just speak. But not all ghosts respond to questions. Some glimmer and vanish; some beckon silently or rattle their chains. Old Hamlet rejects Horatio's over-tures. He keeps his counsel until the third time he appears, when he leads the prince to a more secluded place. The dead king speaks only to Hamlet and in response to Hamlet's direct appeal. Tell me, the prince urges, your reason for leaving your tomb. 'Say why is this? Wherefore? What should we do?'

The Ghost's repeated injunction is to listen. His opening words are 'Mark me.' 'Lend thy serious hearing / To what I shall unfold'; 'List, list, O list!'; 'Now, Hamlet, hear.' He has, after all, a tale to divulge. So suppose we obey the Ghost's command and listen to him, what would we hear?

Voices

In the first place, how would he sound? Some ghosts must speak exactly like the living, since their addressees don't always realise they're dead. But others give away their spectrality in voices that seem to come from a distant place or another time. The ancient Scots ghosts of 'Ossian', for instance, are muted. When Shilric's dead lover speaks to him from the tomb, her voice is 'weak', like the wind in the reeds. Connal's dead comrade in arms comes to warn him, making a sound like a distant stream.

Ossian's poems also include ghosts who shriek like the banshee when a death is imminent. In 1904 M. R. James describes a singing phantom in 'Number 13': 'It was a high, thin voice that they heard, and it seemed dry, as if from long disuse . . . It went sailing up to a surprising height, and was carried down with a despairing moan as of a winter wind in a hollow chimney, or an organ whose wind fails suddenly.' The voice of the ghost in E. Nesbit's story, 'From the Dead', first published in 1893, is 'hollow and faint', 'thin, monotonous'. Marjorie Bowen's revenant in 'The Crown Derby Plate' of 1931 seems very old and speaks in a 'thin, treble voice'.

While these sounds are eerie, they also register the frailty of the dead, who maintain only a tenuous and intermittent hold on vitality from beyond the grave. Alternatively, ghostly voices echo from unnamed depths or as if they resonated from inside the tomb. *The Castle of Otranto* describes the hollow utterance that comes from a hooded skeleton. M. G. Lewis's bleeding nun speaks in a low sepulchral voice; his Antonia hears her dead mother as 'faint, hollow and sepulchral'.

Either way, these distorted voices distinguish their speakers from all that is familiar. A troubled spirit in Arthur Conan Doyle's novel *The Land of Mist*, published in 1926, makes 'such a sound as neither of the auditors had heard before – a guttural, rasping, croaking utterance, indescribably menacing'. When modern directors of *Hamlet* want to create ghosts their audiences can be expected to experience as uncanny, they commonly follow one of these options. In Franco Zeffirelli's film version of 1990, Paul Scofield's voice is thin and papery, faint in contrast to the vigorous action hero, Mel Gibson's Hamlet. Conversely, the Ghost in Laurence Olivier's classic version of 1948 makes a hoarse sound that resounds against his raised visor. In Kenneth Branagh's film, made in 1996, the Ghost delivers his message in a sonorous whisper.

Voices matter. In their materiality, they link us to others at a visceral level. The physiology of the sound has its impact alongside what is said, or perhaps in defiance of it. Pitch, resonance, inflection all elicit a response. The deaf may sense percussion – and sign language has its own physicality. For all of us speech crosses the line between sensation on the one hand and the transmission of meanings on the other. To hearing people, a specific voice can thrill – or irritate – even when its utterance is banal. Conversely, the most honeyed words in a voice that has no charms for us may fail to persuade.

What about the figure that walked the stage of the Globe in 1601? We can't be sure. At least two traditions meet in

Shakespeare's theatre. On the one hand, the classical heritage was familiar from Virgil's role in the education system and also from Seneca's tragedies. These plays, in print in English translation since the 1560s, exerted a major influence on the emerging early modern genre. Greek and Roman ghosts were traditionally high-pitched, faint and attenuated. Lucian's Menippus, who visited the underworld, reiterates a commonplace of his time when he refers to the thin voices of the shades. On the other hand, the suspense that builds in *Hamlet* with the terror of the guards owes more to tales told by the fireside in the long winter evenings. These vernacular spectres were more likely to speak in a hollow tone. Which line of descent prevailed with Old Hamlet?

Perhaps the play itself provides a hint when Horatio invokes the classical past. Among the omens that heralded the murder of Julius Caesar, he says, were the revenants that conventionally appear before a death: 'the sheeted dead / Did squeak and gibber in the Roman streets'. Did Old Hamlet squeak? Surely not. Even with every concession to historical difference, a squeaking king is hard to imagine. He certainly doesn't gibber. Instead, his manner is magisterial, perhaps excessive, but grand.

Shakespeare's *Julius Caesar* tells the same story about the Roman dead, but with a slightly different nuance. There the ghosts 'shriek and squeal'. The efforts of early modern stage spectres to reproduce the classical tradition were easily satirised. In the anonymous *Warning for Fair Women*, printed in 1599, when we think Shakespeare's *Hamlet* was in the making, a figure personifying Comedy derides revenge plays. There, she complains, 'a filthy whining ghost' comes in 'screaming' like a half-slaughtered pig. Thomas Lodge had already ridiculed the old, pre-Shakespearean *Hamlet* for its shrill ghost 'which cried . . . like an oyster-wife'. Did Shakespeare's dead king shriek at his son?

Perhaps not, if he was defined by the fireside tradition. According to the local tales collected by the monk of Byland Abbey, the spirit that appeared at the dead of night to Snowball the tailor was said to have formed its words in its intestines and not with its tongue. This sounds more like Conan Doyle's rasping ghost. In the same collection, Robert of Boltby came out of his grave to speak from his entrails, as if from an empty jar. Reginald Scot, discussing in 1584 the biblical case of the ghost of Samuel summoned by the witch of Endor, concluded that the whole thing was faked. The ghost Saul imagined he heard was the witch herself, speaking in a 'counterfeit hollow voice', 'as it were from the bottom of her belly'. This was evidently how believers expected ghosts to communicate.

Although Scot's argument annoyed promoters of the witch craze, who wanted to find the witch in league with the devil, his suggestion went down well with other Protestants, eager to disavow what appeared to be biblical support for the existence of ghosts. In 1601, the year we think *Hamlet* was first performed, two clerics repeated Scot's argument. Although the Bible itself has nothing to say about the way the dead Samuel spoke, they reiterated that the witch must have fooled Saul by speaking in the bottom of her belly with a counterfeit hollow voice.

Such sepulchral accents seem to have prevailed in popular culture. The Rev. Edmund Jones records two instances in eighteenth-century Wales: a dead woman's tone was hollow, 'different from a human voice'; a woman who had hanged herself spoke with a dry sound, 'as if it were out of a drum'.

Resemblance

If Shakespeare himself played the Ghost, did he counterfeit a hollow voice, as if formed in his entrails? Like so much of what actually took place on the Shakespearean stage, the sound the Ghost makes remains conjectural. We do know, however, what he says. Indeed, once he has isolated his chosen addressee, the Ghost breaks his silence to talk at length and in detail. Compared with the prince's own speech rhythms, his verse is archaic, befitting an earlier time and place. This manner of speaking confirms the sense of distance. At the same time, the Ghost appeals to a paradoxical familiarity: 'If thou did'st ever thy dear father love – '.

Ghosts that speak, however strangely, are to a degree like us, even while they differ from us in the way that all interlocutors do. Speech in a shared language establishes a similarity between speakers. But it also registers a distinction: the sound issues from someone else, which is one of the reasons why hearing our own speech played back to us can feel uncanny. The voice that comes from outside our heads sounds unfamiliar, other than we think we are. Speaking ghosts both differ from and resemble us.

Medieval ghosts offered their seers a mirror, they claimed, returning as the predecessors of their living witnesses but presenting, at the same time, a glimpse of their future fate: I came before you; I was once like you; you will in due course be like me. A mirror image is at once the same, identical, a reflection of the self, and distinct, reversed, outside the self, in the glass. Old Hamlet addresses the prince from the position of the young man's own inevitable destiny, as well as the dead father he mourns, back from the past. Mirrored in the Ghost who shares his name, Hamlet confronts his own estranged resemblance in a premonition of his afterlife. The deadly mission the Ghost confers on the prince brings that afterlife closer.

Speaking beings necessarily live in the awareness of death, even if to name it is not the same as to know it for what it is. And our own mirror image proves unstable, comes and goes, changes, flickers and vanishes – like a ghost. The looking glass can puncture narcissism. 'I am you' is the message delivered by a succession of spectral figures to anyone who will listen in Peter Straub's *Ghost Story*, published in 1979. Human beings are always incipient ghosts. That, Straub's Don Wanderley reflects, is 'one of the unhappy perceptions at the center of every ghost story'.

Afterlives

What do ghosts reveal about life after death? Old Hamlet could unfold a tale of his prison-house – but that is forbidden. All he can say is that he is doomed to walk by night and fast in fires by day. This Ghost comes from a conventional afterlife of bodily pain, but the world of the dead is subject to history. Already in a new generation the prince hesitates to characterise the next world in the approved, traditional way. Instead, he calls it an undiscovered country, unmapped, beyond the reach of travellers' tales.

Listening to ghosts reveals that the condition of the dead was changing. The old netherworlds of Chapter 2 were gradually giving way to a different kind of suffering, more mental than physical. It is not entirely clear which of these most characterises the condition of William Clarkson. Is he happy in the next world, asks his former landlord. 'I am lost', the ghost replies, '– lost, – lost, for ever!' Are we to think of him as simply adrift, or in hell? He brings with him a strong smell of sulphur.

Twentieth-century stories decisively psychologise the world of the dead: what imprisons modern ghosts is more likely to be an attachment that also constrained them in life. Marjorie Bowen's story of 'The Crown Derby Plate' shows the dead Sir James Sewell tied to his house and garden by the imperative to guard his precious possessions from the living. In May Sinclair's story 'Where their Fire is not Quenched' in 1922, Harriott Leigh repeatedly finds her dead self in the hotel room where she formerly conducted a liaison with a married man. The door is locked, just as it was in their lifetime, but now to keep the lovers in, not others out. Here the tormenting flames that afflicted Old Hamlet have become the pyre of a dead romance endlessly rekindled. In life, Harriott's illicit passion for Oscar Wade soon turned sour and, bored and irritated by one another, they broke off the relationship. But after death they refind each other again and again. Harriott runs away to escape him but all the people she seeks to take his place soon morph into the same hated figure.

The prison walls close in gradually but irresistibly. To Harriott's despair, Oscar's ghost tells her:

> In the last death we shall be shut up in this room, behind that locked door, together. We shall lie here together, for ever and ever, joined so fast that even God can't put us asunder. We shall be one flesh and one spirit, one sin repeated for ever, and ever; spirit loathing flesh, flesh loathing spirit; you and I loathing each other.

This is hell in its modern form. Susie Salmon, by contrast, is in heaven – and yet the distinction is not immediately clear. In 2002 Alice Sebold's *The Lovely Bones* sends its innocent 14-year-old to a subjective afterlife where all individual, personal desires are instantly met. Even so, Susie is dissatisfied, constricted: the teenager's imagination cannot encompass much to wish for that doesn't rapidly bore her.

What they want

'Ask them politely what they want', the hotel manager's granny recommended. When the dead seek contact, it may be because they want the living to act on their behalf. 'Say why is this? . . . What should we do?' is Hamlet first question. Ghosts make claims on those they leave behind. Patroclus and Elpenor want their comrades to give them proper funeral rites; Adam de Lond's sister urges her brother to restore her family's property; Robert of Boltby seeks a priest who can give him absolution; old Hamlet impels his son to avenge him. Any number of revenants require others to execute their wills or acknowledge the rightful heir. Still more want the authorities to bring murderers to book.

Spectres police this world when they impel the living to do the right thing. Such ghosts have high moral standards but phantoms can also mislead, reinforcing irrational impulses, legitimating cruelty. If Catherine haunts Heathcliff, she does not make him kinder. Listening to ghosts can authorise error. The jealousy first wives arouse may in practice be unfounded; conversely, femmes fatales and demon lovers encourage false hopes; apparitions can generate madness.

They incite self-destruction when they claim ghost-seers for the afterlife. This is their mission in Straub's *Ghost Story*, where they return to debilitate and consume the living. There they bring despair. Jack Torrance's descent into psychosis in Stanley Kubrick's film *The Shining* in 1980 is also precipitated by the troubled dead. They impel him to 'correct' his innocent wife and children, only in order to embrace him as one of themselves.

Impotence

Because in most cases they need others to act for them, ghosts are commonly ineffectual, to the point where they are reduced to making contact through intermediaries. In *Hamlet* the Ghost first appears to the guards and Horatio. Adam de Lond's sister, who wants the land restored to her husband and children, does not in the first instance appeal directly to her brother to return the deeds. Instead, she approaches him through old William Trower. James Haddock, who wants his widow's new husband to do right by his son, tackles Francis Taverner, not the stepfather himself. Madam Bendish delivers her message about her son's lost estate to an aged gentlewoman, not the heir. In a modern twist on the old tales, the wife in Ambrose Bierce's tale of 'The Moonlit Road' tells her version of the story through a medium. Sam Wheat in the film *Ghost* can approach the living Molly only through the psychic, Oda Mae Brown.

Like the mother of Odysseus, like Patroclus and Creüsa, the disembodied dead cannot embrace the living. Modernity, however, has found a solution to this problem. Sam shares a last dance with his living lover when Oda Mae Brown lends him her body. In an episode that I personally find more uncomfortable than uncanny, Susie Salmon in *The Lovely Bones* borrows a living body in order to experience sex with her boyfriend. When Edgar Allan Poe's 'Ligeia' puts forward such an option, the story finds it appalling, as does Audrey Niffenegger's novel *Her Fearful Symmetry*, but perhaps the difference is that Susie's appropriation of the body is temporary. In any case, it seems that some of us have come to terms with this option.

The ultimate instance of spectral impotence has to be the movie *Ghosts Can't Do It*, directed by John Derek in 1989. This deservedly obscure work offers in addition a cameo appearance by Donald J. Trump. The main protagonist is an extremely voluble spectre, who repeatedly appears on screen, with flames flickering round his image, to give instructions to his young widow on how to arrange her future. As a ghost, he can't make love to his grieving wife but it turns out that a young Italian fisherman, who is vigorously alive, would very much like to do so. (Trump, playing himself, hints that he too is available but no one takes up his offer.) The ghost urges his widow to kill the fisherman so that, as her dead husband, he can occupy the youthful body and return to full sexual capability. In the event, murder is averted: the fisherman is drowned, entangled in his own net. The widow resuscitates him for long enough to permit the dead husband to appropriate his flesh and on these terms the couple live happily ever after.

Communication

Dying takes away the only life we know for sure and so represents the ultimate deprivation. Ghost stories, it's worth remembering, are relayed by the living, and what the troubled dead want can reveal much about what a culture values and most fears to lose. While sex rates highly now, it was not always the most pressing concern. Instead, a desire to retain control drove earlier ghosts to pursue earthly justice or revenge, restitution of property or the execution of their wills. None of these imperatives has gone away in current ghost stories but the most commonly recurring desire of the dead in Western culture is neither sex nor power but communication. Is it possible that this, the exchange of meanings, is what in the end seems most precious? And is it a perennial object of desire because, in death as in life, mutual understanding is so rarely complete?

The dead want their stories to be heard. Old Hamlet impels the prince to listen to his, the poisoning recounted in vivid detail. As soon as Homer's ghosts recover their consciousness, they tell Odysseus their histories. Their stories, recounted by Dante's ghosts, make up the main material of *The Divine Comedy*. Liza Hempstock in Neil Gaiman's delightful *Graveyard Book* of 2008 tells the living Bod how she lived and died. Now what she wants is a memorial: 'It's not much to ask, is it? Something to mark my grave. I'm just down there, see? With nothing but nettles to show where I rest.'

Headstones outline a life. Henry Wadsworth Longfellow's 'Skeleton in Armor', duly asked to say what he wants, declares that he seeks a teller who will do full justice to his unsung tale, a poet to recount how he fought, loved and died:

> I was a Viking old!
> My deeds, though manifold,
> No Skald in song has told,
>   No Saga taught thee!
> Take heed, that in thy verse
> Thou dost the tale rehearse,
> Else dread a dead man's curse;
>   For this I sought thee.

Heroic or not, ghosts commonly want the past put on record.

The dead linger among the scenes of their former lives, or walk to revisit their houses. But it is hard to gain entrance. Old Hamlet is first seen on the outer walls of the castle. In the fourteenth century, Robert of Boltby's ghost would stand at doors and windows, perhaps waiting for someone to come out and attend to his wants. Mr Lockwood dreams Catherine's ghost appears at the window of Wuthering Heights: 'Let me in – let me in', she begs. 'I'm come home, I'd lost my way on the moor.' Peter Quint in *The Turn of the Screw* of 1898 stares in through the windows at Bly. By night, says the ghost in 'The Moonlit Road', 'we can venture from our places of concealment to move unafraid about our old homes, to look in at the windows, even to enter and gaze upon your faces as you sleep'.

Modern afterlives are characterised above all by solitude. In 'The Moonlit Road', the dead cower and shiver 'in an altered world', where Bierce's ghost feels desperately alone. There is no companionship among the dead, she complains; they are invisible even to themselves and one another, 'forlorn in lonely places'. 'I am so lonely and so unhappy', Oscar Wilde's Canterville ghost grumbles in 1887. 'Do come in', urges Sir James Sewell in his haunted house, 'I get so few people to visit me, I'm really very lonely.'

The desire for dialogue is pressing: perhaps identity depends on continued access to language. Psychics complain that they are besieged by the voices of the dead, clamouring for attention. When Oda Mae Brown discovers that she has genuine second sight, she finds herself surrounded by spectral figures wanting to make contact. The dead yearn for conversation with their loved ones, complains the ghost in 'The Moonlit Road'. Sometimes language is the last thing to fall away. As they lose sensation, the dying in Graham Joyce's *The Silent Land* in 2010 can recover tastes and smells, as long as they describe them to one another in words.

Point of view

Traditional ghost stories centre on the point of view of the haunted, dwelling on their reactions, whether frightened, guilty or resolute in the face of their unearthly visitants. But when ghosts make themselves intelligible, they tell their stories from their own perspective, inviting sympathy. 'Alas, poor ghost', Hamlet responds.

But 'Pity me not', the spectre replies firmly. Instead, 'lend thy serious hearing / To what I shall unfold'. The tale he goes on to deliver is not an impartial rehearsal of the facts but an impassioned account of an unnatural murder: 'O horrible! O horrible! Most horrible!' For the moment the audience's attention is directed to the anguish of the dead father before it reverts to the outrage of the living son.

Hamlet himself does his thinking in soliloquies that are spoken directly to the audience. The psychological realism that emerged in the eighteenth century encouraged storytellers to incorporate into the narrative the unspoken thoughts of the characters. While this convention permitted detailed treatment of the effects of apparitions on their seers, in due course it also allowed the reader access to the minds of ghosts themselves. In 2009 Audrey Niffenegger's *Her Fearful Symmetry* includes the thoughts and feelings of the phantom Elspeth Noblin: 'She had no idea how much time had passed. Had she died months ago? Years? . . . Even the sunlight seemed dimmer than she remembered; the windows needed washing'. *'I've got to get more serious about this'*, Elspeth reflects, as she determines to make her presence felt. *'I wish I'd read more ghost stories, I'm sure I could have found some tips in Le Fanu and that lot.'*

The inner speech of this well-read ghost establishes a relationship with the sophisticated reader, who recognises the reference to previous ghost stories. The film *Ghost* tells its story from the perspective of the dead Sam, inviting viewers to share his anxiety. The residents of the cemetery carry most of the narrative in *Lincoln in the Bardo* and readers learn to inhabit their world.

If the point of view of the ghost familiarises mortality, it also emphasises the privations death imposes. Wilde's 'Canterville Ghost' dwells on the spectre's frustration that the down-to-earth Americans remain undismayed by his wide repertoire of grisly appearances. And comedy does not erase the pathos. 'For three hundred years I have not slept, and I am so tired', Wilde's phantom complains. 'Poor, poor ghost', responds the living Virginia.

Spectral storytellers

It was inevitable that the longing to tell their stories would in due course turn ghosts themselves into first-person narrators. 'My name was Salmon, like the fish', begins *The Lovely Bones*, 'first name, Susie. I was fourteen when I was murdered on December 6, 1973'. In 'Since I Died', by Elizabeth Stuart Phelps in 1873, the narrator has returned to explain to a loved one the experience of death. Olivia Howard Dunbar's 'The Shell of Sense', another American short story from 1908, records in the first person the jealousy of a dead wife who learns that her widowed husband and her sister have silently been in love all along.

Since then, any number of spectral narrators have told their own tales, among them, Muriel Spark's Needle in 'The Portobello Road' from the 1950s. There the storyteller confides: 'I must explain that I departed this life nearly five years ago. But', she adds, 'I did not altogether depart this world. There were . . . odd things still to be done . . .' Among the odd things is the haunting of her unconvicted killer, a task she carries out on a weekly basis, greeting him with a breezy, 'Hallo, George!' until he finally loses his mind. George had strangled her and left her body concealed in a haystack.

Spark characteristically sets proverbial meanings in motion. The narrator is known as Needle because she had once found a needle in a haystack. George had photographed the moment. Now she herself becomes the found object. Reporting the discovery of her body, the newspapers announce triumphantly, '"Needle" is found: in a haystack!' Spark's story refers back repeatedly to

George's picture: his three young friends in high summer, lolling on the heap of dried grass. The unwritten proverbial implication is that they were making – or at least enjoying – hay while the sun shone. And, although the ghost is jaunty, the story ends with the irony of the murderer brooding over his snapshot, to see its subjects 'reflecting fearlessly in the face of George's camera the glory of the world, as if it would never pass'.

When she describes her life, Needle is bound, like all realist first-person storytellers, to events where she herself is present. After death, however, she becomes all-knowing, privy to the exchanges of others and even what goes on in their heads. Susie Salmon, too, can witness everything that passes between those she has left behind, all their actions, each inner thought, including her murderer's.

We might find this idea of ghostly surveillance unnerving, justifying the reaction of the policewoman in *Ghost*: 'I'll never undress again.' But, of course, these stories are fiction and the omniscience of the ghost-storytellers a device for telling the tale. But in that case, aren't all conventional third-person narrators with access to the truth of the story in one sense spectral too – invisible presences in the world of their characters, writing from a vantage point outside earthly time and space? In that sense, at least, first-person ghost stories represent the type of all narrative.

The missed encounter

We never learn for certain whether Old Hamlet is a spirit of health or a goblin damned. Although telling their stories goes some way to bring the dead closer, diminishing their eeriness, communication frequently remains incomplete. Whether they exist in the world or in the minds of their seers, ghosts come from outside what we know. They speak from an inaccessible place and their demands may be correspondingly obscure.

Something in their stories often remains unstated or unmastered. An element is withheld from readers or audiences: the motive for returning, the secrets of the prison-house or the details of the disclosure. Robert of Boltby tells the priest what he has done but we are not privy to his confession. Some say he was an accessory to murder . . . The crimes of the old woman who haunts 'The Tapestried Chamber' are too horrible to recite. Is the man in Henry James's 'The Friends of the Friends' visited by a ghost or an illicit lover? Ghosts that preserve an element of mystery retain a corresponding degree of otherness: what is not explained remains uncanny.

Command of the narrative does not guarantee communication with the characters. In 'Since I Died' the dead narrator cannot make contact with her living addressee. 'Is there an alphabet between us?' she asks plaintively. But there is none, because 'the riddle which no soul has read steps between your substance and my soul'. Cornelia Comer's 'Little Gray Ghost' in 1912 has cried out to be audible: '"I have tried so hard to make them hear . . . so hard and so long!"' 'All I could do was talk, but no one on Earth could hear me', laments Susie Salmon.

Ghosts that come to comfort may succeed only in generating fear. The dead wife in 'The Moonlit Road' does not know who killed her: she walks to comfort her husband in his bereavement, to 'restore the broken bonds between the living and the dead'. He does know – and turns away from her in guilt and terror. Miscommunication, always a hazard, is deepened between the inhabitants of different worlds. In W. F. Harvey's tale of 1909, 'Across the Moors', a governess obliged to walk over moorland by night is particularly fearful of Redman's Cross, where a murder took place some years since. She is reassured, however, when a clergyman catches up with her and offers to escort her back. On the way, he will tell her his story, he says: 'I don't want you to be frightened when you are out on the moors again.'

But it turns out that he was the victim of the murder at Redman's Cross. The ghost's purpose is to convince her that death is nothing to be afraid of; his own was painless and happy. The dead man's perspective is not admissible to the living governess, however. Now terrified of the teller, she flees to the light and humanity of the house. Understanding the story, the governess refuses the proffered message and the bonds between the two realms stay broken.

The eeriest voices make sounds that have no meaning at all but come from somewhere outside the reach of the intellect, resonating, once again, with our own wordless prehistory. Predictably, M. R. James is the specialist here. The thin moan that comes from room 'Number 13' is the all more disturbing because it defies any pattern we might recognise: the tale calls it song, but 'Of words or tune there was no question.' According to 'A Neighbour's Landmark', published in 1924, something appalling walks in what was once Betton Wood. This figure is glimpsed in tattered garments, stretching out her arms before her with a piercing cry. The unearthly shriek that is heard at dusk in Betton Wood is 'hideous . . . beyond anything I had heard or have heard since, but I could read no emotion in it, and doubted if I could read any intelligence'.

If stories recounted by all-knowing ghosts share the characteristics of conventional third-person narrative, perhaps listening to ghosts echoes the difficulties of reading. Emissaries from the past, and from the world of the dead, ghosts inhabit an alien realm. It comes as no surprise, then, when they speak in a way that is not fully intelligible, communicating imperfectly, if at all.

In those instances, the exchange of meanings remains incomplete or uncompleted.

We can't count on stories for full communication, either, and not only because so many of the authors concerned are dead themselves. In the first place, however insistent the voice of the author in the story, he or she is not present to direct our attention. And in the second, narratives always belong to history, however recent or immediate: the past is the conventional tense of storytelling. Stories depict a world that does not belong to us, however closely it resembles our own.

More important, the words of a story cannot determine how it should be read. The tale may leave to conjecture the very thing we most want to know. Playgoers cannot be sure how far to trust the Ghost in *Hamlet* and critics continue to disagree radically about how best to interpret Shakespeare's tragedy. Moreover, we are not bound to accept a work at face value: with the virtue of hindsight, we may know something the teller doesn't, like the guilty husband on the moonlit road, and choose to read against the grain of the narrative. We may refuse the work's designs on us, as the governess rejects the ghost's intentions in 'Across the Moors'. Like M. R. James's narrators, we may fail to find intelligible sense at a crucial point of the narrative. If all storytellers play a spectral part in their narratives, reading stories, like listening to ghosts, always risks a missed encounter.

TEN

Strange to Tell

Horrid pleasures

Ghost stories sell. Susan Hill, Toni Morrison, Alice Sebold, Peter Ackroyd and George Saunders would all testify to that. In the nineteenth century Washington Irving and Charles Dickens could count on it. Amelia Edwards, Charlotte Riddell and Mary E. Wilkins Freeman all sold well in their day. Earlier, Horace Walpole must have been astonished by the success of *The Castle of Otranto* and the Gothic tradition it initiated.

Before long, Jane Austen's innocent Catherine Morland would declare herself engrossed in Ann Radcliffe's *The Mysteries of Udolpho*. 'I should like to spend my whole life in reading it', she tells her friend Isabella in *Northanger Abbey*, begun in the 1790s at the height of Radcliffe's fame. 'I assure you', she continues, 'if it had not been to meet you, I would not have come away from it for all the world.' Naivety is not a requirement, however: in the first years of the twentieth century, M. R. James gratified an expectant audience with ghost stories at King's College, Cambridge. From the 1960s, Christmas partygoers called on Robertson Davies for a new ghost story every year at Massey College in the University of Toronto.

Modernity has not done away with the genre's hold, especially on Hollywood. *The Shining*, *Ghost* and *The Sixth Sense* all triumphed at the box office. Centuries earlier, medieval preachers terrified

Figure 9 An old wife spins a yarn in Daniel Maclise's *A Winter Night's Tale*, c. 1867

their audiences with records of revenants. And, if tradition is to be believed, old wives held listeners spellbound by the hearth with tales of the uncanny. *A Winter Night's Tale*, painted in about 1867, shows grown-ups and children intent on an elderly storyteller, while one girl is moved by what she hears to look anxiously into the darkness beyond the circle. The old woman's shadow is ominously magnified by the firelight.

This cottage is prosperously furnished and the family well dressed, but the picture shows one curtain drawn back to reveal a skeletal tree against the dying light. The cold out of doors deepens the comfort within – and the sense of threat. A fitting context for a ghost story, maintains the narrator of Sheridan Le Fanu's 'An Account of Some Strange Disturbances in Aungier Street' is 'a good after-dinner fire on a winter's evening, with a cold wind rising and wailing outside, and all snug and cosy within'. The sense of well-being indoors depends on the keening of the gale beyond the walls, invoked for the reader only to be held (just) at bay.

In what might easily be read as a commentary on Maclise's painting, the narrator of E. Nesbit's 'The Shadow' explains that

> the stillness of the manor house, broken only by the whisper of the wind in the cedar branches, and the scraping of their harsh fingers against our windowpanes, had pricked us to such luxurious confidence in our surroundings of bright chintz and candle-flame and firelight, that we had dared to talk of ghosts.

Maclise's bare tree, Le Fanu's moaning wind and Nesbit's harsh fingers warn us not to count on the security they throw into relief. If the warmth inside encourages indulgence, the storyteller is careful to define the chill that is kept out – or perhaps lured across the threshold by the topic of conversation. Practised readers of ghost stories relish the knowledge that whispers and wailing will find their way in, to bring worse than bad weather.

Henry James's *The Turn of the Screw* also opens with a group round the fire, 'breathless' from a story about an apparition in an old house much like the one they are in now. These listeners are eager for another unnerving tale, just as soon as Douglas can lay hands on the manuscript, their desire only intensified by his promise that the subject matter is 'horrible'. Jane Austen's Isabella delights Catherine with a list of Gothic novels still to be read. 'But are they all horrid?' Catherine asks; 'are you sure they are all horrid?'

Etymologically, *horrid* means fearsome. Why do readers, listeners and viewers want to be frightened in this way? What is the enduring appeal of terror? I have suggested that ghost stories give shadowy substance to hopes and fears that elude exact definition. But part of the reason why we are drawn to ghost stories (if we are) must also lie in the telling: the economy of folk narrative and ballad, or the calculated build-up of suspense in the well-crafted tale, and in each case the depiction of a vulnerability we are invited to share from a place of safety, indoors, by a hearth, real or metaphorical. Ghost stories raise a shiver by propelling us from the familiar into the unknown as firelight gives way to the shadows beyond. One minute, events conform to the patterns of everyday reality; the next, they defy the norms of logic and the laws of nature, so that we find ourselves in a world where anything could happen.

Changing conventions

Or almost anything. In practice, the unknown gradually accumulates its own repeated patterns, varying with time and place. Icelandic revenants are corporeal, larger than life and violent; they menace the halls and farms they have known; the solution is to dismember or dispose of their bodies. Medieval ghosts commonly appear out of doors, in graveyards, or on the moors as lone travellers approach blind summits. Twilight, eclipses, sudden mist and fog are their settings. In popular lore, marginal or empty spaces are haunted, among them crossroads, causeways, forests, ships, disused mine workings. The Arctic encourages apparitions.

When in the ballads the dead return to their home, there may at first be nothing outlandish to differentiate them. The only distinguishing feature of three sons of the Wife of Usher's Well is their hats made of the birch-wood that grows at the gates of paradise. Like the Wife, lovers often refuse to acknowledge the finality – and the physicality – of death. But appearances prove deceptive. The ghost of Clerk Saunders comes back in a Scots ballad to visit

Margaret. But she cannot grasp her loss. If you are my true love, Margaret demands, where are the bonny arms that used to hold me? 'By worms they're eaten, in mools [mould] they're rotten', he replies.

In the Middle Ages this form of the macabre prevails. A spectral knight reports on his place in the grave, where 'the wee worms are my bedfellows, / And cold clay is my sheets'. The Three Dead decompose; Guenevere's dead mother is hung about with toads and serpents. A close encounter with a ghost heralds sickness and death: 'If you have one kiss of my clay-cold lips, / Your time will not be long.'

Familiarity breeds contempt, however. Once the unknown world acquires its own predictability, the uncanny loses its hold, and each epoch renews the genre accordingly. Senecan ghosts in the sixteenth century dwell on the torments of the next world from a location outside time and space. Old Hamlet, by contrast, returns to a specific place. Although he alludes to his painful purgation, he now walks the margins of his former castle. The Gothic brings the dead back indoors, to lodge them among ancient buildings, themselves survivals of a lost past. Along with battlements, Gothic ghosts haunt long-closed, tapestried chambers or decaying underground passages now out of use. They opt for dusty attics and damp cellars; their time is midnight, when the firelight has faded and the candle burned down. And their missions are ancestral, the revelation of family secrets and the exposure of crime.

In the first instance, these recognised conventions serve to heighten suspense. A suit of armour hangs menacingly on the wall of Daniel Maclise's cottage. Vaulted chambers or ramparts in the moonlight guarantee terrors to come; arrival at an old mansion by night promises unearthly encounters. But with repetition the same textual ingredients begin to lose their edge, provoking indifference or, worse, laughter, as horror topples into absurdity. Comic ghosts parody the existing conventions. Oscar Wilde's Canterville phantom hopes a metal-clad spectre will terrify the Americans, evoking Longfellow's 'Skeleton in Armor'. But the Canterville ghost falls over in his effort to get into his old suit of mail and vanishes ruefully to console himself with recollections of past horrid triumphs.

Wilde's story was published in 1891. By this time, the dead had branched out. Ghosts now haunted city streets and town houses, as well as medieval buildings and country mansions. But the boundary between inside and outside retained its menace: the face at the window, a turning door handle, the figure in the garden seen from the house or an unexplained movement inside it perceived from the street.

Modern spectres are mostly disembodied. Sam Wheat has to learn to kick a can. Invisible in the mirror, free to float at will while people pass through her, the dead Elspeth Noblin puzzles over what it is to be a wraith: *'What am I made of . . . ?'* she wonders in Audrey Niffenegger's *Her Fearful Symmetry*. Some kind of energy, perhaps. She finds she can make light bulbs glow. Perhaps she is a collection of electrical impulses? Elspeth gradually learns to propel very small things; in the hope of alleviating her loneliness, she manages to assemble particles of dust into a message on a polished surface. She is bitterly cold; moreover, she drains the vitality of those who come in contact with her, as if she absorbs their being to reinforce her own. But the minimal energy she comprises can be turned into matter: Elspeth is eventually able to make herself perceptible to some, if only faintly.

Disclaimers

Her Fearful Symmetry does not pretend to be anything but fiction. Not requiring belief, ghost stories need not encourage it either. Instead, whether accredited or invented, or hovering uncertainly

between the two, they often build into the telling an acknowledgement of their own improbability. Seventeenth-century printed
tales of the supernatural are commonly promoted on that basis:
Strange and Wonderful [astonishing] *News from*' Lincolnshire or
Exeter; *A Most Strange and Dreadful Apparition* in London in
1680. At the same time, however tall the tale, we are incited to
suspend incredulity: *Strange and True News from Long-Ally in
Moorfields* in 1661; *A Strange, but True, Relation . . . from the West
of England* in 1678.

Unlikely and also trustworthy. Later avowedly fictional tales
will exploit this ambiguity. By candlelight in E. Nesbit's 'The
Shadow', the young women round the fire begin to talk of ghosts
'in which we did not believe one bit'. In 1865 Dickens subtitles
'The Trial for Murder', 'To be taken with a grain of salt' – and
then goes on to tell the tale of a haunting made persuasive by the
accumulation of circumstantial detail. 'Although every word of
this story is as true as despair, I do not expect people to believe it',
concedes the narrator of Nesbit's 'Man-Size in Marble' in 1893.
Alternatively, 'I don't believe in the supernatural, but just the
same I wouldn't live in Shawley Rectory', begins Ruth Rendell's
storyteller in 1972.

Perhaps outright credibility is at odds with the uncanny. Cultural
historians who claim that ghosts mingled comfortably with the
living in the Middle Ages would do well to look again at stories
from the time. The Enlightenment paradoxically saved the uncanny
when it banished the paranormal to self-proclaimed fiction. And
perhaps reason too easily dismissed the Gothic as naive. Any opposition between fact and fiction may be unduly simple. Although
realist fiction is the invention of the writer, we conventionally claim
that it offers insights into human behaviour, emotions, relationships. Ghost stories, I have suggested, illuminate evolving cultural

values, along with grief or guilt, and our varying relation to our own mortality.

Conventional criticism, wedded to realism, often dismisses the genre as childish, mere diversion, nothing but fantasy. And yet conventional criticism does not always have the last word. Anxiety finds a basis in the indefinite and unresolved. Disclaimers, registering an ambivalence towards the events they describe, allow ghost stories to resonate with readers in a special way – by embracing uncertainty.

Distance

Confirmation withheld sustains the uncanny. Relegation of the tale to a bygone age offers one way of deflecting the question of truth. 'In the time of Richard II', begins the Byland monk in the following reign, or 'old people relate . . .' After recounting the tale of the clerical revenant James Tankerlay, he pleads in extenuation, 'it is only what I have heard from my elders'. M. R. James confirms that 'a slight haze of distance is desirable' in a ghost story. '"Thirty years ago", "Not long before the war", are very proper openings', he adds.

The precise arithmetic does not matter, except to imply the passing of time, preferably at least a decade or two. 'Twenty years . . . have gone by since that night', affirms the narrator of 'The Phantom Coach', by Amelia B. Edwards in 1864. In 1861 Le Fanu places 'Ultor de Lacy' in a receding past. The narrator heard the story forty years before, from an old woman who had conversed with one of the participants, of a haunting that took place in the wake of the Jacobite rebellion of 1745, in revenge for an execution for treason in 1601. The events recorded in the eighteenth-century *Castle of Otranto* must have happened, the Preface declares, between 1095 and 1243. Written down in the thirteenth century, the Icelandic sagas depict a time two centuries earlier. *Hamlet* is set long ago and far away in tenth-century Denmark, *Macbeth* in medieval Scotland.

In these instances the stories reanimate a world perceived as lost or forgotten. Gothic fiction opts for what it imagines as the more credulous Middle Ages in preference to the Enlightened present. Alternatively, its overgrown churchyards and ivy-clad ruins show current civilisation in the process of reverting to nature. Ghost stories propose a departure from the terrain mapped by an urbane culture into an unrecovered past, or an irrecoverable prehistory.

Such a world, as shadowy as the figures that haunt it, is necessarily disclaimed even while it is embraced. How else, in culture, can stories, as elements of culture, legitimately put pressure on the boundaries of culture itself? Storytellers hesitate, apologise, make concessions to disbelief. 'It is said' or 'It is alleged' begins the Byland monk around 1400. In other words, the story is someone else's. Pliny has heard the tale of the haunted house from an unidentified friend. Schiller's *The Ghost-Seer* is recounted by Count O – but it concerns the Prince of –, while the German editor intervenes in square brackets to explain or abridge. Sometimes, an old book purchased in a strange town tells an extraordinary tale, which is here reprinted. A distant heir to the property finds a memoir, which he offers as a curiosity. A psychiatrist prises the story out of his patient, who delivers it haltingly. Or a publisher has been sent a typescript; he is not sure whether he believes it; readers must judge.

Unreliability

Framing of this kind places the story beyond immediate reach, as do the multiple voices on which the narrative may depend. Three distinct perspectives make up Ambrose Bierce's story of 'The Moonlit Road'. Because a rich range of voices composes George

Saunders's prize-winning *Lincoln in the Bardo*, the story has no single point of origin. If, on the one hand, there is no solitary witness whose credibility can be called into question, there is on the other no master-narrative, no unitary, authoritative account of what occurs. The more individual reports it includes, the harder the events are to verify. Reality as the story defines it slips through the reader's fingers; ghosts, appropriately enough, change their shapes, begin to flicker or dissolve at the edges. In *Wuthering Heights* is Heathcliff genuinely haunted or sadly deluded? The answer, if there is one, may lie buried in layers of storytelling, Lockwood's enclosing Nelly's, which incorporates Isabella's and Zillah's.

Single storytellers may be no more reliable, however. Edgar Allan Poe is a master here. Does the corpse emit a sound anywhere outside the head of the killer in 'The Tell-Tale Heart'? Does the dead Ligeia genuinely take possession of her successor's corpse, or is her return from the grave confined to her husband's opium dream? 'Ligeia' leaves the options open. The storyteller in Maclise's painting of *A Winter Night's Tale* is spinning a yarn. An old wives' tale is by definition not to be trusted. The conventional attribution of ghost stories to women, while it places marginal figures at the centre of attention for once, also has the paradoxical effect of reminding their audiences not to ascribe much authority to what they say.

Even so, Maclise's listeners are rapt – or anxious: old wives evidently tell a good tale. Elizabeth Gaskell's Old Nurse and Emily Brontë's Nelly Dean perpetuate the tradition in fiction. How far, then, can we trust the narrators who feature inside the story? Does Nelly make full sense of all she sees and hears? But whether she does or not, we share Lockwood's desire to hear more. Are we to see Sir Walter Scott's Wandering Willie, a blind fiddler and another accomplished storyteller, as a reliable source? Perhaps Steenie only dreamed he tracked the ghost of Sir Robert Redgauntlet down to hell to secure evidence that he had paid the rent; on the other hand, Steenie has the receipt, dated after the death of the signatory. However unreliable, Wandering Willie's tale lingers in the mind, threatening to eclipse the rest of *Redgauntlet*, published in 1824.

In these instances, we have no sure way of knowing who is inventing what. In 1838 Nathaniel Hawthorne claims to owe the grim story of 'Howe's Masquerade' to a regular at the bar of The Old Province House. The teller, in turn, says he heard it 'at one or two removes' from an eye-witness. 'But', comments the author of the frame narrative,

> this derivation, together with the lapse of time, must have afforded opportunities for many variations of the narrative; so that, despairing of literal and absolute truth, I have not scrupled to make such further changes as seemed conducive to the reader's profit and delight.

In this Preface, Hawthorne seems to discredit his own tale – and yet he tells it. Perhaps the ultimate ironist is Washington Irving. The conclusion of 'The Adventure of a German Student' cuts the ground away neatly: 'I had it from the best authority. The student told it to me himself. I saw him in a madhouse in Paris.'

Distrust in these cases does not amount to dismissal. Two distinct and perhaps contrasting pleasures are available here. Sophisticated as we readers are, we doubt whether we should take the uncanny tale seriously. Even so, we read on (if we do).

The unresolved

Perhaps evasion is the point. 'We chose to live in your dreams and imaginations', insists the timeless and shape-shifting femme fatale of Peter Straub's *Ghost Story*. This novel links haunting with fiction, films as well as writing. In this instance it is not clear which causes which. The denouement begins while *Night of the Living Dead* is screened to an empty cinema. 'Although we live in your fantasies', the voice continues, 'we are implacably real.' This ghost and her avatars come to solicit a desire that propels people towards death.

What is it like to be dead? No one knows for sure and reason says we can't know. But rational scepticism doesn't eliminate curiosity, conjecture, speculation. People have their ideas: eternal bliss, perpetual torment, a twilit half-life, non-existence. But, when it comes to our personal fate, all these are notoriously difficult to picture in convincing detail, including – or perhaps especially – nothingness. If, as I indicated in Chapter 1, Freud is right to say that, when we attempt to imagine our own death we see ourselves present as spectators, we already envisage ourselves as our own phantoms. 'I am you', reiterate Straub's revenants. In this sense, ghosts are our own future, but in a condition it is hard to visualise. No wonder, then, that when we try to do so, what presents itself to the mind's eye is unclear, shifting, unreliable. The shadows that inhabit the world of the dead hover uncertainly on the borders of actuality.

Moviegoers were to encounter ghost stories of a wholly new kind in *The Sixth Sense*, directed by M. Night Shyamalan in 1999, and *The Others*, directed by Alejandro Amenábar in 2001. The first of these brilliantly plays with expectation, turning viewers into detectives by supplying clues that become evident only in retrospect. Young Cole Sear [seer?] is surrounded by people who don't know they're dead. On the other hand, the main point of view is not Cole's. *The Sixth Sense* eventually reaches closure when Malcolm Crowe comes to terms with his state. But who exactly in *The Others* are the others? This more disturbing film leaves it harder to relinquish the range of perspectives the screenplay has built up: there are ghosts who know they're dead, ghosts who think they're alive, and living psychics who pester them with questions they can't answer. Do the living ever attain the independence the plot projects for them? Who, in the end, does the house belong to?

Is this what it means to be dead? That issue goes to the heart of the lure of the genre for viewers and readers. Beyond – or perhaps in – the hope of being frightened in safety lies a desire to penetrate a world closed to mortal knowledge. Ghost stories give names to the unnameable – in stories, *as* stories and, ultimately, as fiction.

Behind the opening titles of *The Others* are drawings from a Victorian children's storybook. The pictures foreshadow the events the film depicts. As she teaches her own children, Grace makes them rehearse four traditional accounts of the next life: hell where the damned go; purgatory; Abraham's bosom, where the just go; and limbo. These destinies, merited in this life, Grace insists, last for ever, '*for ever*'. The older child tells her little brother a different tale: ghosts go about in white sheets and carry chains; they come out at night. 'Now Anne, why do you make up such stories?' asks Mrs Mills, the housekeeper. She reads them in books, Anne replies; her mother tells her not to credit them, but she expects the children to believe the stories written in the Bible. Meanwhile, the film itself tells yet another story – of the next life as an attenuated version of this one, the dead and the living side-by-side *for ever*, sometimes aware of one another, sometimes not. 'Where are we?'

asks Grace. No one answers. The ghost of Lydia, who died of tuberculosis, asked the same question – and never spoke again.

Equivocation

In other words, the uncanny evades answers. That is why ghosts belong in stories and, supremely, in stories that keep secrets. Perhaps no ghost story keeps them better than *The Turn of the Screw*. Here is an account of Henry James's short novel, first published in 1898. An unnamed narrator tells of a group gathered by the fire in an old house to hear ghost stories on Christmas Eve. Douglas, this narrator records, promises another tale, still more horrible, but they will have to wait while he sends away for the work. In due course, after giving the beginning of the story in his own words, Douglas reads out by the hearth a manuscript that has been locked away for forty years, the memoir of a woman, dead these twenty years, concerning the hauntings that took place in her youth in an old country house. Douglas himself has since died, it turns out, but not before giving the document to the narrator, whose transcription we are now reading.

Despite the illusion of specificity, the exact chronology is elusive. At all events, no one living claims direct access to anyone who features in the main story. Postponed, framed by a series of narrators and repeated transmissions, distanced by time and dispossessed by successive deaths, the main tale, when we finally reach it, is told by an unnamed governess placed at Bly by their uncle in sole control of two seemingly innocent children, Miles and Flora. It concerns her struggle to protect the boy and girl from the ghosts of the previous governess and her valet-lover.

In other words, the memoir records a contest between a virtuous young heroine and the evil dead. But perhaps not. Alternatively, the account of the hauntings can be read as a story of puritanical repression. A country vicar's daughter, appointed as a governess at the age of twenty by a man she falls in love with, takes on two little wards he does not want. Anxious to please him but with no one but the housekeeper to turn to in a remote and unfamiliar country house, the governess is overwhelmed by an impossible convergence of desire and moral responsibility. As the victim of her own fearful, sexualised imaginings, she ends by harming the children she sets out to save.

Henry James's story supports either interpretation. Although in the hope of mastering the story's enigmas, post-Freudian criticism has longed to uncover what remains obscure, nothing entitles us, most critics now concede, to rule out definitively either account. *The Turn of the Screw* equivocates – and revels in its own undecidability. On the one hand, the governess gives a sufficiently detailed account of Peter Quint's appearance to convince the housekeeper that she has seen his ghost. On the other, she bases her conviction that the children are in contact with the dead on their apparent blindness to the apparitions. What she takes for calculated efforts to allay her suspicions could equally represent genuine innocence.

The mystery of Bly is not ancestral but where in the present the children stand. They are beautiful, charming, docile pupils but little Miles has been expelled from his school without explanation and the enigma of his dismissal threads its way through the narrative. Miles himself is vague: 'Well – I said things.' Mrs Grose, the housekeeper, is finally convinced that Flora is possessed by evil: 'On my honour, Miss, she says things – !'

We never learn quite what things. And if Miles and Flora keep their counsel, the story too evades full disclosure. Will the memoir be a romance, the group gathered to hear it by the fire want to know, and who is it that the governess is in love with? Surely the story will tell. '"The story *won't* tell," said Douglas; "not in any literal, vulgar way."' In the event, there is a complex relay of love stories – between Douglas and the narrator in the present of the frame story, Douglas and the governess in the past, the governess and her employer, and before them between her predecessor Miss Jessel and Peter Quint. Not one of them is told in a literal, vulgar way: each is indicated by hints, uncompleted sentences, or unspecified conjectures.

Where so little is finally confirmed, the work has left room for speculation. Is the governess also in love with the dead Peter Quint, as some have suggested? Or with the 10-year-old Miles, as the film version implies? In a narrative so reticent, much that concerns the ghosts also remains unsaid, indicated only by negative prefixes. The governess's impressions are 'unspeakable'; Miss Jessel's gaze at Flora is 'indescribable'; what the children know remains 'unnamed and untouched'; the governess believes they see 'things terrible and unguessable'.

Her memoir finally reaches a moment of reckoning but not of revelation. No detective is available to assemble the evidence and name the offenders. Perhaps, then, the governess is deluded. What is the balance here between illusion and reality? The first apparition fulfils, with whatever irony, a romantic wish. Strolling alone in the grounds, the governess muses on the possibility that she might meet 'the master' at the turn of a path, to see him smile approval of her work, with 'the kind light of it, in his handsome face'. To her astonishment, 'my imagination . . . turned real'. A second glance reveals not her employer, however, but the spectre of an evil double who wears his clothes, Peter Quint the valet, brash, womanising, intrusive, 'Too free with everyone', as Mrs Grose puts it. Is the dead Quint the antithesis of the children's absent uncle, or his similitude on a lower level of the social hierarchy?

Imagination is repeatedly juxtaposed with reality. As Flora conducts her round Bly, the governess encounters 'a castle of romance'. Perhaps, she reflects now, the building was no more than a storybook that had lulled her to dream? But the facts correct her at once: 'No, it was a big ugly antique but convenient house.' At the same time, the governess relives the anxieties of imaginary heroines, Emily St Aubert and Jane Eyre: 'Was there a "secret" at Bly – a mystery of Udolpho, or an insane, an unmentionable relative kept in unsuspected confinement?'

These references also allow us to see her as a latter-day Catherine Morland, at the mercy of expectations shaped by Gothic fiction. Catherine, another parson's daughter transported to a big country house, searches the depths of a cabinet at Northanger Abbey for a record of false imprisonment but, in Jane Austen's romantic comedy, the precious manuscript turns out to be nothing but a laundry list. Are the governess's phantoms no more than the effects of a power struggle, on the one hand her wish to constitute the sole influence on the minds of her charges, on the other the legitimate desire of Miles and Flora to free themselves now and then from her relentless surveillance?

The story never settles the question whether the children's virtue is a masquerade or the good behaviour it appears to be. When they 'say things', are they taken over by corrupt presences, or innocently repeating a coarse vocabulary once learnt from the living Peter Quint? Or not so innocently? Do the spectral figures genuinely reanimate a formative and dangerous influence? In support of the ghosts, it might be said that, apart from his choosing to appear on the battlements like Old Hamlet, the valet is an unusual apparition. With his hard stare, he comes across as too cocksure for a wraith, a profligate resembling, in the governess's account, an actor in stolen garb. As a spectre, this figure has, to my knowledge, no conventional history, no obvious source in romance to encourage a predisposition to see him. Conversely, Miss Jessel typifies the tragic fallen woman in black of the Gothic imagination, exactly the kind of phantom a susceptible governess who has read ghost stories might expect to see.

Uncertainty only deepens when the governess herself insists that she is not imagining what the children know: her denial has the paradoxical effect of invoking exactly that possibility. She understands how her moral rigour looks from the outside and names it as 'my obsession'. Should she summon the children's uncle, as Mrs Grose urges?

> 'By writing to him that his house is poisoned and his little nephew and niece mad?'
>   'But if they *are*, Miss?'
>   'If I am myself, you mean?'

Was Miles just what he seemed after all, she wonders in the final chapter. The possibility 'was for the instant confounding and bottomless, for if he *were* innocent, what then on earth was *I*?'

The *Turn of the Screw* brings into sharp focus the question that so many ghost stories refuse to resolve, even within the fiction. Is the supernatural real or imaginary? Do ghosts belong in the world or in our heads? Perhaps for that reason, Henry James's short novel has had, appropriately enough, an extensive afterlife. Next to *Hamlet*, *The Turn of the Screw* must be the most reworked, rewritten and recreated of all ghost stories. Among the best-known examples, it has been an opera, a play, a film, a TV drama; the plot has resurfaced in other novels and at least one short story.

And then there are variations on the theme. Does *The Woman in Black* find a starting point in Miss Jessel's story?

The greatest tribute to the novel must be *The Others*, which, on a hint from the original, turns the story of Bly inside out. In *The Turn of the Screw* the governess calls the ghosts 'the others, the outsiders' but, facing Miss Jessel at her table in the schoolroom, she feels for a moment that she is the intruder. Amenábar's film shows a woman in a big, isolated house, missing her husband, and threatened by intruders her two children take for ghosts. Grace struggles to instil in the children a rigorous sense of the difference between good and evil. Alone and isolated from the village, she finds herself in the hands of the housekeeper, this time one who knows when she doesn't, and who recognises that 'there isn't always an answer for everything'.

There isn't. And, in consequence, a story as unresolved as *The Turn of the Screw* seems to provoke retelling. Peter Straub's knowing *Ghost Story* incorporates a tale recounted by Sears James to an audience that includes his colleague Ricky Hawthorne. In his youth, when James spent time as a village schoolmaster, he did his best to rescue two strange children from their incestuous dead brother, whose ghost is 'free', unrestrained, self-assured. But in what seems like the moment of victory, the teacher finds he holds the boy dead in his arms, a 'dispossessed' body – although here this is not the last we hear of the dead child. That James and Hawthorne, partners in business and themselves storytellers, share their last names with famous authors of ghost stories is no accident in this playful but properly horrid novel. In due course, their law firm will be sold off and renamed Hawthorne, James and Whittacker. '"Pity his name isn't Poe," Ricky said.'

In another acknowledgement of the fascination exerted by *The Turn of the Screw*, in 1992 Joyce Carol Oates inventively rewrites

the tale from the perspective of the ghosts in 'The Accursed
Inhabitants of the House of Bly'. There Quint and Miss Jessel live
on as ghouls in the cellar. They compete with the new governess
for the allegiance of the children in a desire to recreate in death
the perverse but loving 'family' the four made up in life. While it
respects some of the details given in the original, this is an independent work of fiction, whatever the temptation to take it for the
exposition of a paedophile 'truth' Victorian propriety forbids
Henry James to divulge.

Silence

What seem like more faithful remakes respond variously to the
questions posed by the original. Jack Clayton's film *The Innocents*
in 1961 removes the distancing frame. In other respects it preserves
the ambiguity of the novel but not the reticence, showing distinctly
sinister children in the care of a seriously overwrought governess.
While the unknown is powerfully indicated by shadows and a
menacing darkness at the edge of the picture frame, much that
the novel leaves to the reader is spelt out in the movie. The BBC
TV film of *The Turn of the Screw* in 2009 is still more explicit,
conscientiously filling in the many blanks in the original, including the living Quint's past sexual predations. Here the governess's
reluctant confession to a doctor in the asylum frames the story. A.
N. Wilson's *A Jealous Ghost* in 2005 modernises the tale to centre
on a psychotic nanny. The more comprehensive the exposition, it
seems to me, the more banal the effect. As Walter Scott knew,
monstrosity in full view rarely lives up to expectation. Instead, the
uncanny expands in the silent spaces between utterances.

The Turn of the Screw is full of such silences. There is plenty of
chatter with the children, and a succession of confidences

exchanged with Mrs Grose. But in neither instance does the governess meet her match. She herself is doubly restrained by the instructions of her employer and the injunction of those who blamed old wives, nursemaids and servants for inculcating superstition in the young. She must not write to the master; she must not be the first to name the ghosts to Miles and Flora. Instead, as her conviction deepens of an unholy contract between the children and their late minders, stretches of conversational territory are prohibited: 'Forbidden ground was the question of the return of the dead in general and of whatever, in especial, might survive, for memory, of the friends little children had lost.'

This propriety checks the governess in her conversations with the children: '*They* have the manners to be silent'; how can she, in a position of trust, be so crude as to say what she fears? The children, in turn, say nothing in her presence on the topics that most concern her: they never mention the past. Miles charmingly covers over the spaces she offers him to explain his expulsion. Flora, on the other side of the lake, smiles as Mrs Grose and the governess approach, 'but it was all done in a silence by this time flagrantly ominous'. Beneath her exchanges with her charges, the governess intuits 'prodigious palpable hushes' that signal the presence of the ghosts. For her, the sustained muteness of the children is proof of their supernatural communion; for the reader it remains a place of doubt.

Silences pervade the story. These ghosts do not speak to say what they want. When the governess encounters Quint on the stairs:

It was the dead silence of our long gaze at such close quarters that gave the whole horror, huge as it was, its only note of the unnatural. If I had met a murderer in such a place and at such an hour we still at least would have spoken. Something would have passed, in life, between us.

But silence is not merely imposed by others. The governess repeatedly insists on the gap between her experiences and her capacity to represent them. They are 'unspeakable', 'indescribable'. Recurring negatives remove them from the world we know. 'I scarce know how to put my story into words that shall be a credible picture of my state of mind'; 'I try for terms!'; 'I can't express what followed'; 'I scarce know what to call it'. Gaps the remakes treat as instances of Victorian inhibition might instead be seen as wily storytelling. Henry James himself thought so. In the Preface to the New York edition in 1908, he commented on the importance of leaving it to the reader to supply the nature of the threat. Make the reader *'think the evil . . . and you are released from weak specifications'*.

Naming sets out to master the uncanny. What is specified or spoken begins in the process to be brought inside the realm of the intelligible, classifiable and knowable. This was the project of the Society for Psychical Research, which subjected reported sightings to independent analysis. Henry James took an interest in its work but, as he pointed out in his Preface, investigated phantoms barely did anything worth recording; they had become so inert, he complained, as to prompt surprise that they had the energy to appear at all. The more a case was respectably accredited, 'the less it seemed of a nature to rouse the dear old sacred terror'. Fictional ghost stories, by contrast, are able to penetrate another terrain, pressing at or beyond the limits of the language that enables us to know and so master the world.

At Bly the master is absent, releasing the old sacred terror. If spectres include us in another dimension, projections of our own imagined future, where are they drawn from? Not actuality, presumably. Instead, ghost stories are set in the unmastered margins of what we take for reality. Those margins may be tenanted by impulses looking for a name; they were once populated – in our own forgotten past, our prehistory – by figures that loomed over us in infancy when no names were available. Mysterious, inexplicable, such shapes represented objects of dependency, attachment or dread. The infant world is full of comings and goings, occurrences and sensations at that stage unaccountable, perplexing, to varying degrees strange.

Infans, the Latin source of our own term, means *belonging to a child* but also *mute*: the infant has no access to speech. We don't lay down conscious memories for the future until names for them distinguish people, places, events. But the obscure world leaves its traces, ready to return under pressure – in loss and grief, in loneliness, remorse, the fear of death, or simply in the dark.

Some experiences lie beyond words. Although language displaces infancy, it does not wholly dispel it: even while the named world comes into differentiated view, the old, populated muteness lives on in the depths of anxiety, its shapes ready to be systematised in cultures as spirits, demons, aliens – or the revenants they actually are. Henry James's ghosts are not the product of systems. On the contrary, as Virginia Woolf proposes, 'They have their origin within us.' 'They are present', she continues, 'whenever the significant overflows our powers of expressing it; whenever the ordinary appears ringed by the strange.' His apparitions are made up of 'the baffling things that are left over, the frightening ones that persist'.

Oddly enough, it is not the ghosts themselves that most alarm the governess. She confronts them heroically, faces them in what she perceives as a battle for the good. The ghosts she sees are not unnameable: she identifies them and describes their appearance in detail. What exceeds her grasp remains a less distinct presence, their place in the lives of the children. Are Miles and Flora troubled, possessed by the troubled dead? This is the mystery she longs to elucidate, or subject to the intelligibility of utterance. What do the children know of the ghosts?

But what do we any of us, believers or sceptics, know of ghosts? What is there to know? The world of the dead, of prehistory, or of unacknowledged desires and fears, is by definition unknown – but menacing. The children, themselves barely past infancy at 8 and 10, do not, perhaps cannot, name a trouble their governess herself 'dared but half-phrase'. How could they, when whatever it is emanates from a place she herself hesitates to approach, 'depths and possibilities that I lacked resolution to sound'.

If ghost stories maintain their appeal in our own sceptical, scientific times, when answers to all imaginable questions are readily available from Google at the stroke of a key, perhaps that is because tall tales continue to give tenuous substance to hopes and fears that remain outside the reach of science or psychology. Unmastered by orthodoxy and just beyond the reach of language, nameless shapes may return, taking on wavering identities, at times of anxiety or distress. And ghost stories place such shape-shifting revenants where they can come and go at will, in the changing shadows created by flickering firelight, indefinite, equivocal, uncertain, in every sense uncanny.

CODA

Figurative Phantoms

Metaphorical ghosts

Whether or not ghosts exist, the English language seems unable to manage without them. *The ghost of a smile flitted across her face. Leaves stirred in the ghost of a breeze. Residents fled, leaving a ghost town. Racism survives in Britain as the ghost of empire.* A *ghost ship* is derelict, found floating without its crew. At a *ghost station* the trains never stop and no passengers wait on the platforms. *Ghost patients* remain on the list after death, as do *ghost voters.* Certain armies are said to include *ghost soldiers*, their names preserved in the records and their salaries pocketed by the officers. *Ghost populations* survive only in their DNA, leaving no other remains. Shakespeare's plays include *ghost characters*, named in the cast lists but allotted no entrances or speeches. Facebook acknowledges that some of its users are *social media ghosts.*

'I don't stand a ghost of a chance with you', Bing Crosby and after him Frank Sinatra, Billie Holiday, Ella Fitzgerald and others lament. These recurring metaphors point to what is there and not there: named but not present, located but not lived in, a trace, a residue, incomplete. Are so many phantasmic allusions no more than old habits of speech that have lost their force, leftovers not quite yet driven out by reason and science? Are metaphorical ghosts themselves residual, in other words, inert remainders of belief that once had currency? After all, the souls that once walked on Hallowe'en are now impersonated for fun by children. As a child myself at the fair, when I paid for a trip on the ghost train, I counted on terrifying moans and screams and the sudden luminous appearance, as we rounded a corner, of a skeleton or a shrouded corpse. There was no doubt in my 8-year-old mind that these creatures were devised for my entertainment: the journey brought fiction to life in three dimensions and was the more thrilling for that.

By analogy, figurative phantoms are widely invoked as a way of naming fictions in order to dismiss fallacies. Walter Skeat coined the compound *ghost-word* to name terms that had no real existence. Delivering the Presidential Address to the Philological Society in 1886, he was scathing (in a suitably academic way) about gullible scholars who had given elaborate explanations of the origins of old 'words' that were in practice no more than the result of scribal errors and poor transcription. Meanwhile, the metaphoric spectre of communism that Karl Marx perceived haunting Europe in 1848 was merely, he insisted, the effect of a horror story, to be replaced by the truth explained in the *Communist Manifesto* that followed this opening assertion. Attacking mind–body dualism in 1949, Gilbert Ryle admitted to a 'deliberate abusiveness' when he described the prevailing belief that the mind was a distinct but shadowy counterpart of the body as 'the dogma of the Ghost in the Machine'. 'I hope', he continued, 'to prove that it is entirely false, and false not in detail but in principle. It is not merely an assemblage of particular mistakes. It is one big mistake.'

Although such phantom presences were evidently a byword for superstitious error, these instances ironically confirm that ghost metaphors retain an active role in the vocabulary of our debates. And, in the process, they may also allow for a more complex world, by challenging the familiar distinctions that define our knowledge. A phantom pregnancy is imagined and yet can have material effects on the body; a phantom limb arouses physical sensations in the amputee. Skeat's rejected ghost-words were a product of ignorance but they appeared, large as life, on the printed page. The spectre of communism that haunted Europe in 1848 might have been a figment of the imagination, but communism still carries a threat today, and with more justification in the light of the totalitarianism subsequently practised in its name. When in 1967 Arthur Koestler set out to attack the behaviourism he ascribed to Gilbert Ryle among others, he appropriated the philosopher's image as the title of his own book *The Ghost in the Machine*, revaluing the phrase to affirm an updated consciousness.

Making ghosts

Since other metaphorical ghosts commemorate what once existed, figurative phantoms have a value for conservationists. Current civilisation is busy creating ghosts, as species disappear when their habitats are taken over or despoiled. A vanishing creature haunts a late work, something of a curiosity, by William Burroughs. His short novel *Ghost of Chance*, published in 1991, is set in Madagascar, where isolation from the continent of Africa has allowed a separate evolution. Many of the island's species are unique, including the lemur, called after the Latin word for *ghost* because that is the meaning of its Madagascan name. In about 1700, the aptly named Captain Mission, whose colonial regime confirms the native taboo on killing these sad-eyed, vegetarian primates, sets off into the interior in quest of a larger species, known to the indigenous population as Big Ghost.

Under the influence of the local mind-altering substance, what Captain Mission finds in this terrain without predators, cut off from the mainland, is the biological Garden of Lost Chances, full of 'creatures too trusting and gentle to survive'. On the other side of the water that protects the island from the continent, Homo Sap [*sic*], born in time and wedded to killing, follows his characteristic path of destruction. When Homo Sap's artillery takes over Madagascar, Captain Mission's settlement is destroyed and his own special ghost/lemur dies in his arms.

Burroughs here remakes the myth of paradise lost to reveal actuality. Hunting and deforestation between them have endangered the lemurs of Madagascar to the point where they may genuinely end as the ghosts their name designates. Homo Sap differs from the ghosts thanks above all to language, or what Burroughs calls the representation of a thing 'by *something it is not*'. Language makes a division in the organism, like the channel that separates Madagascar from the mainland. 'One side of the rift drifted into enchanted timeless innocence. The other moved inexorably toward language, time, tool use, weapon use, war, exploitation, and slavery.'

The past in the present

The ghosts of Madagascar are disarming emanations from a world prior to culture. Other apparitions allow the past a role in the present when they bring to light what is unacknowledged by the community. Unlike the lemurs, products, indeed, of Homo Sap, such spectres may instead be deadly – and shocking. Among the works that propelled drama into modernity, Ibsen's play *Ghosts* unsettled its own epoch in the 1880s. Scandinavia refused to stage it; the London reviewers were outraged by the subject matter.

There are no ghosts in *Ghosts*, and yet, as the title might lead us to expect, metaphorical spectres structure the play. When he seeks the joy of life in opposition to the prevailing morality, Osvald reincarnates his dead father; in trying to make love to Regina, he repeats his father's sexual adventure in his own home. And his mother shivers, 'Ghosts! The couple in the conservatory – walking again.' This theatrical moment at the end of Act 1, coming so soon after Mrs Alving's revelation to Pastor Manders that her husband impregnated their housemaid, is surely as eerie as any literal haunting depicted in Gothic fiction.

Ibsen was not happy with the English title: his own Norwegian name for the play, *Gengangere*, means *those who walk again*. The dead Captain Alving returns in the person of his son, and the syphilis he bequeaths to Osvald represents the penalty for the sins of the father, paid in the next generation. But the revenants of the title go deeper: they also represent the old joyless pieties that haunt the living, the inexorable demands of duty that impelled Mrs Alving to marry without love and Pastor Manders to drive her back to her husband when she appealed to him for refuge.

Theology, convention, orthodox morality all deplete people's vitality. The ghosts of such adherences 'are not actually alive in us, but they're rooted there all the same, and we can't rid ourselves of them', Mrs Alving complains. Like Skeat's and Ryle's, Ibsen's revenants are aligned with superstition and falsehood, and yet, as Osvald succumbs to the ravages of his inherited disease, the tragedy seems much less confident that scepticism will dispatch the ghosts. The past, in other words, is not easily cast off in the present.

Figurative phantoms, resurrected after their own lifetime, register the play's acknowledgement that history continues to trouble the current moment. When Jacques Derrida wrote a book in response to the fall of the Berlin Wall, he called it *Specters of*

Marx and the metaphorical spirits Derrida raises lie at the heart of his argument. If Marx's own writing is based on the view that the ghosts of religion and ideology could be dispelled by the truth, our own epoch, older and wiser, knows it's not that straightforward. As Mrs Alving recognises, anachronistic allegiances are still rooted in the living. The major conflicts of the modern world are justified, if not generated, by religious and ideological identifications, the ghost of an archaic ethnicity among them.

Derrida's point in *Specters of Marx* is that reason has not so far succeeded in exorcising error. Instead, the material consequences of dogma promoted as certainty have had the effect of making us doubt how far the denunciation of falsehood takes us. Derrida did not live to encounter the circulation on social media of conspiracy theories, 'fake news' and 'alternative facts' but he might have pointed out that dismissing these figments does not do away with their political purchase. Perhaps what drives convictions is not truth alone, or the rational beliefs of a sovereign consciousness, but hopes and fears, desires and anxieties that are not so easily named. These imperatives, at once insubstantial and powerful, press to find form in regret for a lost purity, or in the ghosts of inherited cultures and nationalities.

Marx, who understood the relationship between the prevailing values and the existing social order, knew that thinking was subject to unacknowledged pressures. For that reason, we should engage with the radical spirit of Marxism, Derrida urges, as a way of confronting what he calls the 'arch-ghost'. This, the greatest surviving illusion, is the sovereignty of consciousness itself, master of all it surveys, the essence of Man as the unconstrained hero of Enlightenment humanism. We cannot, Derrida argues, in the light of Copernicus, Darwin, Freud and Marx himself, continue to believe in this privileged, uniquely created and divinely endowed figure, a phantom among phantoms. Nor, in view of our humanist intellectual heritage, can we simply lay it to rest either, as if by calling it a fiction we dissipate its power. Past ideas, hovering uncertainly between life and death, return to exert an influence in the present. 'They are always *there*, specters, even if they do not exist' – there to be questioned, learned from, challenged, as well as called to account.

The ghosts of past injustices, too, demand a reckoning. Avery Gordon's *Ghostly Matters: Haunting and the Sociological Imagination* was first published in 1997, three years after the English translation of *Specters of Marx*. Its declared aim is to understand the dispossession and exploitation, exclusion and violence rendered invisible by a consumer culture that apparently puts everything on display. Social science aspires to present impartial fact but is haunted, Gordon argues, by stories the statistics repress. Unsystematically, unscientifically, ghosts of the disappeared or the enslaved return to animate historic injustice with the effect of unsettling current complacency. Phantoms not only register what happened; they also make claims on us, inciting action now.

Atrocities – empire, slavery, genocide – apparently done with, seek reparations. Ancestral identities – black, white, Islamic – demand their due. But, in my view, it does not follow that we should let the dead capture us for themselves in a politics of nostalgia or victimhood. 'Just ask them what they want.' And bear in mind in the process that, while some ghosts seek remedy or proper commemoration, others demand blood, lives, the next generation. Recognition is one thing, revenge quite another. The dead are entitled to tell their stories, but it can be just as crucial to create a different future in the light of the information they bring.

Ghosts and storytelling

If death makes a hole in the real that can't quite be filled by the practices of memorialisation, apparitions in their very ghostliness represent an absence, I have suggested: not so much the return of what is gone as its irretrievable loss. Philip Roth's novel *Exit Ghost* in 2007 invokes the metaphor to show its central figure living what, quoting Keats, he calls 'a posthumous existence'. At 71, the reclusive novelist Nathan Zuckerman, now impotent, incontinent and uncertain of his memory, returns to New York to make one last bid for energy, 'to recover something lost'. Painfully for Nathan, the sexual drive persists in a body not now equipped to satisfy it. As a self-confessed 'revenant' in the city, he is drawn back into the turmoil of life above all by a young woman who exerts what he describes as 'a huge gravitational pull on the ghost of my desire'.

Exit Ghost puzzles over the contest between the insubstantial nature of organic existence, an unsatisfying, incomplete actuality, and the imaginative power of fiction. Is there consolation to be found in art? That is a question many authors have asked. Nathan himself eventually retreats to finish the script of his play, *He and She*, in which She yields to His overtures. Only in fiction is anything possible. Where else can we 'wish what is into what is not', except on the page? The writer finds 'the imaginary "She" vividly at the centre of her character as the actual "she" will never be'.

It seems, then, as if storytelling compensates for the living death that is Nathan's old age, offering another kind of apparition instead. 'For some very, very few that amplification, evolving uncertainly out of nothing, constitutes their only assurance, and the unlived, the surmise, fully drawn in print on paper, is the life whose meaning comes to matter most.'

But the book does not end there. If the fictional *He and She* has the last word in Roth's novel, *its* last word is of a missed encounter. In the play She agrees to come to his hotel but He evades their meeting: '(*She's on her way and he leaves. Gone for good.*)' Exit ghost. Writing does not deliver gratification after all, or not, at least, at the thematic level: fiction is not, it seems, reducible to a form of wish-fulfilment. Instead, it too aligns itself with ghostliness, conjuring presences only to record a loss. The defining metaphor of *Exit Ghost* permits the novel to leave unresolved the question it repeatedly poses: where is *life* to be found? Its characters are all what the novel calls 'no-longers' or 'not-yets'. When, if ever, do shadows give way to substance, whether literal or figurative?

What is the relation between the human animal subject to decay and the language in which it both finds and loses its place? It seems that Roth hasn't much more confidence in the main tool of his trade than William Burroughs, who aligned it with death. In Hilary Mantel's memoir *Giving Up the Ghost*, published in 2003, language is just as inadequate to its task. Ghosts weave their way through the fabric of this autobiography as remainders from the past or alternative lives not lived. But they also figure as impressions that escape the definitions available. She is writing, Mantel maintains, 'in order to locate myself . . . in the narrow space between one letter and the next, between the lines where the ghosts of meaning are'. Meanings themselves lead a spectral life, glimpsed in language but not fully present there. They slip through the writer's embrace. The self that could be depicted in a memoir, if it could, exists only in language, but not in the language available to define it.

Ghost writers

Roth's *Exit Ghost* treats spectrality not as an archaic survival but as a current condition. In his earlier novel *The Ghost Writer* in 1979, Nathan, then an aspiring author of 23, sought legitimation from the famous writer E. I. Lonoff, long dead by the time of the later work but a phantom presence in it, even so. *The Ghost Writer* begins, like so many good ghost stories, by the fire, as a December dusk falls in a secluded old farmhouse. And yet there are no ghosts in *The Ghost Writer* either. The characters include a range of candidates for the title role (given as two words), among them the reclusive Lonoff, the writer who has outlived his own success. In addition, perhaps the title alludes to Anne Frank, the ideal Jewish writer who haunts Nathan's fantasies. Anne's *Diary* lives on as a masterpiece on condition that its author did not.

Anne Frank, the dead child writer, still has a story to tell, in contrast to the living Nathan, who wants to be a writer but, guilty of a safe, suburban childhood in Newark, NJ, can only *ghost* other people's tales. *The Ghost Writer* turns on the affinities between spectrality and writing: author as ghost, ghost as author, author as ghostwriter of other people's tales. In the process, it draws out all the paradoxes of the phrase itself. A ghostwriter (one word) is at once present in and absent from the finished work. As one who does the writing on behalf of another, he or she is no more than an invisible intermediary, while the story belongs to the central figure whose experiences are recounted. On the other hand, the ghostwriter is the maker of the piece of writing readers hold in their hands. In that sense, all novelists are ghostwriters, I have suggested, at once there in the writing and absent from the tale, drawing on imagination to tell stories that are not their own.

The Ghost, Robert Harris's best-seller of 2007, exploits this ambiguity in another key. Here the storyteller is a professional ghostwriter, hired to make readable the memoirs of an ex-prime minister who bears more than a passing resemblance to Tony Blair. So spectral does the ghostwriter appear to the other characters that he is never named: his role is too insubstantial, his appellation too immaterial for anyone to remember. At first, then, the distinction seems clear between the leader who shaped history itself and the ghostwriter paid to shape the record of that history. At the same time, we are to understand, the quality of the ghost's research and writing will make all the difference to the book's impact, and so to its influence on popular opinion. Harris's novel reflects repeatedly on the relationship between ghostwriter and named author. Whose book will it be? How far does the ghost himself create the memories he records? Who in the end makes history?

As he works, however, the narrator gets caught up in a plot to bring the former premier to trial for war crimes and, in the event, the central adventure he recounts turns out to be his own. Ironically, the anonymous ghostwriter becomes the hero of his own story. By the time his book is finally completed, the truth about the ex-prime minister cannot safely be told. As a result, the ghosted memoir, marketed as history, is in practice predominantly fictitious. Conversely, the ghostwriter's own tale, as he records it for us, is, we are to understand, true.

At the same time, of course, this anonymous narrator is imaginary and the book is a work of fiction. The ex-premier, however, is not entirely fictitious. Both characters inhabit a popular novel and yet the mystery of a British prime minister's unquestioning allegiance to a disastrous American policy in the Middle East belongs to history. Harris's book leaves us to ponder the possibility that writing creates much of what it appears to document and at the same time transcribes a good deal of what it seems to invent.

If so, where exactly is the boundary between fact and fiction, or between history as one kind of story and the novel as another? On the one hand, good history writing requires imagination. On the other, political thrillers may capture the misgivings of their own moment, while Philip Roth's fiction at once imagines and records a social and cultural history of contemporary America. The invocation of *ghostwriting* expands the options, suggesting that imaginative writing is able to cross back and forth between invention and reality, without collapsing the difference between them.

Haunted writing

While so many authors are ghostwriters, all writing is haunted by earlier written works, the textual past returning in the present. T. S. Eliot's poem *Four Quartets* makes a sudden appearance in *Exit Ghost* over half a century after its publication, at the moment when the now 71-year-old Nathan recognises traces of Lonoff:

> I thought, 'What! Are *you* here?' and then remembered where that very line appears in Eliot's 'Little Gidding', at the point where the poet, walking the streets before dawn, meets the 'compound ghost', who tells him what pain he will encounter.

In 'Little Gidding' the pain the spectre points to is old age and its ills, the theme of *Exit Ghost*. But the allusion also acknowledges a debt. In the eyes of its ghost, Eliot's poem finds 'the sudden look of some dead master', a poet, certainly, and, from the evidence, W. B. Yeats, who had died three years earlier. When Yeats also rages against old age in 'The Tower', he calls on the dead to testify, Homer among them. A ghost writer, then, summons a relay of ghostly writers here – from Nathan to his fictitious master, Lonoff, from Eliot to Yeats and, beyond him, through all dead writers back to Homer. Eliot's compound ghost, 'Both intimate and unidentifiable', as he calls it, surely represents the cumulative tradition that in Eliot's account makes individual talent possible. Last year's words are inevitably superseded by next year's, delivered in another voice but always in the light of what has gone before.

A ghost, however palpable, can never resume the identity of the living being. Dispossessed or disembodied, not the thing itself, the revenant is irreversibly changed. In that sense, isn't all writing haunted? While previous writings inhabit a work, they are at the same time no more than shadows of themselves, rewritten with an inevitable difference. Marx rewrites Hegel, Derrida reinterprets Marx. Burroughs reimagines the book of Genesis. Ibsen's *Ghosts* rewrites the sagas of his native Norway, where the ancestors come back from their graves, malign and larger than life, to spread death.

Ghosts also invokes the arch-fictional-ghost *Hamlet*, that earlier story of a dead father who revisits his son with fatal consequences, while his mother stands by helpless to intervene. Roth's *Ghost Writer*, meanwhile, also alludes to *Hamlet* in its story of Nathan's longing for a (literary) father who turns out to be living as the ghost of his former self. The title of *Exit Ghost* quotes *Hamlet* directly. This time the comparison is between Nathan and the old king, Shakespeare's own Ghost, powerless now to effect his will in his own person but reluctant to surrender control. *Hamlet* also forms the thread that binds the argument of *Specters of Marx*. Derrida's book begins and ends with quotations from the play and reverts at intervals to the story of a time that is radically 'out of joint'. In none of these cases has Shakespeare's play been laid to rest.

Evidently, the dead continue to walk, however anachronistically, in the twenty-first century, introducing a strangeness into what is familiar. Whether or not we believe in literal revenants, we cannot easily give up their figurative successors. These metaphorical spectres register a contemporary uncertainty, not only as a loss, an element missing from the completeness of the current moment, but also as an additional presence, a shadowy past still making itself felt now. Such ghosts menace the autonomy of the present, the self-sufficiency of consciousness and the independence of the writer's work. But they also challenge the rigid distinctions it is easy to take for granted between truth and error, fact and fiction.

In other words, figurative phantoms allow us to think beyond the limited categories orthodoxy takes for granted because they unsettle conventional ways of understanding the world. For better and worse, then, ghosts still haunt the exchange of meanings, even among those who suppose the troubled dead long since safely interred.

Sources

Readers eager to pursue the cultural history of ghosts, especially in pictures, would enjoy Susan Owens, *The Ghost: A Cultural History* (London: Tate Publishing, 2017). Lisa Morton, *Ghosts: A Haunted History* (London: Reaktion, 2015) is wider in scope and correspondingly less tightly focused.

Many of the short stories I cite are reprinted in the classic collections, among them *The Oxford Book of English Ghost Stories*, ed. Michael Cox and R. A. Gilbert (Oxford: Oxford University Press, 1986); *The Virago Book of Ghost Stories*, ed. Richard Dalby (London: Virago, 2006); *The Penguin Book of Ghost Stories*, ed. Michael Newton (London: Penguin, 2010); *Tales from the Dead of Night*, ed. Cecily Gayford (London: Profile, 2013). Numbers of the older tales can be read free online.

Where the stories are readily available or widely anthologised, I have not generally specified particular editions. In what follows, I name sources not already made clear in the course of the book. I give them in the order in which they appear in each chapter and have indexed them for ease of reference. For novels in print in different editions, I have given chapter references. Drama references may vary slightly from one edition to another.

PRELUDE. THE CHANGING SHAPES OF DOROTHY DINGLEY

Dorothy Dingley makes an early appearance in print in 'A Remarkable Passage of an Apparition. 1665', *The History of the Life and Adventures of Mr Duncan Campbell* (London: E. Curll, 1720), second edition, 20–33.

She reappears in C. S. Gilbert, *An Historical Survey of the County of Cornwall* (London: Longman, 1817), 2 vols, vol. 1, 115–19; Fortescue Hitchins [and Samuel Drew], *History of Cornwall* (Helston: William Penaluna, 1824), 2 vols, vol. 2, 548–51; T. M. Jarvis, *Accredited Ghost Stories* (London: J. Andrews, 1823), 218–35.

See Anna Eliza Bray, *Trelawny of Trelawne* (London: Longman, 1845); R. S. Hawker, 'The Bothathen Ghost', *All the Year Round* 17 (1867), 501–4.

For the folklore, see Christina Hole, *English Folklore* (London: Batsford), 162–3; K. M. Briggs, *A Dictionary of British Folk-Tales* (London: Routledge and Kegan Paul, 1970–1), 4 vols, Part B, vol. 1, 504–5; Robert Hunt, *Popular Romances of the West of England* (London: J. C. Hotten, 1865), 2 vols, vol. 1, 295–6.

Oliver Onions, 'The Woman in the Way', *Ghosts in Daylight* (London: Chapman and Hall, 1924), 209–36.

CHAPTER 1. A DEAD KING WALKS

Barabas mentions winter's tales in Christopher Marlowe, *The Jew of Malta*, 2.1.24–6. Banquo's ghost prompts Lady Macbeth's comments in William Shakespeare, *Macbeth*, 3.4. For Mamillius, see Shakespeare, *The Winter's Tale*, 2.1.25–30.

Brutus addresses the ghost in Shakespeare, *Julius Caesar*, 4.3.278. Puck reminds Oberon in Shakespeare, *A Midsummer Night's Dream*, 3.2.381–2.

For the props of the Rose theatre, see R. A. Foakes, ed., *Henslowe's Diary* (Cambridge: Cambridge University Press, 2002), 319.

Faustus fears hell in *Doctor Faustus* (1604 text), 5.2.121.

Augustine's views are translated in *Saint Austins Care for the Dead* (English Secret Press, 1636).

For the ghost stories of Gregory the Great, see Jacques Le Goff, *The Birth of Purgatory*, trans. Arthur Goldhammer (London: Scolar Press, 1984), 91–2.

The letter from the Bishop of Durham is reproduced in Matthew Parker, *Correspondence* (Cambridge: Cambridge University Press, 1853), 222.

Banquo makes his observation in *Macbeth*, 1.3.123–4.

I have quoted Rowe from David Farley-Hills, ed., *Critical Responses to Hamlet, 1600–1900* (New York: AMS Press, 1997-), 5 vols, vol. 1, 30–1.

I have quoted Sigmund Freud, 'The "Uncanny"', *Art and Literature*, ed. Albert Dickson (London: Penguin, 1990), 364 and 'Thoughts for the Times on War and Death', *Civilization, Society and Religion*, ed. Albert Dickson (London: Penguin, 1991), 77.

Claudio fears death in Shakespeare, *Measure for Measure*, 3.1.117–231.

CHAPTER 2. HAUNTED PASTS

For Patroclus, see Homer, *Iliad*, 16, 23. Elpenor's story is told in Homer, *Odyssey*, 10–11. Odysseus visits the underworld in *Odyssey*, 11.

Flavius Philostratus, *On Heroes*, is available online, trans. Ellen Bradshaw Aitken and Jennifer K. Berenson Maclean, http://chs.harvard.edu/CHS/article/display/3565#onheroestext

Creüsa features in Virgil, *Aeneid*, 2.721–94.

His mother threatens Nero in *Octavia*, lines 593–645.

The story of Euthymus is told by Pausanias in his *Guide to Greece*, trans. Peter Levi (Harmondsworth: Penguin, 1979), 2 vols, vol. 2, 6.6.7–11.

The child-eating revenant can be found in *Phlegon of Tralles' Book of Marvels*, ed. William Hansen (Exeter: University of Exeter Press, 1996), 28–32.

Saxo Grammaticus tells the story of Aswid and Asmund in Book 5 of *The History of the Danes.*

For the Drakelow peasants, see Geoffrey of Burton, *Life and Miracles of St Modwenna* (Oxford: Clarendon Press, 2002), 193–9.

William records his ghost stories in *The History of William of Newburgh*, trans. Joseph Stevenson, *The Church Historians of England*, vol. 4, Part 2 (London: Seeleys, 1856), 5.22–4.

The Byland tales were unearthed by M. R. James and published in Latin in *English Historical Review* 37 (1922), 413–22. The translations are mine but the most faithful English version I have found is by John Shinners in his *Medieval Popular Religion, 1000–1500: A Reader* (Peterborough, ON: Broadview Press, 2007), 252–61.

Socrates describes the afterlife in Plato, *Phaedo*, 113d–114d.

Virgil's underworld, including Palinurus, is in *Aeneid*, 6.

For the ghost stories of Caesarius of Heisterbach, see *The Dialogue on Miracles*, trans. H. von Scott and C. C. Swinton Bland (London: Routledge, 1929), Book 12.

Father Pilchard's story is recorded in *Unpublished Documents Relating to the English Martyrs* (London: Catholic Record Society, 1908), vol. 1, 288–9.

The witch of Endor summons the ghost in 1 Samuel. 28.

The Unquiet Grave is no. 78A in F. J. Child, *The English and Scottish Popular Ballads* (New York: Folklore Press, 1957).

The story of the corpse possessed by the devil is told in *John Mirk's Festial*, ed. Susan Powell (Oxford: Oxford University Press, 2011), 2 vols, vol. 2, 258.

For Elizabethan scepticism, see Reginald Scot, *The Discovery of Witchcraft* and *A Discourse upon Devils and Spirits* (London, 1584), esp. 532–3, 152–3; Thomas Nashe, *The Terrors of the Night*, in *Pierce Penniless, his Supplication to the Devil and Selected Writings*, ed. Stanley Wells (London: Edward Arnold, 1964), 141–75, esp. 169.

For the haunted house, see Pliny the Younger, *Letters and Panegyrics*, trans. Betty Radice (London: Heinemann, 1969), Letter 7.27.

CHAPTER 3. THE GHOST OF MRS MILTON

For the quotations from Shakespeare's *Richard III*, see 5.3.205–6, 231–2, 217–19.

The dream in Chaucer's *Book of the Duchess* begins at line 291.

I have quoted Henry More, *An Antidote against Atheism* (London, 1653), 41, 164 and *The Immortality of the Soul* (London, 1659), 289, 296.

James I pronounces on Sadducism in *Daemonologie* (Edinburgh; Edinburgh University Press, 1966), xi–xii, 55, and on ghosts, 61.

I have quoted Thomas Bromhall, *A Treatise of Specters* (London, 1658), sig. A2r. For the story of the restored wife, see 38 and for St Augustine, 335.

I have quoted Isaac Ambrose, *Ministration of, and Communion with Angels*, in *Complete Works of Isaac Ambrose* (London, 1674), 129; John Webster, *The Displaying of Supposed Witchcraft* (London, 1677), 311, 297; Joseph Glanvill, *Saducismus Triumphatus: Or, Full and Plain Evidence Concerning Witches and Apparitions* (London, 1681), Part 2, Preface, sig. Aa2, and, for the story of Mr Watkinson, 228–9.

John Aubrey tells the story of Mr T. M. in *Miscellanies* (London, 1696), 68–9.

For Thomas Hussey's ghost, see Richard Holland, *Cambridgeshire Ghost Stories* (Sheffield: Bradwell, 2013), 57.

I have quoted Daniel Defoe, *An Essay on the History and Reality of Apparitions*, ed. Kit Kincade (New York: AMS Press, 2007), 92–3.

CHAPTER 4. WOMEN IN WHITE

Jacob Postlethwaite stands in the corner in *The Woman in White*, Epoch 1, Chapter 12. Walter first sees Anne Catherick in 1, 4. His valediction is in 3, 2.

I have quoted *The Winter's Tale*, 3.3.22. Evelina appears in *The Castle Spectre*, 4.2. Elvira haunts vol. 3, Chapter 9 of *The Monk*.

Peter Ackroyd tells the story of the Micklegate phantoms in *The English Ghost* (London: Chatto and Windus, 2010), 147–52.

For Miss L. of Dalkeith, see Catherine Crowe, *The Night Side of Nature* (London: T. C. Newby, 1848), 2 vols, vol. 1, 83. The Willington ghost is described in vol. 2, 135. For the woman in the Edinburgh kitchen, see vol. 1, 325–5. The banshee is recorded in vol. 2, 188–9.

The Torquay apparition is recorded in C. W. Leadbeater, *The Other Side of Death* (Madras: Theosophical Publishing House, 1928), 354–5. The White Lady of Neuhaus walks on 435–6.

The Brown Lady appears in Roger Clarke, *A Natural History of Ghosts* (London: Penguin, 2013), 233–47.

I have quoted Cornelia A. P. Cromer, 'The Little Gray Ghost', in *Restless Spirits: Ghost Stories by American Women, 1872–1926*, ed. Catherine A. Lundie (Amherst: University of Massachusetts Press, 1996), 103.

William Lovett features in Carl Watkins, *The Undiscovered Country: Journeys among the Dead* (London: Vintage, 2014), 123–4.

Reginald Scot makes the distinction in *The Discovery of Witchcraft*, 534–5.

For heavenly dress see Revelation 7. 9, 13–14; 15. 6; Matt. 28. 3. David Keck discusses the afterlife of saints in *Angels and Angelology in the Middle Ages* (New York: Oxford University Press, 1998), 27, 44.

The heroine of *The Lady's Tragedy* rises at 4.4.42 SD; for Dorothea, see *The Virgin Martyr*, 5.2.219 SD.

Polly Allen sees the apparition in Charles Lindley, Viscount Halifax, *Lord Halifax's Ghost Book* (London: Geoffrey Bles, 1936), 151–3. For the white lady of Glamis Castle see 32–3.

Sir Thomas Wise's story is told in Peter Marshall, *Beliefs and the Dead in Reformation England* (Oxford: Oxford University Press, 2002), 251–2.

Milton considers the sex of spirits in *Paradise Lost* 1, 423–31.

I have quoted Randall Hutchins, *Of Specters*, trans. Virgil B. Heltzel and Clyde Murley, *Huntington Library Quarterly* 11 (1947–8), 407–29, 419.

I have quoted Alfred Tennyson, *Maud*, Part 2, line 159 and Part 3, line 10.

Jane sees the vision of her mother in *Jane Eyre*, Chapter 27. Bertha Mason appears in Chapter 25.

Jane Pugh tells the story of HMS *Asp* in *Welsh Ghosts, Poltergeists and Demons: A Collection of Stories, Ancient and Modern* ([Connah's Quay]: the Author, 1978), 46–51. For the young Welsh squire, see 55–8. For the faceless Catrin Wen, see 71–3.

For the haunting of Highlow Hall, see Clarence Daniel, *Ghosts of Derbyshire* (Clapham: Dalesman Publishing, 1973), 18–19. The jilted bride is on p. 25.

Virginia Woolf comments in 'Henry James's Ghost Stories', *Collected Essays, Volume One* (London: Hogarth Press, 1966), 291–2.

For the ghost in a foul sheet, see *A Warning for Fair Women*, ed. Charles Dale Cannon (The Hague: Mouton, 1975), Induction, lines 54–5.

For Caesarius of Heisterbach, see *The Dialogue on Miracles*, Book 11, Chapter 63.

Priscilla Beauty's story is told by Laura Gowing, 'The Haunting of Susan Lay: Servants and Mistresses in Seventeenth-Century England', *Gender and History* 14 (2002), 183–201.

The ghost of Ogmore Castle features in Jane Beck, 'The White Lady of Great Britain and Ireland', *Folk-Lore* 81 (1970), 297.

Pip describes Miss Havisham in *Great Expectations*, Chapter 8. She haunts her brother in Chapter 42.

CHAPTER 5. DANGEROUS DEAD WOMEN

Thorgunna's story is translated by Judy Quinn in *The Saga of the People of Eyri*, in *Gisli Sursson's Saga and The Saga of the People of Eyri*, ed. Vésteinn Ólason (London: Penguin, 2003), 165–76.

'The Romance of Certain Old Clothes' can be found in *The Complete Tales of Henry James*, ed. Leon Edel, vol. 1 (London: Rupert Hart-Davis, 1962), 297–319. I have quoted 318–19, 300, 301, 302.

Walter Scott comments 'On the Supernatural' in *Sir Walter Scott on Novelists and Fiction*, ed. Ioan Williams (London: Routledge and Kegan Paul, 1968), 314.

Herodotus tells the story of Melissa in his *Histories*, 5.92(g).

For David Person's story, see Marshall, *Beliefs and the Dead*, 253.

The violent dead wife and the story of John True feature in Sasha Handley, *Visions of an Unseen World: Ghost Beliefs and Ghost Stories in Eighteenth-Century England* (London: Pickering and Chatto, 2007), 90, 52–3.

For the Danish folk tale, see Joan Rockwell, 'The Ghosts of Evald Tang Kristensen', in *The Folklore of Ghosts*, ed. Hilda R. Ellis Davidson and W. M. S. Russell (Cambridge: D. S. Brewer, 1981), 43–72, esp. 61.

The story of Lady Onkhari is told in Andrew Lang, *Cock Lane and Common-Sense* (London: Longmans Green, 1894), 2.

The trial of George Burroughs ('G. B.') is recorded by Cotton Mather in *Wonders of the Invisible World* and extracted in Charles L. Crow, ed., *American Gothic* (Oxford: Wiley-Blackwell, 2013), 4–8.

For the Japanese folk tale, see Lafcadio Hearn, 'The Reconciliation', *Shadowings* (London: Sampson Low, Marston, 1900), 5–11.

For Cynthia, see Propertius, Elegy 4.7.

The ballad of *Fair Margaret and Sweet William* is quoted in *The Knight of the Burning Pestle*, 2.2.485-8. It can be found in Child, *English and Scottish Popular Ballads*, 74, where *The Twa Sisters* is no. 10.

Anne Walker's story is told by Henry More in Glanvill, *Saducismus Triumphatus*, Part 1, 3–11.

For the courting widower, see Briggs, *A Dictionary of British Folk-Tales*, Part B, vol. 1, 480.

Mrs Wilson Woodrow's 'Secret Chambers' is reprinted in Lundie, ed., *Restless Spirits*, 175–91.

I have quoted Audrey Niffenegger, *Her Fearful Symmetry* (London: Jonathan Cape, 2009), 292.

The malevolence is described in Susan Hill, 'Across the Causeway', *The Woman in Black*.

For ancient Greece, see Sarah Iles Johnston, *Restless Dead* (Berkeley: University of California Press, 1999), esp. 161–99.

Defoe comments in *An Essay on the History and Reality of Apparitions*, 280.

For Persius, see Satire 5, line 92.

Scot pronounces in *A Discovery of Witchcraft*, 152–3. John Aubrey praises his nurse in *Three Prose Works*, ed. John Buchanan-Brown (Fontwell: Centaur, 1972), 445.

Locke's comment is from *An Essay Concerning Human Understanding*, 2.33.10.

For Addison, see *The Spectator* 12 (14 March 1711) and 419 (1 July 1712), ed. Donald F. Bond (Oxford: Oxford University Press, 1965), 5 vols.

I have quoted Anne Brontë, *The Tenant of Wildfell Hall*, Chapter 2. Jane is frightened in *Jane Eyre*, Chapters 2 and 3.

Catherine Crowe praises women and children in *The Night Side of Nature*, vol. 1, 362, 384; vol. 2, 24.

CHAPTER 6. UNQUIET GOTHIC CASTLES

Mlle Bearn characterises the Gothic in Ann Radcliffe, *The Mysteries of Udolpho*, 4 vols, vol. 3, Chapter 6. Annette frightens Emily in vol. 2, Chapter 5. Signora Laurentini's story concludes in vol. 4, Chapters 16 and 17.

Antonio hears his dead wife speak in John Webster, *The Duchess of Malfi*, 5.3.9–45. Another Antonio visits St Mark's in John Marston, *Antonio's Revenge*, 3.1.

The abbey is described as castellated (and moated) in Thomas Love Peacock, *Nightmare Abbey*, Chapter 1.

Peter Quint appears in Chapter 3 of Henry James, *The Turn of the Screw*.

The heroine crosses the haunted hall in *The Castle of Ehrenstein*, Chapter 25.

The Kenilworth ghost appears in Ann Radcliffe, 'The Seventh Night', *Gaston de Blondeville*, 3 vols, vol. 3. The Provençal tale features in *The Mysteries of Udolpho*, vol. 4, Chapter 6.

Partridge comments on *Hamlet* in Henry Fielding, *Tom Jones*, Book 16, Chapter 5.

For the German visitor's account of Garrick's *Hamlet*, see Farley Hills, ed., *Critical Responses to Hamlet*, vol. 1, xxvi–xxvii. Critics puzzled over the armed Ghost in vol. 1, 103–4, 224. See vol. 1 for George Stubbes (102) and Elizabeth Montagu (195–200); the Ghost is praised as 'sublime' on 169, 110; for the uncertainty of the Ghost, see 245.

Joseph Addison writes about the supernatural on the stage in *The Spectator* 44 (20 April 1711) and in fiction in 419 (1 July 1712). The fireside storytelling is described in 12 (14 March 1711).

Ann Radcliffe's dialogue, written 1811–15, was originally part of the framing prelude to *Gaston de Blondeville* but 'On the Supernatural in Poetry' was extracted and published posthumously in *The New Monthly Magazine* in 1826, when *Gaston* also appeared in print for the first time. I have quoted it from E. J. Clery and Robert Miles, *Gothic Documents: A Sourcebook, 1700–1820* (Manchester: Manchester University Press, 2000), 166–8.

The portrait of Sir Malise Ravenswood features in Walter Scott, *The Bride of Lammermoor*, Chapters 18, 34 and 35. Wolf's Crag is described in Chapter 7. For Old Alice's warning, see Chapters 19 and 23.

I have quoted René Descartes, *Discourse on Method*, Discourse 4 and *Meditations*, Fifth Meditation.

David Hume's 'Of Superstition and Enthusiasm' appears in his *Essays Moral, Political, and Literary*, ed. Eugene F. Miller (Indianapolis, IN: Liberty Classics, 1987), 73–9. I have quoted 73–4.

I have drawn on Edmund Burke, *A Philosophical Enquiry into the Sublime and Beautiful*, 2.4, 4.14 and 2.3.

Coleridge gives his verdict in Farley Hills, ed., *Critical Responses to Hamlet*, vol. 2, 67.

For magic lantern shows and more, see Marina Warner, *Phantasmagoria* (Oxford: Oxford University Press, 2006), esp. 149.

For Fuseli's image of the Ghost, see Walter Pape and Frederick Burwall, eds, *The Boydell Shakespeare Gallery* (Bottrop: Peter Pomp, 1996), 285.

Dr Johnson calls Hamlet confused in his note on 1.4.46. See Samuel Johnson, *Notes to Shakespeare*, vol. 3, *Tragedies*, ed. Arthur Sherbo (Los Angeles: University of California, 1958).

Jesus says he is not a ghost in Luke 24. 39.

Sasha Handley records the question from the *Norwich Gazette* in *Visions of an Unseen World*, 134. For the apparition in court see 136 and for the return of John Croxford, see 156. The Newcastle Catholic is on 157 and the anti-Revolutionary ghost on 169–70.

Roger Clarke tells the story of the Cock Lane ghost in *A Natural History of Ghosts*, 129–46.

The story of Frederick of Kelle is in Caesarius of Heisterbach, *The Dialogue on Miracles*, Book 12, Chapter 14.

The Bishop of Lincoln's apparition is recorded in John Capgrave, *Chronicle of England* (HMSO, 1858), 210–11.

Edmund Jones tells Thomas Cadogan's story in *A Relation of Apparitions of Spirits in the County of Monmouth and the Principality of Wales* (Newport: Etheridge and Tibbins, 1813), 50.

For James Haddock, see Glanvill, *Saducismus Triumphatus*, Part 2, 276–84. (The pagination is duplicated here.)

For further discussion, see E. J. Clery, *The Rise of Supernatural Fiction, 1762–1800* (Cambridge: Cambridge University Press, 1995).

CHAPTER 7. SPECTRES OF DESIRE

The story of the bleeding nun is told in Chapter 4 of M. G. Lewis, *The Monk*. 'Alonzo the Brave and Fair Imogine' is in Chapter 9.

Philinnion's story, along with 'The Bride of Corinth' is available in Hansen, ed, *Phlegon of Tralles' Book of Marvels*, 35–8, 200, 201–7.

Rudyard Kipling's 'A Madonna of the Trenches' is in his *Debits and Credits* (London: Macmillan, 1926), 239–61.

Ballads of demon lovers can be found in Child, *English and Scottish Popular Ballads*, 243E, F, G.

For an analysis of *Death and the Lascivious Couple*, see John H. Astington, *Stage and Picture in the English Renaissance* (Cambridge: Cambridge University Press, 2017), 109–12.

Maria Manning's story is told in Clarke, *A Natural History of Ghosts*, 165–7.

Washington Irving's 'The Adventure of a German Student' is in Part 1 of his *Tales of a Traveller*.

I have quoted *Wuthering Heights*, Chapters 16, 29, 9, 4.

May Sinclair comments on *Wuthering Heights* in *The Three Brontës* (London: Hutchinson, 1912), 209–37. 'The Intercessor' is reprinted in May Sinclair, *Uncanny Stories* (Ware: Wordsworth Editions, 2006), 177–216.

CHAPTER 8. ALL IN THE MIND?

Cassius distrusts the senses in Plutarch's *Life of Marcus Brutus*, reprinted in Shakespeare, *Julius Caesar*, ed. David Daniell (London: Thomson Learning, 1998), see 351.

Kant denounced superstition in *Dreams of a Spirit-Seer* (1766).

The ghost appears in Chapter 12 of *Nightmare Abbey*.

Hector warns Aeneas in Virgil, *Aeneid*, 2.270–97.

For Woodstock's dream, see *Thomas of Woodstock or Richard II, Part One*, ed. Peter Corbin and Douglas Sedge (Manchester: Manchester University Press, 2002). I have quoted 5.1.65, 80 and 103.

Thomas Nashe comments on dreams in *Terrors of the Night*, 153.

I have quoted *Richard III*, 5.3.177 SD, 178, 179.

Charlemont sees the ghost in *The Atheist's Tragedy*, 2.6.

For 'The Dead Woman', see Guy de Maupassant, *Complete Short Stories* (London: Cassell, 1970), 3 vols, vol. 3, 577–82.

I have quoted Propertius, Elegy 4.7, line 1.

Jacques Lacan names the hole in the real in 'Desire and the Interpretation of Desire in *Hamlet*', *Literature and Psychoanalysis*, ed. Shoshana Felman (Baltimore, MD: Johns Hopkins University Press, 1982), 11–52, esp. 37–9.

Sigmund Freud writes of hallucinated satisfactions in 'Mourning and Melancholia', *On Metapsychology*, ed. Angela Richards (Harmondsworth; Penguin, 1984), 245–68, esp. 253.

For the Breton story see Leadbeater, *The Other Side of Death*, 484–6.

For ambivalence towards the dead, see Sigmund Freud, *Totem and Taboo* in *The Origins of Religion*, ed. Albert Dickson (London: Penguin, 1985), 71–5.

I have quoted Defoe, *An Essay on the History and Reality of Apparitions*, 80.

Banquo returns in Shakespeare, *Macbeth*, 3. 4.

Oliver St John Gogarty makes his observation in *As I was Going Down Sackville Street* (Harmondsworth: Penguin, 1954), 204.

Milton's Satan comments on the mind in *Paradise Lost*, 1, 254–5. Marvell does so in 'The Garden', lines 43–6.

CHAPTER 9. LISTENING TO GHOSTS

For William Clarkson's story, see *The Primitive Methodist Magazine* 7 (1826), 158–64.

For 'Ossian' see James Macpherson, *The Poems of Ossian and Related Works*, ed. Howard Gaskill (Edinburgh: Edinburgh University Press, 1996), 9, 65.

Antonia's dead mother speaks in *The Monk*, Chapter 9.

Conan Doyle's troubled spirit speaks in *The Land of Mist*, Chapter 8.

Roman ghosts shriek in *Julius Caesar*, 2.2.24.

Comedy mocks screaming stage ghosts in *A Warning for Fair Women*, Induction, line 56.

Thomas Lodge complains of the *Ur-Hamlet* in *Wit's Misery* (London, 1596), 56.

Reginald Scot describes the voice of the counterfeit ghost in *A Discovery of Witchcraft*, 150. His account is endorsed in John Deacon and John Walker, *Dialogicall Discourses of Spirits and Devils* (London, 1601), 126.

Edmund Jones characterises the voices of the dead in *A Relation of Apparitions of Spirits*, 62, 64.

Liza Hempstock tells her story in Neil Gaiman, *The Graveyard Book*, Chapter 4.

Catherine begs to be let in in *Wuthering Heights*, Chapter 3.

For Elspeth's reflections, see *Her Fearful Symmetry*, 73, 134.

'The Little Gray Ghost' laments in Lundie, ed. *Restless Spirits*, 103. 'The Shell of Sense' is reprinted 52–61.

Susie Salmon complains in *The Lovely Bones*, Chapter 2.

CHAPTER 10. STRANGE TO TELL

Robertson Davies gives an account of his Christmas ghost-story readings in *High Spirits* (Harmondsworth: Penguin, 1982), 1–2.

The ballads mentioned here are *The Wife of Usher's Well* (Child 79), *Clerk*

Saunders (Child 77F), *Proud Lady Margaret* (Child 47A) and *The Unquiet Grave* (Child 78A).

M. R. James comments on the chronology depicted in the genre in his *Collected Ghost Stories* (Oxford: Oxford University Press, 2011), 407–8.

'Wandering Willie's Tale' features in Letter 11 of Walter Scott, *Redgauntlet.*

The 1908 version of *The Turn of the Screw* with the author's Preface can be found in the edition by Deborah Esch and Jonathan Warren (New York: Norton, 1999). See also T. J. Lustig, *Henry James and the Ghostly* (Cambridge: Cambridge University Press, 1994).

CODA. FIGURATIVE PHANTOMS

See W. W. Skeat, 'Report upon "Ghost-Words", or Words which Have no Real Existence', *Transactions of the Philological Society* 26 (1885–7), 350–74.

I have quoted Gilbert Ryle, *The Concept of Mind* (London: Hutchinson, 1949), 15–16.

See William S. Burroughs, *Ghost of Chance* (London: Serpent's Tail, 1995), 38, 48, 49.

Jacques Derrida, *Specters of Marx: The State of the Debt, The Work of Mourning, and the New International*, trans. Peggy Kamuf (New York: Routledge, 1994), 175, 176.

I have quoted from all four chapters of Philip Roth, *Exit Ghost* and Part 5 of Hilary Mantel, *Giving Up the Ghost.*

T. S. Eliot's compound ghost appears in section 2 of 'Little Gidding'. See also 'Tradition and the Individual Talent', *Selected Essays* (London: Faber and Faber, 1951), 13–22.

Acknowledgements

My greatest debts are to Andrew Belsey and Nicola Prigg, whose comments I have taken to heart. Helen Phillips also refined my prose. Pamela and Keith McCallum braved the ghosts of Cambridge with me, while Cambridge University Library has provided, as always, a generous haven for wandering scholars. The following have helped with encouragement, advice, information, material or their stories: Chu-chueh, Helen Cooper, Alan Dessen, Cynthia Dessen, Eleanor Fellows, Jennifer Fellows, Andrew Francis, Ann Francis, Ken Head, John Hipkin, Ann Keith, Mel Kohlke, Christa Jansohn, Peter Marx, Hugh Mellor, Laurent Milesi, Francesca Paci, Fred Parker, Susie Paskins, Ed Pechter, Olga Peppercorn, Carl Phelpstead, Jean-Marc Pillière, Neil Reeve, Susanne Reichl, Gwyneth Roberts, Susanna Rostas, Yoko Takakuwa, Wynn Thomas, Ann Thompson, Rhys Tranter, Bob White, Julia Wrigglesworth and Angelika Zirker. Jackie Jones unites the soul of wisdom with the spirit of adventure.

Credits

Fig. 1. The Clopton monument from William Dugdale, *Antiquities of Warwickshire*, 1656. Reproduced by kind permission of the Syndics of Cambridge University Library, Syn.3.65.4

Fig. 2. The Three Living and the Three Dead from the Psalter of Robert De Lisle, 1310–20. The Picture Art Collection / Alamy Stock Photo

Fig. 3. Frontispiece illustration to *The Old English Baron*, 1778. The Picture Art Collection / Alamy Stock Photo

Fig. 4. David Garrick as Hamlet, 1754. Engraving by James McArdell from a painting by Benjamin Wilson. IanDagnall Computing / Alamy Stock Photo

Fig. 5. Brutus and the Ghost of Caesar, 1802. Engraving by Edward Scriven from a painting by Richard Westall. Atlaspix / Alamy Stock Photo

Fig. 6. William Hogarth, *Credulity, Superstition and Fanaticism*, 1762. Photo 12 / Alamy Stock Photo

Fig. 7. Hans Holbein, *The Duchess* from *The Dance of Death*. Bilwissedition Ltd. & Co. KG / Alamy Stock Photo.

Fig 8. Hans Sebald Beham, 'Death and the Lascivious Couple'. Image © Ashmolean Museum, University of Oxford

Fig. 9. Daniel Maclise, *A Winter Night's Tale*, c. 1867. Manchester Art Gallery, UK / Bridgeman Images

Index

Achilles, 34, 35, 37, 44, 179, 183–4

Addison, Joseph, 116, 128, 134, 143–4, 261, 262

Adventures of Arthur, The, 47–8, 219

Aeneas, 34, 36, 45–6, 75, 179, 265

Aeschylus, 35–6

Alan Fitz-Osborne, 120

Alcestis, 58, 59–60, 61, 65, 73

Allen, Polly, 85, 258

Allen, Woody, 28

Alonzo, 158, 264

Ambrose, Isaac, 67, 257

angels, 64, 67, 68, 71, 72–3, 83–4, 85–7, 258

Arminian Magazine, The, 145

Atheist's Tragedy, The, 181, 188, 265

Athenian Mercury, The, 68–9, 141

Athenodorus, 55, 185

Aubrey, John, 69–70, 116, 135, 261; *see also* M., Mr T.

Augustine, Saint, 20–1, 53, 61–2, 64, 65, 66, 71, 74, 255

Austen, Jane
  Northanger Abbey, 122, 177, 215, 217, 231
  Pride and Prejudice, 142

Bacon, Francis, 43

ballads, 218–19, 264, 266–7

banshee, 95, 258

Bavarian widower, 65, 73

Baxter, Richard, 66–7, 69, 72

Beaumont, Francis, 109, 260

Beauty, Priscilla, 93–4, 259

Beham, Hans Sebald, 160–1, 264

Beloved, 112–13, 165, 215

Benson, E. F., 182

Berwick ghost, 51, 53, 54

Betterton, Thomas, 18

Bierce, Ambrose *see* 'Moonlit Road, The'

Blair, Tony, 249

bleeding nun, 148–52, 155, 157, 198, 264

Bleeding Nun of St Catherine's, The, 149

Blithe Spirit, 111

Bowen, Elizabeth
  'The Demon Lover', 158
  'Hand in Glove', 111–12

Bowen, Marjorie, 197, 202–3, 208

Braddon, Mary Elizabeth, 109–10, 113, 159, 182

Branagh, Kenneth, 198

Bray, Anna Eliza, 5

Briggs, Katharine M., 7, 8, 254, 260

Bromhall, Thomas, 64–5, 66, 257; *see also* Bavarian widower

Brontë, Anne, 117, 261

Brontë, Charlotte *see Jane Eyre*

Brontë, Emily *see Wuthering Heights*

Buckinghamshire ghost, 50–1, 54

Burke, Edmund, 136, 137, 263

Burroughs, George, 107–8, 113, 260

Burroughs, William, 241–2, 247, 251, 267

Byland tales, 41, 47, 50, 51–2, 176, 200, 222, 223, 256; *see also* Lond, Adam de; Robert of Boltby; Snowball; Tankerlay, James

Caesarius of Heisterbach, 48, 50, 93, 256, 259; *see also* Frederic of Kelle; usurer of Liège

Campbell, Gordon and Thomas Corns, 61, 74

'Canterville Ghost, The', 208, 209–10, 219–20

Castle of Ehrenstein, The, 120–1, 123, 262

Castle of Otranto, The, 119–20, 129–30, 132–3, 144, 198, 215, 222

Castle of Wolfenbach, The, 132, 133

Chaucer, Geoffrey, 60, 180, 257

Cicero, 180

Clarkson, William, 196, 202, 266

Clytemnestra, 36

Cock Lane ghost, 144, 263

Coleridge, Samuel Taylor, 56, 137, 177, 263

Collins, Wilkie *see Woman in White, The*

consolation, 36, 57–9, 69–70, 72, 73, 85, 91, 92, 93, 212

Creüsa, 36, 75, 205, 255

Cromer, Cornelia A. P., 82, 212, 258, 266

Crowe, Catherine, 81, 117, 258, 261

Croxford, John, 144, 263

Dance of Death, 159–60

Dante, 46, 70, 207

Darius, 35–6

Davies, Robertson, 215, 266

Defoe, Daniel, 3, 70–1, 82, 116, 126, 189, 257, 261, 265

Dekker, Thomas, 84, 258

Derrida, Jacques, 243–5, 251, 267

Descartes, René, 65, 134, 136, 138, 262

Dickens, Charles, 5, 215

  A Christmas Carol, 19

  Great Expectations, 98–9, 259

  'The Trial for Murder', 221

Dingley, Dorothy, 1–10, 33, 82, 145, 254

Doyle, Arthur Conan, 198, 200, 266

dreams, 21, 27, 34, 57, 60, 67–8, 76–7, 80, 81, 84, 87, 108, 111, 178–83, 191, 193, 224, 225, 226, 265

Dunbar, Olivia Howard, 210, 266

Edgar; or, The Phantom of the Castle, 131–2, 133

Edwards, Amelia B., 215, 222

Eliot, T. S., 250–1, 267

Elizabeth of Hungary, 84

Elpenor, 34, 204, 255

Enlightenment, 45, 62, 71, 116, 117, 126, 128, 134–6, 138–42, 147, 175, 176–7, 190, 192, 221, 223, 244

Euripides, 59

Euthymus, 37, 255

Eyre, Richard, 176

Fair Margaret and Sweet William, 108–9, 260

Featley, Daniel, 86

Fellows, Jennifer, 150

Fielding, Henry, 125–6, 262

Frank, Anne, 248

Frederic of Kelle, 145–6, 263

Freud, Sigmund, 28–9, 154, 157, 166, 174, 178–9, 181, 184, 185, 188, 226, 244, 255, 265

Fuseli, Henry, 139, 263

Gaiman, Neil *see Graveyard Book, The*

Garrick, David, 125–8, 139

Gaskell, Elizabeth, 112, 117, 224

Gautier, Théophile, 96

Geoffrey of Burton, 40–1, 256

Ghost, 57, 185, 187, 205, 208, 209, 211, 215, 220

Ghost, The, 249–50

Ghost Story, 202, 204, 226, 233

Ghost Story, A, 93

Ghosts, 242–3, 244, 251

Ghosts Can't Do It, 205–6

Gilbert, C. S., 7, 8, 254

Gilgamesh, 43–4

Gilman, Charlotte Perkins, 163

Giselle, 96–7

Glanvill, Joseph, 68, 72, 81, 119, 134–5, 145, 257; *see also* Haddock, James; Walker, Anne; Watkinson, Mr

Goethe, Johann Wolfgang von, 155–6, 264

Gogarty, Oliver St John, 193, 265

Gordon, Avery, 245

Grammaticus, Saxo, 38–9, 256

Graveyard Book, The, 207, 266

Grettir, 37–8, 39–40

Guenevere, 47–8, 219

Haddock, James, 146–7, 205, 263

Harris, James, 157

Harris, Robert *see Ghost, The*

Harvey, W. F., 212–13, 214

Haunted Castle, The, 121

Hawker, R. S., 5–7, 254

Hawthorne, Nathaniel, 225

Hearn, Lafcadio, 108, 171–2, 174, 188, 260

Hecate, 114

Heine, Heinrich, 96

hell, 20, 22–3, 27, 29, 46, 47–9, 54, 69, 71, 193, 202, 203, 225, 227, 255

Her Fearful Symmetry, 111, 113, 205, 209, 220, 261, 266

Hill, Susan, 215; *see also Woman in Black, The*

Hobbes, Thomas, 62–3, 65, 68, 71

Hobson, Elizabeth, 72–3

Hogarth, William, 152–3

Hogg, James, 95–6, 98, 117

Holbein, Hans, 159–60

Hole, Christina, 7, 254

Homer, 35, 44–5, 61, 74, 207, 251, 255; *see also* Achilles; Elpenor; Odysseus; Patroclus

Hume, David, 135–6, 137, 176, 263

Hunt, Robert, 7, 254

Hussey, Thomas, 70, 257

Hutchins, Randall, 86, 259

Ibsen, Henrik *see Ghosts*

Icelandic sagas, 37, 105–6, 107, 218, 222–3, 251; *see also* Grettir; Thorgunna

Innocents, The, 234

Irving, Washington, 215
  'The Adventure of a German
    Student', 163–4, 225, 264
  'The Knight of Malta', 123, 182
  The Legend of Sleepy Hollow, 90
  'The Spectre Bridegroom',
    177–8

Jackson, Shirley, 178–9
James I and VI, 63–4, 66, 257
James, Henry, 236, 237
  'The Friends of the Friends', 212
  'The Romance of Certain Old
    Clothes', 102–5, 110, 112,
    113, 260
  The Turn of the Screw, 123, 162,
    163, 208, 217, 228–38, 260,
    267
James, M. R., 171, 174, 214, 215,
    222, 267
  'Casting the Runes', 171
  'An Episode of Cathedral
    History', 173
  'Martin's Close', 110, 113
  'A Neighbour's Landmark', 213
  'Number 13', 197, 213
  'Oh, Whistle, and I'll Come to
    You, My Lad', 93, 171, 172,
    179
  'The Treasure of Abbot Thomas',
    172–3

'The Uncommon Prayer Book',
    94
Jane Eyre, 87, 88, 92, 231, 259,
    261
Jarvis, T. M., 4, 145, 146
Johnson, Samuel, 139, 263
Jones, Edmund, 146, 200, 263,
    266
Joyce, Graham, 208

Kant, Immanuel, 176, 264
Kemble, John Philip, 190
Kipling, Rudyard
  'A Madonna of the Trenches',
    156, 264
  'My Own true Ghost Story',
    188
Koestler, Arthur, 241
Kozintsev, Grigori, 16
Kwaidan, 108
Kyd, Thomas, 24, 26, 27

L., Miss, 81, 258
Lacan, Jacques, 184, 265
Lamia, 114, 173
Lark Rise to Candleford, 90
Le Fanu, J. Sheridan
  'An Account of Some Strange
    Disturbances in Aungier
    Street', 216–17
  'Mr Justice Harbottle', 191

'Schalken the Painter', 89, 154–5

'Ultor de Lacy', 222

Leadbeater, C. W., 81, 258, 265

Lee, Vernon, 164–5

Lenore, 157, 158, 178, 187

Lewis, M. G., 190

   The Castle Spectre, 80, 125, 150, 258

   The Monk, 80, 92, 117, 122, 148–9, 158, 198, 258, 266

   Tales of Wonder, 150–1, 157

Lincoln in the Bardo, 186–7, 209, 215, 223–4

Locke, John, 116–17, 261

Lodge, Thomas, 199, 266

Lond, Adam de, 52, 204, 205

Longfellow, Henry Wadsworth, 207, 220

Lovely Bones, The, 203, 205, 210, 212, 215, 266

Lovett, William, 83, 258

Lucian, 199

M., Mr T., 69–70, 74, 182, 257

Maclise, Daniel, 216–17, 219, 224

Macpherson, James *see* 'Ossian'

Mallet, David, 109

Manning, Maria, 162, 264

Mantel, Hilary, 247, 267

Marlowe, Christopher, 11, 20, 115–16, 254, 255

Marston, John, 122, 261

Marvell, Andrew, 193, 265

Marx, Karl, 240, 241, 244, 251

Massinger, Philip, 84

Maupassant, Guy de, 183, 265

Mease, Susan, 108

Melissa, 106–7, 260

Middleton, Thomas, 84, 258

Miller, Jonathan, 179

Milton, John, 57–78, 83, 85, 86, 182, 193, 259, 265

Milton, Katherine, 60–1

Mirk, John, 53, 256

Montagu, Elizabeth, 128–9, 262

'Moonlit Road, The', 91–2, 205, 208, 212, 214, 223

More, Henry, 63–4, 65–6, 68, 70, 257

Morrison, Toni *see Beloved*

Mort Castle, 120

Mosse, Kate, 88–9

Nashe, Thomas, 54, 62, 176, 180, 256, 265

Nesbit, E.

   'The Ebony Frame', 165, 166

   'From the Dead', 93, 197

   'Man-Size in Marble', 117, 221

'Number 17', 178

'The Shadow', 217, 221

netherworlds, 42–5, 202–3

Niffenegger, Audrey *see Her Fearful Symmetry*

Nightmare Abbey, 122, 177, 261, 264

Nonne sanglante, La, 150

Norwich Gazette, 141, 263

Oates, Joyce Carol, 233–4

Odysseus, 34, 44–5, 207

Olivier, Laurence, 16, 198

Onions, Oliver, 8, 254

Onkhari, 107, 260

Orphanage, The, 191

'Ossian', 143, 197, 266

Others, The, 226–8, 233

Palinurus, 34, 256

Patroclus, 34, 179, 183, 184, 204, 205, 255

Peacock, Thomas Love *see Nightmare Abbey*

Pearl, 84, 85

Percy, Thomas, 143

Persius, 116, 261

Person, David, 107, 260

Phelps, Elizabeth Stuart, 210, 212

Philinnion, 154–6, 264

Philostratus, Flavius, 35, 37, 116, 255

Phlegon of Tralles, 37, 155, 255

Pilchard, Thomas, 49–50, 256

Plato, 45, 256

pleasure, 77, 173–4, 217–18

Pliny the Younger, 55–6, 175, 176, 184, 185, 223, 257

Plutarch, 175, 176, 264

Poe, Edgar Allan

    'The Fall of the House of Usher', 98

    'Ligeia', 111, 205, 224

    'The Tell-Tale Heart', 224

Potter, Harry, 82, 97

Proklos, 155

Propertius, 108, 184, 260, 265

purgatory, 21, 45–9, 62, 83, 135, 255

Radcliffe, Ann, 121, 122, 129, 137, 138, 143, 176

    Gaston de Blondeville, 123, 129, 137, 262

    The Mysteries of Udolpho, 119, 121–2, 123–5, 138, 144, 215, 231, 261, 262

    The Romance of the Forest, 123

realism, 12, 192–3, 194, 209, 221–2

Rebecca, 111

Reeve, Clara, 120, 123, 131

Reformation, 58–9, 62, 66

Rendell, Ruth, 221

Ring, 94, 112

Robert of Boltby, 51–2, 200, 204, 207, 212

Rossetti, Dante Gabriel, 158

Roth, Philip, 250
   Exit Ghost, 246–7, 248, 250–1, 267
   The Ghost Writer, 248, 251

Rowe, Nicholas, 25–6

Ryle, Gilbert, 240, 241, 243, 267

Saunders, George *see Lincoln in the Bardo*

scepticism, 54–6, 62–3, 70–2, 128–9, 134, 142, 151, 176–8, 192

Schiller, Friedrich, 176–7, 223

Scot, Reginald, 54, 62, 64, 68, 83, 93, 116, 200, 256, 258, 261, 266

Scott, Sir Walter, 103, 168, 234, 260
   The Bride of Lammermoor, 133, 144, 262
   The Doom of Devorgoil, 120, 123
   Minstrelsy of the Scottish Border, 157
   'The Tapestried Chamber', 182–3, 189, 212

'Wandering Willie's Tale', 224–5, 267

Sebold, Alice *see Lovely Bones, The*

Seneca, 26–7, 36, 44, 199, 219

Shakespeare, William, 46, 62, 126–9, 134, 136–7, 139, 147, 190, 201
   Hamlet, 11–34, 41, 45–6, 52, 53, 54, 55, 57, 62, 76, 93, 125–34, 137, 138, 139, 146, 165, 175–6, 183, 184, 190, 195, 196–7, 198–201, 202, 203, 204, 205, 207, 208–9, 211, 214, 219, 223, 231, 232, 251, 262
   Julius Caesar, 14, 28, 139–40, 176, 181, 182, 199, 254, 266
   King Henry VIII, 84
   King Richard III, 60, 67, 180–1, 257, 265
   Macbeth, 11–12, 22, 52, 76, 116, 151, 188–90, 223, 254, 255, 265
   Measure for Measure, 29–30, 255
   A Midsummer Night's Dream, 15, 254
   Romeo and Juliet, 152, 160
   Titus Andronicus, 24
   The Winter's Tale, 12, 15, 80, 83, 254, 258

Shining, The, 204, 215

Sinclair, May, 169, 174, 264

  'The Intercessor', 169–70, 264

  'The Nature of the Evidence',
    111

  'Where Their Fire is not
    Quenched', 203

Sisyphus, 44

Sixth Sense, The, 215, 226–7

Skeat, Walter W., 240, 241, 243,
    267

Snowball, 41, 200

Society for Psychical Research,
    192, 236

Socrates, 45

Spark, Muriel, 210–11

Spenser, Edmund, 74

spiritualism, 57, 81, 188

Star Wars, 16

Straub, Peter *see Ghost Story*

Stubbes, George, 128, 137, 262

Tankerlay, James, 47, 52, 222

Tantalus, 44

Tennyson, Alfred, 87, 259

Thomas of Woodstock, 180, 181,
    265

Thorgunna, 100–4, 105–6, 113,
    259

Three Living and Three Dead,
    41–2, 93, 219

Timbs, John, 145, 146

Timperley, Rosemary, 162, 163

Tityos, 44, 45

Truly Madly Deeply, 57–8, 185–6

Trump, Donald J., 206

truth, 8–10, 187

Twa Sisters, The, 112, 260

Unquiet Grave, The, 52, 186, 187,
    219, 256

usurer of Liège, 48, 83

Virgil, 45–6, 61, 74, 199, 256; *see
    also* Aeneas; Creüsa;
    Palinurus

Walker, Anne, 110, 113, 260

Walpole, Horace *see Castle of
    Otranto, The*

Warning for Fair Women, A, 93,
    199, 259, 266

Waters, Anne, 67–8

Watkinson, Mr, 73–4, 76, 182,
    257

Webster John (dramatist), 122,
    261

Webster John (physician), 67–8,
    257

Welsh White Lady, 94–5, 259

Wesley, John, 72–3, 86–7, 119

Westall, Richard, 139–40

Wharton, Edith
  'The Lady's Maid's Bell', 117
  'Pomegranate Seed', 110–11
  What Lies Beneath, 110
White Lady of Glamis Castle,
  90, 258
White Lady of Neuhaus, 85,
  258
Wilde, Oscar *see* 'Canterville
  Ghost, The'
Wili, 96–8, 114, 158
William of Newburgh, 40–1, 53,
  54–5, 256; *see also* Berwick
  ghost; Buckinghamshire
  ghost
Wilson, A. N., 234

Wise, Sir Thomas, 85–6, 258
witch of Endor, 52, 200, 256
Woman in Black, The, 82–3, 88,
  113–14, 162–3, 233, 261
Woman in White, The, 78–80, 85,
  88, 91–2, 98, 257
Wood, Mrs Henry, 191
Woodrow, Wilson, 111, 260
Woolf, Virginia, 91, 237, 259
Wuthering Heights, 117, 166–9,
  184–5, 204, 207–8, 224, 264,
  266

Yeats, W. B., 250–1

Zeffirelli, Franco, 16, 198

EU representative:
Easy Access System Europe
Mustamäe tee 50, 10621 Tallinn, Estonia
Gpsr.requests@easproject.com